P9-DJL-051
BROWNSBURG PUBLIC LIBRARY
3 1201 91205 7590
J SCI FIC STE
Stewart, Paul
Vox

THIS BOOK
BELONGS TO:

NEW SANCTAPHRAX
OLD UNDERTOWN
SCREE TOWN
THE STONE GARDENS

THE DEEP WOODS
THE TWILIGHT WOODS
THE EDGELANDS
The Edge.

dfb FICKLING
David Fickling Books
OXFORD · NEW YORK

A DAVID FICKLING BOOK

Published by David Fickling Books
an imprint of Random House Children's Books
a division of Random House, Inc.
New York

Originally published in Great Britain by Doubleday, an imprint of Random House Children's Books, in 2003.

www.randomhouse.com/kids

Library of Congress Cataloging-in-Publication Data
is available upon request.
ISBN 0-385-75080-3 (trade)
ISBN 0-385-75081-1 (lib. bdg.)
Printed in the United States of America
October 2005
10 9 8 7 6 5 4 3 2 1
First American Edition

For Jack, Katy, Anna, Joseph and William

THE EASTERN BASKETS
THE CEREMONIAL CAGE
THE ROCK DEMONS RAVINE
SCREETO
THE SANCTAPHRAX FOREST
THE SUNKEN PALACE
TO THE STONE GARDENS
THE SLAVE TRAIL
ROOK'S CROSSING
THE MISERY HOLE
EASTERN ENTRANCE TO SEWERS
UNDER
TH

OLD UNDERTOWN
THE PALACE OF STATUES
THE MIRE ROAD GATES
ROUTE OF THE GREAT LIBRARY FLEET
THE HIVE TOWERS
WESTERN ENTRANCE TO SEWERS
THE SLAVE MARKET
THE EDGEWATER RIVER
MIRE
S
E
W
N

Introduction

Far far away, jutting out into the emptiness beyond, like the figurehead of a mighty stone ship, is the Edge. A river – the Edgewater – pours down from the overhanging rock. Though broad, the river is slow and sluggish. It has been many long decades since storms brought any significant rainfall in from Open Sky – though now, with the sky overcast and the air hot and heavy with moisture, it feels as though perhaps, at last, all that is about to change.

At the furthest point of the Edge, draped in the dark, swirling cloud, are the Stone Gardens. Once they were the source of the floating rocks which gave birth to sky-flight and formed the great Sanctaphrax rocks themselves. Now the gardens are dead, for stone-sickness struck the Edge, grounding the sky ships, attacking the new Sanctaphrax rock and leaving the Stone Gardens a barren wasteland of broken stacks and rubble. Even the white ravens that once guarded them have gone.

Up in the Tower of Night, perched high on the crumbling Sanctaphrax rock, the Guardians – led by the merciless Orbix Xaxis – still believe that the lightning of a Great Storm will heal the ailing rock. They made preparations for its arrival and have waited impatiently for that day for many a long year.

Meanwhile, down in the library chambers of the underground sewers, their enemies – the librarian academics – disagree that lightning will heal the rock. Under the guidance of the High Librarian, Fenbrus Lodd, they study, learn, conjecture and experiment on pieces of the stricken rock, trying to find an alternative cure – while taking care to defend themselves against any who would seize the library and its secrets for themselves.

And there are many, quite apart from Orbix Xaxis, who would like to do just that. The brutal hammerhead goblin, General Tytugg, for instance, who so often dreams of having the same stranglehold over those who live beneath Undertown as those who live above, and who would fulfil these dreams were it not so perilous to attack. And Mother Muleclaw, shryke Mother of the Eastern Roost; she, too, would like to see an end to the library – to break, once and for all, the link between the librarians and the shrykes' sworn enemies in the Free Glades.

Ever vigilant, librarian knights patrol the skies at dusk and dawn – like young Rook Barkwater, fresh from the Free Glades, but already as seasoned a flier as any of his comrades who patrol in ones and twos each day. They keep to the shadows, skimming over the faded glory of Undertown in their sumpwood skycraft, darting round the jumble of debris and gaping crevices of Screetown, and flitting between the great wooden struts and pillars of the so-called Sanctaphrax Forest, that vast never-ending scaffold construction which keeps the stricken Sanctaphrax rock from ever touching the ground.

At the end of their forays, they return to the library with reports of the world above: strange disturbing reports of fireballs in the sky, and sightings of huge, mutant creatures in Screetown – whilst with every passing day, the weather seems to be getting more humid and oppressive.

Vox Verlix – nominal Leaguesmaster and Most High Academe of Sanctaphrax – knows all about the weather. Once he was the most promising cloudwatcher apprentice of his generation. Bully and genius, it was he who wrested power from Cowlquape Pentephraxis, the Most High Academe of New Sanctaphrax, taking the great chain of high office for himself; he who seized control of the mighty merchant leagues; he who oversaw the construction of the Tower of Night, the Great Mire Road, and the Sanctaphrax Forest.

These days, however, despite his grand titles and grander projects, Vox Verlix has little power. Time and again, he has been double-crossed. Orbix Xaxis seized the Tower of Night for himself, Mother Muleclaw took control of the Great Mire Road, while together with his army of goblins, General Tytugg – although content to keep a powerless puppet in place to hold the threat of a shryke attack at bay – rules Undertown with a rod of iron. Vox Verlix, it is generally believed, is little more than a prisoner in the crumbling Palace of Statues; drunken, powerless and obese.

He is, it is true, befuddled by his housekeeper's endless supply of oblivion for most of the time. Yet there are moments of lucidity; moments when – though Vox finds it hard to recall a single thing from the previous day – his memories of former glories are as fresh in his mind as they ever were.

And during those reveries of the past, he makes plans for the future. Intricate plans. *Vengeful* plans. For, alone and powerless as he is, Vox still cherishes dreams of vengeance on those he blames for his current plight. On the shrykes who strut and squawk on the Mire Road, on the goblins who march through the Undertown streets and on the sinister Guardians of Night, ever watchful from their great tower.

These are strange times. With the weather so hot, so humid, so charged with menace, it is like being trapped within a bubbling cauldron which is threatening at any moment to boil over. Slaves wilt in the suffocating heat. Guards squabble among themselves. In Screetown and the Sanctaphrax Forest, the creatures that live there are jittery and unpredictable.

Something is about to happen. Of that, there is no doubt. But what?

Rumours abound. Suspicions deepen. There are many questions but few answers. What are Orbix Xaxis and his Guardians of Night looking for as they gather each night and scan the skies? What is General Tytugg scheming in his Hive Towers fortress? Why has Mother Muleclaw gathered her shryke-sisters to her makeshift court at the end of the Great Mire Road? And what of the librarians, deep in their sewers, always mindful of those who live above them? What danger is it that they sense?

Only one individual is overlooked, forgotten and alone in his crumbling palace, seemingly oblivious to the world outside and lost in his own bitter dreams. Only one individual, who doesn't seem to care as Undertown simmers in the unbearable heat. Only one.

Vox Verlix.

The Deepwoods, the Stone Gardens, the Edgewater River. Undertown and Sanctaphrax. Names on a map.

Yet behind each name lie a thousand tales – tales that have been recorded in ancient scrolls, tales that have been passed down the generations by word of mouth – tales which even now are being told.

What follows is but one of those tales.

·CHAPTER ONE·

DAWN PATROL

It was cold in the great chamber; bitter cold. Above, through the frost-edged panes of the glass dome overhead, the stars glittered like phraxdust in the black sky. Below, at the large ring-shaped ironwood table, a hulking figure was hunched over a sheaf of sky charts, a carved tankard in front of him, and an upturned telescope by the foot of his chair. Loud snores echoed through the chamber as the figure's head slumped slowly forwards, a red gobbet of spittle bubbling on his lips.

The sky charts rustled like dead leaves as they were caught by an icy draught whistling through the chamber. The academic shivered in his sleep and the light *clink* of a phraxdust medallion tapping the heavy chain of office round his neck mingled with his snores.

He slumped further forward, cheeks wobbling and neck creasing into plump, grublike layers of fat. The dangling phraxdust medallion knocked against the rim of the all but empty tankard. The snores were deep and rumbling now and, as the sleeper's jowly face hovered over the table, the medallion hung down inside the tankard.

All at once, with a volcanic snore, the sagging figure fell completely forwards. He slammed his forehead on the edge of the table with a thud – and sat bolt upright. In front of him, there was a hiss, a crackle, a whiff of toasted wood-almonds – and the tankard abruptly exploded.

The academic was thrown back from his chair. He landed heavily on the other side of the chamber, twisting a leg and knocking his head sharply against the tiled floor.

From high above, like a faulty echo, there came an answering sound of breaking glass and an ear-splitting crash, as something hard and heavy burst through the dome and landed in the middle of the ironwood table, splitting it in two.

The academic coughed throatily as he heaved himself painfully to his feet. The air was thick with dust and smoke. His head throbbed, his ears were ringing, and wherever he looked, the after-image of the explosion flashed before him; now pink, now green. He coughed again and again, great convulsions racking his body.

At last the coughing subsided, and he fumbled for a spidersilk kerchief and wiped his streaming eyes. Above his head, he saw that several of the glass panels had shattered in the blast. At his feet, the jagged fragments glinted in the moonlight. He frowned as his gaze fell on the object nestling amongst the shards of glass and splinters of wood. It was a stone head dislodged from one of the statues on the roof, the thick frost coating its surface already melting and dripping down onto the floor.

Who is it this time? the academic wondered. Which venerable figure of rank has taken a tumble tonight?

He crouched down, seized the slippery head with both hands, rolled it over – and gasped with sudden foreboding. It was his own face staring back at him.

Although it was close to midnight, with the full moon dull and greasy yellow behind the thickening mist, the air – even high up at the top of the Tower of Night – was still clammy and warm. The Most High Guardian, Orbix Xaxis, emerged onto the main upper gantry, looked round uneasily, and began at once to fiddle urgently with the metal muzzle that covered his mouth and nose.

With the vents closed by spidersilk gauze, Orbix's face sweated beneath the mask and his voice took on a muffled and rasping tone – but at least it protected him from the vile contagion of the night. The High Guardian clicked the muzzle-guard securely into place. When the great purifying storm finally arrived, he thought with quiet satisfaction, the air would be fit to breathe again, but until that glorious day . . .

'The chosen ones await your bidding, master,' came a gruff voice behind him.

Orbix turned. The cage-master, Mollus Leddix, stood before him. Behind him, flanked by hulking flathead Guardians, were two young librarians, their faces white and drawn. One, a shock of ginger hair matted by a gash in his eyebrow, tried to stand up straight, but the muscles in his jaw betrayed his fear. His companion, smaller and slightly hunched, stared with pale blue eyes at his feet. Their arms were tied behind their backs.

Orbix thrust his muzzle into the smaller one's face, and took a long, deep sniff. A tear squeezed out from the librarian's eyelashes and slid down his cheek.

'Very good,' said Orbix at last. 'Sweet. Tender . . . Caught them in the sewers, did you?'

'One of them, master,' Leddix nodded. 'The other was shot down over Undertown.'

Orbix Xaxis tutted. 'You librarians,' he said softly. 'Will you never learn that it is we, the Guardians of Night, who are the masters?' He nodded to the flatheads. 'Put them in the cage,' he growled. 'And remove their gags. I want to hear them sing.'

The flatheads tore the knotted rope from the prisoners' mouths and bundled them to the end of the jutting gantry, where a heavy cage hung down from an overhead pulley. One of the Guardians opened the barred door. Another shoved the prisoners inside. The ginger-haired librarian stood stock-still, his head held high. Beside him, his companion followed his example.

Orbix snorted. They were all the same, these young librarians. Trying so hard to be brave, to hide their fear – he had yet to meet a single one prepared to plead for his life. A cold fury gripped him. They would be singing soon enough.

'Lower the cage,' he barked.

Leddix gave a signal, and a Guardian stepped forward, released the locking-bolt on the crank-wheel, and began turning. With a lurch, the cage began its long descent. Orbix Xaxis raised his arms and lifted his head. The moonlight glinted on his mask and tinted glasses.

'Thus perish all those who pollute the Great Sky with blasphemous flight!' his rasping voice rang out. 'For we, the Guardians, shall purify the Sky, ready for that Great Night. Hail, the Great Storm!'

The gantry filled with voices raised in salute. 'Hail, the Great Storm! Hail, the Great Storm!'

Far below them now, the cage continued down. Past the dark angular Tower of Night it went; past the surface of the crumbling Sanctaphrax rock and the vast network of scaffolding erected to support it, and on down into Screetown.

Inside the cage, the two librarians struggled to keep their balance as they stared out.

'Try not to look down,' said the ginger-haired one.

'I . . . I can't,' said his companion. 'I saw something down there in the darkness . . . Waiting . . .'

Created when massive chunks of stone had broken off from the crumbling Sanctaphrax rock, fallen and crushed the area of Undertown directly beneath, Screetown was a rubble-strewn wilderness. Every building had been demolished, every street destroyed, while the weight of the immense boulders crashing down was so great that the shock waves had opened up gaping canyons in the ground.

It was into the deepest of these canyons that the librarians were being lowered. All at once, the cage jerked to a standstill. The two young librarians fell against the bars of the cage as, far above their heads, the voice of the High Guardian rang out.

'Come, Demons of the Deep!' he cried. 'And rid the Sky of its polluters!' He turned to Leddix. 'Release them,' he hissed.

Leddix reached across and pulled on the stout wooden lever by his shoulder. There was a *hiss* as rope slid through the pulley-wheel, and a muffled *clank*. Far below, the bottom of the cage swung open and the librarians toppled down onto the steep, scree-covered slope beneath them with an anguished cry.

'Now, their song begins,' Orbix rasped from behind the mask. He stepped forward and peered down into the canyon.

Far beneath him, he could just make out the two young librarians, sliding and stumbling as they struggled to stop themselves slipping further down into the canyon. And there, emerging from the cracks and crevices all round them – in a shadowy flurry of flapping wings and scurrying claws – were the huge dark shapes of the creatures awaiting them.

The pale, young librarians let out loud, piercing screams. Like the contracting iris of a monstrous eye, the black shapes closed in around them – and blotted them out. From the canyon depths came a low chorus of howls and snarls, and the sound of tearing flesh. The screaming stopped.

Orbix turned away. 'Such a sweet song,' he mused. 'I never tire of it.'

'Master,' gasped Leddix, pointing up at the sky and falling to his knees. 'Look!'

Orbix spun round, to see a bright ball of flame hurtling from one side of the sky to the other in a blaze of blood-red light. Over his head it flew, wailing eerily; past the Stone Gardens and off into Open Sky beyond. Unblinking, Orbix watched it shrink to the size of a marsh-gem, a pinprick – and then disappear.

He held his breath.

The next instant, there was a distant explosion and a

flash of light. The misty clouds seemed to grow denser, dimming the yellow light of the moon. Orbix gripped the wooden lever to steady himself. The air grew heavier than ever.

'It is a sign,' he breathed. 'Look how the clouds grow thick, how the very air around us grows hotter. The sky is preparing for the arrival of that wondrous night.'

'Hail, the Great Storm!' barked Leddix, falling to his knees. The guards took up the cry once more. 'Hail, the Great Storm! Hail, the Great Storm!'

Several storeys below, in his study, Xanth Filatine – assistant to the High Guardian of Night – looked up from a barkscroll and shuddered. There must have been another Purification Ceremony – probably the two librarians he'd interrogated that afternoon. And after he'd specifically told Leddix he couldn't have them! Xanth slammed a fist down on his desk. The evil skyslug had gone over his head to the High Guardian – and everybody knew how much Orbix Xaxis enjoyed his little rituals.

Xanth strode across to the window and looked out. 'Hail to the Great Storm,' he muttered bitterly.

*

As he looked down from the saddle of the *Stormhornet*, Rook Barkwater frowned. Something *was* going on at the Mire Gates. Usually at this time in the morning, there would be half a dozen shrykes at most on guard. Today there were hundreds of them.

Deftly lowering the loftsail and tugging the nether-sail rope hard to his right, he swooped in as close as he dared. He was counting on the thick stifling mist to help conceal him. Keeping low, he skirted the boom-docks. Then, taking both rope-handles in one hand, he raised his telescope to his eye with the other.

'Sky above!' he exclaimed.

Long columns of the bird-creatures were stretched back along the Great Mire Road as far as the eye could see. More ominously, from the way they were kitted out – with their shiny breastplates, plumed battle-helmets and multitude of terrible weapons – this was no mere gathering of the clans. The shrykes seemed to be mobilizing for war.

Rook knew he had to get back to the Great Library and make a report. Then it would be up to the High Librarian, Fenbrus Lodd, to decide what to do for the best. Tugging sharply on the loftsail rope, Rook brought the *Stormhornet* round and, staying low in the sky, headed back over Undertown.

These were, indeed, strange times. There were alleged goblin atrocities in Undertown, rumours of a thwarted slave uprising in the Sanctaphrax Forest and unconfirmed sightings of monstrous creatures emerging from the diseased rock itself. And then there was this strange weather. Like all librarian knights, Rook Barkwater had been briefed to take close note of the weather whilst on patrol.

But what was there to say? he wondered. That it was a little bit hotter than the morning before? A little bit more humid, more sultry, more oppressive? That the dense cover of cloud looked a little bit lower in the sky; the sun behind it, a little dimmer? Certainly he could confirm all these things. But that was all. As for *why* it was happening, that was anyone's guess. All Rook knew was that sunrise had become a drab affair, with the displays of dazzling colour and intricate cloud formations now seemingly things of the past.

Ploughing on through the hot, turgid air, Rook circled the tall, cracked towers of the Palace of Statues and swooped back down over the squalor and degradation of Undertown. He noted the dilapidated stores and run-down workshops opening up for business, the factories and foundries belching smoke, and on every street, the columns of chained slaves being driven by goblin guards from one part of town to the other as the night-shift was replaced by the day-shift.

'Poor creatures,' Rook whispered, his stomach churning.

The whole stinking place sickened him. And yet, as he swooped by unnoticed, Rook saw no sign that the goblins' behaviour was any more atrocious than normal. Nor, when he reached the jumbled framework of beams and pillars that formed the Sanctaphrax Forest, could he detect any hint of a recent uprising. It all looked like business as usual, with the slaves toiling and the goblins keeping them at their backbreaking work with random acts of casual brutality.

Away from the work gangs, the Sanctaphrax Forest was eerily quiet. Only the constant soft creaking of the wood broke the silence. Rook flitted in and out of the shadowy scaffolding uneasily. He'd never liked it here. Ever since the forest had first been erected it had become colonized by numerous unpleasant creatures: flocks of ratbirds, colonies of rabid fromps, weezits, razorflits . . .

Suddenly, from his right, he heard a sucking, slurping noise. He glanced round to see a dwarf-rotsucker on a broad horizontal beam crouched down next to a small egg-like cocoon. It had already drilled a hole in the side with its probing snout, and was now sucking out the putrid soup of a recent victim, now fully decomposed.

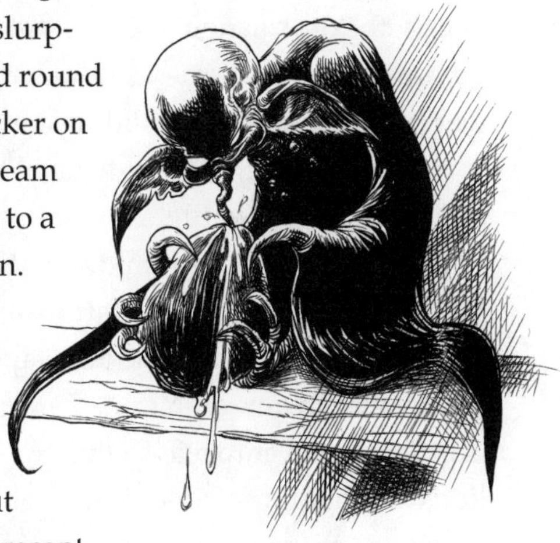

The rank stench of death filled the air. The rotsucker looked up from its meal, its glowing eyes boring into the shadows suspiciously. Rook glided on.

Swooping down lower in the sky, letting the light breeze do the work for him as he crossed the Edgewater

River, Rook found himself thinking about the underground library – and how glad he was not to be there now.

All those years he'd spent down in the dark, dripping sewers had left him with a fierce hunger for the world outside. He loved the freedom, and the space, and the wind in his hair and the sun in his face – and each time he soared up high on the *Stormhornet*, he was overwhelmed by the wonder of the endless expanse of sky all round him.

He looked down, and swallowed uneasily. Screetown.

Rook surveyed the scene of desolation below him. The debris, the destruction, the dark fissures that had opened up in the ground. He shuddered. Everywhere, there were shifting shadows sliding between the rocks, and curious glinting lights that were like eyes glaring back at him; widening greedily, sizing him up. Rook felt the evil of the place weighing him down. He tugged sharply on the sail ropes and the skycraft rose up in the sky.

Higher he flew, past the Sanctaphrax rock and on up above the Tower of Night. Far to his left, the Stone Gardens came into view. Pulling hard on the loftsail, Rook brought the *Stormhornet* about in the sky and prepared for the long swooping descent round the stacks of broken boulders at the furthest tip of the Edge.

His spirits lifted as he left Screetown behind him. It felt good to be high in the sky once more, the whole world spread out below him like a vast intricate map. *This* was where he belonged, up in wide open air. Not trapped below the ground like a piebald rat.

All at once, a sound broke into his thoughts: a great roaring, wailing sound that was coming up fast behind him. The next instant everything was a confusion of noise and heat and light. The *Stormhornet* reared beneath him and spun round. Rook couldn't see a thing. The wind was rushing all round him, tossing him about like a scrap of parchment. The acrid smell of burning spider-silk and toasted wood-almonds filled his nostrils.

'Sky save me,' he murmured, his words whipped away on the rushing air.

The fragile craft had gone into a plummeting tailspin, and together, the pair of them were tumbling out of the sky faster than a stricken flight-rock.

·CHAPTER TWO·

SCREETOWN

Clinging on grimly, Rook fought hard to control the *Stormhornet*'s steep dive. He leaned back in the stirrups and tried desperately to keep her nose up. But it was no good. The skycraft wasn't responding. The ground – a mosaic of rock stacks and ravines – hurtled up to meet them.

The last thing Rook remembered was making himself relax his muscles in preparation for the crash, just as he'd been taught to do in flight training. He released the carved wooden neck, pulled his feet out of the stirrups, and felt the *Stormhornet* slip away from beneath him.

For a moment, everything seemed to be sweeping past him in a smudged blur. There was a roaring of air and a flashing of light – then blackness.

Rook opened his eyes. His head was throbbing, there was something heavy pressing down on his chest, and his mouth was full of foul-tasting dust. But he was alive.

Above him, the chaotic silhouettes of rubble crags stood out against the muddy sky like brooding giants. Where was he? he wondered. Where was the *Stormhornet*? And what in Sky's name had happened? One moment he'd been swooping high in the sky beyond the great rock, the next he was . . .

Screetown!

An icy shiver ran through him. The treacherous winds had driven him back across the sky. Now he was inside that desolate wasteland of wrecked buildings and sprawling rockfalls, home to rubble ghouls and muglumps – and worse. From far above him came the raucous cawing of a lone white raven as it sliced across the dusty sky.

The important thing, he knew, was not to panic. He must stay calm. He must remember his training. After all, he was a librarian knight, he told himself; one of Varis Lodd's finest. He would survive. He had to survive. Varis would expect nothing less of him.

First of all, he must check for any injuries. Gingerly, he felt his head, his neck, and his chest . . . The pressure on his ribs, he discovered, came from a large piece of rubble that was making it hard to breathe. With a grunt, Rook gripped the boulder, slowly eased it off his chest and dropped it beside him. It disappeared into nothingness.

With a gasp, Rook turned to find himself staring down into a deep, dark chasm. He was lying on the very edge of a huge canyon. Far below, he could hear the boulder's clattering descent. Its muffled thuds echoed back – first loud, then softer, and then softer still – as it bounced

from rock to rock. And from the depths of the canyon, there came an answering call; a mewling cry which grew louder and louder, until the air echoed with sinister howls.

Anxiously, Rook rose to his feet and stepped back from the canyon's edge. Whatever lurked down there in those infernal depths, he had clearly awoken it. The cries grew louder, and he thought he heard the sound of shifting scree as something scrabbled closer.

He didn't wait to see what it was. Turning away, Rook began to pick his way through the piles of rubble as quickly as he dared. The treacherous rubble below his feet slipped and slid. The air was thick with choking dust.

'Find shelter,' a voice inside his head whispered. 'Somewhere to hide.'

Rook clambered over the angular rockscape, grazing his fingers and scraping his shins. There were great mountains of rubble looming up everywhere he looked; a chaos of cracked arches, fallen walls and leaning pillars, with jutting roofbeams silhouetted against the sepia-stained sky like the ribs of giant creatures.

The wind, though little more than a hot, malodorous draught, whistled softly between the rocks like an ancient goblin matron sucking air between her gappy teeth. The sun was low behind the cloudcover, with the sky already growing darker, yet the air beneath was hotter than ever. Rook wiped the sweat from his forehead; he was still finding it difficult to breathe. His head ached, and every jarred bone in his body throbbed with pain – but Rook dared not stop, not even for a moment.

The howls were getting closer, and whatever was making them, it was clearly no longer alone. Others had joined it in a chorus of yelps and shrieks. He had to find a hiding-place, and quickly.

Some way ahead a ruined archway poked up from the scree. Beneath it, Rook could see a crevice that looked just large enough for him to crawl through. He only hoped it didn't already have an occupant. He checked his equipment – water-bottle, grappling-hook, notebook, hover tincture, knife . . .

The cries seemed just behind him now; keening, high-pitched, and accompanied by a strange leathery rustling. Rook swallowed anxiously.

He was being hunted.

Drawing his knife, Rook made for the crevice. He crouched down, thrust his head into the entrance and listened. There was nothing. He sniffed. If some creature was using the place as a sanctuary, he should be able to smell its musty bedding or pungent droppings. Again, there was nothing; only the dry, sour odour of the crumbled rock itself.

Behind him, the howls rose up in a swirling discord.

'Earth guard and Sky protect me,' he murmured as he disappeared into the small opening.

It was narrower than he'd first thought and grew narrower still the further he scrambled into the dark, dusty crevice. Soon he was down on his front and wriggling between the great slabs of fallen rock. The gaps between them closed in, pressing into him from both sides, squeezing him

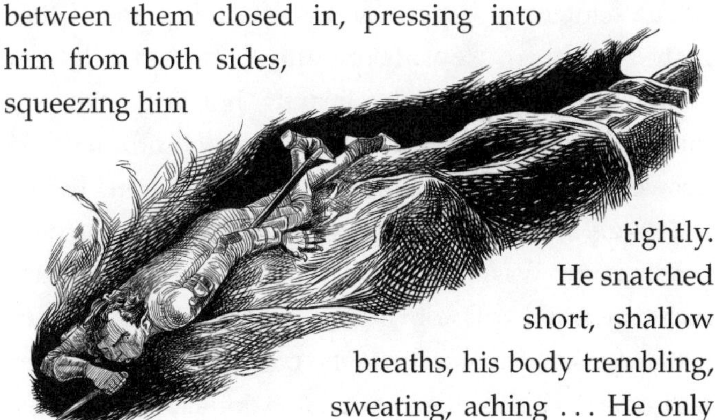

tightly. He snatched short, shallow breaths, his body trembling, sweating, aching ... He only hoped he'd be able to get out again. Had he escaped the howling creatures, only to bury himself in his own grave? The thing was, he had to get far enough in to avoid a probing claw or tentacle.

'Just a few strides more,' he urged himself. 'Just ...'

Rook could go no further. Ahead, the rubble was packed tight. He shifted himself awkwardly round, cracking his knee against a jutting rock. Ignoring the intense pain, he reached out and hurriedly grasped handful after handful of the sour dust, which he rubbed over his clothes, his face, and his hair. It stuck to the sweat, coating every inch of him and should, according to his training, obscure his own smell – at least, that was the theory.

All at once, there came a snuffling, sniffing sound from the opening to the crevice. Rook froze. The sniffing grew louder. Then there was a rough scratching noise, followed by the sound of falling debris. Something – a snout, a claw, a tentacle – was working its way into the crevice, searching for its elusive prey. Rook bit nervously into his lower lip.

The scratching stopped. The sniffing resumed – then it, too, stopped. Rook heard the leathery rustling as something big scuffled off heavily, howling with rage and frustration as it searched elsewhere. A dozen others answered its call. The leathery rustle grew more distant; the howls receded. The hunt seemed to be moving on.

When he was sure they'd gone, Rook began the arduous crawl back out of the crevice. At the end, he pushed aside the rocks that the creature had dislodged, and emerged, dust-covered and shaking. He wiped the sour particles from his lips and breathed in the evening air greedily. Then he peered about him, ready at the first sign of danger to disappear back into the hole.

The ground gave a little tremor – causing the rubble to shift and more dust to rise.

Must get my bearings, Rook thought grimly as he climbed to his feet. He had to get out of this place as soon as he could.

The Sanctaphrax rock loomed in the sky behind him and he could just make out the cracked towers of Undertown's northern heights far ahead. To his left and right, the skeletons of buildings rose up out of the debris like disfigured hands. Before him, a vast mound of stone blocks extended into the distance. Walking was impossible. He would have to clamber up the precariously balanced rocks on his hands and knees.

Rook knew the drill, of course. Test each foothold before committing your whole weight. And if you need to leap, then look carefully first.

By the time he reached the top of the first rubble mound, Rook was sweating heavily and panting like a shryke-sister's prowlgrin after a long patrol. He paused and straightened up. The towers of the northern heights were still in front of him – but by his reckoning it was already late afternoon. At this rate, he faced the very real prospect of having to survive a night in Screetown. He swallowed uneasily.

All at once, a colossal tremor knocked Rook off his feet. The rubble beneath him seemed to boil; great clouds of dust blacked out the evening sky, stinging his eyes and filling his mouth. Rook curled up into a ball and waited for the shaking to stop.

Slowly, the rubble settled and the rattle of shifting pebbles died away. The thick dust still hung in the hot, humid air but, as Rook wiped his eyes, it too began to clear. When he was sure it was over, he climbed shakily to his feet once more and looked around.

The rubble mounds just behind him had been flattened to reveal a line of splintered beams from some long-buried building. Beside them, only half-uncovered, the statue of a great Undertown artisan – long since forgotten – stood at a drunken angle, one arm, broken at the wrist, reaching up to the sky. And in the middle of it all – like a huge clenched fist – lay a massive chunk of rock. Rook looked up at the towering shape of the Sanctaphrax rock above him, propped up on its forest of wooden pillars, like some huge diseased oak-apple.

Despite the neverending work carried out on the Sanctaphrax Forest, crumbling pieces of the great rock were always falling. Most were small and insignificant, but every so often a great slab would break free and come crashing down onto Screetown.

Rook shuddered. 'That was close,' he murmured. 'Too close.'

He turned to go – then froze in his tracks. A hand of ice seemed to grip his heart.

'No,' he whispered. 'No, it can't be.'

But it was. Lying on the ground not half a dozen strides away was the *Stormhornet* – or what was left of it. The mast was blackened and in two pieces. A charred scrap of spidersilk and a twist of rope were all that remained of the sails. And as for the prow . . . Rook picked his way over the uneven ground and, crouching down beside the skycraft, reached out tentatively.

His fingers confirmed what he hoped his eyes had only imagined. The neck of the *Stormhornet* was broken almost in two. Jagged splinters at the top of the stump glinted in the weak sunlight while the angular head – barely attached by a couple of thin, woody fibres – lolled forward.

A painful lump formed in Rook's throat. The sails and ropes could have been replaced; so could the mast. But with the neck of the craft broken, he knew that its spirit had been released. The *Stormhornet* would never fly again.

Rook fell to his knees. He raised the wooden head, held it gently in place, and hugged the prow tightly. Memories from the Free Glades came flooding back: Oakley Gruffbark, the woodtroll master-carver who had helped him find the stormhornet – *his* stormhornet – concealed within the slab of wood he had to carve; varnish-making in the Gardens of Light; sail-setting and ropecraft. Bit by bit, he'd worked on her, and learned to fly her . . .

'I . . . I carved you,' he whispered, his voice faltering. 'I named you. Together we rode the sky, you and I.' He sniffed. 'Farewell . . .' His chest felt tight, as though the boulder was back there, pressing down and making it difficult to breathe. '*Stormhornet . . .*'

Rook knew that his beloved skycraft was now just a piece of wood again. Her spirit had departed. With a heavy heart, he stood up and set off.

He did not look back.

Progress was slow as Rook struggled on. Navigating the jagged, uneven rubble became increasingly difficult and his throat was soon as parched as the rocky landscape he was crossing. Time and again he came to vast craters which took an age to cross. Down he would go, into the echoing bowl of boulders and up the other side, hoping and praying each time that when he emerged at the top, the towers of Undertown would look nearer.

'This time,' he whispered, the sound of his own voice oddly reassuring as he climbed the far side of a particularly large depression. 'This time, they'll look closer, they've got to . . .'

Once again, he was disappointed. The towers appeared as far away as ever. What was more, it was growing darker.

Must keep my head, he reminded himself. I can

survive a night in Screetown if I just follow my training and don't lose my nerve – Earth and Sky willing, he thought anxiously as a raucous shriek echoed round the desolation. The night-creatures were stirring.

He reached for his water-bottle and had it to his lips before remembering that it was empty.

'Stupid,' he muttered to himself, clipping the empty flask back into place. Varis would be disappointed in him for failing to conserve his meagre rations. He shook his head miserably. Perhaps he'd discover some more water and be able to refill it. But until then . . .

He picked up a smooth round pebble and popped it into his mouth. It was supposed to make his mouth water, to provide enough moisture to soothe his burning throat. But it didn't work. Rook spat the claggy stone out in disgust, and as he drove himself on, his thirst nagged at him constantly now that there was no means to slake it.

It was so hot. So humid. He wiped his hand gently across his brow and sucked the sweat from his finger-tips. The salty droplets only made him greedy for more.

Of course, there was water here in Screetown, dry and dusty though it appeared. Rook knew that it was just a matter of finding it. Ruptured pipes and broken fountains continued to flow; wells where, long ago, Undertowners had gathered to draw water and gossip, still tapped into the underground water-table. What he had to do was look out for moss, for grass, and scrubby bushes, whose roots, reaching down through the cracks in the rubble, were a sure sign of the presence of water –

that and the evidence of the Screetown creatures which drank it.

As he forged his way on, their shrieks and cries echoed through the sultry twilight air. Past a cracked tower he went, a great section of its once magnificent dome missing, like a bite from a giant woodsap. To his left, out of the corner of his eye, he caught sight of movement and turned to see something slither into the shadows. Rook moved quickly on.

He made his way over fallen pillars forming makeshift bridges; beneath a crumbling viaduct, its two rows of supports in various stages of collapse; through the lower window of a tall, unsteady facade, and on across a jagged carpet of slates – once a roof, now a treacherous floor. One slip and he would end up tumbling down into the cracks that gaped on either side of him. If he did, he knew that no-one would ever find him – until the scavengers came to pick his bones.

The towers of Undertown were still before him, but flat now against the sky in the fading light. Despite all his efforts, he was still making dismal progress. Every breath was an effort; every step a gamble. Panting noisily, he slipped and stumbled, grazing his knuckles and cracking his shins. And then, just when he thought things couldn't get any worse, something up ahead of him caught his eye; something that reminded him that in Screetown things could *always* get worse.

It was lying on a flat slab of rock: bright blue, furry, crushed. He approached cautiously, a numbing dread pounding in his temples. From its beaky snout and curved claws, Rook recognized the dead creature at once.

'A lemkin,' he gasped, and prodded at the desiccated body with his foot. A fine white dust trickled down from its mouth and empty eye-sockets. Rook looked away, but not before noticing that there was grey-green moss clinging to the rock. There must be water close by! Perhaps the lemkin had come searching for it – and perished in the process. Rook drew his sword and peered into the shadows.

From his left, he heard a soft, murmuring trickle. Water – running water. A broken pipe, maybe; or a little spring. Rook moved towards the sound, his senses on fire and his head spinning – the promise of the cool, refreshing water battling with the need to remain on his guard.

He climbed over a squat, rounded rock that looked like nothing so much as a grazing hammelhorn. The trickling sound grew louder. There, bubbling up from the ground in the shadow of two moss-covered slabs of rock, was a small spring. It overflowed and spread out, before disappearing back into the earth. The muddy ground around it was dappled with the footprints of numerous creatures – both predator and prey. Rook had just seen what had happened to the lemkin. He had no intention of suffering the same fate.

Keeping a close lookout, he crouched down – sword ready at his side – cupped his hands and plunged them into the small pool; and again, and again . . .

Water had never tasted as good!

His thirst quenched at last, Rook unclipped his water-bottle and dunked it into the clear water. Glugging bubbles hit the surface as it filled, and he glanced nervously round, terrified that some prowling Screetown creature might have heard.

Was that something glinting in the shadows? he wondered, his heart racing. And what was that *smell*? Steamy . . . Stagnant . . .

'Hurry up,' he muttered and shook the bottle under the water, trying to force it to fill more quickly. The air bubbles came out in a rush – then stopped completely as the water gushed in. Rook pushed the cork into place and was about to attach it back on his belt when he heard a noise behind him. Soft and slithering, it was – and the steamy, stagnant odour seemed to grow more intense.

Grasping his sword, Rook spun round. At first, he couldn't see anything untoward. Just rocks and shadows.

There's nothing there, he tried to reassure himself. It's just my mind playing tricks.

But even as he thought it, he realized that he was wrong. His gaze fell on a glint of light. It was a tentacle; a moist, translucent tentacle writhing out of a black crevice and probing the rock above. And as he watched – horrified, unable to tear himself away – a second tentacle appeared. Together, the pair of them gripped the rock, quivered and tugged. The next instant, the glistening top of a jelly-like creature appeared from the narrow crack. It squeezed itself up out of the gap, like tilder-fat oozing from a split barrel.

'Earth and Sky!' Rook gasped, stepping back.

With a slimy *squelch*, the last of the great gelatinous creature eased itself out of the crevice. Trembling and wobbling, it resumed its more normal form. With a sickening jolt of recognition, Rook realized just what it was. The three flickering eye-bumps, the slimy transparent skin with the veins pulsing beneath it; the probing tentacles, the fluttering belly-frill, the vast body quivering with anticipation . . .

'A rubble ghoul,' he whispered.

The name was enough to make every hair on his body stand on end. He had pored over descriptions of them in the library treatises he'd read, descriptions that had

revolted him even then. But now, up close, he felt a wave of nausea wash over him.

Slurping loudly, the rubble ghoul slithered over the slab of rock, its three eyes glistening in the gloom. Rook took another step back. At the edge of the slab now, the creature flapped its belly-frill and rose up, seemingly weightless, into the air. It pulsated as it moved, like bellows – in, out, in, out – sucking in the humid air, and blowing it out again, as hot and dry as the blast from an oven.

Rook took yet another step back. The creature came closer. It was clearly thirsty – but then rubble ghouls, he knew, were *always* thirsty. Not for running water though. Even as he edged towards the babbling spring, Rook knew it wouldn't save him. No, the rubble ghoul took its sustenance from living bodies, sucking every drop of moisture from its victims. Lemkins or librarian knights, they weren't fussy what they drank.

At the next faltering step, Rook's back thudded against rock. He could go no further. He was trapped.

The rubble ghoul hovered before him, slurping and hissing. In, out, it went. In out. The air all round grew hotter, drier; the stagnant odour made him gag.

All at once, the great pulsing creature tilted back to reveal a huge iris-like opening at the centre of its quivering belly. Rook stared in horror as, slowly but surely, it began to open. A shower of bright pink suckered tentacles flipped out and danced in the scorching air.

The colour drained from Rook's face. What could he do?

*

Like a clump of noxious toadstools growing out of a grimy Undertown clearing, the Hive Towers – headquarters of General Tytugg and his elite hammerhead guard – gleamed in the fading light. Lamps had already been lit both inside and out. Dull, flickering yellow light glowed from the small windows in the towers and cone-shaped roofs; torches fixed to the walls and the sides of the notorious Gates of Despair blazed. The rank odour of the burning fat mingled with the general filth – fungal, fetid, and foul.

Inside, the shadowy building was one vast, spartan open hall. At its centre was a great fire, the stinkwood logs the goblins preferred blazing fiercely. The flames were intensely hot; the smoke, pungent. Above the brazier hung a series of bubbling pots, each one tended by mobgnome slaves, their chains bolted to the floor. At the sides of the building, there were staircases leading up to platform after platform – all secured to the curving outer-walls but with no inner-walls to close them off into rooms. There were no secrets in the Hive Towers.

The whole place was seething. There were hammer-head goblins in every corner; rough and rowdy, their voices raised, and spoiling for a fight. Even those asleep on their hammocks strung out beneath the roof-beams were snoring, snorting, thrashing about and cursing loudly in their dreams.

Some were on duty, guarding the gates, the walls and the roofs. Some were at table in the slop-corners; others were seated on wooden benches tending to their equipment – patching rents in their jackets and re-soling their boots, cleaning blood from their swords and sharpening the vicious jags on their battle-scythes.

As a mobgnome slave scurried past a group of them, a jug clasped in her scrawny arms, one – a tattooed individual with a ring through his nose – stuck out a boot. The mobgnome went sprawling, her face thudding down into the rank, mouldering straw, her jug smashing and the hammelhorn-milk it had held slopping over the floor.

'Lick that up, clumsy slave-filth,' the hammerhead snarled.

Outside, a dozen or more – massive specimens, each of them, with heavy armour and bearing the scars of numerous hard battles – were locked in mock-combat, so fierce that it looked like the real thing.

Passing between the lot of them, a returning battalion of goblin guards was tramping up the stairs to the bulging armoury with a consignment of seized weapons.

Their victorious voices boomed round the hall.

'That'll teach them Undertown scumsacks not to mess with us,' one grunted. 'Whatever made them think they could get away with manufacturing weapons like that? And right under us noses!'

His neighbour chuckled. 'D'you hear that factory-master squeal when we strung him up?' he said. 'Like a stuck woodhog, he sounded.'

'Bled like one, too,' another chipped in.

'Still, the weapons'll come in useful,' the first hammerhead muttered, patting the great bundle of scythes, swords, maces and crossbows he and his neighbour were carrying between them. 'Rumour has it, there's a fresh contingent coming in from the Goblin Nations.'

Further down the stairs, a couple of goblins snorted dismissively.

'Goblin Nations,' one of them said, hawking and spitting down the stairwell.

'Milksops, the lot of them,' said the other. 'Settled down in villages just like that Free Glade scum, they have!'

Every self-respecting hammerhead goblin prided himself on his independence; with a weapon at his side and his birthing-bundle on his back, a hammerhead was always ready to pick up everything he owned and move on. Or should have been. Recently, though, several of their number had been tempted to settle down in permanent dwellings in the Goblin Nations; they'd become merchants, trappers – some, it was reported, were even taking up farming!

'General Tytugg will soon whip 'em into shape,' came a

voice from further up the stairs, and a cheer of derision and anticipation echoed round the building.

General Tytugg himself was unaware that his name had been mentioned. He didn't hear the raucous cheering, nor the spontaneous boot-pounding of approval that followed. Standing on the raised platform jutting out from the first storey, he only had eyes and ears for his prisoner.

'You *will* tell me, Huffknot,' he said, his voice gruff and menacing as he jerked the lugtroll's head sharply back. 'Of that, I give you my word.' He pulled a long rusty pin from the lapel of his leather battle-jacket and held it close to the lugtroll's terrified face.

'But . . . but I don't . . . I don't know anything,' he protested, his chains jangling. 'Not a single thing. Really, I don't. I'm at the beck and call of any who enlist my services . . .'

'Tut-tut-tut,' Tytugg clicked softly and shook his head. He traced the point of the pin lightly down the lugtroll's bulbous nose. 'I'm disappointed in you, Huffknot.' His voice grew harsh. 'I don't like being disappointed.'

'You've got to believe me!' the lugtroll pleaded.

'When you starts telling me the truth – the *whole* truth, Huffknot – then maybe I shall start believing you,' said the general. He turned and inspected the three small pots set out in a line on a trestle-table. He selected one at random, unstoppered it and sniffed the thick orange liquid inside. 'I wonder what this one does?'

Eyes wide and body quivering, Huffknot watched as the general poked the pin down inside the pot and withdrew it. A bead of orange clung to the sharpened point.

'Hold out your arm,' Tytugg demanded.

Huffknot did as he was told, the chain fixed round his wrist clanking as he moved. General Tytugg seized the arm, jabbed the pin into the skin and stood back to observe.

Almost at once, Huffknot felt the tiny pinprick burn, and he watched helplessly as his arm began to swell.

'Interesting,' said the general. 'Forgive me, Huffknot, but I thought you said the pots contained cosmetics – for the shryke-sisters. Feather-balm, you said. Beak-gloss. Cold cream . . .' He poked at the swollen arm. 'Yet it seems to work like . . . well, poison.'

Huffknot grimaced. 'I . . . I didn't know. She told me that . . .'

'*Who* told you?' General Tytugg demanded. Above and below, the hammerheads paused and looked round as his angry voice rose up above the general hubbub.

'I . . . I don't know her name,' Huffknot whispered.

Without a word, the general seized the second pot, pulled out the stopper and dipped the pin inside. This time, as he pricked the lugtroll's flesh, the skin developed an angry red rash that spread up his arm and down to his fingertips. And, as the pair of them watched, the whole area erupted in a mass of tiny pustules. Tytugg thrust the pin into the bottle a second time and held it close to Huffknot's face.

'Hestera,' he blurted out. 'Hestera Spikesap.'

'I knew it!' the general cried triumphantly. 'Hestera Spikesap . . .' He savoured the words. '*Hestera Spikesap* – the hag what ministers to that parasitic lardbutt, Vox Verlix.' He turned and called down to a hammerhead guard sitting on a wooden bench, hardening his crossbow bolts in the fire. 'I owe you a barrel of woodgrog, Smutt,' he shouted. 'He *was* coming out of the Palace of Statues.'

The hammerhead looked up and grinned toothlessly. 'Sir,' he shouted back.

The general turned back to Huffknot. A thin-lipped smile spread across his leathery face, revealing an incomplete set of brown, jagged teeth. 'Looks like I've struck gold with you,' he said.

'But I don't know anything, believe me. I'm her slave. I have to do what I'm told,' Huffknot babbled. 'I was to deliver the pots to the shrykes, just as I told you, and return with a phial I would be given in return.'

Tytugg shuddered. 'Shrykes,' he muttered. 'One day, so help me, I'm going to wring every one of their scrawny necks. They've got it coming to them . . .' He looked up, eyes blazing. 'A phial of *what*?'

Huffknot shrugged. 'Your guards arrested me before . . .'

The general spat. 'Something to do with that Vox Verlix, no doubt,' he snarled. 'I've been meaning to pay that great fatsack another visit for quite some time.' He ran his fingers up and down his knife. 'Unfinished business, you might say. It's about time he learned who *really* governs Undertown.' He frowned. 'If I could just get into that rat-trap of a palace of his . . .'

He fell silent, deep in thought. Then he turned on Huffknot. His face was grim, his voice menacing.

'But of course!' he said, an evil smile playing on his lips. 'Hestera Spikesap's slave, you say. Well I'm sure *you* know your way round Vox's palace – where those traps are and how to avoid them. How, for instance' – Tytugg leered at the hapless lugtroll – 'a goblin who wanted to pay our so-called Most High Academe an unannounced visit might get into his personal chamber?'

'Unannounced visit?' said Huffknot. 'Personal chamber?' He trembled. 'I . . . I'm just a kitchen slave.'

General Tytugg turned away. He picked up the third pot and tugged the cork free. An acrid odour – like rotting oaksap and tildermusk – filled the air. The lugtroll blanched as the general plunged the pin into the black potion it contained. He stirred it three times, then turned back to the lugtroll and held the steaming pin inches from the bulbous nose.

'No, no!' Huffknot shrieked. 'Not that one! I beg you! Please! I'll tell you everything! *Everything!*'

Grasping his sword, Rook slashed desperately at the hideous gelatinous creature that reared up before him, its huge mouth writhing with tentacles. But it was no good. With a sudden beating of its belly-frill, the rubble ghoul surged forwards and swallowed him whole. It was like being smothered in scalding tar.

Rook couldn't cry out. He could barely breathe. He felt the tentacles attaching themselves to his face, his arms, his legs. He struggled, but could not move. The sword was wrenched from his fingers. Soon, his heart would stop and the suckers would start their work. He would be drained like the hanging carcass of a hammelhorn.

Helpless, he peered through the translucent body of the suffocating creature. He could just make out the towers of Undertown. With a sharp pang of despair, he thought how they looked farther away than ever . . .

All at once, there was a hiss, a shudder – and the rubble ghoul's mouth suddenly gaped in an involuntary spasm. Rook was spat out with such force that he was slammed into the rubble beside the spring. Something round and leathery almost hit him on the head as the creature spat again, and seemed to curl up into itself. Rook looked down. It was his water-bottle – empty now, and dry as a bone.

At that moment, the rubble ghoul let out a bloodcurdling screech and turned from purple to red, three jets of steam hissing noisily from its eyes. Its translucent body bubbled and popped, like water boiling in a cauldron. A glass phial shot out of the writhing rubble ghoul and shattered on the rocks beside Rook.

'The hover tincture,' Rook murmured.

No librarian knight's equipment was complete without the antidote to the bite of the hover worm, the notorious Deepwoods predator. Here in Undertown, they were seldom encountered, and yet the small glass phial was considered a good-luck charm. Rook had good cause to thank it now. The antidote that acted against the horrific swelling caused by the hoverworm's bite was clearly fatal to the rubble ghoul.

With a small sigh, the creature flopped down onto a slab of rock. The last vestiges of moisture evaporated away. There was nothing left but a fine, dry membrane – with Rook's sword resting at the very centre.

Rook climbed to his feet and crossed over to the rock. Already the hot humid air was turning the remains of the rubble ghoul to dust. He stooped down for the sword, wiped the blade on his trousers and returned it to its sheath. Then, as he turned to leave, something caught his eye.

He stopped.

Not some*thing*, he realized, but some*one* – silhouetted against the sky just above him. Rook sank to his knees. He'd been hunted, almost died of thirst, been swallowed whole then spat out again, only to be cornered by . . . By *what*?

'I give up,' he murmured. 'I can't go on . . .'

The figure held out a hand. 'Varis would be very disappointed to hear that,' said a familiar voice.

·CHAPTER THREE·

THE SUNKEN PALACE

Rook could scarcely believe his ears. That voice! He recognized that voice. Shielding his eyes with his hand, he squinted up into the light. He saw an untidy shock of fair hair, a turned-up nose, arched eyebrows over glinting blue eyes . . .

'Felix?' he said. 'Is it you? Is it really you?'

The figure reached forward. Rook hesitated, then grasped the outstretched hand which gripped his own, firmly, warmly, and pulled him to his feet. There in front of him, resplendent in an array of bleached white bone-armour and grey muglump-leather pelts, stood his old friend Felix Lodd.

Attached to his belt were leather pouches and hide ropes. A curved, serrated knife hung at his side next to a sturdy crossbow slung through a faded grey holster. In the ashen dust of Screetown, this tall figure with his fair hair and bleached apparel looked almost ghost-like.

'I might look like a ghost,' laughed Felix, as if reading Rook's thoughts, 'but I'm real enough, Rook, my old friend.'

'Felix!' Rook cried, hugging him warmly. 'I thought you were dead! We all did. Even Varis. She said that nobody can survive for long in Screetown . . .'

'Much as I hate to disappoint my darling sister and all you learned librarians,' said Felix with a smile, 'it *is* possible to survive in Screetown – though not if you stand round a waterhole, chatting like two old washer-gnomes on laundry day.' He winked. 'Come, Rook,' he said, turning and effortlessly scaling a mound of rubble. 'Tonight you're invited to supper in the Sunken Palace!'

Rook scrambled up after him. 'Wait for me, Felix,' he gasped. 'Not so fast!'

Night was falling, and the shadows and the darkness were melting into one, yet Felix navigated his way skilfully and confidently through the broken landscape. He clambered over rockfalls, skirted round gaping crevices and picked his way over uneven rocks and rubble, as agile and sure-footed as a lemkin.

Rook followed close behind – or as close as his stumbling, fumbling efforts allowed. Whenever he fell too far back, Felix would perch on a boulder or lean nonchalantly against a ruined pillar, smiling indulgently and waiting for him to catch up. The going was tough and Rook – hot, dusty and constantly out of breath – was beginning to flag.

'There are quite a number of us now,' Felix was saying as, once again, Rook caught up with him. 'We kowtow to no-one,' he told him, 'be they shryke, Guardian or goblin guard.' He smiled. 'We call ourselves the Ghosts of Screetown.'

'I can . . . can see why,' said Rook, fighting to catch his breath. 'But what do you actually *do* in this terrible place?'

Felix turned and continued, clambering effortlessly up over a jutting spur of broken rock. 'Hunt muglumps,' he laughed. 'Among other things.'

'Such as?' said Rook, wearily following him.

They reached a broad stretch of jagged rocks.

'Well,' said Felix, 'sometimes I organize raids with other ghosts to release those poor beggars in the Sanctaphrax Forest. We get them to Undertown, where you librarians take over, helping to shift them on to the Free Glades. Sometimes, to spice things up a little, I'll ambush a Guardian patrol – and the rest of the time I hunt and trap. All kinds of creatures, from feral lemkins in the ruins of Screetown, to muglumps in the sewers.' He paused and glanced back. 'Careful up ahead, Rook. It gets a bit tricky.'

Rook nodded grimly. He was doing his best.

They passed along a dark, narrow chasm, packed with shifting rubble to negotiate and awkward boulders to get round, and emerged at last beside a broad fluted pillar, cracked and lying on its side. Just beyond it, Rook saw a leaning statue, one arm – severed at the wrist – raised and reaching to the sky . . .

'I recognize this place,' he blurted out, disappointment in his voice. 'You mean, all this time, we've been travelling back the way I came.'

Felix nodded but said nothing. Reaching forward, he shouldered back a slab of rock and pointed down a narrow tunnel behind it. 'It's this way,' he told him.

Rook followed Felix into the dark tunnel and waited as his friend pulled the rock back into place.

'I'll lead,' Felix whispered. 'Put your hand on my shoulder. And don't make a sound.'

Rook did as he was told, shuffling forwards as Felix set off. The ground was bumpy and dropped steeply. Although his friend was steadying him, it was all Rook could do not to slip and pitch forwards. The air grew cooler, damper, and was laced with an acrid odour that grew more pungent with every step he took. Had he been on his own, he would have turned back there and then, but he was with Felix now and, for the first time since the terrible crash, he felt safe.

Beneath his feet came the edge of what seemed like a stone stair. Felix abruptly dropped away from him. Rook's hand grasped at nothing.

'Easy does it,' came Felix's voice, and Rook felt his friend's hand reaching back for him. He seized it gratefully and stepped down gingerly after him. A little further on, there was a second step; followed by a third . . . Then a long flight, which seemed to go deep

down into the rubble. The odour grew more pungent. 'What *is* that horrible smell?' he whispered.

'A ratbird roost,' Felix whispered back. 'And it's the best smell there is in Screetown, believe me.'

As Felix spoke, Rook became aware of the sound of squeaky twittering far above his head and, when he looked up, it was as though the very rocks were squirming. There were thousands of the little creatures. Rook shuddered.

'No desirable residence is complete without a ratbird roost,' said Felix above the rising clamour as the ratbirds raised the alarm. 'If anything unpleasant should come creeping along to pay us a visit, the ratbirds will soon let us know.'

It was darker than ever at the bottom of the stairs, but as the ground levelled out it became easier to walk. They seemed to be in some kind of ancient corridor. Felix increased his pace. Still holding on to him, Rook trotted along behind.

'Nearly there,' said Felix.

The next moment, they came to a thick curtain of animal hide, which Felix pulled aside to reveal a carved lintel set into the wall above a doorway. Rook peered in – and gasped.

He was standing in the entrance to a great chamber. Eyes wide, he followed Felix inside. Despite the dirty walls and blackened beams, the original grandeur of the place was still in evidence. There were marble pillars and a mosaic-tiled floor, and ancient lamps hung from the high moulded ceiling. Clearly this had once been the residence of someone wealthy – a prominent leagues-man, perhaps; or a successful merchant. Not that the contents of the room belonged to either.

There were dried muglump pelts, both large and small, covering every wall; and the implements that Felix must have used to slay them – curved swords, long thin javelins, and heavy nets, ringed with circular weights – hung from rows of great curling hooks. In one corner there were tusks, horns, skins and skulls; some stacked, some hanging, some clustered together in piles. In the other corner, set into an alcove above which a wall-torch flickered, was an ancient carved cistern. It was, Rook thought, similar to the Wodgiss-fonts the woodtrolls used in their celebrations – but made of stone, not wood. Into it – trickling from a crack in the rock – splashed a thin twist of crystal-clear water.

'Welcome to the Sunken Palace,' said Felix. He swept his arm around in a wide arc. 'A modest little palace, but I call it home,' he chuckled. 'But then I don't have to tell you, Rook, that when you've grown up in the sewers of Undertown, anywhere without a leaking roof is absolute luxury.'

Rook shook his head. 'It's amazing,' he murmured.

Felix clapped his hands together. 'Come on then, my old friend. You must be famished. Fetch me a pot of water from the cistern and I'll get a fire started.'

Rook happily did as he was told. He dunked the large pot into the cistern, filling it almost to the brim; then – holding it before him with both hands – staggered back across the dusty tiles, splashing water as he went, to the fireplace, where once huge logs would have burned.

Felix was there, down on his hands and knees. Having arranged the firewood – chopped-up beams, boards and pieces of furniture – he had unfastened one of the leather pouches attached to his belt and was setting out its contents on the hearth. There was a piece of flint, a short length of iron, oakbark dust and a ball of tinderwool.

As Rook watched, Felix teased a few strands of the orange wool from the ball and placed them down on a flat stone. Over this, he sprinkled the oakbark dust. Then, with the flint in one hand and the small iron bar in the other, he struck the two together. A bright spark dropped onto the oakbark and smouldered. Felix crouched down and blew gently. At first nothing happened. Then, with a puff of smoke and a soft crackle, the whole lot abruptly burst into flames.

'The trick is to get it into the firewood without disturbing the pile,' he murmured as he pushed the stone forward. The flames lapped at the twigs and branches.

He nudged the stone right into the centre. The wood caught. 'There,' he grinned. 'Now where's that water?'

'Here,' said Rook, and the two of them hefted the pot up, and hung its handle over the central hook.

With the fire blazing (it was Rook's job to keep adding extra pieces of wood from the pile by the wall) and the water coming to the boil, Felix gathered his ingredients from the hooks and shelves and busied himself with preparations for the meal.

He chopped, cut and tossed handful after handful of vegetables into the pot – diced roots and tubers, woodonions and pinegarlic, the sliced leaves of oak-sprouts and barkgreens, and clumps of the succulent swamp-samphire which grew on the stagnant banks of the Edgewater River. He skinned and filleted three small

creatures – a snowbird, a rock-lizard and something that looked suspiciously like a piebald rat – cut them up into pieces and, having seared the flesh in the flames, tossed them, too, into the boiling pot, then added a cupful of barleyoats for thickening.

'And last but not least . . .' he murmured to himself, as he unclipped a second of the pouches from his belt. 'A little bit of seasoning.' He loosened the drawstring and thrust his fingers inside. 'Some woodpeppercorns, I think. A few dried dellberries, brushsage leaves . . .' He frowned. 'And just a hint of tripweed . . .'

'Oh, not tripweed,' said Rook. 'I hate it, remember? Pickled, dried, salted – it's all disgusting.'

Felix laughed. 'I've always loved it myself. But, all right, since it's you,' he said, 'no tripweed.' He crushed the seeds, berries and dried leaves he'd selected on a stone with the back of his knife, and dropped the whole lot into the steaming broth. A sweet, aromatic fragrance immediately filled the chamber, perfuming the dank air and making Rook's mouth water.

Frowning thoughtfully, Felix searched his belt for something else, opening and closing several other pouches. Rook watched, intrigued.

'Where is it?' Felix muttered. 'Ah, here it is! A corktug,' he cried as, with a flourish, he raised the bone-handled opener in the air. 'Let us have a goblet of winesap together, you and I, Rook, and toast our reunion!'

He seized a bottle from a rough lufwood crate, pulled the cork and poured out two goblets of the thick, dark amber winesap. He handed one to Rook.

'Try that,' he said.

Rook raised the goblet to his lips and sipped. A radiant smile passed across his face as the sweet fruity liquid coated his tongue and slid down his throat. A moment later, a warm glowing feeling coursed round his entire body. He took a second sip and shook his head. 'Delicious,' he said. 'The best I've ever tasted.'

'It should be,' said Felix. 'It was meant for General Tytugg. Drinks only the finest winesap, so he does.' He chuckled. 'Sadly for him, there was a little incident down in the boom-docks a couple of weeks ago and a whole consignment bound for the Hive Towers went missing . . .' He raised his glass and smiled at Rook. 'Here's to the Ghosts of Screetown!'

'The Ghosts of Screetown,' said Rook, raising his own glass high – before draining it in one go.

It was so good to see his best friend again. Rook felt a familiar ache in his chest when he recalled the Announcement Ceremony at which Felix had learned that he would never become a librarian knight like himself. He'd disappeared immediately afterwards without saying a word.

'They miss you, you know,' he said softly.

'Miss me?' said Felix, looking down into his goblet.

'Your father,' said Rook. 'And your sister, Varis. Did you never think of coming back? Or at least letting us know that you were still alive?'

Felix's face clouded over. 'Of course I did, Rook. Many's the time I considered returning to the sewers. But . . .' His voice faltered and he swallowed heavily.

'You have to understand. I was the son of the High Librarian, yet I wasn't picked to become a librarian knight! I let everyone down. My father and Varis. My tutors. Even you, Rook . . .'

'No . . .' Rook protested. 'You've never let me down, Felix . . .'

'You're a good friend,' said Felix. 'You tried your best to help me pass my exams – sitting up with me, night after night. But you know what I'm like with treatises and barkscrolls and all that stuff. I just wasn't cut out to be a librarian knight and I was too ashamed to admit it – so I ran away. And that's something I've had to learn to live with.' He shrugged. 'Besides, I love it out here. This is the life I was born to – not being locked away in some dank library, surrounded by fusty, musty books and barkscrolls – and fustier, mustier professors!'

'But how can anyone love Screetown?' said Rook. 'It's full of rotsuckers and rubble ghouls.' He shuddered. 'And worse.'

'Worse?' said Felix looking up.

'Far worse,' said Rook. 'I crashed near a great canyon north of here and disturbed the creatures living in it. I didn't get a look at them – but they sounded enormous, Felix. Huge scratching claws, leathery wings . . .'

Felix nodded. 'Interesting,' he said. 'This canyon, was it just below the great rock, close to where the Guardians lower their cages?'

Rook nodded.

'It's a bad place, Rook,' Felix told him. 'Usually I avoid it.' He paused thoughtfully. 'But these creatures of yours sound intriguing. I could do with a few new trophies to decorate the place.'

Rook's face broke into a smile. 'You're incorrigible,' he said.

'Yet never bored!' said Felix. 'But enough of me, let's see how our stew is coming along, and then, Rook, you must tell me about yourself. I want to know everything! Especially how a fine young librarian knight like yourself ends up slugging it out with a rubble ghoul down here on the ground in Screetown!'

While Felix stirred the thickening broth, Rook took another slurp of winesap. He shook his head. How *had* he ended up here? It was all so confusing.

'I can remember being on dawn patrol,' he said. 'I'd already checked round Screetown and was heading for the Stone Gardens, when something must have struck the *Stormhornet* – my skycraft – and me.'

Felix looked up from the bubbling pot. 'A Guardian harpoon perhaps?' he suggested.

'I wasn't close enough to the Tower of Night,' said Rook. 'Besides, it was more powerful than a harpoon; *much* more powerful. One minute I was riding the air, sails full and weights swaying . . .'

Felix nodded, his eyes betraying an envious longing to experience flight for himself. Rook's brow furrowed.

'The next,' he went on, 'noise. Deafening noise. And blazing heat. And blinding light. And the stench of burning spidersilk . . . I was thrown across the sky – still clutching onto the prow of the *Stormhornet*, trying desperately to keep her airborne.' He looked at Felix, his eyes filling up. 'We crash-landed. I . . .' He hung his head. 'I survived, but the *Stormhornet* . . . Oh, Felix, I carved her myself from a single piece of sumpwood. We . . .'

Felix stepped away from the fire and placed his hand on Rook's shoulder. 'There, there, old friend. I understand. You were given something precious – the gift of flight. And then it was taken away from you. It's the way I felt at the Announcement Ceremony all that time ago . . .'

Just then, there came a loud squawk and a flurry of flapping wings, and a snow-white bird with glinting eyes and one misshapen foot swooped down from the top of the stairs and landed on Felix's shoulder. It eyed Rook suspiciously.

'Is that a white raven?' gasped Rook. 'I thought they'd all left the Stone Gardens for good.'

'All except Gaarn here,' said Felix, tickling the vicious-beaked creature under its chin. 'He had a little accident when all the others left. I found him lying on the ground, little more than a fledgling; parched, half-starved and with a heavy stone crushing his foot. I nursed him back to health, and he's stuck by me ever since, haven't you, Gaarn?'

'Waaark!' it screeched. 'Felix Gaarn friends.'

Rook started back. 'He can talk,' he said, surprised.

'I taught him,' said Felix. 'I may not be able to fly like you, Rook, but Gaarn here is my skyborne pair of eyes. He sees all and reports his findings.' He paused. 'In fact, it's thanks to Gaarn here that I came to be out looking for a young librarian knight he saw stumbling through Screetown.'

'So that's how you knew where to find me!'

Felix nodded. 'I didn't know it was you though, Rook, old friend,' he said.

'Friend! Friend!' the white raven cawed.

Felix returned to the bubbling pot and stirred the stew with a long wooden ladle. He scooped out a piece of meat, chewed half and gave the rest to Gaarn. 'I think it's ready,' he said.

'Ready!' Gaarn confirmed.

'Are you hungry, Rook?' asked Felix.

'Hungry?' said Rook. 'I could eat a tilder!'

Felix laughed. 'So could I,' he said wistfully. 'But I'm afraid we'll have to make do with snowbird, rock-lizard and . . .'

'It sounds perfect,' Rook broke in. The stew smelled delicious. And if it did contain piebald rat, then he didn't want to know.

Deep down below Undertown, the sewer tunnels echoed to the soft, irregular *drip-drip* of water and the low murmur of voices. It was the end of the day and the professors and under-librarians were busy.

Fenbrus Lodd was deep in conversation with Alquix Venvax on the Lufwood Bridge. A gaggle of raft-hands shared a joke as they moored their vessels. Two guards high up on a jutting gantry exchanged watch. On the floating lecterns, chained in clusters to the heavier Blackwood Bridge, librarian scholars completed their arduous work for the day – putting the finishing touches to their scroll-scribing, capping their inkpots and calling down to the chain-turners to reel them in.

'Hurry up, down there!' came an irate voice. 'I've important business with the Professor of Light.'

'Coming, sir,' a large-eared lugtroll shouted back, as he scurried across the bridge, seized the winding-crank and began turning. 'At once, sir. Sorry, sir . . .'

Away from the Great Storm Chamber Library – dry and airy thanks to its wood-burners and wind-turners – the moist air of the tunnels and outer chambers was warmer than usual. It was as if the searing heat of Undertown above had permeated the sewers, making them clammy, sticky – and deeply unpleasant. Apart from the frisky piebald rats who seemed to revel in the higher temperatures, the sewer-dwellers – from the lowliest lectern-tender to the Professors of Light and Darkness themselves – were finding the atmosphere increasingly oppressive.

Just off the Central Tunnel, two junior librarian knights-elect returned to their sleeping chamber. As one, they slumped down on their hammocks.

'It's so hot,' said one.

'You can say that again, Kern,' came the reply. 'And all

these oil lamps don't help.' He flapped a hand lethargically in front of his face. 'Hot, smelly, smoky – and I swear they create more shadows than they dispel . . .'

Further along the tunnel, an arched door led into a long, vaulted sleeping chamber. The air here was thicker and hotter than ever – and laced with the musty odour of warm fur. A piebald rat scurried boldly across the damp stone floor, making no attempt to conceal itself – as if it knew that the occupants of the room were no threat. It sniffed at the claws of a great hairy paw, twitched its whiskers and sank two long, yellow teeth into the flesh. Blood trickled down into its waiting mouth.

'Wuh!' grunted the creature, more from surprise than pain, and kicked out half-heartedly.

It was a banderbear; a huge male with a thick scar peeking through the greasy, matted fur across his shoulder – one of four banderbears, all huddled together in the corner of the chamber. He kicked again, more viciously this time, and the piebald rat scurried reluctantly away.

'Wurra wollah weera-weer,' he groaned. *Now the vermin drinks my life-blood. My life here is dark indeed.*

His neighbour, a bony old female, groomed him gently – teasing the sewer-ticks from the creases of skin and crushing them between her front teeth. 'Wuh-wuh-wurruhma,' she whispered. *Patience. Soon the full moon shall fill your eyes once more.*

'Wuh?' grunted a third, and shuddered. *But when?* 'Weera-woor-uralowa . . .'

The fourth nodded, her strange facial markings gleaming in the yellow lamplight. 'Wurra,' she trembled. 'Wurrel-lurragool-uralowa.' *Your words are true. If he who took the poisoned dart has fallen, then what is to become of us?*

Just then, the doorflap flew open and a young librarian knight burst in, her tear-stained cheeks gleaming, her eyes red. 'Tell me it isn't true!' Magda Burlix blurted out.

The banderbears looked up.

'Please,' she said. 'Not Rook. It can't be.'

Wumeru, the banderbear female Rook had befriended on his treatise-voyage, climbed to her feet and lumbered towards her. 'Wuh-wuh-weeralah. Uralowa. Wurra-wuh,' she said softly.

Magda hung her head. She knew enough of the banderbear language to understand what Wumeru had told her. It only confirmed what she had overheard the High Librarian telling Alquix Venvax.

There had been reports of a young librarian knight losing control of his skycraft while out on patrol. They had plummeted to the ground. Now Rook had been officially listed as missing.

Magda shook her head, and wiped her eyes. 'I . . . I can't believe it,' she sobbed. 'I spoke to him only last night. In the refectory-chamber. He's the best flier we have. He'd never lose control of the *Stormhornet* . . . He . . .'

Wumeru wrapped her great furry arms around the stricken girl and hugged her warmly. 'Wuh-weera-lowaal,' she said. *Our hearts are also full.*

'Oh, Rook,' Magda murmured, her voice muffled by the thick fur. 'Rook.'

Behind her, the door-covering was drawn back a second time. Magda looked round to see Varis Lodd standing in the doorway, her face sombre.

'I see you've heard the news,' she said. She shook her head sadly. 'I had such hopes for Rook, my finest pupil. It is a terrible loss.'

Magda tore herself away from Wumeru's clutches. 'You talk as if he's dead,' she said. 'You've posted him as missing, Varis; *missing* in Screetown. Not dead.'

Varis stepped into the chamber and laid a hand on Magda's shoulder. 'Believe me, I know it's hard when we lose a comrade; a fellow librarian knight . . . The reports say he was seen struggling to control the *Stormhornet* as it plummeted to earth.'

'But nobody saw the crash,' Magda insisted. 'We don't know he's dead.'

Varis turned away. 'I only hope he didn't survive the crash,' she said quietly. 'Because if he did, there are many far more horrible deaths that await a librarian knight in Screetown.'

'No! No! *No!*' Magda shouted, clamping her hands over her ears and rushing towards the door. 'I won't believe it's true. He's not dead! He's not! *I* haven't given up on him, even if you have!'

Rook opened one eye and looked around. For a moment, he could make no sense of the sumptuous chamber he had woken up in. He was lying on a thick mattress of straw, weighed down by a tilderskin rug. Above him were elegant, fluted pillars, ornate oil-lamps, and gilded ceiling mouldings which glinted in the flickering light. From some way to his left, there came the sound of soft snoring as someone rolled over in his sleep – and everything came flooding back.

He had sat up far into the night talking to his old friend, Felix, telling him of his adventures on the Mire Road, in the Free Glades, and up in the skies above Undertown. He looked over at the figure next to the smouldering fire.

Felix was still asleep, his breathing soft and rasping, and a faint yet familiar smile playing on his lips. Felix had always enjoyed his dreams. Perched by his head on the corner of his pallet was Gaarn, his head tucked under his wing. Rook decided not to waken them. He wished he could go back to sleep but he knew he wouldn't be able to. Already he felt weighed down by the thought of what lay ahead.

They had planned it all the night before, over their bowls of steaming stew. Although it had pained him to leave Felix so soon after their reunion, Rook was still a librarian knight. He had to return to the Great Library and make his report on everything that had happened. After all, the librarians depended on their young knights to keep them informed of life above the sewers. He knew that if Felix helped him to get back to Undertown, he'd be able to find a pipe or an open drain – some entrance that would lead him down into the sewers.

'I know the sprawling underground network of tunnels better than I know the back of my own hand,' Rook had said.

'You always did, but I'll hate to see you go,' Felix had replied sadly. He sighed. 'But then I suppose if you must, you must. I can get you across Screetown, but you're forgetting one thing, Rook.'

'What?' he had asked.

'The Edgewater River,' Felix had replied darkly. 'If *river* is the right name for that curdled cesspit. You'll have to swim across it. The sewers are impassable between Screetown and Undertown. I've had to do it myself . . .' He had shuddered. 'I don't envy you, Rook. I don't envy you at all.'

Rook slipped quietly out from beneath the heavy covers, climbed to his feet and stretched. The wine-sap he'd drunk the previous night had left his mouth parched and claggy, and he crossed the tiled floor to the trickling cistern where he quenched his thirst with cold clear water. Behind him, Felix murmured something soft and indistinct; Gaarn ruffled his feathers – but the two of them slept on.

Rook splashed his face with water. Then, taking care to move quietly, he began to explore.

Although now a cellar, it was clear to Rook that the opulent chamber had previously been an upper storey of a magnificent building. The windows, now shut off with rocks and debris, must once have offered fine views over Undertown – before the crumbling Sanctaphrax rock had covered everything in rubble. The lofty ceiling – decorated with ornately carved league-shields and creatures in various poses – probably gave clues as to who might once have lived here, but it was too high up for Rook to inspect closely. One thing was certain, quite apart from being buried, the place had also suffered from a terrible fire.

The carved beams were charred, the floor tiles cracked, while the walls, he now saw, were blackened by smoke. It was only the hanging muglump hides that concealed the worst effects of the blaze.

Rook crossed over to the wall and ran his hand across its surface. His fingertips were coated with a powdering of soot, which he wiped away on the muglump-pelt to his right.

As he did so, pulling the spongy grey skin to one side, something on the wall behind caught his eye. He looked more closely and recognized the faint but distinctive shape of a painted sky pirate's tricorn hat. His curiosity aroused, Rook pulled a kerchief from his pocket and carefully wiped away the greasy coating of soot.

Below the tricorn hat was a face – a noble face, framed

by curling side-whiskers and a waxed beard. Fascinated, Rook kept wiping. A decorated greatcoat came into view. Were those mire-pearls stitched into the collar? he wondered; were they mire-gems set into the scabbard of his sword? And were those initials stitched into the hem of the garment?

He dabbed at the soot, taking care not to disturb the flaking paint beneath. 'W.J.' he murmured.

Intrigued now, Rook continued across the wall, pulling the great muglump skin away and laying it carefully aside. The proud sky pirate, he soon discovered, stood at one side of a family portrait. His wife stood to his left, tall and elegant. Beside them were six youths, of different heights but with similar faces, each one staring back intently at the artist who had painted them – staring back at Rook.

He continued working on the soot-covered wall, delicately removing every trace of it from their bodies. Their curious old-fashioned waistcoats and baggy breeches were revealed; their high buckled boots. They were standing, Rook discovered, on a tiled floor – the same tiled floor he was now kneeling upon. He exposed it all, little by little, until . . .

'What's this?' he murmured as a painted scroll began to appear directly below the feet of the sky pirate. Scarcely daring to breathe, Rook dabbed at it carefully. The paint was dark – almost as dark as the soot he was removing – but inside the curling frame, picked out in gold, were letters. One by one, Rook exposed them.

Wind Jackal.

Wind Jackal. So that was the name of this prosperous adventurer who had built himself such a fine palace in what was once one of old Undertown's more fashionable districts. Whatever had become of him? Rook wondered.

He returned to the wall, searching for further clues. There were similar plaque-like scrolls painted beneath each of the figures. The wife and mother was Hirmina. The youths, Lucius, Centix, Murix, Pellius, Martilius and, smallest of all, Quintinius. Beneath them all, like a ribbon flapping in the breeze, a painted scroll revealed that this was the *FAMILY ORLIS VERGINIX*.

It must have been so nice to be part of such a family, Rook thought, to have brothers to play with; to grow up in the busy bustle of old Undertown, free from the tyranny of goblins or Guardians. His gaze lingered on the portrait of the youngest son. There was something about the dark eyes and forthright set of the jaw that seemed oddly familiar.

'I wish I'd known you,' he mused softly.

Rook reached up and began cleaning the rest of the wall. Now that he'd started, he wouldn't be satisfied until the entire wonderful mural was revealed.

Above the open section of the great family chamber was the roof of the magnificent building it was housed in; a showy array of twisting spires and swollen minarets. All round it were other majestic structures; turrets and towers, mansions and palaces, forming a great townscape on the banks of the Edgewater River. A scroll, hanging from the beak of a painted caterbird, identified the area as *the Western Quays* – but this was the quays before they had been crushed by falling rocks.

Rook returned his attention to the top of the roof. There was something attached to the side of a minaret which, as he cleaned along it, revealed itself to be a rising length of chain. Link by link appeared as he removed the greasy soot, until he was stretching up as far as he could reach. Abandoning his task for a moment, he seized a nearby stool and jumped onto it. He resumed his feverish wiping – and gasped. For there before him, as the grime fell away, was the most perfectly executed painting of all.

It was an intricately detailed reproduction of a sky pirate ship, accurate to an astonishing degree. He could see every bolt, every lever, every knot of every rope which formed the criss-cross hull-rigging. The sails billowed. The mast gleamed. The brass plate, bearing the name *Galerider*, glinted in the sun. And Rook found himself staring up at the flight-rock wistfully . . .

Would such sky-flight ever again be possible in the Edge? he wondered.

'Waaaark!' came a loud screech, echoing round the chamber.

'Whoooooaa!' Rook cried out as his legs trembled and the stool went over to one side.

'Six hours! Six hours!' screeched Gaarn.

Crash!

'What in Sky's name . . ?' came a puzzled voice from the far side of the chamber. 'Rook? What are you up to?'

Rook picked himself up off the floor, rubbed his aching head and righted the stool. Felix came running over to him – then stopped and looked up at the wall.

'Well I never!' he said. 'I never thought to clean the place up.'

'Beautiful, isn't it?" said Rook, standing back and admiring the wall-painting. 'It was underneath all that soot and grime. Look at the inscriptions, Felix. They're fascinating. We're standing in what was once the palace of a sky pirate captain called Orlis Verginix, also known as Wind Jackal. This is his wife. And those are his sons . . .'

'Yes, yes,' said Felix. 'History never really was my strong point. It's all so sort of *long ago*, if you know what I mean. It's the here and now that I'm interested in, not the past.'

'But the past moulds us, shapes us,' said Rook. 'Look,' he added, sweeping his arm around the great chamber, 'it's all around us.'

'If you say so,' said Felix, yawning. 'Now, how about breakfast? I'm starving!'

As they emerged, blinking, into the daylight outside half an hour later, Rook was struck by the intense heat of the shimmering air. It had been pleasantly cool and damp down in the underground chamber. Now, despite the earliness of the hour, it was stiflingly hot and humid.

With Gaarn perched on his left shoulder, Felix expertly charted a path through the rubble and ruins. Following behind, Rook braced himself for what lay ahead.

'There,' he heard Felix announce some time later as he

reached the top of a great mound of shattered stone. 'The Edgewater River.'

Rook climbed up beside him and peered ahead. Despite the heat, he shivered. The river looked uninviting: thick and sluggish, with a dense swirling mist dancing on her oily surface. Together, he and Felix picked their way down to her banks. A rank odour, like stagnant vegetable matter mixed with stale perfume, permeated the air.

'Good luck, and give my love to my father and Varis,' Felix told him.

'Of course I will,' said Rook, then turned to face his friend. 'It isn't too late for you to come with me!'

'No,' said Felix, shaking his head. 'I . . . I can't go back. This is my world.' He jutted his square jaw towards the river. 'Go now, Rook,' he said. 'Swim hard and fast. Soon the river-mist will rise, and then you'll be spotted easily from the banks . . .'

'Oh, Felix,' said Rook, hugging his friend. 'Take care of yourself!'

Felix pulled away. 'We'll meet again,' he said. 'I'm sure of that.'

Rook nodded mutely, trying hard to stop the welling tears from trickling down over his cheeks. He turned away. The mist swirled; the turgid water slopped at his feet. Gaarn screeched a parting *farewell!* and took to the air.

'Yes, farewell, Rook,' Felix said, clapping his old friend on the back.

Rook glanced back. 'Farewell, Felix,' he said, his voice heavy with sorrow. 'You are a true friend.'

He looked away and took a step forward. Then another, and another . . .

·CHAPTER FOUR·

THE MISERY HOLE

Thick mud squelched and bubbled round his boots as Rook waded down the steeply shelving incline into the treacherous Edgewater River. He felt round his belt, checking that everything was tightly secured – not that there was much he could have done, even if something had not been. The brown water was up to his knees now; a step later and it was swirling around his waist. There was nothing for it. He would have to swim.

With his arms stretched out in front of him, Rook leaned forwards, kicked out with his legs and thrust ahead into the broad, sluggish river. The water felt warm and oily to the touch, and lapped lazily over the leather of his flight-suit.

Keeping his head up, he took long, powerful strokes, sweeping the viscous water behind him and leaving a stream of tiny bubbles in his wake. Sediment coiled up from the riverbed. The air about him smelled brackish and sweet; the water was gritty between his fingers. Stroke after stroke, he forged on to where he hoped the other side lay – though with the thick mist swirling round his head, it was not possible to be absolutely sure.

Rook had never liked swimming as a youth. The water flowing through the Storm Chamber Library had been too foul to venture into without a raft, and he had always avoided the sessions in the overflow-cisterns which his fellow under-librarians seemed to enjoy so much. Yet at the Free Glades, where the crystal-clear waters of the Great Lake had offered perfect conditions, he had grown to love it. Most mornings, he would get up early, dive in off the edge of Lake Landing and swim twice round the lake before breakfast.

'Come on in, Magda!' he remembered calling to his friend. 'The water's lovely!'

The same could not be said of the Edgewater River. And yet as the young librarian knight battled on – his breathing now regular and softly rasping as he slipped into an easy rhythm – he had to admit that the crossing was not as bad as he had feared. The river was warm, like a tepid bath. And while there was certainly a current pulling to his left, it was so weak that, as an experienced swimmer, he remained confident of making it to the other side without being dragged downstream.

More worrying was the thick mist. He couldn't see where he was going, nor how far he still had to swim.

And so he continued blindly, his arms thrusting forwards and sweeping back, his legs kicking, using the direction of the current to guide himself across as best he could. If he kept on like this, he told himself – slow but steady – he was bound to reach the other side before too long.

Towards the centre, however, the river began to grow more choppy. It splashed in his face – warm and cloying. And though he was immersed in water, he began to sweat uncomfortably inside his flight-suit as he battled against the increasing tug of the current. The odour of the mist, coiling off the surface of the river, became pungent, sickly; and when the twisting eddies lapped against his panting mouth, its greasy feel and rotting taste sent shivers of disgust rippling through his body. His arms faltered, his legs grew heavy – yet he urged himself on.

'Not far now,' he encouraged himself breathlessly. 'I'll soon be back on dry land and . . .'

At that moment, his fingers brushed against something soft and slimy. His hand shrank back involuntarily. He looked up. There was something there, bobbing, half-submerged; something with matted patches of white and black fur. Rook shuddered with disgust. It was a dead piebald rat, washed out from the sewers; bloated

and stinking. The stench of its rotting body made him heave as it floated past, and for a moment he sank down beneath the water.

Splashing and spluttering, Rook broke the surface and gulped at the air.

'Idiot,' he muttered angrily. His squeamishness had made him careless. He could have been swept downriver.

Just then, and for the briefest of instants, the swirling mist thinned. Looking ahead, Rook caught a glimpse of the other side of the river. His heart sank. It still looked so, so far away – but turning back was not an option. He had to continue.

Rook struck off once more. The mist closed in around him. He struggled bravely on, keeping at right angles to the current as before, but unable to regain the smooth rhythm of arms and legs he'd got into earlier. Evil-looking clumps of matted weeds floated past him like rafts of broken limbs; unseen objects – some hard, some soft – brushed against him, both above the water and below. Were they mire-leeches squirming like maggots in the cloudy water below him? Was that a waterghoul lurking on the silty riverbed?

Rook tried to push such idle thoughts away, but at that moment – from high above his head – there came the chattering of a passing flock of snowbirds. They seemed to be mocking him.

He'll never make it, he thought he heard them trilling to one another. *He's going to drown! He's going to drown!*

For a second time, the sun burned through the mist –

not for long, but just enough for Rook to see that the far bank, though still horribly distant, was indeed closer than it had been before. He could make out tall workshops and warehouses, dock-workers with wherry-hooks and hard hats, and a swarthy goblin scurrying along the raised jetty, a long hooked pike clasped in his hand.

Again the mist grew thick. Rook trod water, fighting the persistent current whilst he got his breath back. Then he struck out again for the far bank. His legs seemed to be getting heavier and heavier, as though lead weights had been attached to his boots. Every stroke was an effort. Every kick used up a fraction more of his rapidly dwindling strength.

'Easy does it,' he told himself as he drove on through the treacly water. 'Slow and steady. One stroke after the other. Forward . . . back . . . forward . . . back . . .'

The next time the air cleared, it did not thicken up again. Instead the great snakelike coils of dense swirling mist were dwindling to wispy twists. Rook could now see the riverbank clearly. It was fringed with piers and jetties along which he could see figures shuffling to and fro. Although it was a relief to see that he had barely fifty strides to go, he was now seriously worried that some-one might spot him.

With his head low in the water, Rook continued towards the bank. He moved slowly, carefully; pushing the water back with his arms without making so much as the tiniest splash. His legs, heavier than ever, dragged behind him. Not looking up for fear of catching the eye of some dockhand or goblin guard, he swam on as blindly as when the mist had still held him in its grip.

All at once, he felt his boots trail along the squelchy riverbed. The next moment, as he reached down, his searching fingers touched soft mud. Digging in, he pulled himself slowly into the shallows until he was lying half-in half-out of the water. If anyone noticed him, they should think he was simply something that had washed up on the shore. Slowly, cautiously, avoiding any sudden eye-alerting movement, he lifted his head and looked up.

He had been lucky. Very lucky. He was lying in the shadow of a raised platform which jutted out high above his head. It was supported on thick wooden pillars, the closest of which stood half-a-dozen strides or so to his right. He could hear heavy footsteps clomping across the boards above him and, peering closely, saw the broken images of goblins and trogs flashing past the gaps between them.

He'd done it! he thought gratefully as he pulled himself up onto dry land. He'd made it across the Edgewater River. Now he had to find his way back into the sewers. He tried to get to his feet – but found to his horror that he couldn't move his legs.

In a sudden panic, Rook rolled over and looked down. '*Aaeei . . .*' Terrified of giving himself away, he stifled the cry with his hands. Shaking with terror, he stared at his legs. Each had been swallowed up by a great bony fish, which clung tightly up to his knees, like a pair of angler's waders.

Their bodies were gaunt, like canvas stretched over a skeleton, their eyes cold and grey, their sucker mouths – pink and frothing – gripped round the tops of Rook's shins.

'Oozefish,' he breathed.

Rook knew all about oozefish. Petris Fillit's treatise on the subject was a classic of its type. It was housed on a floating-lectern in the Great Library, where disobedient under-librarians were forced to learn its two hundred and thirty-two pages off by heart as a punishment. Oh, yes, Rook knew all about oozefish. He knew how they attached themselves to prey too large to swallow whole; sinking it, drowning it, guarding it, and waiting for it to rot enough for their suckers to begin feeding. He knew that they lived both in the Edgewater River and in the Mire, sliding through mud and water with equal ease. He knew their mating rituals, their gill structure – and of the third lid their eyes possessed. But most relevant of all, he knew how to remove one, should it become attached.

Trying hard to stop his hand from trembling – and thanking the bad-tempered old professor who'd punished him for talking in class, Rook seized his sword, reached down towards his left leg and – taking care not to injure himself – plunged the tip of the blade into the fish's secondary gill, hidden behind its bulging blow hole. There was a soft squelching sound as the sucker instantly released its ferocious grip. The oozefish wriggled down off his leg, flapped wildly for a moment on the mud, then disappeared headfirst into it.

Encouraged, Rook tightened his grip and leaned forwards a second time – but something the first one had done must have alerted the other oozefish to danger, for before he could strike, the creature had already disgorged itself. With a writhing flip, it squirmed down into the soft white mud after its companion. Rook watched its bony tail retreat and the mud plop and fall still.

Still shaking, he climbed to his feet. Though wobbly, his legs seemed none the worse for being swallowed by disgusting oozefish. He took his bearings.

If, as he thought, it was the slave-workshops above his head, then the boom-docks – the obvious way into the sewers – were too far upstream. And he couldn't risk being seen heading up the riverbank. No, his best bet was to go into Undertown itself and find a drain large enough for him to squeeze down. Once he hit one of the main underground tunnels, he'd be back in the Great Library in no time.

He headed up the mudflats, keeping to the shadows, running from one wooden pillar to the next; pausing to catch his breath, before running on to the next. Gradually, the platform drew lower. The sound of pounding boots grew louder and was joined by raised voices; shouting, cursing and barking commands. Rook chewed into his lower lip nervously. The goblin guards were already out, overseeing the change from the night-shift to the day-shift of the work-slaves. It must be seven hours or thereabouts. Soon the whole place would be thronging.

Just then, a snarl and a howl echoed through the air. Rook froze. Not only were they armed, but the goblin guards had white-collar woodwolves with them.

Head down, he darted out from beneath the platform, over to a rear-floodwall and up an old rusty ladder bolted to its vertical side. The metal creaked and threatened to pull free of its moorings as he climbed. Rook felt vulnerable. Exposed. If anyone saw him . . .

No-one *will* see me! he told himself sharply. Just get a move on!

At the top of the ladder, he peeked over the top of the wall. Then, having checked that the coast was clear, he jumped up and made a dash for the nearest buildings – a jumble of rundown warehouses, workhouses and tall slatted lofthouses once used for drying sailcloth and seasoning wood. Between them was a network of dark, narrow alleys, like an intricate maze. Rook took a deep breath and entered.

He turned left. Then right. Then right again. He tried desperately to picture the layout of the place. But it was no use. Despite all the Undertown patrols he'd carried out, he simply could not get his bearings down here on the ground.

As he ran on, the high windowless sides of the buildings seemed to press in about him. It was so hot and close. Sweat poured down his face. It occurred to him that if anything should appear at the ends of the alley, then he'd be trapped. If only he knew the arrangement of streets and alleys of Undertown just half as well as he knew the tunnels and pipes of the sewers below . . .

Just then he heard something that told him *exactly* where he was: the squeaking of an unoiled crank being turned and the low babble of gossip. He paused and listened. The squeaking continued, followed by a *clonk* and a *splash*. Rook smiled. There was no doubt about it; although he couldn't see it, he must be within spitting distance of the Eastern Well. Many was the time he had flown past, noting both the gathering of goblin matrons who would cluster together, deep in conversation, as they filled their jugs and urns from the well-bucket – and the fact that the handle needed oiling!

He crept forwards and, guided by his ears rather than his eyes, squeezed himself into a long, narrow opening between the backs of two wood and stone buildings. The sound of the hushed voices grew louder as he slipped sideways along the gap, which grew narrower and narrower the further he went. At the end at last, he stopped and peered out cautiously from the shadows.

In front of him, just as he'd expected, was the Eastern Well – a tall, ornate structure which was sole source of water for an entire district – and the ancient goblin matrons clustered around it. He peeked out a little further, looking right, left and round the cobbled square. There was a main

drain with a barred gate entrance which lay down the street on the opposite side, Rook remembered – but how could he get to it? Should he work out some circuitous route, keeping to the narrow alleys? Or should he simply make a dash for it across the square? After all, the goblin matrons wouldn't do anything to stop him – *and* it would give them something new to talk about.

He was about to risk it when he noticed one of the matrons look up and murmur to her neighbour; and then the two of them glance round. They'd heard something. The next moment, Rook heard it too – the rising sound of heavy boots marching towards him.

It was a contingent of goblin guards!

Darting back into the narrow gap, Rook crouched down – his knees grazing the stone wall as he did so –

and held his breath. Heart in his mouth, he watched as the first pair of armed guards stomped past the end of the passageway. Their breast armour, helmets and heavy weapons glinted in the early-morning brightness. Next, flanked by a second pair of goblins, Rook saw a ragged slave, head down and back bent, as he shuffled past. He was followed by others – twelve in all, Rook counted – each one yoked by the neck to the one behind. A final pair of goblins brought up the rear. Rook trembled and shrank back as far as he could into the shadows. To his horror, he had noted that they were not alone. Each one had a white-collar woodwolf beside him, straining at the leash.

Praying he would not be noticed, Rook watched first one goblin go past, struggling to control the vicious beast he was holding; then the other. At last, they were both gone from sight. Rook sighed with relief.

That had been close, he realized. Too close . . .

'What's that, Tugger?' the goblin's voice floated back. 'Did you smell something, boy?

'And you, too, Ragger?' came a second voice. 'What's up? Is there something there?'

Rook's heart missed a beat. The wolves had caught his scent. *They knew he was there.*

Turning on his heels, Rook bolted back down the narrow alley, away from the terrible danger. As he scrabbled and stumbled, he shot a look back over his shoulder to see the goblins – their bodies black against the light at the end of the alley – bend down and fiddle with the wolves' collars. They were unclipping the woodwolves from their leashes.

Rook ran for all he was worth.

'He's getting away, Slog,' called one of the goblins.

'Oh, no he's not,' came the reply. 'Ragger, you go that way. Tugger, you go round there, boy. That's it! Head him off at the end of the alley!'

Heart pounding, Rook sped desperately along the narrow alleyway. He had to reach the other end before the wolves did. Twenty strides to go by his reckoning. Not far – but then woodwolves were renowned for their fleetness of foot. He could hear them yelping from his left and his right as they ran down alleys parallel to his own. His head filled with terrible memories from his childhood that he couldn't push away; memories of slavers, and woodwolves, and the last time he had seen his parents alive . . . The yelping grew more excited. Any second now, the terrible creatures would reach the end of the alley and cut him off . . .

'Come on, come on,' he urged himself.

As he neared the end, the passageway became comparatively wide. Rook sprinted the last ten strides, out onto a narrow street and down the alleyway opposite. Behind him, the two wolves met up and resumed the chase. Their excited baying twisted in the air, a discordant duet.

Rook needed to find a means of escape as quickly as possible; a drain that would lead him down into the sewers. A drain-cover! He had to find a drain-cover. And quick!

Sweat drenched his body and soaked his hair, which lay flat and wet against his head. The new day was proving to be the hottest and most humid so far. But he

couldn't stop. Drawing on reserves of strength he hardly knew he had, Rook turned sharp left at a junction and scurried down a dark alley which was full of early-morning merchants and punters, and lined with small workshops. The smell of hot metal and singed wood assaulted his nostrils as he barged his way through, past joiners and turners, past buzzing lathes and screeching circular saws.

'Oi! Watch it!' voices shouted out angrily. 'Watch where you're going!'

But Rook took no notice. Librarian knight though he was, he couldn't afford to be polite or thoughtful. Not just now. His one priority was to escape.

Suddenly this was made easier for him as the trogs and trolls began scattering before him, leaving a path for him to run down. At first he thought they must be clearing a way for him. The next moment, he realized what it was they were shouting as they dived for cover. His heart missed a beat.

'Woodwolves!' 'Woodwolves!'

Rook glanced back over his shoulder. He was hoping against hope that he was outrunning the terrible creatures. But as he saw the flashing eyes and slavering mouth of the first great woodwolf behind him, those hopes were dashed. It was gaining on him. Any second now, it would be snapping at his heels. He raced on – only to discover that the second woodwolf must have circled round to cut him off after all, because now it appeared in front of him at the far end of the alley. As their eyes met, it bared its teeth and snarled menacingly.

Without a second thought, Rook darted into the workshop to his left. A wizened woodtroll with a rubbery nose and a pronounced squint looked up from his lathe indignantly.

'What in bloodoak's name do you think you're doing?' he bellowed as Rook barged past him, sending spindles, table-legs and tools flying. 'I . . . *aaargh!* Woodwolves!'

'Sorry!' Rook called out. Shoving the door aside, he tore through into the back room of the workshop and dived outside, through the far window.

He landed, rolled over and jumped smartly to his feet. The woodwolves were in the room behind him, baying for his blood. Rook reached up, slammed the shutters to and bolted them into place.

There was a loud splintering crash and a howl of pain as the first, then the second of the woodwolves lunged at the wooden shutters. The hinges creaked and the panels buckled and bowed – but the shutters remained in place.

'Thank Sky and Earth for that,' Rook murmured as he took to his heels once more.

The woodwolves howled with rage and Rook heard them pounding back through the woodtroll's workshop to the alley. They weren't about to give up.

And neither am I, thought Rook determinedly.

He darted down an arched opening between two rather grand buildings opposite which – if his memory served him correctly – were Wheelwright's Mansion and the former Leagues' Meeting House. He was right where he wanted to be, at the edge of central Undertown. The place was fairly riddled with drains, both large and small. At the end of the covered passage, he emerged into a second square, far grander than the one housing the Eastern Well. To his left was the Central Fountain – its once glorious cascade of water now reduced to a low, stumpy-looking column. And to his right . . .

'Sky and Earth be thanked,' Rook murmured.

At last he had stumbled across a drain. He dashed towards it and crouched down. Set into the huge flag-stones it was one of the older variety, circular and latticed. He plunged his fingers down into the gaps in the cast-iron grille and tugged.

From the far corner of the square he heard the yelping arrival of the first woodwolf. The second one wouldn't be far behind.

Teeth clenched and legs locked, he grunted out loud with effort. There was the soft grinding sound of grit on metal, and the drain-cover came free. Rook pushed it aside and hurriedly lowered himself down into the dark-ness below.

The wolves, sensing that their quarry was about to escape, sprinted towards him. Rook felt round feverishly with his right foot for the first rung of the iron ladder he knew should be there somewhere, bolted to the inside of the narrow pipe – and found it. He shifted himself round, reached up and slid the drain-cover back into place, just in the nick of time.

The tunnel was plunged into darkness. Above his head, he heard the woodwolves scratching desperately at the metal grille and howling with frustration.

'Too slow,' he taunted softly.

As if the woodwolves themselves knew this to be true, they abruptly stopped their yammer and trotted away. Rook grinned with relief. Then, with a last look up at the pinpricks of light piercing the metal cover above his head, he began the descent. Rung by rung, he climbed down the vertical pipe which would bring him out into one of the great transverse tunnels, deep under the ground. With a bit of luck, he should arrive back at the Great Storm Chamber Library before . . .

'*Aaagh!*' he cried out, as his left foot slipped into thin air. The next rung was missing . . .

It all happened so quickly. His right foot slipped, his hands were torn from their grip, and the next thing he knew, he was tumbling backwards.

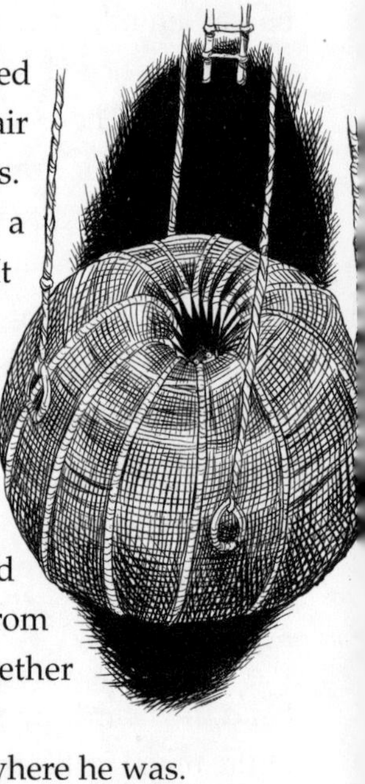

'*Unkh!*' he grunted as he landed with a sudden, heavy thud and the air was forcibly expelled from his lungs.

Where am I? he wondered. Then a horrible thought occurred to him. It couldn't be . . . It *mustn't* be . . .

Cautiously he opened his eyes to see – but the pitch blackness around him was giving nothing away. He felt round gingerly with his hands. He felt walls, round and rigid, and from the feel of it, made from woodwillow withies, woven together like . . . like a huge basket . . .

Rook groaned. He knew *exactly* where he was.

He was inside one of the traps set by the goblin guards

to capture those who tried to escape from Undertown. Misery holes, they were called. Like huge mudlobster-pots, they were set inside the sewer entry pipes beneath deliberately sabotaged ladders. He was a librarian knight: he should have known, been on his guard. Instead, he had blindly climbed down the ladder thinking he was safe.

Misery holes. He shook his head. The traps were well-named, Rook thought bitterly, and he, Rook Barkwater, had become their latest victim. It was little wonder, he realized, that the woodwolves had seemed so unconcerned when he'd escaped them. He'd been such a fool. They hadn't been chasing him at all, they were corralling him to the booby-trapped drain. They'd tricked him, and he had fallen for it, hook, line and sinker. But he wasn't finished yet.

He climbed to his feet and shook the plaited bars of the cage as hard as he could and tried to wrench them apart; he kicked and hammered at them; he drew his knife and tried sawing at the wood – but all to no avail. The misery hole was not about to release its quarry so easily.

'There must be *some* way out,' Rook groaned.

'There isn't,' came a little voice from the far side of the cage. 'I've already tried.'

Rook started with surprise. 'Who's there?' he hissed.

'M-my name's Gilda,' said the little voice tearfully. 'And I'm very frightened. I've been here *ages* and . . .' – she shuddered – 'soon . . . soon, they'll be coming for us.'

·CHAPTER FIVE·

NUMBER ELEVEN

Rook felt the hairs at the back of his neck tingle. There was such fear and despair in the small, childlike voice.

'Are you hungry?' he asked softly. 'I've got some dried dellberries. And a hunk of black bread . . .'

'Water,' said Gilda. 'Have you any water, sir? I'm so thirsty.'

'Yes, yes,' said Rook eagerly. He fumbled at his belt and removed his water-bottle. 'Here,' he said, reaching out towards the sound of the voice.

He felt a hand brushing his fingers as it seized the bottle, then heard the sound of slurping and swallowing. Rook smiled, glad that he'd been able to do something – however small – to help the poor creature.

'Thank you, sir,' said Gilda a moment later. 'Thank you kindly.'

Rook reached out a second time. He felt the water-bottle graze his fingertips; then, just as he was about to close his hand around it, it slipped from his grasp and clattered on the bottom of the cage.

'Oh, mercy me, I'm sorry, sir,' Gilda cried out. 'Indeed I am!'

'It's all right, Gilda,' Rook assured her. 'Don't fret.'

He crouched down and, reaching into the pockets of his flight-suit – both right and left – pulled out a small rough stone from each. As he put them together on the palm of his hand, the whole cage was abruptly bathed in a warm yellow glow. Gilda gasped.

'Mercy me!' she exclaimed. 'Magic rocks!'

Rook smiled. 'They're sky-crystals,' he said. 'Given to me by the Professor of Light himself in the Great Library.'

'So you're a librarian?' said Gilda, her voice trembling with awe. Rook looked at her eager little face, eyes wide and astonished. The shadowy glow from the crystals shone on her pointed ears, her stubby waxen plaits, her broad nose . . .

'Why, you're a gnokgoblin,' Rook said.

'Indeed I am, sir,' said Gilda, 'a poor gnokgoblin from the Eastern Alleys. I was on an errand for my grandmother, I was, sir, when those there goblins set their wolves on me. Just for fun, sir . . . Just for fun . . .' The little gnokgoblin buried her head in her hands and sobbed.

Rook placed a hand on her shoulder and squeezed it gently.

Gilda looked up, her face wet with tears. 'My grandmother's a poor seamstress, sir, always has been. But these days, she's getting frail – and her eyesight is

failing. She relies on me for everything, so she does. Oh, mercy me, sir, if I don't return from my deliveries . . .'

'It's going to be all right, Gilda,' said Rook.

Another sob convulsed the little gnokgoblin and she grasped Rook's hand in hers.'Oh those wolves, sir!' she shuddered. 'Howling, slavering, snarling . . . They chased me, sir. And . . . and I thought I was being so clever hiding beneath the drain-cover . . .' She breathed in noisily. 'And now *this*!' she wailed, the tears streaming down her cheeks.

'There, there,' said Rook. 'I know the feeling, believe me.'

'Oh, sir,' she sobbed, throwing herself forwards and wrapping her skinny arms around his neck. The basket swayed, and from far off in the system of tunnels, Rook heard the sound of squabbling ratbirds. 'But it'll be all right now, won't it, sir?' she said. 'You being a real living and breathing librarian knight with magic rocks and all.' Gilda's grip tightened.

'Of course it will,' said Rook uncertainly, patting her awkwardly on the back.

He glanced up at the inward-pointing spikes of the cage above his head; so easy to fall into, yet impossible to escape. They were well and truly trapped in the misery hole.

Gilda's sobs slowly subsided, and her grip loosened. She wiped her eyes on the back of her hand and sat back. 'What's it like there?' she asked in her small voice.

'What's *what* like *where*?' said Rook.

'The Free Glades,' said Gilda. 'You're a librarian knight, so you must have been there. What are they like? Are they as beautiful as they say? Granny says that everyone is free there, and safe. And no-one goes hungry, and no-one is ever beaten – that it's the most wonderful place in the world!'

'It is,' said Rook dreamily. 'Like a shining beacon in the middle of the dark Deepwoods – the most beautiful place in all the Edge. Glades with towering pinetrees and crystal lakes, and the night sky studded with a million dazzling stars.'

Gilda looked up at him shyly. 'Do you think that one day I might see it for myself?' she asked.

Rook leaned forwards, took both of her hands in his own and squeezed them warmly. 'I'm sure of it,' he said.

Gilda smiled happily, and nodded. 'Me, too,' she said earnestly. 'Now you're here, *everything's* going to be all right.'

Just then, from above their heads, there came a loud sound. Grinding. Metal on stone. Gilda gasped.

'It's them,' she whispered.

Rook nodded. He pulled himself up onto his haunches, quickly returned the sky-crystals to their separate pockets, and looked up. Far above, as the drain-cover was slid aside, a thin sliver of light grew and grew – like the moon going through all its phases, from new to full, in a matter of seconds. The grinding noise set Rook's teeth on edge. The next instant, a great head was thrust down into the hole.

'What have we got here, then?' he muttered gruffly. The light streamed over his shoulders and down into the eyes of the prisoners below. 'Two, by the looks of things.' He clapped his hands together. 'A good catch!'

'Haul 'em in, then,' came a second voice, high-pitched and imperious, 'and let's take a closer look!'

Rook turned to Gilda. 'You'll be all right,' he said. 'I promise.'

Gilda nodded, her eyes wide and trusting. 'Thank you, sir,' she whispered.

Just then, the cage jerked and dropped down a couple of strides. Gilda gasped. Rook clung onto her arm with one hand and the plaited bars of the cage with his other. From above there came a stream of violent curses and the crack of a whip. The cage stopped falling.

'*Pull*, Krote, you great, useless lump,' demanded the high-pitched voice impatiently. 'By Sky, I'll have you boiled down to glue! PULL!'

The voice echoed angrily down the tunnels – where it was answered by a chorus of ratbirds and piebald rats, chattering and squealing in alarm. The cage jolted and slowly began to rise. Gilda whimpered and gripped the side of the cage firmly. Rook looked out through the bars – at the sides of the rusting sewer-pipe sliding past and, a little higher up, at the booby-trapped ladder. Finally, with a bump, the cage came to a halt directly beneath the drain-opening.

A thin leather-covered pole was thrust into the cage, past the inward-pointing spikes, stopping inches from the top of Rook's head. With a click, it opened up, revealing itself to be a heavy umbrella-like object. With much heaving and grunting, the opened umbrella was pulled back out of the cage, springing open the inward-pointing spikes, like the petals of a vicious flower.

A huge hand reached in, grabbed Rook by the scruff of his flight-suit and lifted him bodily into the air – Gilda clinging to his knees. Rook found himself staring into the bloodshot eyes of a hulking great tufted goblin with hairy ears, a jutting jaw and pitted skin that showed the ravages of a hard life and many a savage battle. Dressed in heavy armour, he was still holding the drain-cover under his arm, making it look as light as a the lid of a barrel of woodale.

Behind him, Rook caught a glimpse of a tumbril, the covered wagon fashioned, like the cage, from woodwillow. Two weary prowlgrins were in harness and he could see the driver – a bony mobgnome, by the look of him, a pencil in one hand, reins in the other.

'What have we got, then?' chirped the mobgnome. He licked the point of his stubby pencil and raised his hand ready.

The tufted goblin looked the two of them up and down as they dangled from his fist. 'A big'un and a little'un,' he grunted, his voice deep and guttural.

'If you could be a *little* more specific, Krote,' said the

mobgnome, his voice laden with sarcasm.

Krote's heavy brow furrowed. 'Gnokgoblin,' he called back to the driver, who noted the details on a small scroll of bark.

'Male or female?' said the mobgnome.

'It's a girl,' said Krote. 'And the second . . .' He frowned, and turned his blunt, brutish face towards Rook, who grimaced at the smell – and feel – of the goblin's moist, malodorous breath. 'I's not sure, Mindip,' he said, as a stupid grin spread across his face, 'but I reckon we might've caught usselves a 'brarian knight.'

The mobgnome jumped down from the tumbril and hurried over. 'Are you sure?' he said. 'A librarian knight, you say? Here, let me see.'

Krote turned to his partner and dropped Rook and Gilda, who landed in a heap at the mobgnome's feet.

''Ere, take it easy, Krote, you great lummox! Gotta be careful with the merchandise. If he *is* a librarian, he'll be valuable, see?' Mindip crouched to inspect Rook as he lay, winded, on the greasy cobbles.

As the mobgnome's sneering face came close, Rook saw his chance. He leapt to his feet and drew his sword . . .

But the mobgnome simply laughed. 'Well, well, well,' he said. 'He *is* a librarian knight. No doubt about it! You handle him, Krote, there's a good fellow. I'll take care of the girl.'

Behind him, Rook heard the tufted goblin's low growl. Mindip flourished his evil-looking whip and lunged to Rook's left. There was a sharp *crack!* and Gilda cried out with pain as the end of the mobgnome's whip wound itself around her neck.

'Sir . . . help . . .' Gilda gasped, as the mobgnome tugged hard on the whip, tightening the grip round her neck and pulling her towards him.

Glancing round, Rook saw the tufted goblin raise his great arms. He readied himself.

'Sir . . . *urrrrrgh* . . .' Gilda gurgled.

It was no use. Rook knew he had to do something. Looking back hurriedly, he saw the helpless young gnokgoblin being dragged towards the tumbril by Mindip. At the same moment, Krote lunged. Rook leapt desperately out of his reach and swung his sword. It sliced through the leather whip, freeing Gilda, and caught the mobgnome, Mindip, a glancing blow on the backswing.

Blood spattered down onto the stone flags.

Krote paused to stare down at Mindip and, for a terrible moment, it was as though everything stood still. The next, the furious goblin raised his great head and roared as the mobgnome crumpled to the floor, gripping his belly.

'Mindip!' he bellowed. 'You hurt Mindip!'

His tufted ears trembled. The whites of his eyes turned red.

'Run, Gilda!' Rook cried, gripping his sword as firmly as he could.

Arms raised, the tufted goblin lunged again. He swung the heavy drain-cover through the air in a wide, whistling arc. Rook gasped as he saw the great lump of iron coming towards him. He was frozen to the spot . . .

Out of the corner of his eye, he glimpsed Gilda's green dress fluttering as she made a dash for it . . .

CLONK!

The drain-cover hammered into the side of Rook's head, the sword slipping from his grip and clattering on the cobbles.

There was a flash of intense brightness, a rush of cold – then darkness.

*

Rook woke up with a jolt. Where was he? he wondered. The jolting continued.

He was in motion, that much was certain, bumping and clattering over cobblestones; every movement jarring his body and making his head pound. He was in some kind of a cart. All round him he could hear the sound of soft moaning.

Slowly he opened his eyes. The light poured in. He was inside a tumbril, its wicker roof casting criss-cross shadows over its cargo.

'Mind the pot-holes, you stupid oaf!' came a shrill voice from up at the front. 'Every jolt is agony. I'm bleeding all over my new cloak – and it's all your fault, you useless sack of guts!'

'Sorry, Mindip. He was just a bit quick for me. But I got him in the end, didn't I?' came a gruff reply.

Rook pulled himself onto his elbows, his head throbbing so badly he wanted to cry out, and looked round. He found himself face to face with an old slaughterer lying beside him, his red hair streaked with grey. He shifted round. Apart from the slaughterer, there were others, their faces seeming to blur and smudge as Rook struggled to make sense of it all. There were a couple of waifs, their ears fluttering like woodmoths, a lumpen cloddertrog, snoring loudly, and a strange-looking individual with scaly skin, tiny flute-like ears and a rubbery crest that ran across the centre of his head and halfway down his back.

'E's woken up,' muttered a voice from the back of the tumbril.

'Yeah, poor beggar. Come round just in time to see his new home, innit? The Sanctaphrax Forest . . .'

'If the shrykes don't get to him first!'

Rook shuddered uneasily. Above his head, a solitary white raven circled in the sky, cawing raucously. Its wings looked to Rook like paddles, slicing through the dense, treacly air. It was hot; so stiflingly hot. He could barely breathe. And every time he moved his eyes, the pounding in his head grew more intense.

He raised his hand and touched round his left temple gently. The bone was tender and, when he inspected his fingers, he found them dark with congealed blood.

Outside the clattering tumbril, the streets were getting more and more busy. Peering giddily through the slatted sides, Rook could see merchants, traders and groups of armed guards. Some were standing in clusters. Most were streaming along the road in the same direction he was travelling. From up ahead, there came the hustle and bustle of a great crowd; the sounds of clattering, clanging, dull moans and raised voices, and every now and then a sharp klaxon blast that made Rook wince with pain.

'Left! *Left!*' shouted the mobgnome. 'It's *that* way!' He pointed.

The tufted goblin pulled on the reins, and the tumbril was driven through a low, narrow archway into a broad square, heaving with activity and louder than ever. Rook's head spun all the more. There was movement and colour, and loud noise that seemed to set the very air trembling. The tumbril abruptly lurched to a halt. The goblin turned round.

'Wake up, you idle bunch of sewer-rats!' he bellowed. 'We've arrived.'

The mobgnome climbed down, clutching his belly, hobbled painfully round to the back of the covered wagon and unlocked the door. The tufted goblin appeared beside him – a heavy cudgel in one hand – and reached inside. Rook looked on helplessly as his neighbour, the old slaughterer, was dragged out by the ankles.

Rook was next. The tufted goblin reached out towards him – but he kicked the great hairy hand away. 'I can do it on my own,' he muttered.

Yet as he pulled himself to his feet and the blood drained from his head, he swooned dizzily and stumbled over one of the unconscious waifs.

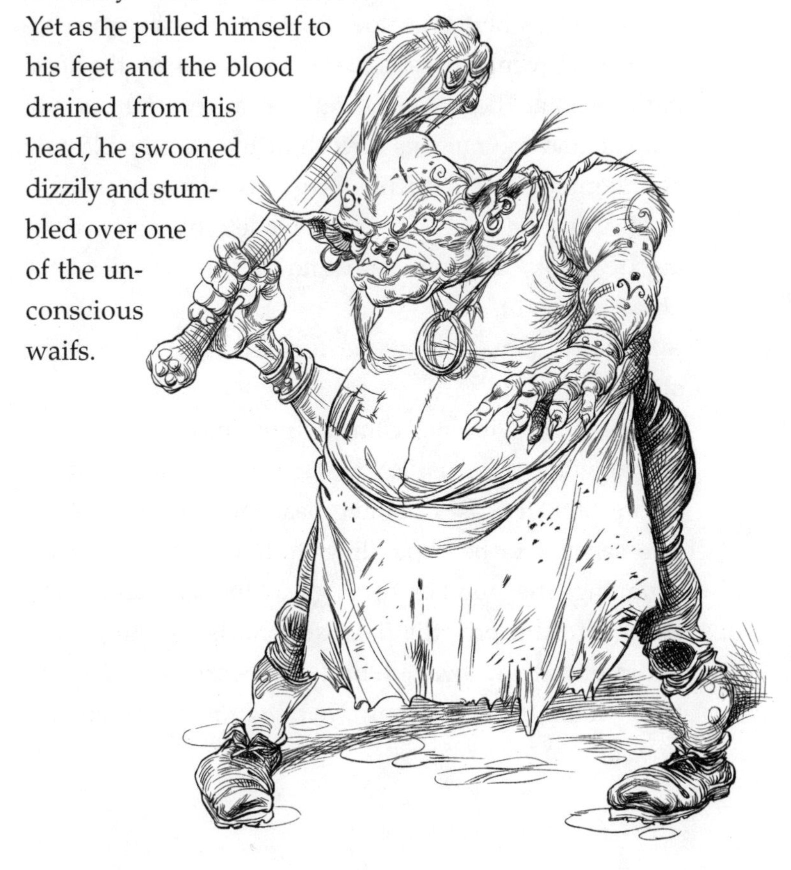

'If you weren't so valuable, I'd slit your throat right here!' snapped the mobgnome, wincing with pain and ticking off a name on his barkscroll ledger. 'Krote, get him out of there!'

The tufted goblin grasped the front of the young librarian knight's jacket and tugged. Rook lurched forwards, banging his head on the top of the doorway as he was pulled from the tumbril and set down on the ground. His legs were wobbly. His head throbbed.

'This way,' came a gruff voice as two flathead goblins seized him by the arms and frogmarched him away.

The cobbles blurred below Rook's feet as he was propelled to the centre of the square. All round him, the noise grew louder. There were shouts of anger and cries of despair, and the raucous screech of the klaxons blasting out intermittently. Suddenly the guards came to a halt.

'Here we are,' said the one to his left, his voice seeming, to Rook, to grow loud and soft as he spoke. 'A librarian knight.'

'Slightly damaged by the look of him,' added the other.

'Leave him with me,' came a third voice.

Struggling to focus, Rook stared ahead at the figure before him. It was a hammerhead goblin. His scarred face seemed to be expanding and shrinking; his eyes spiralling, the number of rings in his ears constantly changing. Abruptly, the flathead guards let him go and withdrew. Rook swayed back and forwards. He felt giddy, bilious. Everything was swimming before his eyes.

The hammerhead seized him by the arm and pulled him upright.

'One of Krote's catch, no doubt,' a voice was saying.

'I don't know what he does to them,' said another.

Rook looked up groggily. Someone was looming towards him, an arm raised. Rook trembled. Was that a dagger in his hand – a dagger still dripping blood? Was his throat about to be cut?

He tried to cry out but no sound emerged.

The dagger came down. Except it wasn't a dagger at all but a brush, dripping with crimson paint. It daubed at the front of Rook's flight-jacket, once, twice; leaving two vertical red stripes.

'Number eleven!' shouted yet another voice and Rook felt himself being bundled on.

Everything swirled and whirled about him as he was dragged forward. He became aware of a new noise – a creaking, jangling sound – and looked up to see a strange contraption hovering above him; in focus one moment, blurred the next. He tried hard to concentrate.

Glimmering in the dazzling heat, a series of great curved hooks hung at regular intervals along a length of chain which was attached to a wide circle of wooden uprights three strides high. A team of flatheads sat on a raised bench at the centre, turning sets of pedals with their feet. As the pedals went round, so too did the chain – taking the hooks with it.

All at once, a huge pair of hands grasped both of his arms at once, and Rook found himself being hoiked high up into the air. From behind him, close to his ear, there came the sound of tearing leather as a hook sliced through the back of his jacket. The sharp point grazed the back of his head. The next instant, the hands let him go and Rook found himself suspended from the hook, his feet dangling above the ground as the chain dragged him round.

All about him, the atmosphere was frenetic; a chaotic hubbub of screeched insults and dark curses; of jabbing elbows, sly dead-legs and the occasional thrown punch. Figures scurried this way and that, fighting to get a good position close to the wooden poles from which the chain hung.

Hands, claws, talons snatched, prodded and poked at Rook as he swung by. Just ahead of him, as the chain jerked momentarily to a halt, a crowd surged round a figure struggling on a hook. Rook could make out voices raised above the hubbub.

'Number nine. Lugtroll for sale. Strong in the shoulder and short in the tooth. Ideal for pulling any chariot, cart or cab. Fifteen gold pieces . . .'

'I'll take him!' cried a voice.

'Sold!' A klaxon sounded. 'To you, sir . . .'

The chain jerked on, swinging Rook with it like a badly laundered shirt on a washing line.

Another voice shouted out, 'Number ten. Who'll buy this flathead goblin? In his prime, he is; ideal for the toughest of construction work . . .' There was a flurry of activity and a chorus of excited shrieking, then, 'Sold!' The klaxon blast echoed round the square. 'Sold to the goblin with the eye-patch!'

Rook trembled. It was just a matter of time before he, too, was sold. His own slave-dealer – the flathead who had hung him up on the hook – was doing his best.

'Number eleven. Young, fit, strong. An academic. A *librarian knight*, no less! Top quality, I'm sure you'll agree!'

Saltflies were buzzing round Rook's head. They landed on his ears, his lips; they crawled round his eyes, lapping at the drops of sweat. Suspended from the hook, his leather flight-jacket tight beneath the arms, Rook was unable to bat them away. He wriggled and screwed up his face but the flies continued to torment him, seemingly aware that he could do nothing about it. He closed his eyes wearily.

'How about this one?' a screeching voice enquired, and Rook felt himself being sharply poked and prodded. 'What do you think?'

'I don't think so, mistress,' came the shrill reply. 'Won't get much sport out of it. Looks half dead already.'

Rook's eyelids fluttered. He saw two tall shrykes – one an elegant matron with purple plumage and a bone flail; the other, at the end of a leash, a drab shryke-mate. As she turned away, the matron thrust her beak in the air and sniffed.

'Come, Mardle,' said the shryke, tugging on the leash. 'Far too over-priced anyway.'

Rook shuddered, relieved that the fierce yellow-eyed creature with the sharp talons had moved away. But his relief was short-lived. As the bird-creatures moved on, they were replaced by a sinister figure in a black cloak with the white emblem of a screaming gloamglozer emblazoned upon it – a Guardian of Night.

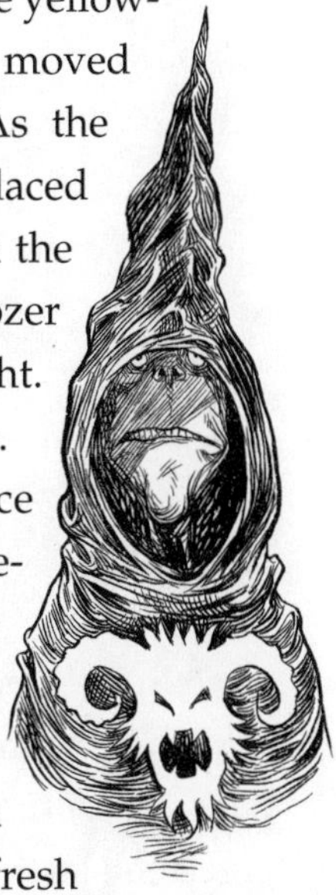

'How much?' said a thin rasping voice.

'To you, sir, seventy-five,' a voice shouted back. It was the flathead slave-dealer who had hung him up on the hook.

'Thirty,' said the Guardian. 'He's damaged, and my master, the High Guardian of Night, likes his librarians fresh as a rule . . .'

'Sixty,' said the voice firmly. 'And that's my final offer.'

'Well . . .' mused the Guardian, his face buried in the shadows of his hood.

Rook felt an icy sweat break out on his forehead. Sold to the Guardians of Night. No, it could not be happening. Not this! Anything but this . . .

Suddenly his head lolled forward. It was all too much. His throbbing temples. The suffocating heat. The breath-taking tightness in his arms and chest . . . And all the while, the prodding and poking and pinching continued – though further away now. Further and further. As if it was happening to someone else, while he – Rook – was in his hammock, all wrapped up in a nice warm blanket . . .

'Seventy!' a voice called.

'Sold!'

Rook opened his eyes and looked round blearily. Beside the slave-dealer stood a stooped figure in an embroidered hooded cape; it had broad ears, doleful eyes and bony fingers which it held out before it like a wood-mantis. It reached forward and took Rook's hands in its own, one after the other. It scratched at the calluses on his palms, it picked at the nails, it scrutinized the fingers from every angle and fingered the leather cuffs of his flight-suit thoughtfully.

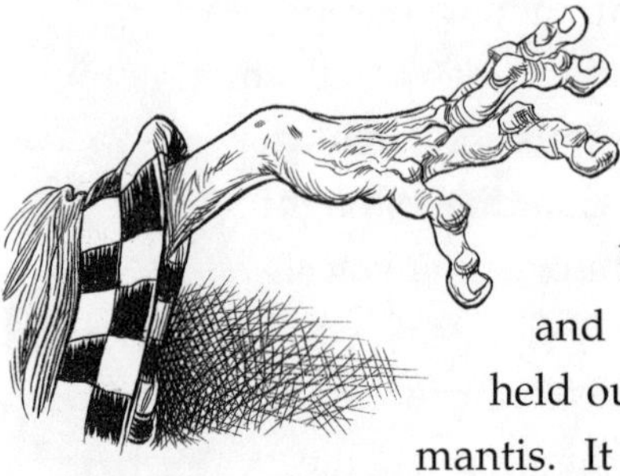

'Yes, he'll do,' the figure said. 'Have him delivered.'

The flathead nodded. There was a soft jingle as the gold coins were passed over and the flathead raised his klaxon.

'Number eleven!' he roared. 'Sold to Hestera Spikesap.' The klaxon bellowed loudly by Rook's ear.

The next instant, Rook was lifted from the hook and placed down on the ground. His legs threatened to crumple. Yet as he breathed in the air – unrestricted at last by the choking jacket – his head began to clear. Behind him, his place on the hook had been taken by a quivering nightwaif; his ears fluttering nervously, his waistcoat daubed with the number 14. As the chain pulled him away, the slave-dealer flathead went with him.

For a moment, Rook considered making a dash for it. But only for a moment. Before he could move so much as a muscle, he was seized by both arms and dragged away by the two hefty hammerheads who had answered the klaxon-call. They bundled him roughly through the crowd and delivered him to the chaingang-master – a leathery-skinned hammerhead with a clipboard and a whip – standing at the head of a line of slaves.

'Number eleven,' he noted, glancing at Rook's front and making a note of it. 'Full chain! Put him at the end.'

Rook was dragged along the row of dejected individuals – creatures from every corner of the Edge, now all yoked together with wooden collars and chains; fifteen in all.

As the wooden yoke clicked shut around his neck, he knew that that was it. He was no longer an individual. Someone had bought him and Rook Barkwater was no more. He was a mere number now. A bonded slave . . .

At the front of the line, the chaingang-master cracked his whip. 'Forward!' he roared.

The chained slaves set off, stumbling at first before getting into a slow, shuffling rhythm. On either side, armed guards marched beside them, barking commands and cracking their whips. Rook shuffled with the other slaves; his legs dragging, his head held rigid by the wooden yoke. Behind him, the sounds of the market receded; far in front, the great Sanctaphrax rock, with the jagged Tower of Night at its top, loomed in the sky.

Rook groaned. Once again – like a boulder-salmon battling against a formidable current – he was being

taken back the way he'd come. Worse than that, he now had no doubt as to where he was bound.

The Sanctaphrax Forest. It had to be.

His whole body was overwhelmed with fearful heaviness at the thought of what lay ahead. Like so many before him, he would be worked to death by the goblins in the Sanctaphrax Forest – for the scaffolding which supported the crumbling rock was as greedy for slaves to labour upon it as it was for the neverending supplies of wood that shored it up. Every pillar, every rafter and every cross-beam was stained with the blood of those who had perished there.

Rook fumbled desperately with the catch of the yoke, hoping to tease it open – but in vain. There was no escape. Ever since his decision to climb down into the sabotaged drain, his fate had been sealed. Already he could see the sluggish Edgewater River – and a large

flat-bottomed boat moored to a wooden jetty. A ferry-goblin with a long pole was seated on the bank, chewing on a straw as he waited idly for his doomed passengers.

It was hot and airless on the ground. Rook looked up into the cool, open sky, where once he had flown his beloved *Stormhornet* high above the streets of Undertown and looked down on tiny specks chained together far below. He had never, even in his darkest dreams, realized what it was to be one of those specks. He'd been too high up, exhilarated by the thrill of flight and the rush of the cool wind in his face, to imagine what it must be like down there . . .

And now I have become one of those specks, Rook noted glumly.

Lost in his own misery, he failed to notice that they had left the main road which led down to the river. It was only when the chaingang-master bellowed *'Halt!'*

that he realized they had ended up in one of the more affluent districts of Undertown. The buildings were tall, elegant and, though now past their best, still evoked the grandeur of their opulent past.

'This is the place,' barked the chaingang-master. 'Unyoke number eleven.'

Rook frowned. Number eleven? But that was him. Who *had* bought him?

The other slaves groaned miserably. A few jangled their chains.

'Be still!' bellowed the chaingang-master and cracked his whip threateningly.

The slaves fell silent.

The flatheads unlocked the yoke around Rook's neck and dragged him towards a small side door set into the wall at the foot of the towering building. Rook looked up; he recognized it at once.

The facade, though cracked and scarred, was ornately decorated, every jutting ledge, every curlicued plinth and every sunken alcove occupied by a statue. Scores of them; hundreds – continuing up as far as Rook could see.

The Palace of Statues. It looked different from down here on the ground; more imposing, more sinister – but unmistakable nonetheless.

'Move!' grunted one of the flatheads, and shoved him hard in the back.

Rook stumbled forwards, tripped over something lying in his path and ended up sprawling on the cobbles.

The first of the flatheads reached the small arched

doorway, raised his fist and hammered loudly. The second seized Rook by the hole in the back of his jacket, pulled him roughly to his feet and marched him to the door – but not before Rook had seen what had tripped him.

It was the remains of a statue of an ancient leagues-man, shattered from its fall from the crowded upper ledges. Its sightless, unblinking eyes met Rook's and he felt a familiar pang of pain deep in his chest.

You're just like me, he thought. I, too, have fallen to earth.

Even now, he could hear the grinding of bolts being slid across from inside the door. At the bottom. At the top. There was a soft click and the door cracked open . . .

·CHAPTER SIX·

HESTERA SPIKESAP

The rusty hinges creaked mournfully as the door before Rook slowly opened. He peered into the darkness of the widening gap. Why had he been brought here to the ancient Palace of Statues?

All at once, a long, bony arm reached out from the shadows and a sinewy hand – all knobbly knuckles and jagged yellow claws – gripped him round the wrist, and tugged. Rook swallowed hard as he was dragged forwards.

Behind him he could hear whips cracking, guards bellowing, and the yoked slaves howling with dismay . . . Then – as the door slammed shut with a loud *bang* – nothing.

Rook's breathing caught in his throat. A heavy silence closed in about him. It seemed to throb in his ears, oppressive and unnatural, with not a single sound from outside penetrating the stillness within; while after the glare of the daylight, his eyes struggled to adjust to the gloomy half-light of the vast, cavernous hall before him.

Compared with the unbearably hot, humid air outside in the street, the air in the hall was wonderfully cool. Rook felt the grip tighten on his wrist.

Before him, standing alone in the vast, gloomy space, was a thin, stooped and – judging by the deep wrinkles creasing his high forehead and the white tips to the whiskers on his ears – *old* goblin. Not that Rook was about to underestimate him. The goblin might look a bit doddery, but he was obviously powerful – like leather, he had been toughened and strengthened by the passing years.

'Number eleven, is it?' the goblin muttered, peering at the daubed numbers on Rook's front. 'Number eleven! Well, Speegspeel had better get number eleven to the kitchen straight away. Speegspeel doesn't want any trouble, oh, no! Speegspeel does as he's told.'

The goblin motioned for Rook to follow him, and set off across the cool, marble floor of the entrance hall.

Rook kept close behind him. As his eyes grew accustomed to the dim, shadowy half-light of the hall which seeped in through the slats of the shuttered windows above, he saw statues – hundreds of statues, in various poses and numerous styles, lurking in every shadow. There were crowds of them all round the sides of the hall, on fluted pedestals and scalloped plinths, with countless others set into alcoves in the walls; there were statues along the balconies, statues lining the grand sweeping staircase and still more disappearing up into the shadowy heights far above his head.

Each one – like those balanced so precariously on the outside of the building – had once been a former leaguesman. Their wealth and status had been captured in stone. Close by was one – short and portly – who was clutching a length of carved rope, symbolic of the material which had made his fortune; another held a stone telescope to his eye; a third had a sculpted hammelhorn standing at his feet. All of them were dressed in marble finery with jewels picked out in the stone, fur-like collars, lacy ruffs and long sweeping cloaks carved from the gleaming white rock. And as he stared closer, so their unblinking eyes appeared to narrow; their mouths, to sneer.

'Oh, they watch old Speegspeel,' the goblin grumbled softly, pushing Rook in front of him. 'They watch, just waiting for the chance to topple over when he least expects it. But old Speegspeel's too clever. They won't get Speegspeel.'

He shoved Rook viciously in the back. Rook stumbled forwards, his footsteps echoing on the cold marble. He gazed up at the grey cloaked shapes of the statues around them and realized with a jolt that they were not cloaked at all, but rather festooned in thick, dusty cobwebs. They webbed every finger, veiled every face and hung down from every outstretched arm like lengths of tattered muslin.

As they approached the other side of the vast hall, Speegspeel motioned towards a small panelled door, set beneath a modest archway ahead. Two cobweb-shrouded statues stood guard on either side. Speegspeel stepped forward, fumbled with the door handle and, with difficulty, pushed the heavy wooden door open.

'Go on, number eleven.' The old goblin chuckled. 'It doesn't do to keep Hestera Spikesap waiting. Speegspeel knows! Oh, yes, he does!'

Rook stumbled inside and found himself at the top of a steep staircase.

'That's the way,' came Speegspeel's voice. 'Down those stairs, number eleven. Hestera's expecting you.'

The door closed and Rook heard the soft shuffle of the old goblin's footsteps receding. He peered down. The stairs disappeared far below him into a noxious, dark orange glow. Gripping the banisters tightly and trying to stop his legs from shaking, he started down the flight of stairs.

Down, down, into the sunken bowels of the palace Rook went. Beneath his feet the wooden stairs – simple boards set into the stone of the palace's supporting walls – were worn and slippery. They creaked and bounced and he had to take enormous care not to lose his footing. As he went deeper, so the air grew hotter and steamier, and filled with a strange odour that Rook was unable to identify. It grew increasingly pungent with every successive step he took; now sour, now metallic, now laced with acrid smoke which coiled up thickly and fuzzed the brightening orange glow.

As he neared the bottom of the stairs, he glanced back and was shocked to see just how far down the rickety open staircase he'd come. The top was swathed in darkness and he couldn't even see the little door. It was a wonder he hadn't broken his neck, he thought giddily as he went down the last few steps.

On solid ground at last, Rook looked round and gasped. He was standing in a vast, seething kitchen. Supported by an intricate brickwork structure of stout pillars and curved arches which criss-crossed above his head, the underground chamber wheezed and heaved with heat and noise, while the intoxicating fumes were stronger than ever. They seemed to be coming from the far side of the kitchen, where the orange-yellow glow was brightest.

Just ahead of him was a long table, its surface gouged and scorched by years of misuse, overflowing with a seeming chaos of utensils, equipment and convoluted paraphernalia. Ladles, spoons, mortars and pestles, stacks of trays and sheaves of paper; scales, scissors, phials of tincture and pots of oily creams; boxes, beakers, skewers and cleavers; rulers, funnels, candles and pipettes . . .

The jumble wasn't limited to the table. The floor around it was littered with crates and sacks, each one overflowing with Deepwoods' fauna and flora; everything from dried razorflit wings to shrivelled globes of pus-fungus. Bundles of herbs and leafy branches and bunches of dried flowering shrubs hung from every wall, every arch and every pillar, giving the whole place the appearance of a vast upside-down forest. There were cupboards and cabinets; their drawers bursting with dried lichens, mosses and various desiccated remains. Racks, stacks and rows of shelving, crammed full with countless bottles – both large and small – all filled to the brim, stoppered and labelled. Some contained bark-chippings, identified by spidery writing – *Lufwood, Leadwood, Lullabee, Sallowdrop, Blookoak* . . . Some contained berries; dried, pickled, steeped in oil; some had nuts, some seeds. Some contained leaves – from the tiny spiky grey foliage of the creeping woodthyme, to the vast heart-shaped leaves from the sweetly aromatic, yet deadly poisonous, black-bay.

Rook frowned. What was so dangerous a herb doing in a kitchen? he wondered. And as he moved slowly round, inspecting the shelves and cabinets more closely, he saw other suspicious ingredients.

A barrel of venomous rosy heartapples; a flagon filled with deadly scrapewortberries, half a dozen of which he knew could kill a fully grown hammelhorn . . .

This kitchen was a poisoner's paradise!

Just then, a thin, wheedling voice rang out. 'Who's creeping round my kitchen? Is that you, Speegspeel, my old loverly . . . I've warned you about creeping round my kitchen, haven't I? Don't want another stomach-ache, do we, dearie?'

Rook's heart missed a beat. He screwed up his eyes and stared in the direction the voice had come from.

In front of him, set on dumpy legs against the blackened back wall, he could see a gargantuan pot-bellied furnace, its glass door at the front seeming to wink at him like a great orange eye. Ornately handled bellows stuck out from a hole in the grate-cover at the bottom; a black, twisting chimney emerged from the top and disappeared into the wall high above. To the right of the furnace was a towering heap of logs; to its left, an even higher pile of uncut branches and trunks – together with the saws and axes to turn it from one to the other. And to the left of that, set into the wall . . .

Rook gasped with amazement. Huge, luminous bell jars fizzed and bubbled above acid-yellow flaming burners, all connected by a seemingly chaotic jumble of interconnecting pipes and tubes which coiled and looped and doubled back on themselves before coming down in a neat row where they dripped slowly into a line of glass pots below them. Rook leaned forward and raised his fingers to the small brass spigot at the end of one of the pipes.

'Don't touch that, dearie,' wheedled the voice. Rook started back. 'Come over 'ere and let me look at you, my loverly!'

A short, wrinkled old crone stepped out from behind the forest of pipes and tubes. Rook recognized her at once from the market; a short, dumpy goblin with grey skin and heavy-lidded eyes. She was clothed in chequer-board livery, a stained pinafore, and a white cowlcap – the high, arched headgear favoured by goblin matrons – on her head. In one hand, she was clutching an opened bottle; in the other, a tiny measuring spoon. She glanced up at Rook.

'Hestera Sp . . . Spikesap?' Rook asked.

'That's right, dearie,' she told him. 'Wait a second. Can't you see I'm trying to concentrate?'

Returning her attention to the bottle, she tipped a level spoonful of red powder down the slender neck. Then another, and another, counting off as she did so. '. . . Six. Seven. Eight.' She stopped and returned the spoon to the small pot. Then, having corked the bottle and shaken it vigorously, she held it up to the light. The colourless contents had turned red. With a satisfied smile playing over her thin lips, Hestera picked up her quill, dipped it in the ink-well and wrote on the label – in the same spidery writing that Rook had noticed before – a single word: *Oblivion*.

'Oblivion?' Rook murmured.

'Never you mind about that, dearie,' Hestera said, putting the bottle to one side and bustling round the table. 'Let's have a good look at you, my loverly.' She dragged him to the light; pinched him and prodded him with her sharp little fingers. 'Wiry but strong,' she said. 'I think you'll do.' Her small eyes narrowed as she

twisted his head round. 'You've taken a nasty blow, dearie? Does your head pain you?'

Rook nodded.

Hestera reached up and placed the flat of her palm across his forehead. It felt oddly dry, like parchment – but pleasantly cool. She nodded, turned away, and Rook heard the sound of clinking glass, pouring liquids and the metallic clatter of stirring. She turned back, and held out a glass of frothing green liquid.

'Drink this, dearie,' she told him.

Rook stared nervously at the glass in her outstretched hand. What was in it? Nectar of rosy heartapple perhaps? Or scrapewortberry juice?

'Go on, my loverly,' said Hestera, thrusting the glass into his hand. 'It won't kill you.'

Slowly Rook raised the glass to his mouth and sipped. It tasted delicious – a tangy mix of flavour after flavour. Pineginger. Rocklime. Dellberry and anisleaf . . .'

'That's right,' said Hestera. 'Every last drop, dearie.'

As the liquid coursed round his body, Rook felt himself being reinvigorated and, by the time the glass was empty, not only had his head stopped throbbing but he had begun to feel fit and well once more. He wiped the back of his hand across his mouth and placed the glass down on the table.

'Amazing,' he said. 'What is it?'

'Just one of my little concoctions, my loverly,' said Hestera, testing his forehead for a second time. 'Feeling better, are we?'

Rook nodded. 'Much better, thank you.'

Hestera smiled, a nasty glint in her eyes. 'Good, then you can get to work and build up that fire!' She strode over to the pot-bellied stove. 'Look at it,' she said. 'It's glowing orange, dearie. *Orange!* It hasn't been touched for three days. Not since Huffknot went missing. And now it needs tending.' She wrapped her shawl tighter about her shoulders. 'My kitchen is growing cold. Can't you feel the chill, my loverly? Why, my teeth are beginning to chatter . . . Feed the furnace! Feed it until it glows white hot! Just the way I like it, dearie.'

Rook picked up a log from the pile and was just about to take it towards the glowing furnace when a voice inside his head spoke. *Not so hasty, my young furnace-keeper!* it said.

Rook froze. The log clattered to the floor. It was as if icy fingers were probing his brain, causing a stabbing pain behind his eyes and making it difficult for him to think clearly.

'I was just getting him to stoke up the furnace with a few logs, dearie,' Hestera protested indignantly. 'Where's the harm in that, Amberfuce? It's freezing in my kitchen. Tell him, Flambusia; *freezing!*'

The unpleasant chilled sensation in Rook's head abruptly stopped. He turned to see not one but two figures standing in the shadows behind him. One was a hulking great creature – possibly of cloddertrog-extraction, and made bigger still by the stacked sandals on her feet and winged hat upon her head. She was dressed in voluminous robes which fluttered and shimmered in the trembling heat. Before her, seated in a buoyant sumpwood chair, was an ancient-looking ghost-waif, hunched and shaking; his skin pale and mottled; his eyes dull and half-closed.

'My dear Hestera Spikesap,' he croaked, his drooping ears and limp barbels trembling. 'How many times must I remind you? We really can't be too careful. If you must go shopping at the slave auction, please, please, *please* bring your purchases directly to me!' His sunken cheeks sucked in and out alarmingly.

'I was going to, dearie,' said Hestera, pushing Rook towards the tiny waif. 'But he's only just arrived. And it's *so* cold – I thought he could feed the furnace first, and then . . .'

'No, no, *no*, Hestera!' The waif fell back in the chair exhausted, choking and gasping for breath. His companion, Flambusia, leaned round.

'Lawks-a-mussy!' she exclaimed. 'You're vexing yourself again. And what did I say about vexing yourself?' She pulled a cloth from her sleeve and mopped Amberfuce's glistening brow. 'Nursie said, don't! It isn't good for your constitution. And nursie knows best.'

The waif closed his eyes. His ears rippled strangely. His breathing became slower, more regular. 'You're right, of course, Flambusia,' he said at last, his words breathy and snatched. 'It's just . . .' He flapped a bony arm in Hestera's direction. 'This . . . this *creature*! She's a law unto herself . . .'

Hestera folded her arms. 'Well, he's here now,' she said sharply. 'What are you waiting for?'

'Bring him closer, Hestera,' said Amberfuce wearily.

'Go on, dearie,' said Hestera, shoving Rook in the back.

Rook stumbled across the tiled floor, and stopped in front of the buoyant chair. An unpleasant smell hung round the sickly-looking creature, a curious mixture of stale milk-rusks and antiseptic which grew stronger as Amberfuce leaned forward in his chair.

'Kneel,' he croaked.

Rook did as he was told. The waif grabbed him by the collar, pulled him closer and stared deep into his eyes. For a second time, Rook felt the icy tingling inside his head.

Let me in, whispered a voice. *Let me in, Rook Barkwater, librarian knight . . .*

The tingling grew more intense. Chilled, numbing; it was as if the icy fingers were searching his mind and reading his thoughts, turning them over like the pages of a book.

A librarian knight . . . Lake Landing . . . the voice inside his head said. *A skycraft; the Stormhornet . . . An approaching storm, a rippled lake . . .* The ancient waif closed his eyes, and his back arched as he threw himself back in the chair. *An under-librarian!* The voice was strong now, insistent. *A lectern-tender, a chain-turner . . . Deep, deep sorrow . . .* The waif gripped Rook's cuffs tight and pulled him closer. *Tears . . . Pain . . . Bad dreams . . .*

Rook shuddered.

Let's clear them all away, the voice inside his head told him. *Let them all go. Give them to me. That's the way. Let all those troubled thoughts disappear for ever . . .*

Rook's head swam as his memories slipped away, one by one, little by little. Soon there would be nothing left.

'No,' he groaned, jerking back and trying to push the numbing fingers away with his thoughts.

Don't fight me! Rook heard inside his head, and he felt the fingers tighten their grip as they continued their searching.

It was tempting to do as the waif had instructed. Anything to bring a hasty end to the terrible jarring of those ice-cold fingers, scraping and scrabbling inside his head. Yet, if he *didn't* fight . . .

His mind was already beginning to resemble a barren landscape of snow and ice. Impressions, thoughts, feelings – Rook seemed to see them staggering across the empty wasteland only to be seized by the probing fingers and frozen solid.

Must try to hide from the icy fingers, Rook thought. Must hide myself. Rook. Rook Barkwater . . .

Like a great searchlight, the waif's probing thoughts swept across Rook's mind, poking into nooks and crannies, prising open cracks and crevices and unlocking door after door after door, on down into the deepest of his most distant thoughts.

Still on his knees, Rook swayed back and forwards, his head lolling from side to side. It was so hot in the kitchen; stiflingly hot, the air laced with miasmic fumes from the furnace.

Yet inside his pounding head, it was cold – bitterly cold – as the icy fingers delved deeper, freezing every part of him.

I . . . am . . . Rook . . .

A blizzard wind seemed to whip away his memories and thoughts like so many snowflakes. Rook . . . I'm Rook . . . He ran away from the icy, probing fingers and fell into the arms of something soft, something warm; something from his earliest memories. A banderbear. *His* banderbear.

The great creature raised a warning claw to her lips, pulled him down into a mossy hollow and wrapped her arms around him. Rook curled up and hid himself away inside the huge creature's warm, furry embrace.

He couldn't be found now. He was safe. Secure . . .

With a jerky shake of his head, Amberfuce sat up straight. His eyes snapped open.

'Well?' said Hestera.

'Oh, I think you'll find he'll be compliant now,' the

waif said, as Flambusia mopped his glistening brow. 'His mind has been cleared. A blank slate, so to speak.' He frowned, and flapped the nurse away irritably. 'A fine mind it was, it must be said,' he remarked thoughtfully. 'A strong mind. It seems such a shame to take all those brave thoughts and noble memories from such an intrepid young lad. Still, Hestera, I'm sure you'll soon teach him afresh – particularly if you treat him as casually as all the oth . . . oth . . . others . . .' His words collapsed into a fit of coughing. He wheezed and gasped for breath.

Flambusia patted him gently on the back. 'There, there,' she said soothingly. 'You've been overdoing it again.'

'Medicine . . .' Amberfuce croaked. 'My . . . medicine . . .' The coughing resumed, louder than ever.

'At once,' said Flambusia, grabbing the buoyant chair and steering it away. Just before she disappeared from sight, she turned and flashed a smile at Hestera. 'I don't know where we'd be without your medicine,' she said.

As the two of them left, Hestera turned her attention to Rook. He was still on his knees, head slumped and eyes staring blindly ahead. She raised his chin with one hand and clicked her fingers with the other. 'I only hope Amberfuce hasn't gone too far,' she muttered. 'It wouldn't be the first time.' She stepped back. 'Stand!' she commanded.

Rook struggled to his feet. 'Yes,' he intoned obediently.

'Good, dearie,' muttered Hestera. 'Right, you've got to

work if you want to earn your daily gruel. To the furnace with you. Stoke the fire! Stoke it up high!'

'Yes.'

'Very good,' said Hestera. She pulled on a heavy glove and opened the door at the front of the furnace. A blast of scorching, sulphurous air struck Rook full in the face. He recoiled – but said nothing. 'Yes, very good, indeed,' said Hestera. 'Amberfuce has done well. *Very* well.'

Rook stood before the furnace, stock-still, unblinking. His mind was blank; so blank that he wasn't even aware that he didn't know what to do next.

'The logs,' came Hestera's voice. 'Take the logs from the pile and feed the fire.'

'Yes.'

He crossed over to the towering heap of logs and seized the one closest to him. It was large, unwieldy, and almost twice his own weight. He dragged it across the floor, grunting and groaning with effort. In front of the furnace, he caught his breath before reaching down, clasping the rough bark and hefting the whole lot up into the air. The log rested precariously on the lip of the circular door-frame for a moment, threatening to fall back and crush him – then keeled forwards onto the glowing embers inside.

'That's it,' Hestera told him. 'Now pump the bellows – up, down, up, down; that's the way . . . Then fetch another log. And then another, and another – and you keep on fetching them and feeding them to the fire until I tell you to stop. Understand?'

'Yes, I understand.'

The work was back-breaking. Time and again, Rook dragged the heavy logs across to the great furnace, hoiked them up and tipped them in. With each one, the fire blazed hotter and hotter. It scorched Rook's lungs and skin. It singed his hair . . .

Yet inside his head it was all still a frozen wasteland that the flames could not touch. Though his body was suffering, his mind was unaware of anything beside the sound of Hestera's voice.

'Another log!' she rasped. 'And hurry! You're slowing down!'

'Yes, Hestera.' He doubled his efforts.

But in the emptiness within, something stirred – a tiny movement in the snow as a buried speck of consciousness flickered. The banderbear's embrace warmed his spirit.

Rook, it whispered. *You are Rook.*

He was curled up in a foetal ball, protected from the arctic chill by the banderbear's reassuring embrace. The waif's icy fingers had taken his memories, his thoughts, his hopes and fears, his nightmares and dreams . . . But there was one thing that had remained out of reach; that most important and precious thing of all. The seed of his existence, the essence of himself – in short, the knowledge of who he was.

Rook Barkwater.

He was still safe in the warm embrace of the banderbear that had once protected him as a child, lost and alone in the Deepwoods . . .

Rook stumbled and dropped the log he was dragging to the furnace. His head was spinning.

The ice was in retreat. Rook crawled from the banderbear's warm arms. The memories, the thoughts, the feelings; they were all beginning to thaw.

Suddenly, with a loud roaring in his ears and a flash of blinding light, everything came flooding back. *Who* he was. *Where* he was . . .

'That's enough for today, dearie,' said Hestera, eyeing him suspiciously. 'You can get to your bed.'

'Thank you,' said Rook, trying hard to conceal his relief. The stifling heat of the blazing furnace was getting to his racked and weary body now. He didn't know how much longer he could have kept going. With a huge effort – using every last reserve of strength – Rook hefted the log he was holding up into the fire and stood waiting for his next instruction.

Hestera slammed the great round furnace-door shut and secured the latch. She turned to Rook. 'You sleep over there,' she said, pointing back to the low table. 'Underneath.'

'Thank you,' said Rook.

He shuffled towards it, crouched down and, taking care not to knock the bump on his head against the table-top, crawled beneath. There was a mattress of woodchips and shavings strewn across the tiles – soft, warm, inviting. Rook lay down, curled up into a ball and breathed in the sweet, aromatic scent of the fragments of wood. His eyelids grew heavy; his body seemed to sink into the floor.

Hestera stood above him. 'Sleep well, little furnace-keeper and build up your strength,' she rasped softly. 'You'll need it. Today you have fed the fire . . .'

Rook wrapped his hands round his knees and pulled them up close to his stomach. 'Thank . . . you . . .' he whispered drowsily.

A darkness descended; the outside was switched off, sense by sense – and Rook slipped into a deep, dreamless sleep. Hestera chuckled unpleasantly.

'. . . But tomorrow you will feed the baby.'

·CHAPTER SEVEN·

FEEDING THE BABY

Early the following morning, Rook was rudely awoken by something hard and pointed jabbing into his back. His eyes snapped open.

For a moment, he was perplexed. He seemed to be lying on a pile of wood-shavings. The sharp, stabbing sensation struck him in the back a second time.

'*Ow!*' he cried out loud, and rolled over.

Peering down at him was a grey-skinned old goblin matron with a stick clutched in her bony hands, its sharp end pointed towards him. 'Look lively, my loverly,' she was saying. 'Get up. There's plenty of work to be done.'

At the sound of her shrill, wheedling voice, everything suddenly came flooding back. Speegspeel the butler, Hestera Spikesap the cook, and the sickly waif, Amberfuce, who had probed his mind and erased his past – or at least, tried to . . .

Mustn't give myself away, Rook cautioned himself as he crawled out from beneath the table and scrambled quickly to his feet. He looked round giddily. The furnace was glowing and the hot, stifling air shimmered like water. Hestera raised the stick and pointed to the table behind him.

'Victuals,' she said.

Rook turned. A place for one had been laid. There was a large bowl of steaming grey gruel with a wooden spoon sticking out of the middle, and a glass of what looked like the same liquid he had drunk the previous evening.

'Eat, drink – and be quick about it, dearie,' said Hestera. 'The furnace is getting low.'

With no stool or bench to sit down on, Rook had his meagre breakfast standing. The gruel tasted as unpleasant as it looked – smoky, salty and with a stale tang of mould about it – but by washing down each claggy spoonful with a slurp of the frothing green juice, he was able to sate his hunger and slake his thirst at the same time.

'Hurry up, dearie,' said Hestera impatiently. 'That furnace needs building up.' She shuddered and pulled her shawl tightly about her. 'My old bones are chilled to the marrow.'

What was she talking about? Rook wondered. The kitchen was scorching. His entire body was damp with sweat. He drained the glass, laid it down next to the half-empty bowl and turned to Hestera. 'Thank you,' he said expressionlessly.

'Better you thank me with deeds not words,' said Hestera. 'Stoke up that fire, dearie. Get it blazing white hot. White hot, d'you hear? As hot as it can possibly be, for today's the day we feed the baby.'

'Yes,' said Rook, taking care that his face betrayed not the faintest flicker of emotion. He turned away and headed for the great mound of logs, Hestera's words echoing in his head.

Feed the baby? he thought. What baby?

By the time Rook had dragged the first of the logs across to the furnace, Hestera had already opened the circular door. As he stepped in front of it, a blast of roaring heat struck him full in the face. He let out a soft, involuntary moan.

Hestera turned and gave Rook a long, searching look. Rook could feel her dark suspicious eyes boring into him. Struggling to remain impassive, he reached down, seized the log and thrust it into the furnace. Then he turned, crouched down and worked the bellows, just as Hestera had shown him – four sharp movements, up, down, up, down. There was a crackle and a hiss and the glow from the fire turned from a deep gold to pale, luminous yellow.

'*White* hot, remember, dearie,' said Hestera. 'More logs, more logs. And keep working those bellows!'

A dozen logs and a deal of back-breaking bellows-pumping later, Rook was relieved to hear Hestera declare herself satisfied at last. The pot-bellied furnace was creaking and juddering as the fire inside blazed more furiously than ever; blinding as the sun and lightning hot.

'Come over 'ere,' my loverly,' she said. 'Observe what I do.'

'Yes,' Rook croaked. His throat, parched and scorched,

felt as though it had been sandpapered; his legs felt weak and heavy. Yet as he left the furnace and headed into the shadows where Hestera was busy fiddling with a length of rope, he found that the air was cooler and his head began to clear.

'Unknot this for me, dearie,' said Hestera. 'I can't reach.'

Rook nodded obediently, stretched up to the wall-mounted cleat and detached the tangled coil of rope. He handed the end to Hestera who, without a word, fed the rope through her hands. From high above, there came a soft clatter and Rook looked up to see a large wooden bucket slowly descending towards them. When it was low enough, Rook reattached the rope to the cleat.

'Make sure it's tied securely, dearie,' said Hestera. 'That's it. Now come and have a look.'

Rook gave the rope an extra tug, then returned to the bucket, now suspended a couple of strides above the floor. Steadying it with one hand, Hestera reached in with the other and pulled out a small, red, bulbous object which glistened as she held it up to the light.

'It's an acorn,' she announced.

Rook frowned. With its red flesh, thin, slimy membrane and thick juice that oozed like blood, it looked like no acorn he had ever seen before. Nor did it smell like one.

It was, he thought, his nose wrinkling at the stale, metallic odour, more like a piece of offal – a hammelhorn liver, perhaps; or a tilder kidney.

'An acorn,' he repeated, trying to mask the surprise in his voice.

'But not just any old acorn, dearie,' said Hestera. 'This here is a *bloodoak* acorn. Harvested in the Deepwoods by woodtrolls, so they are, my loverly. And there's a tricky task, I can tell you! What with the bloodoaks eating all the flesh they can get their tarry-vines on and all, the harvesters often get harvested, if you take my meaning. You want to count yourself lucky you're here working for me.'

'Yes,' said Rook, his stomach churning.

'That's why they're so expensive,' she went on. 'I mean, it stands to reason. But you try telling that to that old tightwad, Amberfuce. Always moaning on about the price, so he is. But as I always tell him, if it keeps the master upstairs happy, then it's gold pieces well spent, and no mistake.'

Hestera carefully placed the acorn in the crook of her apron and, selecting another, held it up to the light. Rook watched queasily as she picked out four more of the quivering crimson blobs and placed them in her bloodstained apron. At last she turned to Rook.

'That should do, my loverly.' She pointed a bloodstained finger across to a rack of hearth-tools – tongs, brushes, shovels; a set of bellows and several small hatchets. 'Fetch me a shovel, dearie,' she said.

Rook did as he was told.

'No, not that one,' came Hestera's voice from behind him as he reached out. 'That one there with the long handle.'

Rook seized the shovel she wanted, and returned to Hestera.

'That's it, my loverly,' she said. 'Now, hold it out flat in front of me. That's the way. Now, we place them out on the shovel-tray, so.' She stared down at the half dozen acorns thoughtfully. 'Maybe one more,' she said at last, turning and retrieving a seventh acorn from the swaying bucket and placing it next to the rest. 'That's better. Now for the roasting. Follow me.'

Hestera headed back to the furnace. Rook went with her, holding the bloodoak acorns out in front of him. Hestera slipped on a pair of heavy gloves, reached up and pulled the furnace-door wide open. The heat blasted out.

'*Ooh*, lovely,' Hestera cooed. 'Nice and warm in my cold, old bones.' She turned back to Rook. 'Pass over the shovel,' she said. 'Careful, now.'

Rook stepped forwards, feeling himself wilt as the heat grew suddenly more intense. He handed over the precious load of bloodoak acorns and retreated.

'Pop it in like so,' said Hestera, plunging the shovel into the white-hot heart of the furnace. There was a hiss and the unmistakable smell of roasting meat. 'And now we wait,' she said. 'A couple of minutes ought to do it.' She turned back to Rook. 'Course, normally you won't be doing such a large batch, dearie,' she said. 'One acorn is enough for at least a hundred bottles of oblivion.'

'Oblivion,' Rook repeated.

'I was making some up when you arrived,' said Hestera, 'do you remember? Oh, no, of course you don't,' she added – thankfully before Rook could give himself away. 'I was forgetting. Silly old Hestera . . .' She picked at a splatter of crusted, blood-coloured sap on her apron. 'Oblivion,' she sighed. 'It's the master's little tipple. Keeps him happy, so it does. And it's all my own recipe,' she added, with obvious pride.

Rook remained still, impassive.

'I distil it from the finest vintage sapwine.' Hestera nodded at the chaos of pipes and tubes, burners and bell jars set into the wall to her right. 'I have some on the go the whole time,' she said. 'But it's my own secret ingredient that makes it so special. Powdered blookoak acorn. It's what gives it the kick the master likes so much . . . ' She pulled Rook close and her eyes narrowed. 'It's our little secret. You won't tell anyone will you, dearie?'

Rook could smell her fetid breath, sour and moist in his face. 'No,' he managed to say.

The goblin released her grip and pushed him away with a laugh. 'Course you won't, my loverly. After all, you're part of our little family now. You won't ever be meeting anyone else to tell Hestera's secret to, not ever again . . .'

She turned back to the furnace, pulled the shovel out and inspected the acorns. 'Hmm, half a minute longer, I think . . .' She thrust them back inside. 'Of course, we shan't be making oblivion today. Oh, no. Today we're going to feed the baby.'

'Feed the baby,' Rook repeated softly, but his mind was still racing from the impact of her words. Never meet anyone else . . . Not ever again?

Hestera pulled the shovel from the furnace a second time. 'Perfect!' she announced. 'Look at it closely, dearie. This is exactly the colour and consistency you should be aiming for, see?'

'Yes,' said Rook, looking down at the shovel. Where the seven slimy offal-like acorns had been, there now lay a single pile of powder; as fine as flour, as crimson as blood.

Hestera pulled the shovel clear of the furnace, pushed the door shut with her shoulder and headed back to the table, the charred handle clasped in her bony hands. 'As I say, normally I'd keep this in a jar until I needed it for the oblivion. But not today . . .'

'No, today we're going to feed the baby,' said Rook, relieved to hear his own voice was still flat and expressionless.

'That's right, dearie,' said Hestera. Her dark eyes glinted behind their hooded lids. 'At least, *you* are.' She rested the end of the shovel on the table-top. 'Now, grab a bell jar, my loverly, and brush all of the bloodoak powder inside. That's the way. Every last speck. And be quick about it! Timing is everything.'

Rook hurried to complete his task, trying his hardest to do exactly what Hestera had told him. Yet despite his best efforts, as he swept the soft bristles over the shovel, some specks of the red powder missed the bell jar and fluttered down to the damp floor. Hestera, thankfully, seemed not to notice.

When the shovel was completely empty, she turned and returned it to the rack. Rook picked up the bell jar and examined the vivid red powder inside. It was so bright it seemed almost to be pulsating . . .

'Put it down,' came a voice by his shoulder.

Hestera was back, a small pot clasped in her hands. She placed it down on the table next to the bell jar and unscrewed the lid. Curious, Rook peered inside. It was half-full of a pale sepia powder that glittered in the dim light of the kitchen.

'Phraxdust,' said Hestera.

'Phraxdust,' repeated Rook flatly, trying desperately to conceal a surge of excitement. He knew all about the stuff – that it came from stormphrax, that precious substance created in a Great Storm, so heavy in darkness that it had once been used to weight down the old floating rock of Sanctaphrax; that it was produced naturally and safely in the half-light of the Twilight Woods as the stormphrax broke down; that it could purify even the most polluted water . . .

'Ay, finest quality phraxdust, dearie,' said Hestera. 'Garnered by the shrykes in the depths of the Twilight

Woods.' She tapped the side of her nose. 'We have a little arrangement . . .' She bustled forwards and handed Rook a pair of tweezers. 'But we are wasting precious time,' she said. 'The bloodoak powder is cooling. See how the colour is growing dimmer. Add some phraxdust to it, dearie; then shake the whole lot up together.'

'Yes,' said Rook. He held the tweezers with his forefinger and thumb and dipped them into the pot. 'How much do I add?' he asked.

'For seven bloodoak acorns, seven pinches of phrax-dust,' came Hestera's reply from the other side of the kitchen. Rook glanced round and was surprised to see that the old goblin matron had slipped away and was now crouched down behind a heavy bench, her white cap just poking up above the worktop. 'Go on!' she snapped.

Rook turned back to the powders, his heart clomping like a skittish tilder. What he was doing must be dangerous, he realized – otherwise, why would Hestera be shielding herself?

He leaned forwards and, with trembling fingers, took a tweezer-pinch of phraxdust and moved it over to the bell jar. Then, breath held, he opened the tweezers and a sprinkling of sepia fell onto the crimson powder inside.

Rook reached in for a second pinch. His palms were wet. Glistening beads lined his forehead, and as he leaned forwards once more, he struggled to focus on the bell jar. Sweat was running into his eyes; his head was throbbing.

'Take care not to drop any of the phraxdust, dearie,' came Hestera's wheedling voice.

Rook opened the tweezers and the tiny particles of phraxdust dropped. As they did so, a single speck broke away from the rest and swirled round in the scorching air-currents. Down towards the table-top it floated, then up again, spinning and glittering – now in lamplight, now in furnace-glow; then down again, floating past the edge of the table and hitting the floor with its traces of bloodoak powder . . .

BANG!!!

The explosion which ripped through the kitchen was as violent as it was sudden. It shook the floor, it rocked the heavy table, it seized Rook and tossed him back across the kitchen like a wet rag. He landed heavily by the wall, the tweezers still clamped in his grip.

'Careless, dearie! Very careless!' came a shrill voice. 'Jaspel was careless, and *he* didn't last long!' She wagged a bony finger at him reproachfully. 'I *told* you to take care!'

'W . . . what just happened?' stammered Rook, picking himself up. His nostrils quivered at a familiar smell – like wood-almonds; toasted wood-almonds . . .

'You must have dropped some bloodoak powder before, and then some phraxdust just now,' said Hestera matter-of-factly. 'Outside the bell jar, they're very unstable – any bit of moisture and . . . *bang!*'

Rook froze. It suddenly occurred to him that if moisture was the cause of the explosion, then his entire body was a detonator. Just one clammy finger; one bead of sweat, and . . . The thought of it made him sweat more heavily than ever. Suddenly he was like a sieve, dripping water from every pore.

'Hurry up!' said Hestera sharply. 'We must feed the baby. Carry on, dearie.'

Wiping his shaking hands as best he could on the front of his jacket, Rook hurried back to the table. He raised the tweezers, reached forwards gingerly and held his breath. Then, with his fingers trembling like a sallowdrop in a storm, he dropped the next tweezer-pinch of sepia phraxdust into the bell jar. He repeated this four more times.

'At last,' said Hestera. 'Now stopper it up and give it a shake.'

'Yes,' said Rook faintly. Feeling sick to the pit of his stomach, he reached forwards, seized the bell jar and held it up. The phraxdust formed a thin layer on top of the bloodoak powder. He pushed the cork into place.

'A good shake, mind,' said Hestera.

'Yes,' said Rook. He could feel the heat from the toasted powder warming his hands – his nervous hands; his *moist, clammy* hands . . . Eyes clamped firmly shut, he shook the glass jar vigorously. Nothing happened.

He looked up. The powders had mixed together.

Just then a tinkling sound echoed round the kitchen. It was coming from the wall behind the table, where a row of bells attached to coiled strips of metal were mounted to a board. Each one was identified by a small plaque beneath – *the Great Hall, the Banquet Hall, the Master's Chamber* . . . It was the one marked *Leagues' Chamber* that had just rung. The bell was still swaying.

'Quickly, dearie! Quickly!' said Hestera. 'Speegspeel is waiting. Bring the bell jar over here, my loverly, and I'll warm it up ready.'

Back at the furnace, Hestera placed the bell jar on the ledge of the door and waited till the powder inside was once again glowing a vivid red. Then, without saying a word, she removed it and hurried off, beckoning to Rook as she went.

He followed behind her as she crossed the kitchen to the opposite corner. There, half-hidden in shadow, was a carved stone head set into the wall and gurning hideously. It was huge, each bulging eye the size of Rook's head and the bulbous nose as large as a hammelhorn. Beneath it, the mouth was vast and snarling. Rook frowned. Hestera seemed to be aiming straight for it.

'Step inside and hold this close to you, dearie,' said Hestera, handing him back the bell jar. 'You're to take it up to the Leagues' Chamber at the very top of the palace. Speegspeel will meet you there. Don't keep him waiting.'

Rook nodded mutely. Hestera pulled a lever set to the right of the stone head, and the bared teeth opened.

Rook stared into the mouth. Inside was a small cupboard-like affair – oddly modest for so grand an entrance – with a length of rope hanging from above.

'It's a pulley-lift,' Hestera told him. 'It connects all the different palace floors. Go on, dearie.'

Despite the heat of the hot bell jar clasped to his chest, Rook shivered. He manoeuvred himself up into the small box-shaped compartment and sat cross-legged on the floor. The rope hung down before his face.

'That's the way, my loverly,' said Hestera. 'Seize the rope and pull. Pull with all your might. And don't stop till you reach the top. The bell jar mustn't be allowed to cool down. If it does, moisture could form on the inside of the glass – and if that happened . . .'

Rook swallowed noisily.

'But then, I'm sure a big strong lad like you won't have any problems. Not like old Gizzlewit. Stopped halfway up at the banquet hall, so he did. Horrible mess! Glass and guts everywhere!'

Rook swallowed again and hugged the bell jar tightly to his chest – anything to keep it warm.

'Go on, then, dearie,' said Hestera, her voice laced with impatience. 'Speegspeel's waiting, remember.'

Rook seized one side of the rope and pulled down hard. The pulley-lift juddered and he felt himself rising up. He pulled again. The kitchen disappeared – and with it the intense heat from the blazing furnace. Higher he rose, in a dark chimney-like space, pulling hand over hand in a regular rhythm. Sweat beaded his forehead and dampened his hair; the muscles in his stomach and

arms began to protest. But he mustn't allow the bell jar to cool. Rook drove himself on.

A dim light above his head grew closer, closer . . . All at once, Rook found himself staring out of a narrow opening into the statue-filled hallway. It was as cavernous and shadowy as he remembered. And as cold! Tightening his grip on the rope, he pulled harder than ever.

A moment later, he glimpsed an ornate reception hall with rugs on the floor, and numerous chairs and benches, each one covered with a ghostly dust-sheet.

He continued up. An upper landing flashed past; then, on the other side of a metal grille, a small library with books lining the walls and display cases in the centre of the room. His arms were throbbing now, each tug on the rope harder than the one before. He wanted to stop, to rest – but he knew he dare not.

A little further up, squinting through the hatch-like opening, Rook saw a grandiose room. The ceilings were tall and vaulted; a crystal chandelier hung low over a long, blackwood table laid out with gold cutlery and silver goblets.

Rook's body was aching; his head throbbed. And he was hot. So hot . . .

'The banquet hall . . . Gizzlewit!' he murmured weakly, and started back, horrified by sight of the misty clouds of breath twisting from his lips as he spoke.

He might be hot, but the banquet hall was freezing. Gizzlewit's terrible end flashed before his eyes.

Doubling his efforts, Rook pulled on the rope with all his might. The banquet-room hatch disappeared as the pulley-lift went back into the square chimney-like stack. For a moment the rope twisted and snagged and the lift slowed. Rook tugged all the harder. There was a slight jerk, and the ascent continued. Up, up, up he went, past a locked hatchway and on. It grew darker, mustier; sticky spiderwebs wrapped themselves round his hands and face. But he kept going. And as he did so, something occurred to him. Something wonderful. It was getting warmer . . .

With a jolt and a loud *clonk!* the lift came to an abrupt halt. Rook looked about him anxiously. It was darker than ever. Pitch black. He couldn't see his hands in front of his face.

Just then, he heard a soft sing-song muttering behind him. He twisted round and cocked his head to one side. The voice grew clearer. '*Keep to the black, not the white, if you want to keep your life,*' it was saying. Rook recognized the slightly hissing voice of the old goblin who had dragged him inside the palace. It was

Speegspeel. *'Keep to the black, not the white, if you want to keep your life.'*

Rook reached forwards, and his fingers closed round a small handle, which he twisted and pushed. The door remained shut. Trying hard not to panic, Rook paused, and listened.

'Keep to the black, not the white . . .' The rhyme broke off abruptly. 'Oh, he'd better be quick, so he had . . .'

'Speegspeel, I'm here!' Rook cried out. 'In the pulley-lift!' He rattled and shook the door, and banged upon it with his fist.

The goblin fell still and Rook heard the sound of hurried, shuffling footsteps approaching. There was the sound of jangling metal and a key being slid into a lock. The next moment, the door burst open, dazzling light flooded in and Rook found himself peering into the expectant face of the butler.

'Number eleven!' he exclaimed, relief splashing across his face. 'Oh, but he's a strong one, that number eleven. Speegspeel knew he would be.' His eyes narrowed. 'And have you got it? Did you bring me food for the baby?'

Rook opened the front of his jacket and pulled out the bell jar. Speegspeel clapped his hands together, making a sound like clacking wood. 'Excellent!' he hissed. 'Jump out, number eleven,' he said. 'Hurry now. Follow me.'

Rook swung his legs round and, holding the bell jar carefully, jumped down onto the floor. The staggering heat of the chamber wrapped itself around him like a suffocating blanket. He found himself standing in a magnificent rooftop chamber.

Above his head, a spectacular panelled-glass dome opened up onto the bright sky beyond. Some of the panes had been broken and lay glittering on the floor around a huge, ring-shaped table – crudely repaired with ropes and wooden splints – which filled the centre of the chamber. On the side nearest him lay a great stone head, its unblinking eyes staring down blindly at the wooden boards; while on the far side of the table, out of place in the rundown finery of the chamber, stood a rickety-looking structure some twenty strides or so high, at the top of which – like an egg in a nest – was cradled a large metal ball. It was there that Speegspeel was heading.

He circled the table, picking his way through the broken glass, and stopped at the foot of the scaffold. Rook stopped beside him, then watched curiously as the old goblin reached for a trumpet-like instrument some fifteen strides long which was leaning up against the wooden framework. With a soft grunt of effort, Speegspeel raised it up into the air, placing the flared bell at one end against the surface of the metal ball and the other end to his ear. His leathery skin creased as a smile spread across his face.

'Baby needs feeding,' he said. 'It's nearly full enough, but not quite . . .' He laid the ear-trumpet aside and turned to Rook. 'Follow me,' he said. 'Follow Speegspeel and we'll feed the baby.'

Rook tucked the bell jar under his left arm and followed the goblin up the tricky ascent. It looked difficult – and was even more difficult than it looked.

The wood was rough and splinters kept jabbing into Rook's fingers; the gaps between the struts were wide and awkward to navigate – particularly with the heavy jar threatening to slip at any moment. He clambered over a long, thick beam set at an angle and on up towards the criss-cross framework which supported the great ball, keeping pace with the goblin.

'We're almost there, number eleven,' Speegspeel called over his shoulder encouragingly.

Rook glanced down. The floor seemed miles below him already. He looked up again. He was level with the ball now. Close up, with its coppery gleam and segmented body, it looked like nothing so much as a giant wood orange, the impression completed by the long, stalk-like length of rope hanging down from a small hole in its underside. Just above, Speegspeel held out a hand.

'That's the way,' he said. 'Now right on up to the platform.'

Rook reached up, took the goblin's hand and pulled himself up beside him. He was standing on a rough, almost-circular platform which ringed the top of the ball.

'Look at baby,' Speegspeel whispered. 'Beautiful, isn't it?' He stroked it softly, feeling the smoothness of its burnished outer casing. 'The master designed baby. But Speegspeel, he made it. Just like master said. Beautiful baby. Beautiful big baby.'

Far above Rook's head, a white raven swooped across the sky on soft, padded wings. Its gimlet eyes bored down through the glass dome of the great statue-covered building.

'See the cap, number eleven? Set into baby's centre,' whispered Speegspeel. 'Remove it. Gently now . . .' Rook did as he was told. 'Now empty the bell jar into it. Every last speck. And quickly, before any nasty moisture gets into baby. We don't want that . . . Not yet.'

With fumbling fingers, Rook slowly tipped the jar up. Then with a deft flick he thrust the neck of the jar down into the hole in the copper casing. It was a perfect fit.

As the powder dropped down into the ball, Rook found himself looking through the glass bottom of the jar and into the so-called baby. It was almost full. He tapped the glass, and the last few specks of red powder dropped down inside. Then, in one movement, he pulled the empty bell jar away, slammed the cap back into place and tightened it.

'All done,' came Speegspeel's voice in his ear. The goblin was stroking the side of the huge ball with pride. 'We'll have the baby full up in no time. The master will be so pleased with us.'

Rook followed the goblin back down the scaffold. At the bottom, Speegspeel clapped him on the shoulder.

'The baby's fed,' he said, 'so you'd best be getting back. You don't want to cross old Hestera Spikesap. Speegspeel knows.' He rubbed a gnarled hand slowly round his stomach. 'Not if you don't want no mysterious stomach-ache,' he said. 'She's good at those. Mark old Speegspeel's words.'

Returning to the kitchen was infinitely easier than leaving it had been. The lift went down all by itself. All

Rook had to do was hold onto the rope to make sure it didn't go too quickly.

'*There* you are, dearie!' said Hestera as he reached the bottom. He climbed out through the stone mouth into the suffocating heat of the kitchen. 'I was wondering where you'd got to,' she said, dragging him back towards the furnace. 'It's got chilly since you've been gone. Stoke up the fire with logs, my loverly. Lots of logs.'

'Yes,' said Rook wearily.

'And get those bellows working again. I need to warm these cold, aching bones.'

'Yes.'

'And when you've done that, you'd better chop some more logs. We're running rather low.'

'Yes,' said Rook. He handed Hestera the empty bell jar and the cork and, with a sigh, marched off towards the heap of logs.

But despite his weariness, Rook's mind was racing; full of questions with no answers and wild speculations. What was *baby*? Why had it been built and what could it possibly be for? One thing he knew for certain; he had to find out. And, as an icy chill gripped him despite the heat of the kitchen, he realized that only one person would have the answers to these questions . . .

The master of the Palace of Statues, Vox Verlix himself.

·CHAPTER EIGHT·

VOX'S EYE

'More logs, dearie! The furnace is getting low,' came Hestera's wheedling voice.

'Yes,' said Rook wearily.

He'd slept fitfully the night before, his troubled dreams filled with complicated recipes for bloodoak acorns and phraxdust, and a fat baby, its burnished copper face twisted up with fiery rage as it screamed, *More! More! More!* Rook had awoken almost as tired as when he'd lain down to sleep. Now it was back to the endless toil in the stifling kitchen and he was really suffering.

As he hefted a great log up into the insatiable furnace, a spasm of weariness racked his body and it was all he could do to keep his eyes open. In the corner of the kitchen, seated on two vast carved rocking chairs, Hestera and Amberfuce's nurse, Flambusia Flodfox, were deep in whispered conversation.

'I gave him three drops of your lufwood tincture, just like you said, Hesty dear,' Flambusia was saying, nodding down at the waif who was dozing in his chair beside them. 'And it didn't seem to have any effect,' she added. 'I swear he's getting used to it, Hesty. I had to add a drop from your, er . . .' – her eyes narrowed and she leaned forwards conspiratorially – '*special* potion.'

'Oh, Flambusia!' clucked Hestera. 'I've told you, that is only for emergencies. Why, one drop too much and . . .'

'Hesty, dear, you know I'm careful. Besides, his constant nagging is so hard to take. But just look at him now.' The huge nurse smiled indulgently at the waif. 'Sleeping like a baby.'

Hestera caught sight of Rook out of the corner of her eye. 'Excuse me, Flambusia,' she said. 'I shan't be a minute.'

The old goblin matron bustled over to the table, poured a glass of the green liquid from a pewter jug and hurried across to the furnace. 'Here we are, dearie,' she said to Rook. 'Drink it all up now.'

Rook looked round blearily. Hestera placed the glass in his hands; he raised it to his lips. At the first taste, Rook felt charged with renewed energy and he gulped down the rest of the green juice greedily. It coursed through his veins, invigorating his body and clearing his head.

'Thank you,' he said.

Hestera was shaking her head in bemusement. 'My word,' she said. 'What a thirst! Why, you remind me of Birdwhistle . . . Poor, *dear* Birdwhistle . . .' she added wistfully. She reached forwards and squeezed Rook's upper arm with a bony thumb and forefinger. 'Feels good, doesn't it?' she said. 'Hestera's little potion's building you up nicely.'

'Yes,' said Rook. It was true; in the short time he'd been in Hestera's kitchen, the hard work and strange diet had certainly had an effect. He could *feel* it. He was definitely broader in the shoulders now; stronger in the arm.

'Come on, then, dearie,' said Hestera. 'Let's see you using those fine young muscles of yours. Stoke up the fire and get those bellows pumping.'

'Yes,' said Rook, keeping his voice flat and toneless.

Hestera turned away. 'Sorry about that, Flambusia, my loverly. Now, where were we? Ah, yes . . .' She rummaged in the folds of her apron and pulled out a small phial of brown liquid. 'Here's a little potion that should be helpful.' Her voice dropped. 'It should make that chesty cough of his just a little worse.'

'Thank you, Hesty dear,' said Flambusia, spiriting it away into the tiny bag which hung from her huge forearm. 'You're always so helpful . . .'

Ding! Ding! Ding! Ding! Ding . . .

The peace of the kitchen was shattered by the sound of insistent ringing. Flambusia stopped mid-sentence and Amberfuce stirred groggily and began coughing. Rook looked round to see the central bell – the one marked *the Master's Chamber* – jiggling up and down on its coiled ribbon of metal like a startled ratbird. Vox Verlix must be summoning someone to his chamber.

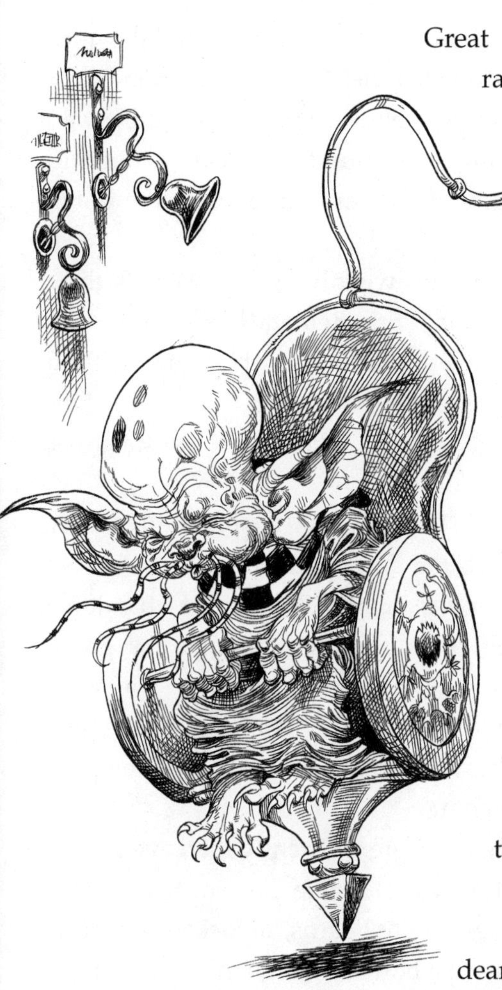

Great hacking coughs racked the waif's body as he slowly emerged from his stupor. Rook would have to watch his thoughts, he realized.

'The master calls,' Hestera announced. 'Flambusia, my loverly, I think you-know-who's awake.' She pointed at the waif.

'Oh, don't I know it, Hesty dear,' said Flambusia, tapping the side of her head and shaking it. She turned to the coughing waif. 'I heard you the first time,' she said. 'Don't you go getting yourself in a state . . . Yes, yes, I know the master wants us upstairs. I was just about to wake you . . .'

The waif fell back in his chair and motioned the nurse to take hold of its long handle. As the two of them set off across the kitchen, they passed Speegspeel sitting on a stool and gnawing at a hunk of meat. Amberfuce motioned for Flambusia to stop and fixed the goblin with a cold stare.

Speegspeel looked up wearily. 'What? What's that?' He sighed. 'Oh, they are demanding of poor old Speegspeel. Can't even let him have his lunch without disturbing him.'

The waif's huge ears twitched, but his stare was unwavering.

'All right, all right, I'm going. Speegspeel will be at the door to greet our visitor, don't you worry.'

Muttering under his breath, Speegspeel abandoned his half-eaten leg of hammelhorn, wiped his greasy fingers down his front, and set off towards the stairs. Flambusia followed him, with Amberfuce the waif directing her to hurry from his chair, whilst attempting to control his coughing.

The bell rang again, more insistently than ever.

'Coming, my treasure,' Hestera purred. She scuttled over to a large chest of cupboards, unlocked one of the doors and pulled out a bottle of oblivion. 'By Sky above and Earth below, he got through that last batch quickly,' she was saying. 'I shall have to make some more up.' She decanted the crimson liquor into a pewter jug with a hinged lid, then placed it on a silver tray.

Rook quickly turned away and busied himself with a log as she hurried back across the kitchen, the tray clasped tightly before her. He didn't want Hestera to see him slacking, or who knows? – he might just end up with a nasty stomach-ache. With a grunt of exertion, Rook hefted the log up onto his shoulders and, doubled over, staggered towards the furnace.

'You can stop doing the logs, dearie,' said Hestera hurriedly as she bustled past him. 'And follow me. I want you to take this up to the master, and mind you don't spill a drop!'

Rook let the log fall to the floor and straightened up. He followed Hestera back to the pulley-lift where she opened the bared teeth of the doorway.

'Look lively, my loverly,' she said.

Rook climbed into the pulley-lift and took hold of the rope. Hestera slid the tray in behind him. 'Ninth floor,' she said. 'And be quick about it. Don't keep the master waiting or you'll have me to answer to.'

'Yes,' said Rook quietly.

The teeth snapped shut and, in the darkness, Rook pulled hard on the rope. The pulley-lift lurched upwards.

'One,' he panted with exertion as he reached the entrance hall. He glimpsed Amberfuce, ears fluttering, gesticulating towards Speegspeel while Flambusia fussed by his side.

Two. The reception chamber. Sweat ran down Rook's back and his breathing was heavy and loud in the confined space. Three, the library; four, the banquet hall; five . . .

Rook's mind was racing. He'd been fortunate;

uncommonly fortunate. There he'd been, wondering how to get to meet Vox Verlix – and now, thanks to Hestera Spikesap, he was about to come face to face with him. He tugged down hard on the rope. Six . . . Seven . . . Eight . . .

'Nine,' said Rook. He pulled the brake-lever. The lift came to a halt. Bathed in sweat, Rook was directly in front of the locked hatchway he'd seen the previous day. From inside came the sound of a ringing bell announcing his arrival, followed by whistling and wheezing and the *thump thump thump* of someone heavy lumbering closer.

There was a jangle of keys, a scraping of metal – and the door swung open. Rook found himself looking out into a vast, shadowy chamber, the candlelit air thick with woodjasmine incense. There were massive dark tapestries covering the walls. Thick rugs and plump silk cushions – one embroidered with a golden tilder – were strewn across the floor. And, in the centre of it all, stood a huge round table made from the whitest marble Rook had ever seen. The next moment, a gigantic figure loomed before him, blocking everything from view.

'Give it to me,' rasped a wheezing voice.

Rook picked up the tray and held it out. Two great podgy hands, studded with jewelled rings, seized the tray.

As Rook watched, the figure wobbled back from the hatch and into the candlelight. There, with shadows flickering across his vast, bloated features and the gold medallion of high office hanging from his neck, stood Vox Verlix himself. He grasped the jug of oblivion in one massive paw and took a long slurp before wiping his mouth on his sleeve. His eyes glazed over.

'You can go,' he mumbled.

Rook was about to say something when the door slammed abruptly shut.

From the other side came a loud burp and a high-pitched, wheezy laugh, followed by the sound of something big and ungainly stumbling into things and knocking them over. Rook hesitated, his ear pressed against the door. He listened and waited . . .

Finally he heard the sound of heavy snoring. He tried the door but it was no good. The hatchway was locked from the other side.

With a sigh, Rook took hold of the rope, released the brake and the pulley-lift began its long descent. Still, he reasoned as the various hatches flashed by, I know where Vox is now. The ninth floor. And even if the hatchway is kept locked, the pulley-lift isn't the only way to get to the master's chamber . . .

'Thank Earth and Sky you're back, dearie,' Hestera cried as he reached the bottom. 'What kept you so long? It's perishing down here.'

Rook climbed out into the searing heat of the kitchen. Hestera fussed about him. 'The fire, dearie,' she wheedled.

'You must see to the fire at once, before these cold old bones of mine seize up completely. How can I be expected to sort through my recipes in a freezing kitchen? Look lively, now.'

'Yes,' said Rook, and traipsed obediently off to the log he'd dropped earlier. Seizing it with both hands, he swung it up off the ground and into the furnace in one movement, then returned to the pile of logs for another.

Hestera, meanwhile, withdrew to a walk-in cupboard at the end of the kitchen, from which she emerged a moment later clutching a great sheaf of parchments and a large empty ironwood box. Struggling with the awkward load, she shuffled back across the kitchen and sat herself down on a chair in front of the furnace with a soft sigh of contentment. Then with the parchments laid out across her aproned lap and the box before her, she began sorting through the recipes, clucking to herself and muttering beneath her breath.

Rook fetched another log and tossed it into the furnace; and then another, and another – pumping the bellows vigorously after each new addition. The furnace glowed brighter. The kitchen grew hotter.

'That's the way, dearie,' Hestera murmured, her eyelids growing heavy. 'Nice and warm, just the way I like it.'

Rook smirked. The goblin was beginning to nod off. I'll give you nice and warm, he thought. I'll have this kitchen hotter than it's ever been before. He gave the bellows a good pump. Hestera's eyes flickered and closed.

Rook kept on feeding the roaring flames until the furnace was so full that he could fit no more inside. The blast was infernal, hotter even than the great industrial furnaces he'd seen in the Foundry Glade from where he'd rescued Wuralo and the other banderbears. How long ago that now seemed. Dripping with sweat, Rook pumped the bellows one last time.

Behind him, Hestera's head lolled forwards and several sheets of parchment slipped from her lap to the floor. A rasping snore echoed through the air.

Rook smiled. Hestera was fast asleep and he had his opportunity to sneak away. As he passed the snoring goblin, he stole a glance at the recipes strewn across the floor by her feet. *Tincture of Ear-ache. Melancholia Salve. Eyeblind Drops* and *Cramp Linctus* . . . The words were picked out in Hestera's spidery writing. He was about to leave when one parchment in particular caught his eye. *Stomach-ache Cordial,* it said.

He scanned the page. *Pour in the sallowberry vinegar and tildermilk and simmer until curdled . . . Allow to cool . . . Add a pinch of dried chundermoss if vomiting is required . . .*

Rook's top lip curled in disgust. In his studies in the Free Glades, Rook had received instruction from gabtrolls and oakelves who had dedicated their lives to the study of the properties of herbs and plants in order to create potions and lotions that would ease suffering and cure pain. But not Hestera Spikesap. The twisted creature was clearly using *her* arts to cause misery and pain. Rook stared down at the hateful 'recipes'. He would have liked nothing better than to sweep the whole lot up in his arms and stuff them all into the furnace . . .

But not now, he told himself, turning away. Now, he had to get out of the kitchen and find the ninth floor.

The sound of Hestera's snoring grew fainter as Rook crept stealthily away. Into the cooler shadows he went, leaving the scorching furnace and the wicked poisoner behind him.

He picked his way through piles of boxes and mountains of sacks, on past long, cluttered tables strewn with pots and pans, jars and glass vessels full of curious liquids. At last, the staircase was before him, its upper steps disappearing into the murky gloom, far above his head. Rook began climbing.

It was only when he was halfway up that a thought struck him. What if the door was locked?

At the top at last, he seized the handle gingerly and turned it slowly, slowly . . . then pulled. The door – thank Sky – opened, its ancient hinges protesting weakly. Rook slipped out through the gap, closed the door quickly behind him – and fell still.

There, on the other side of the huge entrance hall, shivering in the cold air, his back towards him, stood Speegspeel.

Rook edged forwards and peeked round the jutting leg of a dusty, cobweb-strewn statue. The ancient butler was standing alone by the front door, blowing into his hands. The statue tottered unsteadily and, seizing it with both hands, it was all Rook could do to stop it crashing over.

'Who does he think he is? High and mighty librarian keeping old Speegspeel waiting,' Speegspeel grumbled as he stamped his feet up and down and hugged his arms about him. 'Speegspeel's cold,' he muttered sullenly. 'And hungry . . . Everybody puts upon old Speegspeel, so they do. Wouldn't even let him finish off his lunch . . .' He turned back towards the door, slid a silver spy-hole across and peered out. 'Where *is* he?'

With Speegspeel's back turned, Rook emerged from behind the statue and tip-toed across the tiled floor as silently as he could, keeping close to its statue-lined fringes. Darting from statue to statue, Rook made for the great staircase ahead of him, rising up out of the gloom. He was halfway across the hall when the old goblin turned back again. Rook held his breath and froze, blending in with the statues around him.

'At everyone's beck and call the whole time,' the butler was complaining, 'and what thanks does Speegspeel get?' He sniffed and began pacing back and forth. 'A kindly word wouldn't come amiss now and again . . .' He turned away.

From somewhere above him, Rook heard an ominous low creak. Instinctively he dropped to the ground and raised his arms protectively above his head.

CRASH!

The sudden loud noise tore through the great hall, and

around him the cobwebbed statues wobbled, as if in support of their toppled colleague that now lay shattered on the marble floor. The hall fell silent – until Speegspeel's voice cried out; a mixture of triumph and defiance.

'You'll have to try harder than that if you want to catch old Speegspeel!' he bellowed, raising a fist at the statues crowding the alcoves above him.

Rook peered round the plinth of the statue he was cowering behind. The butler kicked at the broken remains of the ancient statue.

'Thought you'd had me that time, didn't you? Waiting till my back was turned. But Speegspeel was too quick for you, wasn't he? Eh?' He chuckled as he headed across to the door leading to the kitchen. 'Now Speegspeel will sweep you up and tip you away. And good riddance!'

The goblin disappeared through the door. Rook seized his chance. Head down, he made a dash for the staircase and, taking the stairs two at a time, he bounded up the first flight and crouched down on the first landing in the shadow of a carved newel post. He looked back to see Speegspeel returning across the great marble floor, a heavy knotted broomstick tucked under one arm. Whistling tunelessly, the goblin set about sweeping the shattered statue into a neat pile.

'Important visitor,' he muttered to himself. 'Got to make the right impression . . .'

Turning away, Rook continued up the elegant staircase, dodging the bright beams of sparkling sunlight which sliced down at an angle from high windows; keeping to the shadows. All round him were the statues. They stood on plinths and platforms on every landing and lined the corridors which radiated away in all directions like the spokes of a great wheel. Hundreds of them, like a great stone army lurking in the gloom; watching, waiting . . .

They're just carvings, Rook told himself. Pieces of rock, no more.

The air was cold, but it wasn't only that which was making him shiver. As he passed them by, the statues creaked and seemed to whisper and sometimes Rook thought he caught them moving out of the corner of his eye – but when he turned to look, they were always standing as motionless as before.

At the sixth landing, the musty air was laced with the mentholated tang of embrocation. Rook heard the sound of distant coughing and Flambusia's disembodied voice – honeyed and sinister – as it echoed down the corridors.

'If you won't keep still, then I can't rub it in properly,' she was cooing. 'And then that cough of yours will never get better.'

Rook hurried on. He didn't stop again until he reached the ninth floor. Pausing for a moment to catch his breath, he looked round.

The landing he was standing on was quite different from the others he had passed. Unlike the patternless marble of the lower levels, the floor here was inlaid with an intricate pattern of tiles. As he looked more closely, he saw that they were not random abstract designs but rather countless creatures – some known, some unknown – all cunningly interlocked.

The ear of a woodhare-like creature formed the mouth

of an oozefish, whose dorsal fin in turn provided the space between the broad legs of a banderbear above it. A lemkin fitted together with a snicket, the dark jutting jaw of the one forming the edge of the white wing of the other; a daggerslash mutated into a razorflit; a muglump into a fromp. And so it continued all the way along the single broad corridor which led away from the landing. Just the one corridor, Rook noticed – unlike the other floors which had corridors leading off from the landings in all direction.

At the far end of the single corridor was a high window. A shaft of sunlight streamed through it, slicing along the length of the corridor, striking the crystal chandelier above Rook's head and sending rainbow-coloured darts of light flashing through the air in all directions. They spun and collided; they skidded over the white marble of the statues and sparkled on the tiled floor.

Halfway down the corridor, to his right, a magnificent doorway was set into the wall. The panelled door it framed was emblazoned with the same symbol of high office – a sun-like circle segmented by jagged bolts of lightning – which Rook had seen on the medallion hanging around Vox's neck.

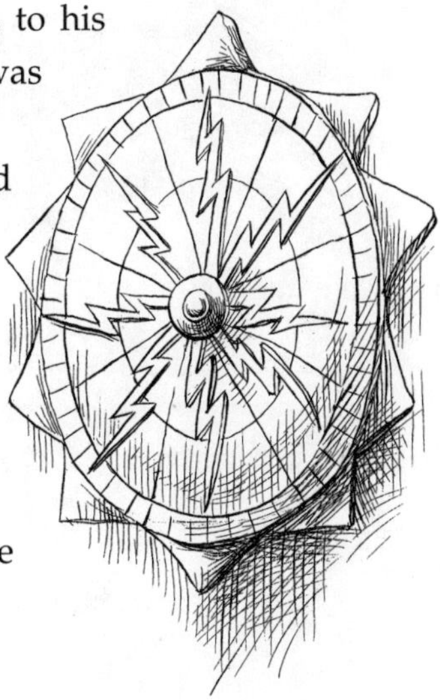

'The Master's Chamber,' he whispered.

He had just set off down the hallway, keeping to the shadows close to the near wall, when a sudden clatter halted him in his tracks. He slipped back into the darkness of a cobweb-filled alcove that must once have housed a statue and watched anxiously. The noise had come from outside – most likely a statue falling down the front of the building.

As the noise died away, it was replaced by another, altogether closer: the low scraping sound of metal on stone. This was followed by a muffled *crunch*, and the silhouette of a goblin guard in battle-dress appeared at the high window. Rook shrank back further into the alcove and held his breath.

The goblin guard pulled the window open, balanced for a moment on the ledge, looking round – before jumping down onto the floor. As he dropped, the sunlight glinted on the serrated blade of the evil-looking scythe clenched between his teeth. He landed lightly, braced his splayed legs and looked round again. Then, glancing suspiciously about him, he advanced along the corridor, his bare feet pattering softly on the tiles.

Rook watched, horrified. It was clear the goblin had only one thing on his mind.

Murder!

He swallowed heavily. The goblin was almost at the door now. He could see the individual bristles of his tufted ears; he could smell his unwashed body. The goblin pulled the scythe from his mouth and gripped it tightly in his hand. Then, with a final glance over his armour-plated shoulders, he took a step forward and . . .

It all happened so quickly. The tile beneath the goblin's feet clicked down as he stepped on it. At the same moment, from up in the shadows of the high ceiling, there came an answering click followed by a hissing *swoosh* as a long pendulum swung down through the air. The goblin never knew what hit him. Before he could move so much as a muscle, the heavy curved blade at the end of the swinging pendulum sliced through him like butter, cleaving the would-be assassin in two.

Rook stared open-mouthed, scarcely able to believe what had just happened. The goblin was dead; his body twin islands in a growing sea of blood. Rook tore his horrified gaze away. Above his head in the shadows, the deadly pendulum clicked back into place as – at exactly the same moment – the tile did the same, merging seamlessly with the others in the treacherous mosaic.

'A booby-trap,' Rook trembled.

He stared at the floor. Each ornate shape now seemed deadly. Any one of the tiles, Rook realized, could unleash the hideous pendulum – or worse. He was trapped, paralysed with fear, unable to take a step forwards or back. At his feet was a white tile – snowy white, shaped like the head of a gloamglozer. Its curling horns formed the underbelly of a black serpent coiled above it.

'Black serpent,' Rook murmured. 'White gloamglozer.' *White* gloamglozer. Black and white . . . Something stirred in his memory: *Keep to the black, not the white, if you want to keep your life.*

It was Speegspeel. Rook had heard him singing the little tune over and over up in the Leagues' Chamber.

Keep to the black, not the white, if you want to keep your life . . .

Emerging from the alcove, Rook stepped tentatively onto the black serpent, then a black hammelhorn, and from that onto a black lemkin, taking care to avoid the white halitoad between them. So far, so good. Trying hard not to look at the bloodied corpse, he skirted round the snow-white head of a huge rotsucker – via a black tilder and a second black lemkin – and arrived at last at the large, ornate door.

Rook put his ear to the carved wooden panel and listened. He could hear nothing; nothing at all. He reached forward, grasped the door handle and turned it. The door slid silently open and Rook slipped gratefully inside.

Rook found himself in the same opulent chamber he had glimpsed from the pulley-lift. Dark, shadowy and reeking of incense and musky perfumes, it was far larger than he'd imagined – a cavernous hall made to seem smaller than it was by the sheer number of items cluttered within it.

There was a forest of racks and stacks, each one bulging with sheaves of parchment; and tall stands with curling hooks sprouting from their tops, draped with sailcloth, silken ropes and lengths of fine material embroidered with gold and silver. On the floor were the fur rugs and plump satin cushions Rook had seen earlier; on the walls were dark tapestries – while dangling from the ceiling, like a library of hanging scrolls, were countless yellowed squares of parchment suspended from ropes and motionless in the still air.

They must be sticky, Rook realized, for on both sides of every parchment, there were countless creatures fixed to the surface: woodmoths, oakbugs, bees and wasps; snickets and ratbirds in various stages of decay; the skeleton of a dwarf-rotsucker, its parchment skin stretched over bony wings ... The traps, it seemed, caught every airborne intruder into Vox Verlix's chamber – though of the master himself, there was no trace.

Keeping to the wall, Rook continued round the chamber. And as he picked his way through the chaos, he began to look more closely at the rows of charts, blueprints and diagrams – sepia ink on tilderhide and thick parchment – which hung from taut wire racks and covered every flat surface. He recognized a detailed plan for the Great Mire Road, annotated with lengths and weights and detailed descriptions of how to sink the great pylons into the soft, shifting mud of the Mire. There were several cross-sections of the Tower of Night, each one subtly different from the one before – and a model of the design that had finally been chosen. And as he went further, he passed a table covered with set-squares and slide-rules, and piles of calculations detailing what was arguably Vox's most ambitious project: the Sanctaphrax Forest.

Next to a long workbench was an easel with a single yellowed piece of scroll pinned to a drawing-board. On it was a complicated design for something large and round with intricate internal chambers, covered with minute annotations. Rook recognized it at once.

'The baby,' he breathed.

His fingers traced the round form beneath which, underscored with an angry red line, were the words, *blast them all to open sky!*

So it was true what they said. Vox Verlix, the greatest engineer and architect there had ever been, was a bitter, broken creature. Rook looked around at the clutter. Vox had been betrayed by everyone he'd had dealings with: Mother Muleclaw, the shryke roost-mother who had seized the Great Mire Road when it was completed; Orbix Xaxis, who had ousted Vox from the Tower of Night and forced him to seek refuge in old Undertown; and finally General Tytugg, the goblin-leader Vox had himself hired to enslave Undertowners and force them to work on the Sanctaphrax Forest, but who instead had taken over Undertown and made Vox a virtual prisoner here in the Palace of Statues. The goblin assassin lying in the hallway was just the latest of many, Rook guessed, sent by the brutal general who made no secret of his contempt for his former master.

Ahead of him, Rook saw an ornate gilt frame fixed to the wall. He moved closer, expecting to see a painting of one of the former occupants of the chamber – perhaps even a likeness of Vox Verlix himself. Instead he found himself looking at a small, blackwood door. It was the entrance to the pulley-lift. He looked round. There was the satin pillow with the embroidered tilder; there, the thick fur rugs, and there, the round white marble table. Behind them, bathed in shadows, was what seemed to be a huge upholstered chair, a heavy throw in blues and purples draped over it and a long rope with a brass ring at its end, hanging down beside.

Rook looked more closely at the chair. It was moving up and down to the unmistakable sound of a soft rasping snore which grew louder and louder until, with a sudden sharp snort, it woke the sleeper up. Rook took a step backwards into the shadowy clutter. Just then the tasselled throw was tossed aside, and what Rook had taken to be a chair clambered to its feet.

'Vox Verlix,' Rook murmured, transfixed.

Vox looked round, bleary-eyed. He scratched his head, jiggled a fat finger in his ear and belched twice. 'That's better,' he muttered.

Rook remembered seeing a picture of Vox Verlix as a cloudwatcher apprentice; young, lean and with a glint of naked ambition in his steely gaze. The bloated drunkard he had become was unrecognizable. Rook watched him with a mixture of pity and disgust as he heaved his great weight across the floor.

He stopped at the table and looked up. Rook followed his gaze to a funnel-shaped contraption with mirrors, chains and levers suspended above him. With a loud grunt of effort, Vox reached up and pulled hard on one of the brass chains. A mirror tilted, and a broad beam of light fell upon the great marble table-top below.

Rook peered out from behind a rack of barkscrolls. Vox was looking down at the illuminated table, his face bathed in light. Rook eased himself forwards, craning his neck for a better view.

Vox reached above his head again, pushing a lever up and lowering a second chain. The image on the table-top shifted – and Rook stifled a gasp as he realized what he was looking at. It was Undertown and its environs. Somehow, Vox Verlix had designed a contraption to bring the view outside into this vast windowless chamber and, as he raised and lowered the sequence of chains and levers one after the other, the image on the vast circular table-top came sharply into focus.

'I can see you all . . .' Vox murmured gleefully. His sweat-drenched face was animated, the small beady eyes glinting coldly. 'There is nowhere to hide, for Vox's Eye sees everything! Everything! The end is coming, you puny woodants,' he cried. 'The end is coming – and only I can see it!'

Rook felt his pulse quicken. Then, curiosity winning over caution, he stepped up onto a padded footstool for a better look at the image on the marble table. There was the Undertown skyline; the Tower of Night; the Mire Road – and, arching above it all, a heavy, cloud-laden sky . . .

The stool wobbled. Rook lost his balance and lurched to one side, knocking into a tall vase which toppled and crashed to the floor.

Vox looked up, the expression on his face a mixture of fear and rage. 'Who's there?' he demanded fiercely.

Rook was about to step forward and introduce himself as Hestera's new assistant – as well as inventing some errand that would explain his presence, when . . .

'Say your prayers, Vox Verlix,' came a low, gruff voice.

Rook froze. The voice came from the shadows near the door.

Vox turned towards the voice. 'Show yourself,' he said, his own voice tinged with unease.

'As you wish, *Vox Verlix – Most High Academe*,' came the voice, spitting out the name and title with contempt. And as Rook watched, a goblin appeared from the shadows. Tall and heftily built, he was dressed – and armed – like the goblin guard Rook had seen in the corridor. He brandished a vicious-looking curved scythe with glinting jags, an evil grin playing round his scarred lips and blackened teeth. 'I come with a message from General Tytugg . . .'

'How . . . How *dare* you!' Vox blustered, his double chins wobbling indignantly. 'Get down on your knees when you address the Most High Academe of Sanctaphrax and all Undertown!'

The goblin's grin widened. 'They said you were fat,' he said, and made a show of running a callused thumb slowly along the curve of the glinting blade. 'I'm going to enjoy hearing you squeal,' he snarled.

'General Tytugg shall hear of your insolence,' said Vox imperiously. 'And you shall *both* regret it!'

Rook shook his head. Vox was in mortal danger and, for all his bluster, there was the unmistakable glint of panic in his deep-set eyes. Rook realized that it was up to him to do something. Slipping back into the shadows, he seized the first object he could find. It felt reassuringly heavy.

'Most High Academe,' the goblin laughed. 'Why, you nasty great big fat useless blubbery parasitic lardbucket!' He lunged at Vox with the scythe.

'Please!' Vox gasped. 'I'll give you anything.' A spasm of desperation flashed across his face. 'Anything at all!' He stumbled backwards, arms raised defensively. 'No, no, no . . .' he cried.

The goblin raised his scythe high in the air, slicing through the dancing particles of dust. The blade glinted. Vox froze.

'Now squeal for General Tytugg . . .'

'Aaaiiieeeeee! Aaaiiieeeeee!' Vox cried out with terror, screeching and squealing like a stuck woodhog. *'AaaiiiEEEEEEE!!'*

Rook leapt from the shadows, the heavy

lump of wood held above his head with both hands. The goblin's sword flashed. Vox toppled backwards. With a grunt of effort, Rook swung the wood through the air and brought it down on the back of the goblin's head with colossal force.

The heavy wooden object struck with a splintering crack. The goblin stiffened but remained standing. Rook swallowed hard. Goblins had skulls as hard as iron-wood. He struck him again – a savage blow to the side of his head . . .

The goblin tottered where he stood, staggering slowly round in a circle. His eyes swam in their sockets, then shot abruptly upwards, leaving only the bloodshot whites showing. With a low groan the goblin fell back-wards, stiff as a board, and crashed noisily to the floor.

Rook poked the body with his foot. The goblin was not dead – but he'd have a headache to remember when he finally woke.

'It's all right,' said Rook to the huge figure cowering before him. 'You're safe now.'

Vox lowered his arm and looked up. 'You . . . you saved my life,' he said. 'Who are you?'

'Rook Barkwater,' said Rook. 'Assistant to Hestera Spikesap.'

'Hestera's slave,' he sniffed. Grunting and groaning with effort, he rolled over onto his front and eased himself up into a standing position. 'I am grateful to you,' he said wheezily and extended a podgy hand. His eyes narrowed. 'What are you doing outside the hatch?'

'I . . . *errm* . . . Hestera . . . that is, Speegspeel . . .' Rook was floundering.

Just then there was a polite, distinctive knock at the door; three light taps, followed by a gap, and then three more. 'About time!' muttered Vox. 'Enter, Speegspeel!' he called out.

Rook watched the ancient butler do a double-take as he emerged from the shadows at the back of the room. His gaze jumped from face to face of the occupants of the room.

'Master,' he said. 'Number eleven. And . . .' He grimaced. '*There* he is!' he gasped. 'Old Speegspeel knew there'd be two of them. Always hunt in pairs, goblins, so they do – when they've got murder in mind. Saw the other one outside in the corridor – knew there'd be a second one somewhere hereabouts.'

'The slave-lad here laid him out,' said Vox, adding sharply, 'It's just as well *someone* around here has their wits about them.' He nodded towards the piece of wood still clutched in Rook's hands and chuckled; a sound like water gurgling down a drain. 'Fortunate indeed that I designed it to be strong.'

Rook looked down and was surprised to find himself holding a finely crafted scale-model of a tower. 'The Tower of Night,' he said softly.

'Ay, the Tower of Night,' said Vox. 'Built to withstand both hurricanes and cannon-balls . . .'

'And the most terrible place ever built upon a Sanctaphrax rock,' came a soft, cracked voice from over by the door.

Vox's eyes narrowed. 'I know that voice . . .' he whispered.

'Ah yes, Speegspeel was forgetting, master; what with all the palaver over goblin assassins, 'n all. Your visitor has arrived.'

As he spoke, a wiry individual stepped forwards from behind Speegspeel. Rook gasped.

The visitor was well-kempt, with trim hair and beard, polished cheeks and fine clothes; for all the world the successful merchant or money-lender. Yet the eyes told a different story; they, and the deep lines that etched his face. This was someone who had known great pain and terrible suffering; someone who had stared down into the yawning chasms of black despair. His gaze bored into Vox's eyes.

Vox looked back at him, puzzlement flickering round his eyebrows. 'You are the emissary from the librarians?' he began.

'You have changed since last we met,' the visitor said. He nodded towards the medallion of high office around Vox Verlix's neck. 'It was the night you stole that little trinket.'

Vox's mouth fell open; the colour drained from his cheeks. 'Cowlquape Pentephraxis,' he gasped in disbelief. His head shook slowly from side to side. 'No . . . No, it can't be!'

But it was, as Rook was only too aware. What could the true Most High Academe of Sanctaphrax be doing here in the Palace of Statues holding court with Vox Verlix?

'But you're . . . you're . . .' Vox paused.

'Dead?' suggested Cowlquape. 'As you can see, Vox, I'm very much alive. When you betrayed me to the Guardians of Night I expect you thought they'd kill me. But no, they kept me alive – if you can call being locked up on a stinking cell-ledge in the depths of the Tower of Night, living. I suppose they enjoyed knowing that while I lived, you could never be the true Most High Academe, despite your claims . . . But enough of this. I am, as we both know, here on behalf of the librarians to discuss important matters; *pressing* matters . . .' He stopped mid-sentence and stared at Rook, who was standing beside Vox – actually seeing him for the first time. His eyebrows arched with surprise. 'Rook,' he said. 'It can't be. But it is! Rook, my boy, what are you doing here?'

Rook grimaced sheepishly. 'It's a long story,' he said.

'You know this slave?' said Vox.

'Slave?' said Cowlquape. 'Rook Barkwater is no slave. He is a librarian knight; the most valiant of his generation – and the person who rescued me from the Tower of Night. It seems we *both* owe him our lives, Vox.'

Vox sighed. 'I thought he handled himself rather well for a mere kitchen assistant.' His narrowing eyes glinted. 'But Hestera bought him at the slave auction, which makes him *my* property . . .'

Cowlquape breathed in sharply. 'Times have changed, Vox,' he said, his voice level and firm. 'The tables are turning . . .' He looked down meaningfully at the unconscious goblin guard.

'Yes, yes, all right,' Vox blustered. 'Consider yourself restored to freedom by the Most High . . .' He caught Cowlquape's steely gaze and coughed awkwardly. 'Er . . . yes . . . well . . . Let's just say, you're free.' He turned to Speegspeel. 'Refreshments for our guests,' he said gruffly. '*Both* our guests.'

Rook's heart soared. He felt a wave of relief, as if a great weight had fallen from his shoulders. Free once more; he was free! Speegspeel nodded, neither his face nor his voice registering any emotion. 'Yes, master,' he said.

'And Speegspeel,' Vox added. 'Send Amberfuce up. I have a little job for him.'

'Yes, master,' Speegspeel repeated. He turned and started away.

'Oh, and one last thing,' Vox called after him. 'You'd better tell Hestera to visit the slave auction right away. We need another slave to help with the baby. Straight away, do you understand?'

'Yes, master,' said the old butler, shuffling off. 'Speegspeel understands.'

As the door clicked shut, Vox turned to Cowlquape. 'And now, old friend, we must let bygones be bygones, don't you agree?' he said. 'Come and look into Vox's Eye.'

·CHAPTER NINE·

THE TWO MOST HIGH ACADEMES

Cowlquape's sunken green eyes flashed with naked delight.

'Rook, my dear lad, I can't tell you how good it is to see you alive and well,' he said, clapping him warmly on the back.

Vox was over by the marble table, muttering to himself and swaying back and forth as he surveyed the sky.

'We heard you'd come down in Screetown,' Cowlquape continued. 'Naturally we feared the worst.' He smiled sympathetically. 'What happened to you?'

'My head's still spinning – I can't quite take it all in,' said Rook. 'Oh, Most High Academe, sir, I . . . I was beginning to think I'd never see another librarian ever again.'

Cowlquape reached forward and touched Rook on the arm reassuringly. 'Easy now, lad. You've clearly been through a lot. But I'm here now and it's all going to be fine, believe me.'

Rook nodded and sniffed and collected himself. 'I did come down in Screetown,' he said at last. 'Something struck the *Stormhornet* when I was on dawn-patrol – something loud and fiery . . .' His voice drifted away.

'And then?' said Cowlquape. 'How did you end up here?'

Rook shook his head slowly, suddenly lost to a series of fleeting images which flashed before his eyes: the rubble ghoul, the oozefish and woodwolves; the Sunken Palace and the misery hole; the tumbril ride to the auction-square . . . 'It's a long story,' he said at last, and smiled apologetically.

'And there'll be time enough to tell it back in the library, Rook, my lad,' said Cowlquape, nodding. 'But right now, I must attend to our fat friend over there. He sent a strange missive to the Great Library, requesting an urgent meeting with an emissary who could speak on behalf of the librarians. It was passed to one of our agents in Undertown by someone from the palace and our experts verified it as genuine.' His voice dropped. 'We had a hastily convened council-meeting, and it was agreed that I – as the true Most High Academe – should represent the librarians. Besides,' he added, 'I was intrigued to see what had become of my former colleague. It is many years since our paths last crossed . . .'

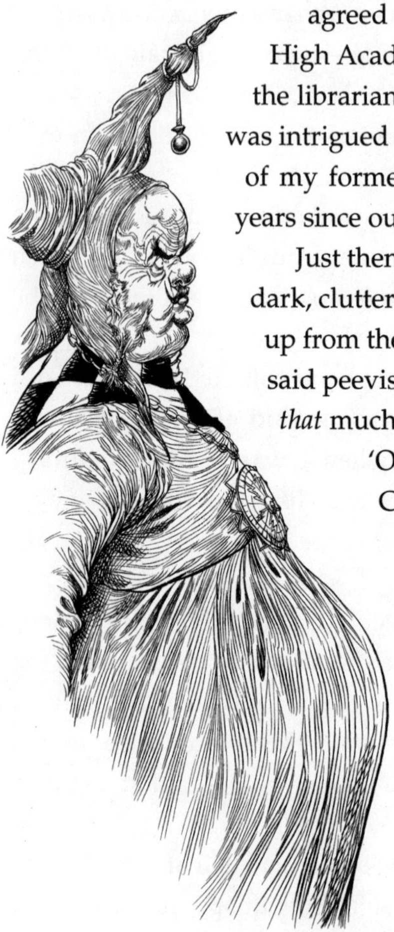

Just then, from the far end of the dark, cluttered chamber, Vox looked up from the Eye. 'Time is short,' he said peevishly. 'I thought I'd made *that* much clear in my message.'

'Oh, you did, Vox,' said Cowlquape, crossing the room and approaching the huge figure. 'You certainly did. What you didn't make clear was why.'

Rook watched with fascination as the two academics stood facing each other. One was morbidly obese, the other painfully thin. One was dressed in flamboyant, though stained, robes of embroidered satin and tasselled silk; the other wore a simple brown gown made of some rough, homespun cloth. Like chalk and cheese, they couldn't have been less similar.

Even the medallions which hung around their necks were different, for whereas Vox's was dull and worn, Cowlquape's one was highly polished and glinted as brightly as his amused eyes. Vox's gaze seemed fixated on it.

Cowlquape smiled. 'I see you've noticed the seal of Old Sanctaphrax,' he said. 'The librarians kindly replaced the one you stole.'

Vox glowered. Rook could feel the tension between them.

'Oh, Vox, Vox, what went wrong?' Cowlquape continued calmly. 'With your skills and my vision, we could have rebuilt Sanctaphrax. Together in partnership . . .'

'Partnership!' Vox blustered. 'You just wanted the glory while I did all the hard work. What was it you were always saying? Ah, yes,' he said, his voice taking on a mocking sing-song quality. 'Everyone's equal and we're all the same; earth-scholars and sky-scholars; professors, apprentices and even Undertowners.' He wagged a flabby finger at Cowlquape. 'A recipe for disaster. It would never have worked.'

'You never gave it a chance, Vox,' said Cowlquape sadly. 'You went behind my back and betrayed me to Orbix Xaxis and the Guardians of Night. Did you really think you could trust them?'

'I did what I had to do,' said Vox. '*Someone* had to assume the role of leader. A proper leader; a leader prepared to lead. It was what you never understood, Cowlquape. All those endless meetings and consultations; trying to keep everyone happy – yet satisfying no-one . . .'

'Someone like you, eh?' said Cowlquape softly. 'A traitor . . . A usurper . . .' He let the words sink in. 'Is it any wonder that things have come to this?'

'I . . . I . . .' Vox blustered hotly.

'You've destroyed everything, Vox. Everything . . .' he said. 'And the sad thing is, it could all have been so different. If you had trusted me as I trusted you, Vox, we could have built a better world together, you and I. And now look at you!' He sighed. 'You had so many wonderful talents, Vox . . .' He shook his head sorrowfully. 'And you've squandered them all. What a waste your life has been.'

Vox looked away, muttering under his breath, and reached for a jug of oblivion. 'You always were a pompous little creature, weren't you?' he growled. 'At least I didn't end up imprisoned for years on end.'

'No? Are you sure?' said Cowlquape evenly. 'Look around you, Vox. When did you last dare to leave this palace, with its barred windows and booby-trapped corridors? When did you last even venture beyond this chamber? You are as much a prisoner as I ever was.' He tutted softly. 'The bully being bullied . . .'

'They double-crossed me,' said Vox quietly. 'All of them. The shrykes, the Guardians, the goblins . . . But they'll soon be smiling on the other side of their faces.' His voice rose. 'For it's all coming to an end. That's what I want to tell you. Undertown is done for. Time is running out . . .' He stared at Cowlquape. 'And it's why I need the librarians. You're the only ones I can trust.'

Cowlquape looked puzzled. 'Undertown, done for?' he said. 'What do you mean, Vox?'

'I mean precisely what I say, Cowlquape,' said Vox, his voice growing louder still. 'Undertown is finished. Doomed! The whole sorry lot will be washed away, and with it all the back-stabbing traitors and treacherous infidels who have sought to destroy me!' He raised the jug, took a noisy glug of the bright red liquor and wiped his mouth on the back on his sleeve. 'A storm is coming!' he announced. 'A mighty storm!'

'A storm?' said Cowlquape.

'Yes, Cowlquape. A storm, the like of which has never been seen before. Can you not feel it in the air; the searing heat, the stifling humidity? Have you not noticed the formations of the clouds?'

Rook found himself nodding. Every day he had been noting the ominous changes in the weather.

'A storm to end all storms,' Vox continued, sweeping his massive arms round dramatically as his voice rose to fill the great chamber. 'No-one shall be spared. And I alone, Vox Verlix, know exactly when it will strike – down to the very second.'

'But how can you possibly know when . . ?' Rook began.

Cowlquape silenced him with a hand on his arm. 'Vox

Verlix was the finest cloudwatcher the College of Cloud ever produced, Rook, my boy,' he said quietly. 'If he says a storm is coming . . .'

'I do! I do say a storm is coming,' said Vox excitedly. He reached forward and seized Cowlquape by the sleeve. 'Look,' he said, tugging him sharply across to the round white marble table and pointing down at the illuminated image from outside laid out across its surface.

Cowlquape looked down. Rook, eager to see for himself, stood beside him and scanned the tabletop. Vox's podgy fingers spread across the sky.

'You see these clouds,' he said, taking a swig at the oblivion. 'Like giant anvils? They're growing all the time, merging, fusing together and gaining power with every passing day. I've consulted my cloud tables,' he continued, the drink staining his lips red. 'I've done the calculations. I alone know when the dark maelstrom will strike!'

Rook glanced at Cowlquape. The true High Academe was deep in thought.

'And when the dark maelstrom does strike,' Vox went on, 'there will be lightning and hail, and torrential driving rain will flood the sewers within minutes. If the librarians are to survive, then you must leave your underground chambers and flee. Leave Undertown, Cowlquape, and head for the Free Glades . . .'

Behind them, the unconscious goblin groaned softly. Again, Rook looked up at Cowlquape – but the old academic's thoughts were difficult to read.

'You're proposing that the librarians leave Undertown?' he said at last, his voice calm and even.

'You must, Cowlquape,' said Vox urgently.

'What, up and go – just like that?' said Cowlquape, fixing Vox with a level stare. 'Tell me, Vox,' he said. 'Just supposing we could get out of the sewers and somehow make it past General Tytugg's goblin guard, and then by some miracle also manage to get through Muleclaw's shrykes and cross the Mire to reach the Free Glades . . .' He paused. 'Why would you help us?' His eyes narrowed. 'What's in it for *you*?'

'For me?' said Vox, an air of injured innocence playing over his blubbery features. He breathed in wheezily. 'If I were to tell you,' he said, 'how you and all the librarians could get safely through Undertown and down the Great Mire Road, I would ask just one thing in return.'

Cowlquape shook his head and smiled. 'And what might that be, Vox?' he said.

Vox returned his gaze, his face deadly serious. 'That you take me with you.'

*

'So this is where you hide when you're not toadying up to the High Master,' came a sneering voice.

Xanth looked up from his desk and sighed. Mollus Leddix, the cage-master, stood in the doorway, his black hood pulled back to reveal his twitchy weasel-like features and small dark eyes. An ugly grin was playing across his face.

'Not that it'll do you much good. Not if the rumours are to be believed,' he added.

'What rumours, Leddix?' said Xanth wearily. He mustn't let the executioner get to him.

'Oh, the rumours that the High Guardian doesn't quite trust his favourite since he got back from spying on the librarians in the Free Glades. They say that all that Free Glade air turned his head, made him soft, unreliable . . .'

And I wonder who put those ideas into the High Guardian's head, Xanth thought bitterly – but he managed a smile as he looked up at Leddix. 'Oh, I wouldn't listen to those rumours, Leddix, if I were you,' he said. 'I'd be more worried about the rumour going round that a certain executioner was overheard hatching a plot with the Captain of the Nightwatch. Now if the High Guardian was to hear about *that* . . .'

'You wouldn't dare,' snarled Leddix.

'Just try me,' said Xanth, rising from his stool.

Leddix stepped back and laughed a thin, weasely chuckle. 'No need to be like that, Xanth,' he said. 'Mustn't let little misunderstandings get in the way of our duty. Talking of which . . .' He straightened up. 'A

fresh young librarian has been apprehended and the High Master has ordered an interrogation. Right up your street, I would have thought, Xanth,' he added, his voice oily and insinuating, 'given your special knowledge of the librarians and their ways.'

Xanth nodded, but said nothing. There it was again. The same underlying implication . . . He was not to be trusted.

Leddix beckoned for Xanth to follow him to the Interrogation Chambers and, as he did so, the executioner muttered, 'The High Master will be observing. And remember, Xanth, when you're finished with her, the prisoner is mine!'

They arrived outside an interrogation chamber deep in the lower recesses of the Tower of Night. A tall heavily-built Guardian – a cloddertrog with swarthy scarred skin and flowercabbage ears – opened the door and Xanth entered the small room. Leddix slunk away down the corridor, chuckling softly as the door swung shut.

In the corner, slumped against the wall, was a librarian knight, unmistakable in green flight-suit and light wood armour. The prisoner looked up, thick plaits falling across her face.

'Xanth?' came a small voice. 'Xanth?'

Xanth froze. The prisoner knew his name.

'Xa-anth?'

'Be silent, prisoner,' Xanth said in a low growl.

He needed time to think. The spy-hole on the opposite wall was open and the High Guardian was observing his every move. How Leddix would love it if he made a slip now . . .

Arms tied behind her back, the prisoner flicked the golden plaits off her face with a toss of her head. She was bruised and battered, with a black eye and one side of her lower jaw badly swollen. A trickle of dried blood ran from the corner of her mouth. She was a mess, certainly – yet Xanth recognized her at once. After all, having spent the best part of eighteen moons studying beside her at Lake Landing, how could he fail to?

'It *is* you, Xanth,' she said. 'I knew it was. It's me, Magda. Magda Burlix . . .'

Xanth stared at her impassively, his face betraying not a single flicker of emotion.

'Xanth?' said Magda. 'Don't you remember me?'

'On your knees!' shouted Xanth roughly. He was clammy and hot, sweat beading his forehead, his cheeks and the top of his shaven head. He'd liked Magda. She'd been good to him at Lake Landing when he'd broken his leg and . . .

No! he told himself sharply. He would have to deal with her as he would *any* prisoner. Orbix Xaxis was watching.

'I said, on your knees!' he snarled, and kicked her viciously in the side.

Magda struggled awkwardly to her knees, the tight ropes biting into her wrists. She looked up at Xanth, her eyes as wide as a tilder doe's, willing him to recognize her. But Xanth was having none of it. Refusing to meet her imploring gaze, he pulled a notebook from one pocket, a thin, sharp ironwood pencil from another; opened one, licked the other and started writing.

'Name,' he said quietly.

'Xanth,' said Magda, her voice breaking with emotion. 'You *know* my name.'

Xanth's scalp prickled. He could feel the accusing glare from the spy-hole burning into the back of his head. 'Name!' he repeated harshly.

'You know my name,' came the tearful reply. She sniffed. 'It's me, Xanth. Magda Burlix.'

Xanth scribbled it down.

'Position,' he said, a moment later.

'I am a librarian knight,' said Magda and, even though he didn't look up, he could tell from her voice that she was glowing with pride as she spoke. 'And as such, you know I can tell you no more – even unto death.'

'You were apprehended by our patrols on the banks of the Edgewater,' said Xanth quietly. 'What were you doing there?'

'I am a librarian knight,' Magda repeated. 'I can tell you no more, even unto . . . *aarrgh!*' she cried out as Xanth slapped her hard across the face.

Her head dropped. Xanth stared down at her, his hand stinging, his head swirling with mixed feelings. Magda was brave and kind. She had been so good to him . . . But the High Master was watching and he mustn't allow his feelings to show, not even for an instant.

He breathed in sharply. 'What – were – you – doing – by – the – Edgewater – River?' he asked, enunciating every word crisply, coldly.

Head still lowered, Magda sighed. 'It can't do any harm,' she said. 'Not now. You're going to kill me anyway, so I'll tell you. I wasn't on librarian business, I was on my own. I was looking for Rook. Rook Barkwater – remember him?' she asked bitterly. 'He went missing. In Screetown. The librarians have given up on him. But I couldn't.' She looked up, her golden plaits trembling. 'And do you know why? Because Rook is my friend.' Her eyes narrowed to angry slits. 'But then you wouldn't understand, would you? Because you don't know what friendship is.'

She turned and spat on the floor.

Behind him, Xanth heard a soft *click* as the cover to the spy-hole closed. With a sigh of relief, he snapped the notebook shut and put the pencil back in his pocket.

He'd passed the test.

'My plan is simple,' said Vox, scanning the Undertown horizon. 'With the librarians' help, I intend to lure the goblin army and the shrykes into a trap of my own devising, leaving the way clear for us . . .' – he laid a podgy hand on Cowlquape's shoulder – '. . . to leave Undertown by the Mire Road unmolested.'

'And what is to be the bait in this trap of yours, Vox?' asked Cowlquape, his brow furrowed.

'Why, my dear Most High Academe, who do the shrykes and the goblins hate even more than each other?'

'The librarians!' said Rook, unable to contain himself.

'Your young friend is correct,' laughed Vox, his chins wobbling in the candlelight. 'I intend to inform both the shrykes *and* the goblins precisely how they might safely penetrate the Great Library itself . . .'

An excellent plan, master, a sibilant voice whispered in Rook's head.

Vox turned, along with Cowlquape and Rook. 'So good of you to join us, my dear Amberfuce,' he said. 'How's that cough of yours? No worse, I trust.'

The waif emerged from the shadows, followed by the massive figure of Flambusia Flodfox, a huge hand on the handle of the sumpwood chair. She blushed and rearranged Amberfuce's shawl fussily. The waif tutted and waved her away.

How may I be of service, master? The sibilant voice sounded again in Rook's head, and he shuddered.

Vox gestured airily towards the prone figure of the goblin, lying beside the marble table. 'I wish you to wash this wretch's mind clean, Amberfuce, and then place a little message in his pathetic brain . . . This message . . .'

Vox stared into Amberfuce's large dark eyes. The waif's ears twitched as he stared back.

Understood, master. Very cunning. Very cunning indeed . . . came the sibilant whisper.

'Yes, yes,' said Vox, turning back to the table. 'Get on with it, then!'

The waif's eyes closed and his head lolled back. At Rook's feet, the goblin flinched and shook his head. Spasms racked his body; his jaw clenched and unclenched; his eyeballs swivelled round in their sockets independent of each other – and Rook trembled, knowing exactly what the goblin was going through. Little by little, the waif was sifting through his thoughts; discarding ones he had no use for and replacing them with those of his master, Vox.

'It is time, it is time,' the goblin mumbled, his head lolling from side to side. 'General Tytugg . . . I have the secret route into the Great Library . . . It lies defenceless before us . . . Attack from the eastern entrance to the sewers and show no mercy . . . Death to the librarian scum!'

The waif glanced round at Vox who was standing

watching; a self-satisfied smirk played over his blubbery face. 'Very good, Amberfuce,' he said. 'Now the rest of it.'

Amberfuce nodded and returned his attention to the goblin, whose head jerked back so hard that his neck cracked.

'Dead,' he cried. 'Vox is dead . . . I killed him . . . With my own bare hands . . . I heard him squeal like a great fat woodhog . . . A mound of blubbery . . .'

'Yes, yes,' Vox interrupted testily. 'I think he's got the message, Amberfuce. Now send him back to the Hive Towers.'

Amberfuce concentrated. The goblin nodded, his eyes staring ahead, unblinking. 'Must return to General Tytugg,' he muttered. 'At once.'

The goblin climbed to his feet and, without another word, set off across the cluttered chamber. As the door clicked shut, Vox chuckled to himself unpleasantly.

'That's General Tytugg taken care of,' he said. 'Now

for the shrykes. I need someone to go to the court of the Shryke Sisterhood and tell that feathered monster, Mother Muleclaw, that the goblins have the Great Library within their grasp. It is vital that this someone convinces her that she has the goblins *and* the librarians at her mercy. I was thinking, er . . .' Vox's gaze fell on Rook. 'A runaway slave, perhaps? With nothing to lose? Prepared to sell his friends and comrades out for a pouchful of shryke gold?'

Cowlquape turned to Rook. 'You have been through so much, Rook, lad,' he said, his eyes glistening with emotion. 'Would you do this, Rook?' he said. 'Would you pay a visit to Mother Muleclaw? For the librarians? For me . . ?'

Rook swallowed hard. The thought of Mother Muleclaw and the court of the Shryke Sisterhood filled him with dread; just as impersonating a treacherous slave sickened him, and yet . . . He looked into Cowlquape's concerned, kindly eyes.

'I'd be honoured to,' he said.

·CHAPTER TEN·

THE ELEVENTH HOUR

i
The Hive Towers

It was steamy, smoky and scorchingly hot inside the cavernous Hive Towers. The rank air hummed with the odours of unwashed goblins, burning lamp-oil and boiling tripweed, and the smoke from the foul stinkwood logs which burned intensely in the central brazier, their acid-green flames lapping at a tilder turning on the spit above. Drips of fat oozed from the revolving carcass and fell hissing into the fire, and puffs of acrid smoke rose up to join the dense miasmic cloud writhing in the conical towers far above. The goblins themselves were listless and irritable. Tempers were fraying.

'Turn that spit faster, scum!' roared a goblin undermaster, and cracked his whip. The mobgnome slave cowered miserably and struggled to obey.

From the shadows of a far corner came a loud groan,

followed by a parched, rasping cry. 'Woodale! More woodale! I'm dying of thirst, here.'

'Me, too,' said another. 'It's so blasted hot.'

'Yeah, where's that accursed slave?' bellowed a third.

'Coming, sirs. I'm coming,' said a weary voice, and a dumpy mobgnome pulled away from the communal ale-vat, climbed down the rickety ladder propped up against it, and – a slopping jug of woodale clasped in her callused hands – scurried across the hall to top up the goblins' tankards.

High above them, on one of the jutting stanchions, a look-out guard was bellowing at his replacement. 'You're late!' he roared. 'Shryke-loving dunggrub!'

'Who are you calling a dunggrub?' the second guard shouted back, his face red with rage. 'You stinking woodhog!'

He shoved the first guard hard in the chest. The guard lashed back. A scuffle broke out. Meanwhile, below them on the sleeping platforms, a second fight was in progress. With teeth bared and fists flying, three hefty tufted goblin guards were rolling about, crashing into the sleeping-pallets and sending the laden guard-racks tumbling – and all, apparently, over some dispute about mattress straw.

Down on the first-storey platform, General Tytugg was well aware of the state of his troops. Tension was high; morale low. He knew that the problem was nothing to do with spits or shifts, or who had the biggest wad of clean straw, but rather the terrible airless heat – both inside and outside the Hive Towers – that was

driving each and every one of his goblin guard to distraction. He himself was suffering, and he paced up and down the platform, his brow furrowed, his fists clenched.

'Get out of my way!' The angry voice cut through the general hubbub. It was coming from the entrance gates, where a group of guards were clustered round a new arrival.

'Out of my way!' roared the goblin a second time and attempted to brush the crowd aside. 'I have important information for General Tytugg . . .'

'Clodwit?' bellowed a voice from above them. 'Is that you?'

The goblins turned as one, to see General Tytugg's furious face glaring down at them. 'Ay, sire,' Clodwit shouted back. 'I bear news!'

'Step aside!' the general roared. 'Let him through!'

The goblins did as they were told and Clodwit hurried through the gap in the grumbling crowd, wiping the sweat from his brow as he went. The general, having climbed down the steep flight of stairs from the platform, was waiting for him at the bottom. Head lowered, Clodwit approached and greeted him as goblinlore required, with one fist raised and the other pressed to his heart.

'Make your report,' said General Tytugg. 'And for your sake, I hope it's a good one, or you'll join that tilder over there on the roasting-spit.'

Clodwit smiled and looked up. 'Vox Verlix is dead, master.'

'Dead,' whispered General Tytugg, his eyes widening with pleasure. 'Are you sure?'

'Killed him with me own hands,' said Clodwit proudly, patting the sheathed scythe at his belt. 'Squealed like a great woodhog when I stuck the blade in, so he did . . . One, two, three, four . . .' He jabbed at the air, demonstrating where the blade had struck.

All round the cavernous Hive Towers, the news was spreading. Vox Verlix was dead.

Clodwit's face clouded over. 'Glitch was sliced in two outside the chamber,' he said. 'The place was booby-trapped, just like you said – but I sneaked in behind a slave and waited for my opportunity to strike!'

'You've done well, Clodwit,' said General Tytugg. 'Very well.' He clapped the goblin on the shoulders. 'Vox Verlix called himself my master,' he went on, 'just because he had once paid me for my services.' He hawked and spat, a great glistening ball that landed in the stinkwood fire with a hiss. 'But who's the master now, eh?' he said, and laughed unpleasantly. 'With Vox Verlix in his grave, Tytugg is the Master of Undertown!'

'And there's more, sire,' said Clodwit in a low voice, as a rising swell of cheering began to echo round the great towers. Tytugg listened closely. 'Before he died, Vox pleaded for his life. He said he could help the goblins defeat the librarians, master. He told me that there was a secret route into the sewers which leads directly to the Great Chamber; showed me where it was in exchange for his life.'

'A secret route!' Tytugg exclaimed, his eyes glinting. 'Where is this secret route?'

The goblin crouched down and began to draw in the dust of the hard mud floor. 'Here's the underground library chamber and here's the central tunnel,' he said, drawing first a circle, then bisecting it with a long, horizontal line. 'And the main entrances are here, here and here,' he continued, marking the ground with crosses to represent the Great Eastern and Western Entrances, and the broad pipes which emerged in the boom-docks. 'But according to Vox, there is another entrance here,' he said, stabbing at the ground just above the Great Eastern Entrance.

Tytugg he looked at the spot thoughtfully. 'There's a small sink-hole there,' he said. 'I thought it was blocked.'

'That's what they wanted us to think,' said Clodwit. 'Vox learned of it from a librarian slave he employs in his kitchen.'

'Cunning old woodfox,' chuckled General Tytugg, his uneven brown teeth gleaming in the light from the brazier. 'To think that it was there all the time.'

All round the Hive Towers, the watching goblin

guards were cheering Clodwit's success and the scatter of applause was turning to a loud, rhythmic clapping.

General Tytugg frowned. 'Secret or no,' he said, 'surely the librarians don't leave it unguarded.'

'Not normally,' said Clodwit, 'but Vox reckoned they're about to have one of their ceremonies. The true Most High Academe is to make an important announcement. Two nights from now. At the eleventh hour.'

'The eleventh hour,' Tytugg repeated, furrows creasing his scarred brow.

'Apart from a skeleton guard posted at the main entrances, Vox said that everyone will be down in the Great Library Chamber at that time,' said Clodwit. 'Trapped. Defenceless. They'll be like sitting ducks; just waiting to be picked off, he said.' The goblin frowned as the false memories jostled for position inside his head. 'He claimed he was going to tell his old friend and ally, General Tytugg, all about it – and let you take all the glory. He was on his knees, pleading for me to spare his life.'

The general gave a derisory snort. 'I'm sure he was,' he said. 'Did he say anything else?'

A cruel smile stretched the goblin's thin lips. 'No, master,' he said, fingering his scythe. 'Your name was the last thing he uttered.'

General Tytugg threw back his head and roared with laughter. 'Wonderful! Wonderful!' he roared. 'Vox Verlix is no more, and now I'm going to destroy the librarians as well. Once and for all! Even Mother Muleclaw and her scabby shryke-sisters haven't been able to penetrate the

Great Library. Truly I shall become the greatest ruler of all the Edge. "General Tytugg" shall be the last words *many* shall utter.'

Around the hall, the goblin guards were picking up on the latest snippets of information as the eavesdropped conversation between Clodwit and the general passed from one to the other. The thick, stifling air was becoming charged with excitement and expectation.

'Death to librarian scum!' someone shouted and a great cheer went up, so loud and so long it set the beams overhead rattling. The heavy hand-clapping grew louder and a chant started up, quiet at first, but growing louder with ever passing second as the goblins whipped themselves up into a frenzy of battle-rage.

'Ty-tugg! Ty-tugg! Ty-tugg! Ty-tugg . . .'

ii
The Great Storm Chamber Library

'Order! Order!' bellowed Fenbrus Lodd, trying to make himself heard above the agitated babble of voices echoing round the tall ceiling of the underground library chamber. He raised his heavy blackwood gavel high in the air. *'Order!'*

Despite the lateness of the hour, the Great Storm Chamber Library was packed – and in uproar. There were librarians everywhere; crowded together on the Blackwood Bridge, clinging precariously to the jutting gantries overhead, crammed into the floating buoyant lecterns and onto the bobbing rafts in the main water channel below. Every one of them was staring across at the old Lufwood Bridge where the council members were all assembled, standing before high-backed chairs laid out in a broad semi-circle. Every one of them was shouting.

'Never!'

'Heresy!'

'Blasphemy!'

The atmosphere had been charged ever since the Open Council Session had first been called. Now it was at fever-pitch. It had been strange to be summoned to the library so late; stranger still to be witnessing the High Librarians in open session. But strangest – and most disturbing of all – was what Cowlquape Pentephraxis, the true Most High Academe, had just proposed.

'Leave the Great Library?' shouted a middle-aged

librarian, spluttering with rage. His side-whiskers flapped and the tasselled mortar-board jiggled about loosely on his long, pointed head.

'Shame! Shame!' bellowed another indignantly.

'Over my dead body!' croaked an ancient research-librarian, the buoyant lectern he was wedged within dipping wildly as he brandished his bony fists at the row of High Council members before him.

Bang! Bang! Bang! Bang!

Fenbrus Lodd's gavel hammered down like a volley of heavy hailstones. Unchecked, the librarians continued to berate their superiors who, for their part, remained in dignified silence.

There was Alquix Venvax and the other senior professors, Varis Lodd, captain of the librarian knights, and the Professors of Light and Darkness, Ulbus Vespius and Tallus Penitax. In the middle of the curved line, standing before his especially high-backed chair, was Cowlquape Pentephraxis, true Most High Academe – and object of most of the assembled librarians' outrage and indignation.

He looked stooped, uncertain and oddly frail in the face of such obvious hostility. His brown robes trembled. Fenbrus Lodd, the High Librarian – standing apart from the others at the top of a tall, carved blackwood lectern – could feel the meeting was slipping out of his control. He slammed the heavy blackwood gavel down – *Bang! Bang! Bang!* – and bellowed furiously at the top of his voice.

'Order! *Order!* I will not have these disturbances!'

The raucous hubbub dropped a notch.

Bang! Bang! Bang!

'I shall clear this chamber if I do not have immediate silence,' he warned, his eyes blazing. *'Order! Order!'*

The din subsided further.

'The true Most High Academe wanted you here – professors, sub-professors, librarians, apprentices and under-librarians – to bear witness to what we, the High Council, debate this night; for our final decision affects us all. Such rabble-rousing behaviour is unfitting.'

The chamber became quieter still with only a low, intermittent murmuring breaking the silence. With a short nod of satisfaction, Fenbrus Lodd turned to Cowlquape.

'My apologies, Most High Academe,' he said. 'Pray, proceed.'

Cowlquape raised his head and faced the sea of hostile faces before him. He stepped forwards, scanning the crowd for the ancient research-librarian who had cried out.

'Ah, there you are, Surlix,' he said, his gaze fixing on the wizened individual in the buoyant lectern. 'Over your dead body, you say.' His soft voice was audible in every corner of the now silent chamber. 'I tell you, Surlix; I tell you all . . .' He glanced back at the row of librarian dignitaries. 'If we do not leave the Great Library Chamber, then it will be over *all* our dead bodies – for I have it on good authority that a mighty storm is imminent.'

'A storm? A storm?' the librarians muttered among themselves.

Bang! Bang! Bang!

'That is why it's been getting so hot, so humid,' Cowlquape continued. 'The storm is gathering. I have been shown the cloud charts. It will strike at midnight in two nights' time. If we have not left the Great Library before the eleventh hour, we will all surely drown.'

'What nonsense is this?' shouted a red-haired librarian, unable to keep silent a moment longer. 'We've weathered storms before!'

'Yes, that's what the sluice-gates are for,' one of the raft-hands shouted up from the flowing waters below.

'I, for one, refuse to leave the sacred library!' cried an angry voice. And a chant began somewhere to the left of the Blackwood Bridge, which soon spread. 'Stay! Stay! Stay! . . .'

Bang! Bang! Bang!

'This is no ordinary storm,' Cowlquape shouted above the rising din. 'It is a . . .'

Bang! Bang! Bang!

'Silence!' roared Fenbrus Lodd.

Cowlquape breathed in sharply. 'It is a dark maelstrom,' he said.

There was a gasp from all sides which rose up and echoed round the vaulted ceiling.

'A . . . a dark maelstrom?' said Fenbrus Lodd uneasily, looking round from his lectern. 'Are you sure?'

Cowlquape nodded earnestly. 'Vox Verlix, the greatest cloudwatcher there has ever been, showed me his calculations. There can be no doubt about it – in two nights' time, the maelstrom will strike.'

'Vox Verlix!' shouted an angry voice. 'Why should we believe anything *he* says?'

Cowlquape raised his hand. 'Because he *needs* us. In exchange for taking him with us, he has worked out a plan to enable us to escape from the sewers and take this great library of ours to a new home in the Free Glades!'

Alquix Venvax pushed his steel-rimmed glasses up nose with trembling fingers. His lower lip, too, was trembling. 'But this is my home,' he said in a soft, quavering voice. 'I don't want to leave it.'

A murmur of agreement spread out across the crowded chamber like ripples on a lake. Fenbrus Lodd glared round darkly, raised his gavel and was about to bring it down when Varis suddenly sprang forward.

'The Free Glades is the most wonderful place in all the Edge!' she exclaimed. 'I know,' she added, 'for I have been there. It is a sparkling jewel in the Deepwoods; a beacon of light and hope for academics everywhere.'

The librarians listened intently. Varis Lodd was renowned both for her academic rigour and for her selfless bravery. If *she* thought moving to the Free Glades was a good idea . . .

'Just think of it,' she was saying. 'A new beginning in a place where learning is valued and academics are revered.' She turned round to face Alquix. 'You say that this place is your home. But look at it. Why should you have to remain down here in the sewers? In the *sewers*, for Sky's sake! Hiding away, too frightened to show your face above ground.' Her voice softened. 'When did you last feel the warm sun on your back, Alquix Venvax?' she asked. 'Or rain in your face, or the wind in your beard? When did you last see the stars?'

Alquix remained seated. 'It is true,' he murmured sadly. 'I miss all these things.'

'We are academics,' Varis continued, turning her attention to the crowd, now hanging on her every word. 'We have dedicated our lives to the pursuit of knowledge – knowledge of the Edgeworld. Yet we skulk down here, beneath the ground, in this dark, damp hole, cut off from the world we claim to hold so dear. Librarians, one and all, I second the Most High Academe's proposal. We should leave the sewers and build a new library in the Free Glades!'

A loud cheer went up. This time, Fenbrus Lodd made no attempt to quieten the librarians down, either with threat or gavel. His daughter's impassioned speech had not only won over the librarians but it had also persuaded him of the wisdom of Cowlquape's proposal.

He turned to Cowlquape, his voice thick with emotion. 'If you think we can trust the usurper, Vox Verlix, then, Most High Academe, that is good enough for me and . . .' – he looked around at his fellow council members – 'for all of us.'

Bang! Bang! Bang!

Fenbrus Lodd brought the great gathering back to order with his heavy gavel. 'There is much to do and two days is all we have,' he said. 'Panniers must be loaded. Crates and boxes must be filled. And everything must be packed up securely in waterproof tarpaulins and loaded onto the rafts and barges . . .'

Cowlquape looked at the High Librarian, grateful to him – and his daughter, Varis Lodd – for swaying the librarians in favour of his proposal. Now all he could do was hope, and pray to Earth and Sky that everything would go smoothly.

'Two days' time, at the eleventh hour,' he murmured to himself. It seemed so terribly close.

iii
The Court of the Shryke Sisterhood

As well as the tollgate towers, tally-huts and talon-shaped barriers – familiar landmarks, all – there was a new construction at the eastern end of the Great Mire Road. It stood tall and imposing, an immense ironwood pine, uprooted from the rich soil of the distant Deepwoods and transported whole to its current site. Here it had been erected, supported by myriad ropes and staves, its branches stripped, polished and bedecked with the ornate perches beloved by the Shryke Sisterhood.

The Roosting Tree towered above the Mire Road and, in its branches, the High Sisterhood were gathered, their screeching voices raised in increasingly raucous debate. Mother Muleclaw herself, resplendent on a suspended gilded throne, wound the plaited leash she was holding in and out of her talons as she listened closely.

'The verminous goblin scum are swarming round the Hive Huts like crazed woodants!' one of the shryke-sisters, a tall individual with gaudy plumage and gaudier gowns, was saying.

'They're up to something, sisters! The hammerhead guard is said to be gathering at the Great Eastern sewer entrance,' added a second sister, her tall purple crest quivering violently.

'Indeed,' commented a third. 'Tytugg's definitely up to something. I can feel it in my tail feathers!'

'Which is why I say we should attack now, sisters, and bathe our claws in goblin blood!' said the purple-crested one adamantly, talking louder to be heard above the shrieks and battle-screeches of the battalions of shrykes performing their drill-manoeuvres below. 'Attack, I say. *Attack!*'

'And I say again that we must wait, Sister Talonscratch,' interrupted an angular shryke perched opposite her. She shook her long, mottled face slowly. 'Tytugg is clever. We must send out our spies; we must curb our impatience until we are certain of his plans, sisters.'

'My dear *cautious* Sister Hookbill,' said Sister Talonscratch, her voice soft and honeyed, 'always pecking at the seeds on the ground rather than reaching for the fruits in the branches!'

'Indeed, *venerable* sister,' replied Sister Hookbill gently, her voice laced with the stirrings of impatience. 'As I peck at the seeds on the ground, as you so delicately put it, I hear the whispers in the forest – while the fruit-seekers risk breaking their fine feathered necks on untested boughs.'

Sister Talonscratch's eyes blazed. 'You squawk of untested boughs, Sister Hookbill,' she said sharply, her feathers ruffling menacingly, 'when there is goblin blood to be tasted!'

'Sisters, sisters,' said Mother Muleclaw. Her hanging-throne swung from side to side. 'Calm yourselves. We need clear heads and sharp eyes in these dangerous times . . .'

Just then there was a loud disturbance below as a party of shryke guards approached the Roosting Tree. The entire circle of sisters spun round indignantly.

'A thousand apologies, sweet sisters,' said one of the guards.

'But we found *this*,' said the second, dragging a bedraggled youth by the scruff of the neck. Throwing him down roughly onto the boards at the base of the tree, the guard squawked up to the roost-mother above. 'Caught him snooping around by the tally-huts at the Mire Gates, your supreme Highness.'

The shrykes squawked and clucked with rage. The youth raised his head nervously and looked up. There was a loud *crack* as the first of the guards struck him on the shoulder with her bone-flail. 'How dare you cast your gaze upon the shryke-sisters!' she screeched. 'Librarian filth!'

The youth lowered his head. 'I . . . I'm sorry,' he said. 'But I must speak with . . .'

A second *crack* sounded, as the other guard brought her flail down heavily on his back. 'You will only speak when spoken to!' she shrieked.

'Let the librarian speak,' clucked Sister Hookbill. 'Seed-pecker that I am, I sense we might learn something from him.'

'He dared to meet our gaze!' shrieked Sister Talon-scratch. 'I say we tear out his liver and gorge on it!'

'Enough!' commanded Mother Muleclaw as her yellow eyes fell on the cowering figure of the youth. She lowered her hanging-throne. 'What business does a librarian knight have at the tally-huts?' she said. 'Speak, wretch, or my sister here shall feast on your liver!'

Keeping his head down, the youth replied, 'My name is Rook Barkwater,' he said. 'I am a librarian knight no longer. I spit on their rules and restrictions. Sewer rats, the lot of them! I seek the freedom of the Deepwoods and I'm prepared to sell out every last one of them to get it!'

The clucking grew louder. Mother Muleclaw's yellow eyes narrowed. 'Stand up,' she said. 'Explain yourself.'

Rook did as he was told, taking care to keep his gaze fixed firmly on the floor below him. He didn't want to feel the searing pain of the bone-flail again.

'They accused me of forging my treatise and stealing barkscrolls,' he said, his voice little more than a murmur. 'Lies, all of it. And for that, they shall pay dearly.'

The shrykes fell still. Mother Muleclaw leaned forwards, pressed a vicious talon against the underside of his chin and jerked his head upwards. Rook found himself staring into the cold, unblinking eyes of the formidable creature.

'Pay dearly?' she said. 'How, pray?'

'The librarians are in great danger, if they only knew it,' he said with a bitter smile. 'The goblins have discovered a secret passageway into the Great Library and they intend to attack and take it for themselves.'

'You see!' screeched one of the shrykes. 'I *told* you Tytugg was up to something!'

Mother Muleclaw silenced her with a flap of her taloned hand. 'Why should we believe you, librarian scum?' she growled.

'Because I hate the librarians, and with the gold you shall pay me for the information I give you, I can buy a passage back to the Deepwoods,' said Rook, head still bowed. 'Fifty gold pieces is all I ask. A cheap price for the chance to destroy the goblins and the librarians at a stroke . . . And I know the shrykes understand the value of a good spy. I could be even more useful to you once I reach the Free Glades.' He paused. 'For the right price.'

'Go on,' said Mother Muleclaw, leaning forward in her roost throne. Around her, the other sisters had fallen quiet.

'First the gold,' said Rook, looking up and meeting her gaze.

For a moment, Mother Muleclaw said nothing. Then, with a savage jerk of the plaited leash, she yanked her puny shryke-mate up beside her. Rook noticed the leather coffer strapped to his back.

'Stand still, Burdle,' snapped Mother Muleclaw as she pushed a key into the lock of the coffer and turned it. 'Fifty, you say,' she said, and thrust her hand inside. She counted out the coins. 'There,' she squawked and tossed the gold to the floor at Rook's feet. 'There's thirty. That's *plenty*. Unless you *want* to see the colour of your own insides . . .'

Rook crouched down and began stuffing his pockets with the gold pieces. As the final coin clinked down beside the others, he climbed to his feet.

'The goblins will attack from the east,' he began, 'and I can show you an entrance from the Great Western Tunnel that will lead you straight to the Great Storm Chamber Library. Attack at the right moment and you will trap the goblins *and* the librarians.'

Mother Muleclaw clucked excitedly. 'Tell me when to attack and you shall be escorted along the Mire Road in my own personal carriage!' she said.

Rook smiled, his gaze as unblinking as that of the shrykes themselves. 'Attack in two nights' time,' he said. 'At the eleventh hour!'

·CHAPTER ELEVEN·

XANTH FILATINE

Xanth stood by the window of his study looking out at the new day dawning, his head in turmoil. It was hotter than ever that morning, with the atmosphere so still that, although the window was wide open, not the faintest breath of fresh air penetrated the stifling room.

Mopping his glistening brow, he surveyed the huge, dark, anvil-shaped clouds which lined the horizon with a mounting sense of dread. They were vast and dense, their horizontal upper reaches silhouetted against the heavy blood-red sky. Xanth shuddered. Was this the storm the Guardians had been awaiting for so long? It looked so menacing, so evil . . .

At least, Xanth thought, if the storm *did* strike, the air might clear and the temperature drop. It had been so hot the night before that he'd barely slept a wink, tossing and turning beneath sweat-drenched covers, his dreams troubled and disturbing.

Far below him, Screetown was stirring. Further off, the lights of Undertown were going out, one by one, and on the narrow streets between the clutter of rundown buildings he saw Undertowners and goblins – as tiny as woodants – going about their daily business. Further still and he could just make out the signs of activity at the end of the Great Mire Road.

He pulled a telescope from the folds of his gown and focused on the tally-huts, the gateway towers – and the writhing mass of the bird-creatures clustered together in groups on the great platform beneath the towers and the curious tree-like construction which had sprung up a couple of days earlier. What was more, he realized as he switched his attention to the road itself, there were more arriving all the time. Like the clouds, the entire shryke army seemed to be advancing on Undertown.

The Eastern Roost must be almost deserted, he thought. But why? Did they also sense an impending storm?

Just then, a white raven flew past the window, cawing loudly. Xanth lowered the telescope and watched as the creature flapped past the Tower of Night, over Screetown and on towards the Stone Gardens.

Xanth sighed wistfully, wishing that he, too, could fly away from the dark evil tower. He no longer belonged here. Perhaps he never had . . .

If he *could* fly, however, it wouldn't be to the Stone Gardens. No, if Xanth had wings, he would head off in the opposite direction; to the Deepwoods. He smiled to himself. Maybe Leddix was right, after all; maybe the Free Glade air had turned his head . . .

He'd flown there, of course, in the Free Glades; soaring above the Great Lake on the *Ratbird*, the skycraft he had built with his own hands. He sighed again. How differently things might have been if that maiden flight hadn't ended up with him crashing into Lake Landing and breaking his leg . . .

Xanth turned away from the window, crossed the stone floor and sat down on the stool at his desk. He had work to complete. A barkscroll lay before him, half-translated from the ancient tongue of the first academics. He picked up his pencil and read over the last sentence.

Et syth thit lyghtninge bleue slamme to thit steyne strykenard, yereby to makke sund.

And his transcription.

And so the blue lightning strikes the stricken stone, thereby making it . . .

'*Sund,*' he murmured. 'Healthy? Well? . . .'

His mind – already muzzy with the airless heat and

lack of sleep – began to wander. And as he traced his fingers over the pattern of whorls and knots in the surface of the wooden desktop, he remembered Oakley Barkgruff, the kindly woodtroll who had helped him carve his skycraft from the great slab of sumpwood; what a thrill it had been to feel the wood beneath his hands take on the shape of a ratbird . . .

And the slaughterer, Brisket, scarcely older than himself, who had taught him everything he knew of sail-setting and ropecraft. How he'd loved those intricate rope-knots and the subtle shapes of a billowing sail . . .

And, most of all, Tweezel, the ancient spindlebug who had shown him how to varnish his craft – and with whom he had spent so many indulgent hours, sipping aromatic teas and listening to the wise old creature's stories. Even now, he could recall that thin, reedy voice telling him of far-off days when the spindlebug had walked the streets of old Sanctaphrax . . .

Then there was Parsimmon, the Master of the Lake Landing Academy; and Varis Lodd; and his fellow students, Stob Lummus, Rook Barkwater . . .

And, of course, Magda. Magda Burlix; the librarian knight he had interrogated so cruelly the day before, acting as though he didn't know her, and sealing her fate.

'Oh, Magda! Magda! Magda!' he cried out, slamming the pencil down on the table and pushing the barkscroll away. He couldn't work. Not now.

The stool scraped loudly on the stone floor as he pushed it back and climbed to his feet. He began pacing the small room, to and fro from bed-pallet to window and back again, rubbing his hands over his shaven scalp and muttering under his breath.

'I've tried so hard to be a good Guardian. Nobody can say that I haven't. Obedient. Loyal. Ruthless . . . And then *you* come along, Magda, stirring up all kinds of stuff I thought I'd forgotten about. Why did you have to get caught? Eh, why *you*?' His face hardened. 'Sky blast you!'

Yet even as he cursed her, Xanth knew it wasn't Magda's fault that he was feeling the way he did. He clutched at his head. How had it ever come to this?

Back at the window, he glanced across at the Palace of Statues. It had been many long years since Orbix Xaxis had first taken him into his confidence, flattering him, tempting him and finally luring him away from Vox Verlix whom he'd been serving as a young apprentice.

Whenever he could, Orbix had taken Xanth aside. 'There could be an excellent future in the Tower of Night for a quick-witted lad such as yourself,' he would tell him. 'You could go down in history, my boy, as the one who healed the stricken rock and returned Sanctaphrax to its former glory.'

Though alarmed by the mask and dark glasses which concealed Orbix's face and muffled his voice, Xanth had listened keenly, his heart thumping with excitement.

Then one cold morning, as Vox struggled with the construction of the Sanctaphrax Forest, Orbix had gone further. 'Vox Verlix is finished, I tell you,' he'd said softly. 'And those arrogant buffoons, the librarians, will never manage to find a cure for the rock with their poultices and potions. *We* are the future.' His voice had dropped to a gruff whisper. '. . . The Guardians of Night, are the true heirs of the sky-scholars,' he'd said. 'Join us, Xanth. Join us.'

And he had. That night, in the darkest hour just before daybreak, he had stolen away from his quarters and met with Orbix Xaxis's shadowy followers on the upper gantries of the tower. There he had joined the breakaway faction of Guardians, signing his name to the Oath of Allegiance with his own blood.

Xanth turned away and crossed the room slowly, the painful memories coming thick and fast.

Before the blood on the parchment was even dry, Orbix had whisked him away and quizzed him relentlessly about every aspect of Vox Verlix's apartments in the tower, the layout of corridors and staircases, the exact timing of his daily routine, the movements of his palace guards – and of Vox himself . . .

Three days later, Orbix Xaxis had launched his attack, massacring all those loyal to Vox Verlix, who had fled for his life; seizing the Tower of Night for himself and declaring himself its High Guardian.

Xanth sat down heavily on the corner of his bed-pallet, knees clutched tightly to his chest, and began rocking slowly backwards and forwards. Although he hadn't realized it at the time, he'd been used . . . Used . . .

From deep down in the bowels of the tower, he heard muffled thuds as doors were slammed, one after the other, and in between, the intermittent wail of desperate voices. The prisoners were being fed. Each time a door was unlocked for their daily ration of gruel and water to be pushed inside, mournful cries escaped the atrium and echoed up into the higher reaches of the tower. Xanth put his head in his hands. Soon the terrible prison stench, wafting out through the opened doors, would also fill the air.

Prisoners! Yes, under Orbix Xaxis, there were many prisoners; captured librarians, Undertowners and denounced Guardians accused of plotting against him. Nobody was safe. Xanth had earned his new master's trust by interrogating prisoners. He was, he realized guiltily, good at it; getting them to talk through a mixture of brutality and kindness.

It was how he'd first met Cowlquape, the hapless Most High Academe, betrayed by Vox to Orbix Xaxis, who had imprisoned him. The High Academe was free now, but Xanth couldn't help missing him – after the initial interrogation, he had grown to like and admire the resilient old academic.

Cowlquape it was who had buoyed him up so many times over the years when his spirits were low: with no-one else to talk to, Xanth had often crept down to the dungeons to hear the professor talk of his love for the Deepwoods. He had held Xanth spellbound with his stories of that mysterious place, far from Undertown, with its exotic fauna and flora, and tales of the tribes and forest-folk that dwelt there. And when the opportunity had arisen for Xanth to travel there himself, he'd seized it – though he had been too ashamed to tell Cowlquape that he was travelling there as a spy for the Guardians of Night.

Despite the sultry heat of the small chamber, Xanth shivered with a mixture of sadness and remorse. He *had* left the sinister tower and travelled to the Free Glades. And there, for the first time in his life, he had tasted happiness, just as Cowlquape had promised he would. But in the end, he had had to return. He'd had no choice. At risk of being unmasked as a spy, he'd had to flee back to the Guardians. It had broken his heart to leave, and on his return it had been too painful to see Cowlquape. Never again did Xanth visit him in his cell. So far as he knew, the old professor did not even know that he had returned.

Now, of course, the tables had been turned. Cowlquape Pentephraxis, former Most High Academe of New Sanctaphrax, was free, while *he* . . .

Just then, Xanth heard the soft clinking of chains. He jumped to his feet and hurried to the window. It was one of the terrible cages, empty now, being raised up from the deep ravine below.

Xanth turned away and slammed his fist down onto the desk. If he'd had his doubts about the High Guardian before – with his tortured prisoners, his summary executions and his fanatical hatred of the librarians – now that Orbix had begun feeding the poor, helpless librarians to the terrible rock demons, Xanth knew that his master had gone beyond the bounds of brutal tyrant. The so-called Purification Ceremonies were nothing more than an excuse for the High Guardian's twisted sport. Orbix Xaxis was a madman, a maniac. A monster.

Returning to the window, Xanth paused. By daylight, the approaching clouds looked darker and more imposing than ever. Perhaps this time, after decades of drought, the Edge was about to be struck by a mighty storm – with driving rain, thunder and lightning . . .

Lightning!

Despite himself, Xanth felt a shiver of excitement. *Sacred* lightning. The lightning which every Guardian believed would strike Midnight's Spike and so pass down through the crumbling Sanctaphrax rock, healing it as it went.

What if Orbix was right? Xanth wondered anxiously. What if a storm did break, and the lightning did strike, and did heal the Sanctaphrax rock? What then? The power struggle between the warring factions of shrykes and goblins, Guardians and librarians was in the balance at the moment – as it had been for many years.

But if the Guardians of Night *were* to cure stone-sickness, then all that would change at a stroke. The Guardians would both govern New Sanctaphrax *and* take control of the sky, as buoyant flight-rocks began once more to grow in the Stone Gardens.

And, if *that* happened, then who would become the most powerful figure in all the Edge? Why none other than the High Guardian himself, Orbix Xaxis! Did he, Xanth, really want that to happen?

Thud! Thud! Thud!

The three heavy blows at the door echoed round the small study-chamber and brought Xanth out of his reveries with a start. The door burst open.

'You're wanted up on the Upper Gantry, now,' said a surly-looking guard gruffly. 'Come with me.'

As Xanth stepped into the corridor, the rank odour from the dungeons made him grimace. Poor creatures, he thought. And Magda was one of them; down there in the putrid depths, perched on her jutting prison-ledge. Alone. Frightened . . .

Oh, Magda, he thought sorrowfully as he followed the armed Guardian up the flights of stairs to the High Guardian's quarters. I should thank you, not curse you, for stirring such memories and doubts and emotions. Ever since returning from the Free Glades, I've tried desperately to keep my feelings under control, but you . . . you, Magda, have brought them flooding back. I cannot stay in this evil place. I must leave – and somehow take you with me.

*

Xanth's footsteps echoed round the High Guardian's sumptuous stately chamber as he made his way across the polished leadwood floor. The place was as luxurious as his own study was austere. It was crammed full of priceless items, all plundered from the ruined palaces of Screetown.

There were gilt framed mirrors and intricate tapestries, sparkling with gold and silver thread, on every wall; ornate vases, candelabras and dancing figurines on shelves, plinths and podiums, and in tall, elegant glass-fronted cabinets. Huge turquoise and magenta porcelain urns stood in every corner, a crystal chandelier hung overhead, while at the far end of the room, on either side of the gantry-doors, stood two ferocious banderbears, carved from the same heavy leadwood as the floor – and looking for all the world as though they were rearing out of it.

'There you are, Xanth,' came a steely, yet slightly muffled voice and a sinister black-gowned figure appeared between them.

'High Guardian,' said Xanth.

'Join us,' said Orbix, turning away.

At the far end of the gantry, crouched down beside the ceremonial cage like a great woodcrow hunched over carrion, was Leddix. He looked up, but his sallow face was impossible to read.

'Come closer,' snapped Orbix.

Xanth approached. The mask clamped over the High Guardian's mouth hissed ominously; the dark glasses reflected Xanth's own anxious face back at him.

'I've had my doubts about you, Xanth,' Orbix said. 'You may have noticed. Ever since you returned from the Free Glades . . .' His voice trailed away.

Xanth swallowed nervously.

'But my doubts were clearly misplaced,' Orbix continued. Xanth tried not to show his relief. 'When I saw you kicking that librarian scum, I knew that the rumours about your loyalty were . . . were . . .' He glanced round at Leddix. 'Were less than well-founded.'

'By the Oath of Allegiance, I did my duty as a Guardian of Night,' said Xanth solemnly.

'Indeed, indeed,' said Orbix. 'You acted admirably.' He stepped forwards, clapped an arm around Xanth's shoulder and steered him towards the balustrade at the end of the broad, jutting gantry. Behind him, Xanth heard Leddix – sullen and disgruntled – muttering under his breath.

'The Great Storm is almost upon us,' said Orbix, nodding towards the towering stacks of cloud before them. 'We must be ready for it.' He pulled Xanth round and drew his muzzled face close. 'I want you to prepare Midnight's Spike. Clean the cogs, oil the levers, check the winding-chains. At the precise moment the storm breaks, the spike must rise smoothly up to its full extent to receive the healing power of the lightning bolt. Nothing must go wrong, do you understand?'

Xanth nodded dumbly.

The High Guardian relaxed his grip on Xanth's shoulder, and from behind the muzzle came a muffled grunt of satisfaction. 'I know you will not fail me.' He straightened up. 'Go now. See to the spike.'

'Sir,' said Xanth. He turned away and headed back towards the gantry-doors.

Orbix turned his attention to his cage-master. Behind the muzzle, his breathing was rasping and heavy. 'Leddix,' he hissed. 'I trust everything is in place.'

'Yes, High Guardian,' said Leddix, giving a small, cringing bow. 'The tunnel between the ravine and the sewers has been completed. I supervised it myself.'

'And have you inspected the bait?' he said.

Leddix nodded enthusiastically. 'Such sweet, tender young flesh, High Guardian,' he simpered. 'They're really going to go for her, I can promise you that.'

Orbix strode over to the balustrade and stared down for a long time as if deep in thought. Leddix hovered behind him.

'They'll tear her to shreds,' he said keenly. 'How they'll cheer from the upper gantries. It'll be the best Purification Ceremony yet.'

The High Guardian turned and regarded the cage-master. Behind his muzzle, unseen by Leddix, his lip curled. 'Leddix, Leddix,' he said, his voice dripping with contempt. 'You have understood nothing. This will be no ordinary Purification Ceremony. I don't intend this young librarian to be torn to shreds for the mere delectation of the upper gantries . . .' He paused, and beneath his mask, the rasping breathing quickened.

'You don't, High Guardian?' said Leddix, a puzzled disappointment in his voice.

'No, you fool!' snapped Orbix. 'Why do you think your work gangs have been labouring day and night these past months, digging a tunnel between the ravine and the sewers? Why do you think we've been nurturing the rock demons, feeding them only the sweetest, most tender librarian flesh? Simply to keep you and your bloodthirsty cronies on the upper gantries entertained?'

Leddix shrugged uneasily.

'Of course not!' Orbix sneered. 'I intend her to flee down the tunnel we have so kindly provided. She will run for her life, run to the Great Library – and after her, snapping at her heels and shrieking for the succulent flesh, will come the pursuing rock demons.'

His voice became louder. Leddix seemed almost to shrink into himself.

'They'll infest every tunnel,' the High Guardian told him. 'Every nook, every cranny. They'll run amok, driven into a frenzy of bloodlust by the scent of all that tender librarian flesh around them; a scent they have grown to love so well. There will be no escape! Not a single librarian will survive!'

Leddix bowed low. 'A stroke of genius, High Master,' he said, his voice oily, fawning. 'Truly the Guardians are blessed by your inspired leadership.'

From behind the mask there came a thin, cackling laugh. 'Tomorrow at noon, when the sun is at its highest, the last and greatest Purification Ceremony of them all will begin.'

·CHAPTER TWELVE·

THE GREAT LIBRARY FLEET

The ceiling fans, their blades whirring like agitated woodmoths in moonlight, were having little effect in the Great Storm Chamber Library. Rather than cooling the stifling atmosphere, their frantic beating seemed to be making the air even hotter. Below them, on the library bridges and numerous gantries, the librarians – their clothes damp and their faces glistening with sweat – worked with grim determination.

Groups of conical-hatted professors hurried over the bridges and along the long, winding sewer tunnels, clutching boxes and crates and huge bundles of barkscrolls. Under-librarians, their robes flapping behind them, were racing up and down from the jutting gantries overhead to the channels of water below with heavy rolls of waterproof oil-cloth slung between them. The lectern-keepers, marshalled by the bridge-masters' barked commands, were expertly winding in the skittish buoyant lecterns, one after the other. They were chained together in vast bobbing bunches, waiting to be attached to the huge vessels which were taking shape on the water below as hundreds of barge-hands and sewer-rafters feverishly lashed their craft together to form a fleet of five massive flat-bottomed ships.

Above them, on the Lufwood Bridge, the Council stood poring over barkscroll blueprints and library inventories. There was Fenbrus Lodd the High Librarian, short and gruff, his shock of curly white hair forming a glowing halo round his head. And Varis Lodd, his daughter, captain of the librarian knights, looking curiously cool and collected in her leather flight-suit despite the heat; her green eyes darted here and there, missing nothing. Beside her, deep in conversation, were the Professors of Darkness and of Light; Tallus Penitax in heavy dark robes, and Ulbus Vespius, his cloak glowing white in the shadows.

Behind them all, the aged figure of Alquix Venvax hopped from foot to foot, unable to contain his agitation at the sight of his beloved library being packed up and entrusted to the treacherous waters of the Edgewater River. It was all proving too much for him.

'This is madness!' his querulous voice rang out above the clamour all round. 'Madness! We shall all drown and this great library we have fought and died for will be lost for ever!' His voice cracked with emotion as tears streamed down his face. 'Please, there must be another way . . .'

The council turned and Varis sprang to the old

professor's side as he crumpled to his knees. Below them, an uneasy silence fell as under-librarians, professors, barge-hands and sewer-rafters suddenly stopped what they were doing and looked up at the group on the Lufwood Bridge.

'There is no other way, Alquix, my old friend,' came an equally frail voice – though unlike the old professor's, this one had a calm, steely determination about it that cut through the stifling air and echoed round the Storm Chamber. The council stepped aside as Cowlquape, the Most High Academe, in full regalia, stepped up to the balustrade of the Lufwood Bridge and spread his arms wide.

'I know there are many amongst you who are loath to leave this great library of ours,' he said, addressing the crowd.

There were murmurs and whispers from the upper gantries and barges below.

'It has been our refuge and haven against those who have sought to destroy us for so long. The sewers have kept us safe, it is true, but now, as the dark maelstrom approaches, they will flood, and all we have fought and died for will be lost. So we must leave this place we've called home, the only place many of you have ever known, and make this perilous and terrible journey. Remember . . .' – Cowlquape's voice rose to a crescendo – 'the Storm Chamber will soon be no more. But with your help, my dear brave librarians, the Great Library will live on!'

There was utter silence. All eyes were on the Most

High Academe. Above, the monotonous whirring of the ceiling fans seemed louder than ever. Suddenly Fenbrus Lodd stepped up beside Cowlquape and raised a fist.

'Long live the Great Library!' he roared.

'The Great Library! The Great Library!' The words rang out as the librarians took up the chant; professors throwing their conical hats in the air, under-librarians banging on the wooden boards of the gantries and the barge-hands hoisting their oars above their heads.

At last Cowlquape raised his hand and the cheering subsided. 'Thank you, brave librarians. Now back to work, all of you,' he commanded. 'The eleventh hour approaches.'

Everyone returned to their tasks with renewed vigour. The five great vessels were nearing completion. Each was broad and flat, braced with thick ironwood staves in the middle, and tapering to a long thin point at either end. The prows were fitted with anchor weights and grappling-hooks, while each stern had been raised high with a platform for

the helmsman. Rows of benches lined the sides, already bristling with oars. In the centre of each boat, the lecterns were being loaded, jostling and clashing together as the nets being used to restrain the buoyant wood were strapped into place.

'The work is going well,' said Fenbrus Lodd, turning to Varis who was busy overseeing the storage of the fragile skycraft onto the fourth barge with the Professors of Light and Darkness.

She looked up. 'Yes, Father,' she said, 'though I'd be happier leading a squadron in the air than trusting myself to the water. Besides, the fleet should have airborne cover.'

'It's far too dangerous,' said the Professor of Darkness, shaking his head. 'Even for you, Varis.'

'Tallus is right,' said the Professor of Light. 'With the storm about to break, no skycraft would last five minutes out there.'

'And we'll need them later,' the Professor of Darkness reminded her. 'Once we have left Undertown . . .'

'*If* we ever leave!' interrupted Fenbrus. 'All this discussion! For the love of Earth and Sky, hurry it along, all of you. Varis, you heard the professors. No skycraft! We'll just have to hope and pray that we meet no resistance on our way to the Mire Gates.'

'You shall not, I promise,' a voice rang out.

Unnoticed, a cloaked figure had emerged from the shadows of the tunnel at the far end of the Lufwood Bridge, and stepped into the frantic atmosphere of the Great Storm Chamber. Now the figure strode boldly forwards onto the bridge and pulled back the hood that masked his face.

'Rook!' Fenbrus exclaimed. 'I can't tell you how good it is to see you, lad!'

'And for me to see you, High Librarian,' said Rook. 'I have much to tell.'

'Make your report,' said Fenbrus Lodd. 'For everything depends on it!'

The council gathered round the white-faced youth, Cowlquape offering him a lufwood stool.

'Don't crowd him,' Fenbrus Lodd said, as he climbed down from the lectern. 'You there,' he gestured to an under-librarian. 'Get the lad some water.'

'Sit,' said Cowlquape, placing a hand on his shoulder, 'and catch your breath, that's the way.'

Rook sat down shakily and tried to suppress a shudder. 'It was terrible,' he began. 'I'd almost forgotten how truly monstrous the shrykes are. The stench, the noise – and the way their unblinking eyes bore into you.' He shuddered again. 'I could have sworn that they saw right through me . . .'

'You've been very brave, Rook,' said Cowlquape gently. 'You're safe now.' He paused. 'And if they had seen through you, you wouldn't be here.'

Rook nodded and managed a smile. 'I stuck to the story Vox gave me, about hating librarians and wanting to betray them . . .'

'Shrykes understand treachery,' Varis broke in. 'They find it easy to believe.'

'I told them where and when to attack the library, just like we agreed . . .' Rook continued, looking round at the faces of the High Librarian and the Professors of Light and Darkness uneasily.

'Now there is truly no going back,' said Fenbrus, looking askance at the worried face of Alquix Venvax, who shook his head sadly. The Professors of Light and Darkness exchanged glances.

'And Mother Muleclaw believed you?' the Professor of Darkness asked.

'She did when I demanded fifty gold pieces,' said Rook. 'And offered me safe passage down the Mire Road in her own personal carriage into the bargain when I gave her the details. She thinks she has a spy who will continue working for her – so let me live, thank Sky.'

'Like I said,' Varis muttered, 'shrykes understand treachery.'

Cowlquape turned back to Rook. 'So you think the path down the Mire Road will be clear?' he said.

'Yes, I'm sure of it,' said Rook. 'As I was leaving, I saw vast numbers of armed shrykes streaming in from the Eastern Roost. The entire shryke army is massing. They plan to swarm down into the sewers at the eleventh hour, leaving only fledglings and puny shryke-mates guarding the Mire Gates.'

'We can handle them,' said Varis firmly.

Cowlquape leant forward and rested a hand on Rook's shoulder. 'This is excellent,' he said. 'I had my doubts, but Vox's plan seems to be working.'

'The fat barkslug,' muttered Fenbrus Lodd darkly.

'You have served the Librarians well, Rook,' Cowlquape continued. 'Refresh yourself and then make your way down to the jetties. There is a place on one of the boats for you.'

Rook smiled. Although he would have willingly done anything asked of him to help with the grand exodus, he was exhausted. And though proud to have played his part in Vox's plan, he was relieved that it was now over.

Varis stepped forward and wrapped an arm around his shoulder. 'Come, Rook,' she said. 'Let's go and find you something to eat.'

Just then, there came a plaintive yodel from the far end of the Lufwood Bridge. 'Wuh-wuh, Ru-wuh-uk, Uralowa. Wurra!'

Rook recognized it at once. *Welcome back, Rook, he who took the poison-stick. We have missed you.*

'Oh, banderbears!' he cried.

There was Molleen, an old female, the light glinting on her gappy smile and chipped tusk as she grinned at him lopsidedly. And Weeg, the huge shambling male with the ugly scar across his shoulder. And Wuralo, dear Wuralo, the female with the curious markings which encircled one eye and crossed her snout, that he had rescued from the Foundry Glade – taking a poisoned arrow to the shoulder for his pains. And last but not least, there was Wumeru, his friend. How many moons had passed since that first Deepwoods encounter . . ?

Forgetting how weary he had been feeling only moments before, Rook dashed towards them, arms outstretched, and fell into Wumeru's tight embrace. The others clustered round them, hugging tightly, and forming a huge moss-speckled dome of fur.

At the middle of it all, scarcely able to breathe, Rook smelled the warm, comforting odour of musty fur. It calmed his anxiously beating heart and brought back vivid memories, both good and bad. Of banderbear slaves. Of the great convocation. And of a single banderbear female who, years before, when he was a small orphaned child, lost and alone in the dark Deepwoods, had found him and cared for him until one of his own kind had come to take him away . . .

'My friends . . .' he mumbled, struggling to free himself from their powerful arms. 'Wurra-wuh, meerala!' *My heart sings loudly to be with you again!*

'Wuh-wuh!' 'Wurra-weeg!' 'Larra-weera-wuh!' The banderbears were all speaking at once.

Wumeru silenced them with a slight tilt of her head.

'Wuh-wella-loom,' she said gravely. *Our hearts are glad to be with you, too.* 'Weera-wullara.' *But they also grieve that we must leave you.*

Rook stepped back. 'Leave me?' he asked, touching his chest with an open hand and tilting his head. 'Why must you leave when we have only just been reunited?'

Wumeru held out a vast paw and clasped Rook's face, drawing it close to her own. He could smell her sweet breath, and see the sorrow in her eyes.

'Wurra-weeg, wurra-woolah,' the banderbear said softly. *We must take the fat one to the Mire Gates. It has been agreed.*

'It's true,' said Varis, appearing at Rook's side. 'As part of our agreement, you know we must take that great oaf, Vox, with us. The banderbears have agreed to go to the Palace of Statues and carry him to safety in a specially constructed bower. It will be dangerous, but we gave our word, as librarians.'

'Wuh-wuh wooralah,' Rook said softly. *This mission is perilous. No-one would blame you for refusing.*

'Wurra-weeg!' said Wumeru sharply, her teeth bared. 'Wurroo-leera!' *Our own hearts would break with shame.* Varis smiled. 'They won't let us down, Rook,' she said. 'And Sky willing, we'll all meet up again at the Mire Gates.' She motioned to the banderbears who, each in turn, embraced Rook, then left the bridge.

Rook turned to see a tall, ornate bower standing in the shadows of the tunnel. It had a wide padded bench, surrounded with plush curtains, all mounted on a carved frame. Two broad, varnished poles stuck out from the sides; one at the front, one at the back.

The banderbears bent down, seized a length of pole each in their great clawed paws and, on Varis's command, lifted the bower up in the air.

'Wuh-wuh, weeralah-loog-wuh,' muttered Molleen, smiling bravely. *Light as a feather, even for an old bag of bones like me.*

Rook smiled back. They were so brave, all of them. The librarians were fortunate indeed to have the help of such noble creatures. He could only hope that Molleen would be able to carry the bower as easily when it bore the weight of that great, bloated mountain of flesh, Vox Verlix.

'Wuh-wuh!' he whispered, his hand brushing lightly against his chest and forehead. *Fare you well.* There were tears welling in his eyes.

Fare you well, Rook, came the banderbears' reply as they set off along the tunnel. *And soon may the moon shine down brightly on our next meeting.*

Rook swallowed hard, but the painful lump in his throat remained. They would meet again, he told himself.

Wouldn't they?

Fenbrus took his arm and guided him from the bridge. 'You have done well, Rook Barkwater,' he said kindly. 'Eat well, then take your place on a bench in one of the great vessels, next to your old professor, Alquix Venvax. He needs a steady shoulder to lean on. Go, and Earth and Sky blessings be upon us all in the Great Library fleet!'

·CHAPTER THIRTEEN·

THE CLODDERTROG GUARD

As Xanth Filatine climbed down the narrow ladder from the flimsy spike-ledge at the very top of the Tower of Night, the tooled-leather box slipped from his shoulder. It knocked against the side of the ladder with a loud *clunk*.

'Gloamglozer blast you,' Xanth muttered under his breath as he paused and lifted it back onto his shoulder.

The box was heavy. Inside it were spanners and steel-brushes and an oil-can with a long, slender spout, as well as numerous more delicate instruments – a spindly plumb-line spirit-level to ensure the vertical ascent of the spike; a ratchet-grip used for aligning the teeth of the many interlocking cogs; and most important of all, a calibrated barometric astrolabe made of brass, the readings from which Xanth had to record faithfully and pass on to his master. The High Guardian's instructions had been clear.

Nothing must go wrong.

With a grim smile tugging at the corners of his mouth, Xanth wiped a hand over his sweaty brow and continued down the ladder. He realized he was panting.

Xanth had been up at the crack of dawn that morning, and though it was still early, the air was already hot and humid. It sapped his strength, leaving his body weary and making it difficult to concentrate.

He glanced round as he descended, pausing for a moment to take in the best view – aside from a skycraft saddle – in all of the Edge. He saw Undertown swarming, not with Undertowners, but with battalions of goblins. Reports had reached the tower that a curfew had been called, and the goblins were marching through the deserted streets and congregating in a large square to the east of the city. Far off in the opposite direction, he could just make out the shrykes also amassing in huge numbers, the colourful battle-flocks seeming to glow in the hazy light. And beyond all of this, he could see the great stacks of cloud beginning to coalesce to form a vast wall of swirling darkness.

Reaching the bottom of the ladder, Xanth stepped down onto the lookout-platform and opened the toolbox. He searched its contents for a moment before removing a metal bar, pointed at one end and with the metal head of a gloamglozer decorating the other. He examined it briefly, turning it over in his hand, the same grim smile playing on his lips. Suddenly a gruff voice spoke, making the hairs at the back of his neck stand on end.

'Who goes there?' it demanded.

Xanth spun round – slipping the metal implement into his pocket as he did so – to find himself confronted by a hulking cloddertrog guard, one hairy ham of a hand hovering near the handle of the great curved sword which hung at his belt. The cloddertrog's small red eyes narrowed and his nostrils flared.

Xanth glared back at him. 'It's me,' he retorted crossly. 'Xanth Filatine. You challenged me on my way up, you great oaf!'

'Password,' grunted the cloddertrog, his face betraying not a hint of emotion.

Xanth sighed. *'The rock demons screech,'* he intoned in a bored voice.

The cloddertrog guard's gruff voice grunted back the response mechanically. *'For soon they will be free.'*

'Satisfied?' said Xanth. 'Made absolutely sure it's the same Xanth Filatine you challenged half an hour ago?'

The cloddertrog's small eyes stared back, hard and stony. He made no move to let Xanth pass. 'Rules is rules,' he grunted. 'Even for a librarian-loving pet of the High Guardian . . .'

'What did you say?' thundered Xanth, his violet eyes blazing. 'I have the authority of the High Guardian of Night!'

'Rules is rules,' muttered the guard, a slight quiver in his voice.

'I could have you thrown into the foulest dungeon-ledge in the tower, you insolent wretch – and don't think I wouldn't,' Xanth continued, his eyes boring into the cloddertrog's. 'Go on, take a good look at this face and remember, the next time you show such insolence, you'll be seeing it from the other side of a dungeon peephole. Understand?'

The cloddertrog looked down at his heavy iron-shod boots, and moved to let Xanth pass.

'Understand?' the youth repeated.

'Yes,' said the guard in a low growl.

'That's better,' said Xanth, sweeping past, and disappearing from view down the winding staircase.

The cloddertrog stared after him. 'Xanth Filatine,' he growled, spitting out the youth's name. 'I'll remember your face, don't you worry about that.'

The tower was swarming with black-cloaked Guardians. They were on the gantry-landings, keeping watch, and on the jutting weapon platforms, tending to the harpoon-turrets and swivel catapults, in constant readiness for any attack. It seemed to Xanth, as he made his way down the winding staircase from Midnight's Spike, that just like the goblins and the shrykes, the Guardians of Night, too, were massing. Why, the entire guard seemed to have been turned out today.

'Step aside!' he barked time and again as he barged his way down the great tower. 'Make way! I'm on important business for the High Guardian!'

Past the spy-turrets and guard-decks he went, and down past the great gantry with the sinister feeding-cage glinting at the far end. The bars of the cage seemed to tremble in the hot, shimmering air. He was indeed on important business, he thought bitterly, but not for the High Guardian, Sky curse him. Right now, his master was probably laughing to himself behind that evil metal muzzle as he anticipated the Purification Ceremony scheduled to take place at noon.

But it wouldn't – not if he, Xanth Filatine, could do something about it. Magda, his friend, would not end up as bait for the rock demons, he would see to that! But time, Xanth realized, his pulse quickening, was not on their side. The minutes were ticking by.

'Move aside!' he shouted, barging his way through a group of Guardians, standing on an open landing.

As he hurried down lower still, the tower broadened and the single stairway became one of many. The air grew heavier and more oppressive, laced now with the scent of newly sawn wood and the odour of unwashed bodies. He passed Orbix Xaxis's living quarters, studies and stores, guardrooms and interrogation chambers, coming at last to the point where the tower divided up into an outer and inner section. The rooms and chambers formed the outer shell to the tower, with gantries of various lengths and widths protruding from their windows, while an inner wall encased the cavernous central atrium which housed the terrible prison-ledges. Xanth was sandwiched between the two of them, on a high, rectangular landing dimly lit by cowled oil-lanterns.

'Password,' demanded a tall flathead goblin, stepping from the flickering shadows.

'The rock demons screech,' said Xanth, catching his breath with difficulty. The air down here was stifling.

'For soon they will be free,' the goblin intoned. 'Pass, Guardian.'

Without so much as a backward glance, Xanth continued on his way. The further down he went into the shadowy depths, the hotter and more pungent the atmosphere became. Eerie sighs and moans penetrated the air from the other side of the wall.

Half walking, half running, Xanth entered the maze of narrow walkways and rickety flights of stairs zigzagging off in all directions around him. Each staircase led to a door set into the inner wall. Behind one of these doors was Magda Burlix – and Xanth knew exactly which one. It was a cell he knew well, for it had once belonged to his old friend, Cowlquape. Now, however, it was set aside for the librarian victims of the evil Purification Ceremony.

Arriving at the bottom of a familiar sloping flight of stairs, Xanth ran headlong into two hefty flathead guards standing in front of a low, studded door. One of them stepped forward, a heavy club in his hand, while the other lowered the crossbow he was carrying and pointed it at Xanth's chest.

'Halt, who goes there?' said the first.

'Xanth Filatine,' came the breathless reply. 'On important business for the High Guardian.'

The guard frowned. 'Password?' he said.

Xanth tutted impatiently. *'The rock demons screech,'* he said.

'For soon . . .'

'Yes, yes, just get on with it,' snapped Xanth with all the bluster he could manage. 'Orbix Xaxis himself has sent me here. He wishes to interrogate the prisoner personally.'

The guards exchanged glances, and the one with the crossbow shook his head uncertainly. 'Orbix Xaxis, you say,' he said slowly. 'We haven't been told anything . . .'

'Are you challenging my authority?' said Xanth, his voice dropping to a low, menacing growl. 'If you are, I shall make sure that the High Guardian hears of your insubordination.'

The guards exchanged looks again. Xanth seized his chance, brushing the club and crossbow aside as he strode between them. Before him stood the door to the cell, the names of its former occupants carved into the thick, dark wood. *Cowlquape Pentephraxis* was at the top; below it others, librarian knights who had paid the ultimate price for their steadfast loyalty to the Great Library. *Torvalt Limbus, Misha Blix, Estina Flembel* . . . And there, at the bottom of the terrible list, the name he had been hoping to see.

Magda Burlix.

He slid the bolts across, top and bottom. Then, ignoring the troubled muttering of the guards behind him, he straightened up, grasped the handle firmly and pushed the door open. It struck the back wall with an echoing thud.

Xanth stood in the doorway, reeling giddily. He would never get used to the yawning chasm which opened up before him – nor the appalling stench of sewage and death. Prisoners, perched on nearby ledges, who had heard the door being opened, fell to their knees, clasped their hands together beseechingly and pleaded with this newcomer to set them free.

'Have mercy, sweet master!' they cried, their eyes staring imploringly.

'Release me!' cried a one-eyed lugtroll.

'This is all a mistake! A terrible mistake!' wailed a grizzled former professor, his spangled robes hanging in filthy tatters.

Xanth tore his gaze away from the hapless prisoners and looked down the narrow open-staircase to the jutting ledge. There, sitting motionless in the middle – her face turned away and her long plaits hanging down the back of her flight-suit – was Magda.

'You stand when a Guardian enters!' Xanth barked, as he descended the flight of stairs.

Magda looked round wearily.

'Get up, scum!' he ordered, in a hard cold voice. 'And come with me. The High Guardian wishes to interrogate you further.'

Magda turned away but made no move to stand up. Xanth strode across the ledge and prodded her roughly with his boot.

'I said, get up!' he repeated. Magda didn't move. With a grunt of irritation, Xanth bent down, grabbed her by the arms and dragged her to her feet.

'Aaagh-*ow*!' Magda cried out, as Xanth twisted her arm round behind her back. 'You're hurting me!'

'Shut up, Sky curse you,' Xanth hissed in her ear, 'and do exactly as I say.'

At the top of the stairs, he shoved her roughly through the doorway, past the guards, and bundled her on up the next flight of stairs. Only when he reached the top and the guards were out of sight did he relax the upward pressure on her arm. He leaned forwards.

'Just keep walking,' he whispered into her ear. 'Don't say a word.'

Outside the open cell door, the two guards turned to one another.

'I don't like this one little bit,' said one, his finger stroking the trigger of his crossbow. 'What do you think old muzzle-face is up to?'

'Dunno,' said the other. He tapped the club down in his open palm; once, twice, three times, before thrusting it decisively into the sheath at his belt. 'I don't know about you,' he announced, 'but High Guardian or no

High Guardian, I'm going to find Leddix. After all, as cage-master, the librarian is *his* prisoner, strictly speaking.'

Meanwhile, in the dark walkways above, Xanth and Magda had come to an abrupt halt.

'I'm not going another step!' Magda said, turning on Xanth.

Xanth released her. 'Magda,' he said softly, 'I'm trying to save your life.'

'Save my life?' said Magda, breathless with disbelief. 'You struck me, remember? You called me librarian scum . . .'

'I'm sorry,' said Xanth brusquely. 'But I had to. I was being watched. If they'd suspected anything, I'd have joined you in the ceremonial cage as rock demon bait. I still might, if we don't hurry,' he added.

'You almost broke my arm!' Magda complained, rubbing her throbbing elbow.

'Magda, *please,*' said Xanth. 'When they realize you've escaped, they'll sound the tilderhorn alarm and then we'll be done for. We'll have the whole tower-guard after us. I'm telling you, we must get out of here as quickly as we possibly can.'

'But why should I trust you, Xanth?' Magda persisted obstinately, her green eyes flashing with anger. 'You betrayed the librarians at Lake Landing. You serve the High Guardian of Night. You lie. You deceive.' She shook her head. 'Why should I believe anyone who wears the sign of the accursed gloamglozer emblazoned on his front?'

Xanth looked up, his violet eyes full of sorrow. 'It is true,' he admitted. 'I have done many bad things. Terrible, unforgivable things. Yet you – *you*, Magda – you awoke in me memories of a better life, and with them the dream of leaving this place – for ever. Come with me, Magda, and I shall make sure you get back to the librarians.' His voice faltered. 'It is time I made amends for the terrible crimes I have committed.'

Magda's mouth pursed as she searched the shaven-headed youth's face. 'You'll get me back to the librarians?' she asked. 'Promise?'

Xanth smiled. 'I give you my word,' he said.

Magda held out her hand, and Xanth took it gratefully.

'We'll take the baskets used by Guardian patrols heading into Undertown,' he explained. 'The Eastern baskets. They'll bring us down close to the Edge, not far from the Stone Gardens. I know a path that'll take us to Undertown without having to venture through Screetown . . .'

'Come on then,' said Magda, striding ahead. 'What are we waiting for?'

'Not that way,' said Xanth, halting her in her tracks. '*This* way!'

With Xanth in front and Magda following close behind, the pair of them made their way through the labyrinth of staircases and walkways. Xanth never faltered for a moment – now taking a right-hand turning, now a corner to the left, now continuing straight on – without a second thought. Down here, close to the base of the tower, there seemed to be almost no Guardians at all – which wasn't surprising, Magda thought, as the air was so foul that breathing it was almost intolerable. Xanth turned sharply to his right and hurried down a long narrow corridor with light streaming in from the far end.

'This is it,' he said. 'The Eastern Gate.' He stopped abruptly and grabbed Magda's arm. 'I almost forgot,' he whispered. 'The baskets are guarded.'

Magda watched, bemused, as he reached up and pulled the black hooded gown over his head. Underneath it was a second gown, identical in every detail. Magda looked at the garment with distaste as Xanth held it out to her.

'It's for you,' he said. He nodded toward the green flight-suit. 'Make you a little less conspicuous.'

Magda pulled the heavy gown – still warm from Xanth's body-heat – over her head. She tugged at the cuffs and smoothed the material down, shuddering uneasily as her hand passed over the symbol of the screeching gloamglozer, now emblazoning her own chest.

'Raise the hood,' Xanth said, doing the same. 'And when we're outside, let me do all the talking.'

Together, the two of them stepped out, wincing involuntarily at the daylight, so blindingly bright after the subdued lampglow within the tower. At the far end of the long, broad gantry were half a dozen baskets, each one suspended from overhead pulley-wheels mounted at the top of jutting struts, three on each side. A single guard – a wizened gnokgoblin – looked up as they marched towards him.

He was dressed in a black gown the same as their own

– but several sizes too big for him. Pushing his sleeves halfway up his scrawny arms, he gripped his sword.

'Password,' he said.

'The rock demons screech,' said Xanth.

'For . . . for soon . . .' The gnokgoblin frowned, a look of confusion flitting across his features. 'Very good,' he said, his voice quavering as if in fear of a reprimand. 'Business in Undertown, Guardians?'

'That's no concern of yours,' said Xanth, striding past him, Magda at his heels.

The gnokgoblin moved aside, stumbling over the trailing hem of the gown as he did so. Xanth was already at the baskets. He climbed into furthermost one and helped Magda in after him.

Xanth took up a position on the raised winding-stool and unhitched the chain from the mooring-cleat. 'Hold tight,' he whispered to Magda. He let the links of the chain slide through his hands and slipped his feet into the winding-pedals.

The gnokgoblin watched them from the tower entrance. Once he had been fierce in battle, fighting alongside flatheads and hammerheads twice his size, and often taking the greatest trophy. These days, though, battles were no more than distant memories. His bones were old and his muscles shrivelled. Too weak to fight and too blind to operate the gantry weapons, he'd been appointed a basket-guard. It was one of the lowliest positions in the Tower of Night – yet it had its compensations. Leddix paid him well to keep his eyes and ears open.

The gnokgoblin smiled as the two Guardians disappeared from sight. *Business in Undertown,* indeed! Approaching the edge of the landing, he gave a long, low whistle.

Below, Magda gasped as the basket dropped down, concerned at the alarming way it twisted and lurched. Although she had countless flights to her name, there was a world of difference between being airborne in her beloved *Woodmoth* – the skycraft she had created with her own bare hands and which obeyed her every flight-command – and being suspended in this creaking basket from a disturbingly rusty-looking length of chain.

The lower they dropped, the closer the diseased Sanctaphrax rock came. At one point, Magda could have reached out and touched the crumbling rock – and would have, were it not for her fear of setting the unstable basket rocking. The porous rock was riven with cracks and fissures and huge boulder-shaped chunks threatened to break away at any moment. A small, grey creature with long twitching ears caught her eye as it scampered over the pitted surface in a flurry of dust and was gone.

'We'll soon be level with the Sanctaphrax Forest,' said

Xanth. The winding-pedals creaked softly as they turned.

Magda nodded. A moment later, the dark and damaged rock gave way to the vast wooden cross-beams and pillars constructed to support it.

'The Sanctaphrax Forest,' she whispered, her voice trembling with awe.

No wonder they called it a forest, Magda thought. Half the Deepwoods must have been cut down to build it. As she stared at the great vertical pylons thrusting up from the ground like mighty tree-trunks, and the chaotic jumble of branch-like struts and supports, transoms, rafters and beams, it seemed that *forest* was exactly the right word for the place.

A dark forest. An endless forest. A *living* forest . . .

It was almost as if the very spirit of the Deepwoods themselves had been transported here along with the trees that had been felled.

The so-called *forest*, she knew, served a dual purpose. Originally, it had been constructed to prevent the stricken rock from crushing Undertown below. The endeavour had not been entirely successful – as the ruins of Screetown bore terrible witness; yet, thanks to the vision of Vox Verlix and the endless backbreaking toil of the slave-workers, damage had been kept to a minimum. The other purpose was altogether more contentious. As everyone knew, the Guardians – in stark contrast to the librarians – believed that the rock must be kept from touching the ground if the coming lightning bolt was to heal it. It had been the cause of their terrible rift and the reason why the Guardians still hated the librarians.

Magda turned to Xanth. 'So you believe in the sacred lightning bolt, do you?' she said. 'Curing stone-sickness.'

Xanth hesitated and looked up. The basket turned around again. 'As a Guardian, I do,' he said, 'though my studies at Lake Landing with the librarians left me less certain . . .' He shrugged and resumed the long descent. 'Maybe none of them are right,' he said a moment later. 'Maybe there really is no cure for stone-sickness, in the sky *or* in the Deepwoods.'

Magda shook her head. 'As a librarian knight, I have to believe there is a cure out there in the Deepwoods somewhere. But what I don't understand is why the Guardians hate us so much for believing that. After all, we all want the same thing, don't we?'

Xanth looked away. 'I used to believe that, Magda. But the minds of the Guardians have been poisoned by sky-watching and envy. It is not only the stone that is sick. I only wish I had realized that sooner,' he added softly.

The basket lurched to one side, then righted itself. Magda swallowed nervously and gripped the sides of the basket till her knuckles went white. As the basket slowly turned, she found herself staring into the shadowy depths of the great wooden structure and heard a curious *whiffling* noise, like air passing through a narrow opening. She turned to see a bat-like creature with hooks on its wings and a long rubbery snout soaring through the criss-cross shadows and coming in to land on a tatty nest, one of many lined up along the broad crossbeam. It was a dwarf-rotsucker.

The breathy whistling sounds grew louder, and Magda realized that the creature was not alone. Dozens of others, their leathery wings wrapped tightly round them, filled the shadows behind it. An acrid smell of droppings made her nostrils quiver. This was clearly a regular roosting spot for the whole flock; a place they came to every morning, to rest up in the dark shadows and wait for nightfall – the creature she had watched must have been a straggler . . .

With a lurch, the basket dropped further and the dwarf-rotsuckers disappeared. A new sound filled the air. The sound of hard toil. There was sawing and chopping, and the shifting rhythm of numerous pounding hammers – and underlying it all, a constant low moaning: the sound of despair.

'Right, now try again,' bellowed a deep, throaty voice. 'And this time, put your backs into it!' A whip cracked and the moaning grew louder. 'Lift it higher! *Higher!*'

'Slave gang,' Xanth muttered grimly. 'The work on the forest never stops.'

The slave-master's furious voice echoed up through the air. 'Imbecile!' he bellowed and the whip cracked louder than ever. 'Do that again, and I'll snap your scrawny neck!'

Magda shuddered.

Xanth continued turning the winding-pedals steadily, and as the basket dropped Magda found herself face to face with the slave gang itself. She gasped and clapped her hands to her mouth.

Magda knew, of course, that the life of a slave was

harsh, particularly those assigned to work on the Sanctaphrax Forest. Nothing, though, could have prepared her for the sight of the group of pitiful unfortunates before her.

There were a dozen or so of them in all, from every part of the Edge. Beneath the grimy skin and matted hair, she could make out mobgnomes, gyle-goblins; a cloddertrog, a lugtroll, a pair of flatheads . . . Here, however, as slave-labour in the Sanctaphrax Forest, their backgrounds counted for nothing.

Wearing nothing but filthy loin-cloths, the hapless slaves were balanced precariously on rickety scaffolding and flimsy boards, their arms raised, struggling under the weight of the massive ironwood crossbeam they were attempting to push into place. Magda watched them, tears welling in her eyes. Their straining muscles were like knots of rope; their protruding bones, like sticks – for if there was one thing that the slaves had in common, it was this. They were all being starved to death.

'There's nothing you can do,' said Xanth softly.

Magda's face crumpled. 'I know,' she said. 'That's the worst thing of all.'

The moaning rose and fell in waves as the slaves tried, again and again, to raise the heavy crossbeam high enough.

'Higher! Higher!' bellowed a voice, and a great hammerhead goblin with a horned brass helmet and heavy leather armour stepped out of the shadows. He cracked his whip. 'Half a stride more!' he roared, urging the slaves forward.

Just then there was a muffled cry and Magda saw one of the gyle-goblins stumble and fall to his knees. Moaning loudly, the other slaves wobbled precariously, desperately trying not to let go of the ironwood beam. The hammerhead slave-master strode forward furiously, seized the quivering gyle-goblin by the scruff of his neck and raised him high up into the air.

'I warned you!' he hissed. 'You're more trouble than you're worth.' He twisted the terrified gyle-goblin round and gripped him tightly in the crook of his elbow. He turned to the others. 'You're going to have to work even harder now!' he bellowed.

He seized the goblin's head and wrenched it sharply to the right. There was a dull crack.

Magda let out a cry of horror.

The hammerhead spun round and glared at her. 'Guardians, eh?' he sneered.

Magda looked down, grateful for the hooded gown which concealed her tear-stained face.

'Greetings,' Xanth called back, easing up on the winding-pedals for a moment. 'It is good to know that the welfare of the sacred Sanctaphrax rock is in such competent hands. The High Guardian himself shall hear of your excellent work.'

The slave-master tossed the limp body of the dead gyle-goblin off the platform and placed his hands on his hips.

'So long as old muzzle-face keeps paying, then we'll look after his precious rock,' he snarled. A crooked smile, all broken teeth and dark intent, flashed across his face. 'Perhaps *you'd* like to lend a hand . . .'

Xanth said nothing. He turned the winding-pedals with renewed vigour.

Magda could not speak. The condition of the slaves, condemned to labour until they dropped, had shocked her to the core; while the casual brutality of the slave-master played over and over in her mind. Although the moaning of the slaves soon faded away as the basket dropped lower, their memory would linger on so long as she lived.

'Magda,' said Xanth, turning to the young librarian. She didn't stir, lost in her own thoughts. 'Magda! We've arrived.' The basket touched down on the ground with a soft thud and Xanth secured the brake-lever before any more chain could unwind. He jumped down from the winding-stool and climbed out of the basket. 'Magda,' he said a third time, grasping her shoulders tightly with both hands. 'We've almost made it. The worst is over.'

'For us, maybe,' said Magda bleakly.

With Xanth's help, she climbed out of the basket and looked about her distractedly.

'Looking for something?' came a gruff voice.

Magda started back with surprise. Xanth spun round to see a cloddertrog guard standing before him, his thick heavy arms folded in front of him.

'*The rock demons screech*,' he said.

The guard eyed him dismissively, a sneer playing over his mouth. 'I recognize that face,' he said with an evil leer. He unfolded his arms and drew a heavy club from his belt. Vicious studs glinted in the heavy sunlight.

'Step aside this instant!' Xanth commanded, his voice breaking with outrage. 'I am Xanth Filatine, following orders given to me by the High Guardian himself. If he were to find out . . .'

Just then there was a stirring from the shadows behind him and a wiry individual with lank hair and weasely features stepped from the shadow.

'The High Guardian will find out soon enough,' came a thin voice.

'Leddix,' said Xanth, the colour draining from his cheeks.

'Surprised to see me, eh, Xanth?' the cage-master asked. 'Did you not realize that I have been having you watched?' He chuckled softly. 'I've been waiting for this moment for a long time, my treacherous friend. A very long time . . .'

'You're . . . you're making a big mistake, Leddix,' said Xanth. 'I'm warning you.'

'*You* warning *me*?' Leddix said, his face creasing with amusement. 'Oh, but you're a slippery one, Xanth Filatine. Sucking up to the High Guardian; poisoning his mind against me with your traitorous lies.' His expression hardened. 'But now I've got you, like a fat oozefish wriggling at the end of a line . . .'

'How *dare* you!' said Xanth with all the cold fury he could muster.

Leddix clicked his fingers and the cloddertrog guard leapt forward, his club raised and swinging.

'Watch out!' Magda cried.

But too late. The heavy studded club struck Xanth hard on the back of his head with a sickening crunch. The last thing Xanth saw was Leddix's goading smile, cruel in victory. Thin lips. Brown teeth. Dead eyes . . .

Then nothing.

·CHAPTER FOURTEEN·

AMBERFUCE

Nobody but a waif could understand how difficult it was, thought Amberfuce bitterly. His barbels quivered as he drew a circle in the thick dust that coated the crowded medicine stand beside his buoyant chair.

Needs dusting!

His icy thought cut through the muddle in his nurse's huge head.

'Ooh,' came a screech from the room next door, accompanied by the sound of a glass stopper being dropped. 'How many times must I tell you, Ambey, dear?' Flambusia called out. 'Nursie doesn't like you barging into her head!'

'Sorry, Flambusia,' whispered the waif in a pathetic voice.

Not even Flambusia – big, beautiful Flambusia, who nursed him, soothing his aches and easing his pains – not even *she* understood how difficult it was being a waif. All those thoughts in all those heads; whispering, moaning, shouting, without a moment's respite . . .

Eighty years ago, in the dark marshy waiflands, far off in the furthest reaches of the known Edgelands, it had been so different. Amberfuce's eyes glazed over and a smile set his barbels quivering. He remembered the delicious silence that had surrounded him as a waifling; so empty, so comforting – and broken only by the occasional whispering of another ghostwaif out there somewhere in the endless distance.

Amberfuce sighed.

Like so many before him, he'd been drawn to Undertown, lured by the promise of a better life and riches beyond imagining. Most found only misery and despair. But not Amberfuce.

The waif's smile widened and his eyes twinkled.

He had found employment. There was always employment to be found for a clever waif who was good at keeping quiet and listening. Amberfuce had kept his huge ears open and had soon secured himself a lucrative position in the School of Light and Darkness, snooping on the gossiping academics for his master, an ambitious High Professor.

Long dead now, Amberfuce thought darkly.

The professor had been the first of many masters, all interested and ready to pay for what he overheard in the gabbling, gossiping, endlessly noisy old Sanctaphrax. So many thoughts! So much noise!

Amberfuce leaned across to scratch at a dry, flaky patch of skin itching at the back of his knee.

He'd soon learned though; learned how to blot out the incessant babble and listen selectively. It had been hard.

Many waifs were driven insane after a few years in Undertown. But not Amberfuce. He was made of sterner stuff – and besides, he had his medicine.

A cough racked his frail body as he surveyed the rows of dusty bottles, nestling on the medicine stand. The large jars contained his tinctures; potent concoctions which soothed his poor, tired ears. The tall slender vessels were filled with salves and balms. And then there were the embrocations, greasy and black – how he enjoyed Flambusia's rough hands applying them . . .

Amberfuce chuckled throatily – and collapsed into a fit of coughing which, this time, showed no sign of abating.

'Oh, dearie-dearie me!' said Flambusia, bustling into the chamber, her heavy stack-heels clacking on the marble tiles. 'Can I never get a moment's peace and quiet?'

She hurried across the floor to the quivering waif, unstoppering a squat blue pot as she went. A pungent whiff of eye-watering sagemint and woodcamphor filled the air.

'Now, shirt up for Nursie,' Flambusia said calmly, 'and let's rub a little vapour embrocation into that chest of yours.'

She opened his gown and tugged at his undershirt with one hand then, dipping the other into the jar, she loomed in above the waif. As her plump, deliciously rough fingers worked the embrocation into his pallid, mottled skin, Amberfuce could feel his lungs being soothed. The coughing eased. He sat back in his chair, eyes closed.

He could make out Flambusia's thoughts in the background; fussy, cluttered and . . . what was that?

He stopped himself probing – he knew how she hated that – and tried to think of something else.

Professors! What a noisy squabbling rabble they were, the whole lot of them, with their petty grievances and niggling dislikes . . . But then he had met Vox Verlix, a junior professor in the College of Cloud; tall and opinionated, a braggart and a bully, never happier than when throwing his weight about. Young and callow though Vox was, Amberfuce had sensed something about him – something beyond the naked ambition, the base desires . . .

The waif smiled. It was Vox's mind – his brilliant, unfathomable mind – that had fascinated him. He had known at once that he could really *work* with this professor and that is exactly what he had set about doing.

'That should do you for now,' Flambusia announced, pulling the waif's undershirt back down and straightening his gown. 'Now don't you go getting yourself all excited again,' she chided him. 'You know it's not good for you.'

'Tea,' Amberfuce murmured, his eyes fluttering open for a moment. 'I'd like some nice herb tea.'

'Presently,' said Flambusia, turning away. 'Nursie's a bit busy at the moment. You get some rest, Ambey, dear.'

Amberfuce nodded resignedly, and closed his eyes again.

Ah yes, those early days as Vox's assistant . . . They'd

certainly been eventful. There had been the Mother Storm, and the loss of old Sanctaphrax, and the birth of the new rock. What times they'd been! Amberfuce rocked backwards and forwards in the buoyant chair.

Vox had ingratiated himself with the young fool of a High Academe, Cowlquape Pentephraxis. He'd pretended to believe in all that academics-and-Undertowners-being-the-same nonsense. And all the while, he, Amberfuce, had been listening and reporting back to Vox so that when the opportunity arose, the pair of them had been ready and waiting.

Stone-sickness had taken hold of the Edge, the new Sanctaphrax rock had begun to crumble and the leaguesmen's once mighty fleet had been decimated by the failing flight-rocks. Undertown and New Sanctaphrax had been in turmoil, and Cowlquape in despair. Vox had come up with a brilliant plan – the construction of a vast single tower on the Sanctaphrax rock, to replace the smaller buildings that the various squabbling schools and academies had built. The earth-scholars – their numbers increasing and influence growing – could have the lower levels for their Great Library. From there they could continue to search the Deepwoods for a cure for stone-sickness. The sky-scholars could inhabit the upper levels, establishing laboratories and workrooms and, most importantly, supervising the building of a mighty spike. This, they believed, would harness the power of any passing lightning and heal the stricken rock beneath.

It had been a masterly plan. Vox's plans always were.

Yet it was he, Amberfuce – negotiator, manipulator, deal-breaker – who, as always, had been charged with putting it into effect.

The smile on the ghostwaif's pale face broadened. He had been clever; very clever. He had persuaded the most important leaguesmen of Undertown to use their few remaining ships to carry one last cargo of Deepwoods timber into the city. Then, when the tower's construction had consumed the last of this, he had organized gangs of Undertowners to tear down entire districts to furnish the rest. And of course, while acting for Vox, Amberfuce had been careful to skim off fees and commissions for himself. The work had almost bankrupted the academics, but the Tower of Night had been completed.

From the ante-chamber, there came the sound of liquids being poured and the clinking of a spoon stirring. Amberfuce opened his eyes and glanced round hopefully – but there was no sign of Flambusia, with or without the herb tea. Ahead of him was the window, with the fuzzy outline of the tall, imposing tower seeming almost to mock him from behind the billowing lace curtain.

'Ah, me, the Tower of Night,' he murmured ruefully. 'Our first great masterpiece.' His voice was soft and rasping. 'How did it go so wrong?'

Looking back at it, of course, it was perfectly obvious. The earth-scholars had hated the tower from the start, and the Knights Academy had split into sky and earth factions. Once the library had been established, those knights sympathetic to the ideals of the earth-scholars had joined them. Together, they became known as the librarians. They had been opposed by the sky-scholars, who had gathered under the leadership of a wall-eyed, pasty-faced individual by the name of Orbix Xaxis. They had called themelves the Guardians of Night.

Librarians and Guardians; the two sides had prepared themselves for a showdown.

Amberfuce chuckled. He'd never heard such a hub-bub! Such dark thoughts and high emotion! He'd told Vox to side with the Guardians – and had taken a nice fee from Orbix into the bargain.

What a night that had been! thought Amberfuce, sitting back in his buoyant chair. *The Night of the Gloam-glozers.*

In their new black uniforms, emblazoned with the screeching evil creatures, the Guardians had launched their attack. All those openly loyal to Cowlquape had been swept from power, many paying with their lives – while the Most High Academe himself had disappeared.

Vox, Amberfuce remembered, had declared himself the new Most High Academe, and made him – Amberfuce – his chancellor. It made him tremble just to think of it. A small ghostwaif from the Deepwoods, High Chancellor of New Sanctaphrax and Undertown!

Where was his herb tea? he wondered, looking back towards the ante-chamber and strumming his fingers impatiently on the arms of the buoyant chair. What was taking Flambusia so long?

Of course it hadn't lasted. The Guardians had seen to that.

'Accursed ingrates!' Amberfuce wheezed bitterly.

He should have seen it coming, of course. He should have read Orbix Xaxis's dark thoughts more carefully but, drunk on power, he'd become negligent. It was more by luck than judgement that, on that fateful night when Orbix had made his move and sent Guardians to throw Vox and his chancellor from the high gantry to their deaths, he had been alert . . .

Orbix had wanted the tower all for himself and had planned to slaughter the increasingly obstructive librarians, always carping and complaining, and blocking his plans. It had been Amberfuce who, sensing that they might yet prove of use, had sent the librarians word, just in time – and together they had all fled to Undertown.

Vox and Amberfuce had taken refuge in the Palace of Statues which, with the collapse of the great merchant leagues, had been abandoned and was lying empty. That was when Amberfuce had first moved into his precious little chamber . . .

The waif sighed wearily. Where *had* all the years gone?

At first, the pair of them had prospered in the Palace of Statues. Vox, the new Most High Academe, had been accepted by the Undertowners and, with his chancellor Amberfuce in charge of trade and taxes, the gold had soon been flowing in. The Guardians of Night had kept themselves to themselves, holed up in the Tower of Night and waiting for their blessed storm. A queasy equilibrium seemed to have been established.

But Amberfuce had known that it couldn't last, for Undertown was all but cut off from the Deepwoods. Dealings with the sky pirates had continued for a while longer, but soon – as their sky ships also fell prey to the relentlessly advancing stone-sickness – business in Undertown had ground to a halt. Panic-buying turned to looting. Mobs had taken to the streets. The economy had been on the verge of total collapse . . .

With noon approaching and the sun high in the sky, the motes of dust in the chamber fluttered like particles of gold in the shafts of light streaming in from outside.

Amberfuce felt a tickle in his throat and put his handkerchief to his mouth to filter out the dust, cursing Flambusia for being such a poor housekeeper. The whole chamber needed a good clean. Time was when he would have done it himself – removing every medicine bottle and tincture pot and dusting them with fastidious care. But not now . . .

Amberfuce sighed, and closed his eyes to the neglected room. Vox! he thought. What an incredible talent for invention he had possessed!

He recalled Vox's face when he'd come to him late one night, his hair all sticking up, and his eyes burning with excitement. He'd pulled a roll of parchment from a tube and flattened it out on Amberfuce's desk, to reveal the blueprint for a long complicated construction, mounted upon stilts.

'It's a kind of bridge. It'll extend all the way from the Deepwoods to Undertown. I'm going to called it the Great Mire Road,' Vox had explained, his hands flapping about animatedly. 'Just think of it, Amberfuce. It will be Undertown's connection with the riches of the Deep-woods. I've already enlisted the help of the librarians. They're only too delighted to restore our links with the Deepwoods. We'll need their expertise with wood – you know what they're like; they know everything, from which acorn sprouts in summer, to which part of the ironwood log is strongest . . .'

'I hate to pour cold water on this brilliant scheme of yours,' Amberfuce had replied. 'It's all well and good building a bridge across the Mire, but how do you propose to get through the Twilight Woods?'

'The shrykes!' Vox had exclaimed, his eyes blazing. 'We'll do a deal with the shrykes! They're immune to the effects of the Twilight Woods. They can build a road through them to connect with our bridge! And then, Amberfuce, the riches of the Deepwoods will be in our hands.'

'And in the claws of the shrykes,' Amberfuce had added darkly.

'You can do a deal, Amberfuce,' Vox had replied. 'If anyone can, *you* can.'

Vox was right. Amberfuce had done a deal with the leathery, golden-eyed old bird, Mother Feathergizzard. As roost-mother of the vast nomadic shryke flock, she had agreed – admittedly, for a high price – to construct the Great Mire Road through the Twilight Woods.

Thereafter, in return, she would be allowed to tax that part of the road.

Everything had gone perfectly, Amberfuce remembered. The Twilight Woods stretch of the new road had been finished within six months, enabling fresh timber to be brought in from the Deepwoods so that the librarians and Undertowners could work on the longer section which crossed the Mire. It had taken three years to complete. Mother Feathergizzard had taken her tax – both in gold and in kind – and Amberfuce, as ever, had skimmed his own fee off the top.

'Ah, happy days,' he sighed, his voice muffled by the handkerchief. 'Happy days.'

It was only when the final section of the road had been put into place, joining the easternmost point of the road to the westernmost end of Undertown, that Vox had discovered just how high a price he had had to pay for the shrykes' help. The first wagons had just begun to roll when a shryke army had swarmed down the road and seized the whole Great Mire Road for themselves.

Still, it could have been worse, Amberfuce conceded. The shrykes had taken control of the road to the Deepwoods, it was true, but at least he and Vox had still had the citizens of Undertown to squeeze for taxes. And squeeze they had. Amberfuce had become richer than ever, forcing the dealers and merchants to pay duty on the Deepwoods' materials the moment they entered Undertown; then again before they could take their merchandise – fine cloth, tools and weaponry – from the workshops of Undertown back out of the city. By the time they had paid off the shrykes as well, there had been barely any profit left. No wonder they had always been complaining.

Amberfuce had listened to the mutterings, the threats and curses. The mood had grown ugly. There had been talk of rebellion; of revolution; of the Undertowners rising up and overthrowing Vox. And at the head of this mob – inciting an uprising and sowing the seeds of discontent – had been the librarians, Sky curse them!

Amberfuce's brow furrowed. The librarians had been useful in building the Mire Road certainly, but afterwards they had begun getting above themselves. What was more, still believing in all the nonsense Cowlquape had preached about Undertowners and academics being equal, they had proved themselves to be as dangerous as they were foolish. They had had to be stopped.

Amberfuce gazed from the window at the Tower of Night on the crumbling rock, propped up by the scaffolding of the Sanctaphrax Forest.

It had been a good bargain. Even now, he still believed that. Amberfuce had overheard talk of a great meeting being held at the Chantry Palace; the grand riverside building the librarians had made their headquarters. The leading Undertown merchants would be there, as well as the entire librarian faculty. It was too good an opportunity to miss. The traitorous vermin could be destroyed in one fell swoop . . . But they would need an army of ruthless killers to carry out the deed.

Amberfuce turned away from the window. 'Orbix Xaxis and the Guardians of Night,' he muttered. Yes, it had been a good bargain. He'd convinced Vox of that.

'The sacred rock is sinking,' he remembered his master saying at that fateful meeting between him and his enemy, Orbix Xaxis. 'But I can stop it before it touches the earth. Just think of it, Orbix,' Vox had said. 'The thing you fear most; the sacred rock touching the ground – and I'm offering to prevent that.'

'How?' the voice had rasped from behind the metal muzzle.

'By designing a great cradle of wood – the Sanctaphrax Forest – to hold the sacred rock in place. You know I can do it, Orbix . . . If I so choose.'

'And if you build such a thing, what price would I have to pay?' Orbix had growled.

'Oh, you'll enjoy this,' Vox had chuckled, his three chins wobbling – for he had been growing fat even back then, Amberfuce remembered. 'All you have to do is slaughter the whole librarian faculty and their cronies, the merchants. I trust you can handle that, Xaxis, my dear fellow.'

Amberfuce shivered. Xaxis *had* handled that. His Guardians had surrounded the palace where the librarians had been holed up three nights later, and there had been a mighty slaughter. The streets around the great building had run red with librarian blood, and yet . . .

There always seemed to be an *and yet*, Amberfuce thought bitterly.

And yet, some librarians had managed to fight their way out and had disappeared down into the sewers, where they had remained, like piebald rats, to this very day.

'Sky bless the librarians,' smiled Amberfuce; for even now, they had their uses . . .

'Soon be with you, sweet'ums,' Flambusia called from the ante-chamber. 'The pot's just coming to the boil.'

Amberfuce coughed weakly. Herb tea was just what he needed to soothe his parched throat. He looked around. Now, did he have everything he needed? It would be a long journey . . . Yes, it was all here. Flambusia could sweep all his medicines into that great bag of hers in two seconds. Dear, sweet Flambusia. Of course, she must come with him. He couldn't possibly leave *her* behind. Oh, no! Though there were plenty of others he would be glad to see the back of . . .

General Tytugg for one.

Amberfuce remembered his first meeting with the wily old hammerhead thug. He'd been introduced by Amberfuce's business partner, Hemuel Spume of the Foundry Glade. Hemuel looked after the Deepwoods side of Amberfuce's operation – and highly profitable it had become, too.

'Meet Tytugg,' Spume had smiled. 'He's visiting Undertown from the Goblin Nations, and I think he might be just what you're looking for.'

Amberfuce had looked at Tytugg's battle-scarred face,

ears ragged with sword cuts; tattooed arms and dented armour. He'd been impressed.

Needless to say, getting rid of the librarians hadn't been quite the answer to their problems that Amberfuce had hoped. In fact, even without the librarians' influence, the population of Undertown had proven maddeningly unco-operative – and the Guardians had been demanding that work on the Sanctaphrax Forest begin at once. There had been walkouts and pay-demands and a downing of tools. It had all been bad for business.

Of course, Vox hadn't seemed to notice. He had been working on his drawings and blueprints, absurdly happy to have another great project underway. No, it had been down to Amberfuce, as usual, to make Vox's plans a reality. There had been only one thing for it . . .

A small tingle ran down the waif's puny back. 'Slavery,' he whispered.

Since the Undertowners hadn't been prepared to work voluntarily, they had to be made to work. They'd had it too easy for too long. Amberfuce had decided to turn them into slaves. To do that, though, he had needed slave-drivers; an army of slave-drivers.

'*I* have an army,' Tytugg had said, 'out in the Goblin Nations. And none of your rabble of tufteds and long-hairs either. These are trained hammerheads and battle-hardened flatheads. But I warn you, Mister High Chancellor, sir,' he'd added darkly. 'We don't come cheap.'

'Oh, there'll be plenty of money for all of us,' Amberfuce had laughed. 'Just get your army to Undertown and

I promise you healthy profits for your trouble.'

Over the next few weeks, hammerhead and flathead goblins had travelled down the Great Mire Road in twos and threes, disguised as tinkers and tailors, trappers and traders, and merchants of every description. The shrykes had never suspected a thing. The ghostwaif chancellor had been there to receive them all in Undertown, ticking off the numbers. Soon, there had been a great army of the goblins dispersed in every part of Undertown, laying low – until Amberfuce had given General Tytugg the signal to act.

The waif rocked in his chair, rubbing his long spidery hands together as he thought of it. *The Week of Blood!* Over the next seven days, every single Undertowner had been systematically rounded up. Those unable to work – the elderly, the infirm – had been slaughtered on the spot. The rest had been enslaved. They were to be forced to work on the Sanctaphrax Forest – but first, there had been mass graves to dig . . .

Amberfuce yawned. 'Ends and means,' he muttered, nibbling at a fingernail, more ragged than the rest. He smirked to himself. Vox had been happy with the way things had turned out. And he, Amberfuce, had made a mint!

And yet . . .

There it was again. Amberfuce stopped his rocking and let his hands fall limply in his lap. If only Tytugg hadn't been so greedy. He should have detected that greed in the goblin general when they'd first met. It had spoiled everything. Instead of being happy sharing the profits from the sweatshops and foundries, and supplying the Sanctaphrax Forest workforce, General Tytugg had wanted it all.

He had simply cut Vox and Amberfuce out of the loop. Then he had maintained the Forest *and* run Undertown single-handed. There had been rumours – Amberfuce had heard them – that Tytugg had wanted Vox's chain of office so that he could declare himself Most High Academe.

The cheek of it! he thought indignantly. An uncouth hammerhead from the Goblin Nations, Most High Academe! It was absurd! But he also knew Tytugg wouldn't stop until Vox, and he, were dead. Amberfuce shook his head. Those two goblin assassins had come perilously close . . .

And so, it had come to this. Vox was a prisoner in the Palace of Statues with a handful of faithful servants to watch over him and a series of traps and murder-holes to keep the goblins at bay. That might be all right for Hestera the poisoner, besotted with her master; and old

Speegspeel, stupid but faithful – but not Amberfuce. He had a fortune salted away with Hemuel Spume in the Foundry Glade, and no way to get to it.

Vox was finished. Undertown was finished. It was high time he looked out for himself.

Just then, Flambusia bustled back into the room, a steaming glass of herb tea held in one hand, a plate of wafer-biscuits in the other. She placed them both down on a tall, slender table and pulled Amberfuce's buoyant chair over beside it.

'There,' she said. 'Herb tea and a little treat. But first you've got to be good and take your special medicine.' She pulled a small glass bottle from her apron, unstoppered the cork and poured out a spoonful of dark red liquid. Then, having returned the bottle to the apron-pocket, she stepped towards him. 'Open wide!' she chirped.

I don't think so, Flambusia. Amberfuce's icy thought entered the nurse's head. *I need to keep my thoughts clear. So, no special medicine, not today. Understand?*

'Ambey, dear,' the nurse protested. 'Stop it, you know I don't like it when you . . .'

Understand, Flambusia? The waif's eyes narrowed and the barbels at the corners of his thin mouth quivered. *Clear away the clutter. Empty your mind . . . completely . . .*

Flambusia dropped the spoon and sank to her knees with a whimper.

Give me the medicine. The waif's thought numbed the inside of Flambusia Flodfox's head. She held out the bottle and a thin, spidery hand took it. *Now pack up the rest of my bottles – carefully, mind. Then take me to Speegspeel. I have one last little errand for him.* He looked at the medicine bottle in his hand and laughed, darkly.

The nurse's huge head nodded dumbly.

'Excellent,' Amberfuce said, smiling. 'And Flambusia, my sweet . . .' The nurse hesitated, her eyes blank and stony. 'Do hurry, for time is short.'

·CHAPTER FIFTEEN·

SLAD, SLASHTALON AND STYX

i
The Goblin Army

'It's time, Slad, the phalanx is forming!' The gruff voice was followed by a booted prod to the legs. The swarthy hammerhead goblin looked up to see his comrade, Dunkrigg, staring down at him. 'Look sharp!' he grunted.

Slad sat up. 'I must have nodded off,' he muttered. He pulled himself stiffly to his feet and, still groggy from his short nap, reached for the heavy curved shield and distinctive horned helmet of the elite hammerhead guard. He strapped the helmet in place between his wide-set eyes and raised the shield to his shoulder. 'I'm ready,' he said.

Dunkrigg nodded.

Around them, packed into the large gloomy square,

were goblins of all shapes and sizes – squat, stocky gnokgoblins in simple armour; hefty flatheads carrying heavy clubs; tufteds and long-haired goblins armed with curved bows and bristling quivers of arrows; ridge-browed and lop-eared goblins, and saw-toothed goblins with their distinctive carved stabbing spears. Each one was inked, branded or ringed with the specific marks of his individual tribe: each one was ready for battle.

At their head, the hammerhead guards formed up into the awesome battle phalanx, two hundred wide and three hundred deep, their shields overlapping and forming an impenetrable wall.

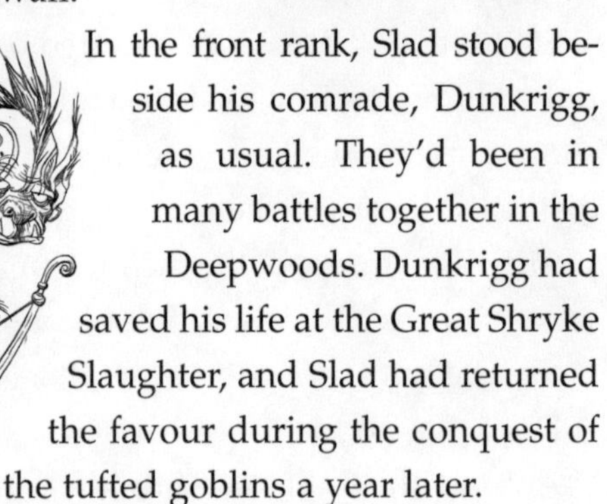

In the front rank, Slad stood beside his comrade, Dunkrigg, as usual. They'd been in many battles together in the Deepwoods. Dunkrigg had saved his life at the Great Shryke Slaughter, and Slad had returned the favour during the conquest of the tufted goblins a year later.

They were hammerheads. They lived for battle. Here in Undertown, however, life was far less dramatic. Here it was endless drill and the tedium of long hours in the Hive Towers, with only the occasional skirmish with a runaway slave or an errant factory-master to look forward to. Tonight, however, would be different; tonight their enemy would have nowhere to run and nowhere to hide.

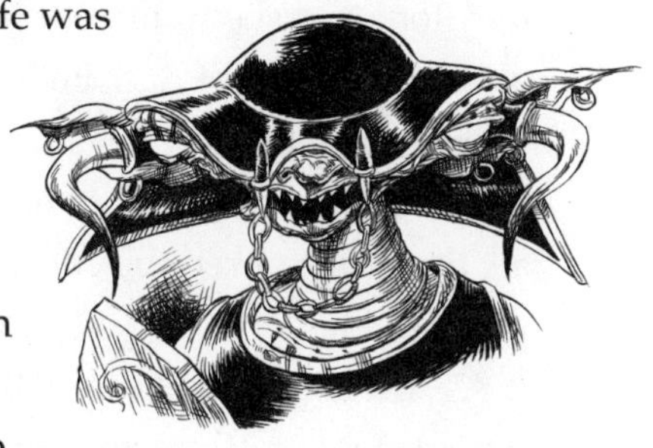

'Librarian scum,' growled Slad.

In front of him, the phalanx leader looked across to where General Tytugg stood on a raised stone plinth, waiting for an order. The general raised his curved sword.

'*Phalanx!*' he roared. '*Advance!*'

Slad grunted with approval as he fell into step with the others. No more drill, no more patrols, no more unsatisfying skirmishes. Finally the great battle they'd all been promised was about to begin. As the phalanx strode noisily out of the square and down the broad thoroughfare, Slad raised his head proudly. He liked the feel of his muscles, powerful and strong, as he marched. How they tingled, how they clenched; how they longed to be tested out in brutal armed-combat. He liked the weight of his armour, the solid tramping of his boots – and the fact that there were so many of them marching in step that the very ground trembled. Most of all, though, he liked the effect the great army was having on the inhabitants of Undertown.

As they marched past the ramshackle buildings, setting doors rattling and tiles falling, Slad caught sight of innumerable Undertowners woken from their sleep, peeking furtively from behind shuttered windows. Their faces were shot with confusion, with fear, with horror . . .

Slad chuckled to himself. This was more like it! Just like the old days, he felt invincible!

The phalanx turned left and was soon heading into a second square, smaller than the one the goblins had assembled in, and dominated by a huge arch. An open channel, running round the square and bubbling with water, flowed through the arch and cascaded down into the deep shaft beyond like a waterfall. With the sculpted flames on top of the arch and the rows of bars sealing the front, this was the infamous Great Eastern Entrance to the sewers beneath Undertown. The phalanx came to a halt in front of it.

'I don't understand, Slad,' Dunkrigg whispered from beneath the cover of Slad's raised shield. 'It's certain death to enter the sewers through the Great Eastern Entrance. Everybody knows that.'

Slad nodded. It was true. The barred entrance led through to a vertical drop where a torrent of water poured down into a vast black tank – the so-called Drowning Pool. Many goblins had perished there in an attempt to enter the sewers – and the few who had made it to the other side had been summarily dispatched by the librarian guards. Not one of their number had ever got through.

'So, what are we doing here?' hissed Dunkrigg.

Slad shook his head. 'Don't know, 'Rigg, mate,' he said.

Just then General Tytugg strode up from the rear, accompanied by a cowering goblin. They stopped in front of a low trough behind which was a tall curved obelisk, ornately carved and with a dark plaque screwed into the front.

Slad watched, bemused, as the general motioned to the goblin, who walked forward. What was he up to?

Without saying a word, the goblin reached up and pressed the plaque firmly with both hands. There was a soft *click*, a grinding of stone on stone and the curved obelisk swung round to reveal a long dark shaft beneath it. The general motioned to the phalanx leader, who approached and received his orders before returning to the hammerhead guard.

The leader spoke to the front rank in a low voice tinged with urgency. 'The secret route into the sewers lies open to us at last,' he said. 'But the librarians are ingenious. The entrance is so narrow that we must enter it in single file. You, the front rank of the guard, have the honour of going first!'

Slad licked his lips and stepped forward, Dunkrigg behind, followed by the rest of the phalanx's front rank. At the entrance to the shaft, the phalanx leader thrust a blazing torch into Slad's hand.

Slad crouched down, shield over his shoulder, and gripped the torch firmly. Then, having kissed the carved bone amulet he wore at his neck for good luck, he stepped into the darkness. Instead of the ladder he was expecting, he found himself on a steep metal chute and, for a moment as he hurtled downwards, the flames of the torch flickered and threatened to go out.

After several long, unnerving seconds, his boots landed with a heavy thud on the floor below, and the flame once again flared brightly. Slad raised the torch in his hand, straightened up and stepped cautiously forwards. He was, he saw, in a vast underground vault with dark tunnels leading off in various directions.

Behind him, he heard the roaring of the water cascading down into the drowning-pool. In front, guarding the tunnel, was a large crossbow on a raised metal platform.

It seemed to be unmanned – but you could never be sure . . .

Slad moved cautiously forwards, plunging the flaming torch into every dark corner and shadowy alcove he came to. He didn't like this dark, dripping, subterranean cavern. It was no place for him, a hammerhead guard. It was a place for sewer rats – both piebald *and* academic . . .

'There's no point hiding,' he growled. 'I'll sniff you out wherever you are.'

Just then something moved to his left. He heard it, and saw it out of the corner of his eye. Drawing his sword, he spun round, lunged forwards – and sliced off the head of a scrawny piebald rat. Slad breathed out noisily and grinned with relief.

So far as he could tell, the place was deserted. He kicked the dead rat out of the way – just as Dunkrigg thudded down the chute behind him.

'It's all clear!' Slad called out over his shoulder, his voice echoing round the cavernous vault.

Almost at once, a third hammerhead appeared, followed by another, and another, as goblin after goblin slid down into the underground chamber. All round, the chamber soon echoed with coughs and grunts and shuffling of boots as the other goblins entered the vault and took up their positions; gnokgoblins, flatheads, tufteds, saw-tootheds . . . They hurriedly reformed themselves into their individual battalions and the phalanx rapidly resumed its shape.

Slad grinned. The battle was very close now. His temples throbbed with the blood coursing through his veins; his heart was beating wildly. Yes, it was just like old times. Beside him, he could sense a similar excitement in Dunkrigg who, eyes blazing, was licking his lips and clutching his shield with a white-knuckled grip.

Finally, the last of the goblin army passed through the narrow entrance and into the great vault. General Tytugg strode to the front, drew his sword and raised it high. He threw back his head as if to shout yet, when it came, his order to move was little more than a whisper.

'Phalanx, to battle!' His sinister words hissed round the glistening walls. 'Death to the librarians!'

ii
The Battle-Flocks

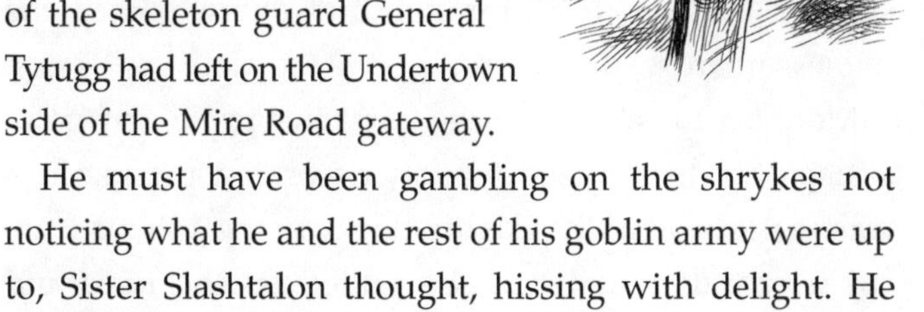

Perched high up on a jutting stanchion, Sister Slashtalon scratched at the feathery tufts beside her beak; with the weather so hot, the parasitic woodfleas were more active than usual. Her eyes, yellow and unblinking, bored down into the back of the armed goblin below her – one of the skeleton guard General Tytugg had left on the Undertown side of the Mire Road gateway.

He must have been gambling on the shrykes not noticing what he and the rest of his goblin army were up to, Sister Slashtalon thought, hissing with delight. He had gambled wrong.

Just then, behind her, she heard a low whistle. It was Sister Feathermane. She had reached her position at the bottom of the left tower. An answering call announced that Sister Beakscreech was also ready.

With a loud shriek, Sister Slashtalon launched herself off the stanchion of the Great Mire Gates and landed in goblin-controlled Undertown. The flathead guard spun round, a look of surprise etched into his brutal features. One hand flew to his sword; the other to his knife. Neither found their mark. Sister Slashtalon saw to that.

In one graceful move, she leapt up into the air and kicked out with her taloned feet. The razor-sharp claws slashed through the goblin's belly, ripping it open. Then, as he stumbled forwards, hands vainly grasping at his spilled guts, she struck him again. His neck snapped and his head was left hanging on by a knot of stringy tendons.

To her left and right, Sisters Feathermane and Beak-screech had dispatched their own guards with the same ruthless efficiency. More goblins were coming, swords drawn and clubs swinging – but it was already too late. Sister Slashtalon had unchained the great Mire Gates and pushed them open. A vast army of the bloodthirsty shrykes came pouring through and overwhelmed the hapless guards.

Mother Muleclaw – resplendent in purple and gold, sitting astride a huge, ornately-decorated prowlgrin – was at the head of the mighty flock. As the goblins were cut down all round her, she pulled on the reins and turned her prowlgrin round.

'Come, sisters!' she screeched. 'Tonight we shall feed on goblins' hearts and librarians' livers! You all know what you must do. Forwards, sisters! Forwards!'

Sister Feathermane gathered her battle-flock around her, as did Sister Beakscreech, and the pair of them set out towards the southern boom-docks. With low whistles and guttural clucks, Sister Slashtalon assembled her own battle-flock. They were to take the northern route to the boom-docks, seeking out and destroying any goblins they encountered on their way, for there must be none left who

might later try to cut them off. Having taken a final headcount of her squadron and issued last-minute instructions, Sister Slashtalon set off, while behind her the mighty Mire Gates were secured once more.

A motley collection of fledglings, their feathers still drab and downy, cowered in the shadows and chirruped their encouragement. Beside them, the weedy shryke-mates jangled their thin silver chains and squawked feebly.

Keeping close together, the squadron of shrykes left the Mire Road platform and entered Undertown itself. Once they hit the network of roads, they divided into smaller groups. At the head of each junction they came to, they split up again, inspecting the darkened narrow alleys and twittens in pairs – keeping in touch with each other with their reedy whistles and muted shrieks then reuniting at the far ends. Road by road, alley by alley, they inspected the whole area. Apart from the cowardly Undertowners peering out from the windows of their dilapidated dwellings, the shrykes saw no-one.

This part of Undertown, at least, was clear of any goblins. Sister Slashtalon was prepared to stake her life on it.

Their mission complete, the patrol-squadron headed along a narrow path between tall, wooden buildings which led down towards the Edgewater River. From there, where the West Wall of the city met the river, they made their way to the boom-docks.

Up ahead, Sister Slashtalon could see the other brightly coloured battle-flocks already milling about on the muddy banks beside the jutting pipes; some dry, some gushing water. And coming closer, she could make out Mother Muleclaw herself, still perched atop her battle-prowlgrin. As she got within earshot, Sister Slashtalon realized the roost-mother was already addressing the flock.

'... treacherous ... Do not stray ...' she was saying, her words whipped away by the rising wind. Sister Slashtalon trotted closer; the words became clearer. 'For the pipes are not to be trusted,' Mother Muleclaw was saying. 'Some lead to dead-ends. Many are booby-trapped ...'

Sister Slashtalon nodded. As one of the High Sisterhood, she had been present when that traitorous youth ... What was his name? Rook ... When he had come amongst them ...

She remembered his description of the sewer pipes only too well. He'd explained how, in a system modified by the librarians themselves, the pipes were operated by a series of valves, each one opening or closing a different sluice and directing the water in ever-changing routes. It had kept them safe for years ... Not a single shryke had ever breached this simple, yet deadly, defence.

The youth had told them something else, however. Something crucial. Something which, even now, made Sister Slashtalon's eyes glint with anticipation. He had told them how, at ten hours that night, the librarians would all be in the Great Storm Chamber Library, attending some ceremony or other. From that moment until the conclusion of the meeting, the valves would remain untouched. Those already open would stay open; those shut would stay shut. The shrykes would therefore be able to proceed safely through the network of pipes with no fear of being washed away and drowned. All they had to do was find a way through.

Sister Slashtalon raised her head and sniffed the air. The musty odour of fusty librarian emerging from the pipes made her tongue quiver. A smile passed across her face.

At Mother Muleclaw's screeched command, the shryke squadrons and battle-flocks proceeded into the pipes – keeping to the dry or almost dry ones. There was a gentle trickle coming from the pipe Sister Slashtalon led her shryke-sisters into. Although she hated the way the water swilled round the feathers between her claws, she knew that the running water would help lead them to their goal.

On into the pipes she took them, now left, now right, her keen eyesight and unerring sense of smell helping her to navigate the labyrinth of pipes. As she went, she heard water coursing through other pipes close by; fast gushing water that no-one could ever withstand – water that, if the valves were to change, would drown them in an instant and flush them back down to the mudflats of the boom-docks.

As she passed yet another of the valved-junctions – the torrent of water roaring behind it – Sister Slashtalon clucked, grateful that the treacherous youth's information had proved reliable. They were making good progress – as were all the shryke battle-flocks. One by one, they were emerging into a vast sub-chamber situated at the far western end of the Central Tunnel. Some were already beginning to explore the pipes and channels which led from it.

Mother Muleclaw raised her feathered arms and hissed for silence. 'Wait, sisters,' she called. 'Wait!'

Sister Slashtalon – about to try a tunnel for herself – paused, and fought down the disappointment which rose within her. Wait? When they were so close? It was almost too much to expect of them. Why, she could smell the librarians so clearly. She could almost *taste* them! Their plump, fatty hearts . . . Their tangy livers . . .

'We must not forget ourselves, sisters, for at the eleventh hour, the goblins will strike,' Mother Muleclaw continued. 'And we must let them. We shall let the predators catch their prey; for then, when they are done, the predators shall themselves become prey. *Our* prey! And we shall gorge upon them all!'

iii
The Guardians of Night

Orbix Xaxis, the High Guardian of the Tower of Night, was taking his time all right. The noon deadline had come and gone, and still the Purification Ceremony had not taken place. Now night had fallen, and Styx – a stocky gnokgoblin with tufted hair at his ears and a scar which passed down his cheek and over his jutting chin – was beginning to flag. Almost ten hours he had been waiting at his post, waiting for the signal to be given for the ceremonial cage to be lowered. Ten hours! He was beginning to wonder whether it would take place this day at all . . .

Just then – as far below him an Undertown bell rang out nine hours – Styx noticed a movement at the gantry-doors, and Orbix strode onto the gantry, his black gown flapping behind him. He sat up straight as the master stormed towards him. Behind the muzzle and dark glasses, it was impossible to tell what the High Guardian was thinking but the gnokgoblin didn't want to give the impression that he had been slacking.

'I asked for you, specially, Styx,' Orbix announced. 'I

want the cage descent to be as smooth and silent as possible. Make sure everything's set accordingly.'

'Sir,' muttered the gnokgoblin, leaning forwards in the raised seat at the top of the cage winching-gear. He reeled in a length of surplus plaited rope and checked the balance-weights.

Behind him, Leddix emerged onto the gantry, followed by two pairs of hefty flathead guards. Styx turned. Between the guards were the prisoners; two of them. One was a girl – pale and drawn, with sunken eyes and quivering lips, her plaits hanging limply onto her shoulders. The other was a youth. Thin. Wiry. Bruised. He was rubbing the side of his shaven skull tentatively. Styx recognized him; he was one of the High Guardian's special advisers. What was his name?

'Courage, Magda,' Styx heard him muttering as, flanked by the hulking guards, the two of them approached the cage. 'Don't give them what they want. You're better than they are, remember that!'

Orbix Xaxis turned towards them. 'You think so?' he sneered, and pushed his muzzled face into the youth's. 'You have disappointed me, Xanth,' he said, his voice hissing behind the muzzle. 'Disappointed me more than you will ever know.' He nodded towards Magda and tutted dismissively. 'It is a shame you have allowed your head to be turned by this librarian scum.'

Xanth lowered his head but said nothing.

'Yet even now, you still have a sporting chance. For it is the sweet meat of the librarians that the rock demons crave. If you ditch the girl, you might still manage to escape.' He chuckled. 'What will you do, Xanth? Abandon her and save yourself? Or stay with her and be eaten?'

Still Xanth remained silent.

Orbix grunted with irritation. 'Put them in the cage,' he cried. 'Let the ceremony begin.'

The pale girl and thin youth were bundled into the barred contraption which swayed precariously as the door was slammed shut and locked. The gnokgoblin's nostrils twitched.

Fresh meat, he thought. The rock demons *will* be happy.

The High Guardian raised his arms. 'Hail, the Great Storm!' he bellowed. 'Lower the cage!'

Styx seized the winding-levers and started turning. After an initial jolt, the cage began to go down, travelling slowly, smoothly and in complete silence – for, at the High Guardian's instructions, Styx had plaited strips of cloth into the winding-chain to muffle the tell-tale clanking sound of the cage's long descent. The rock demons should not be alerted too soon.

'Hail, the Great Storm! Hail, the Great Storm!' the chanting voices of the High Guardian, the cage-master and the four Guardians rang out.

Styx shuddered. He knew he had to be careful. Not only must the cage descend in silence but he also had to calculate the exact moment to apply the brakes. Too soon and the prisoners would drop down through the air. Too late and the cage could crash against the side of the canyon. Either way, the rock demons would be alerted before the prisoners had a chance to make a run for it. And that, as Orbix Xaxis had stressed, his eyes blazing behind the dark glasses, must not happen.

'Must get it right,' Styx murmured anxiously. 'Mustn't mess up.'

Leddix had whipped him so soundly the last time he'd made a mistake, he'd thought the flayed skin on his back would never heal. If he got *this* wrong . . .

'Hail, the Great Storm! Hail, the Great Storm!'

'Gently does it,' Styx whispered to himself, trying not to be distracted by the Guardians' chants as the cage below him began to swing in the rising wind. 'Mind that rock there. That's the way . . . A little lower. Just a little bit more . . .' He pulled the brake-lever and, as he looked down into the canyon below, sighed with relief. The cage had come to rest against a slab of rock, not fifty strides from the dark, jagged hole in the side of the canyon. 'Perfect,' he breathed.

Orbix, leaning over the balustrade, a telescope raised, monitoring the situation for himself, turned to the gnokgoblin. 'Open the cage,' he told him.

Styx reached up above his head, uncleated the plaited rope and tugged it hard. He heard a soft *click* below him and looked down to see the cage door swing open. Then as he continued to watch, scarcely daring to breathe, he saw the two figures emerge. They paused. They looked around, and for a moment Styx thought that they were about to split up . . .

'Come, Demons of the Deep,' Orbix Xaxis intoned. 'Come, now . . .'

Apparently deciding to stick together after all, the two ant-like figures set off, leaving the cage behind them. They can't have noticed the hole in the rock,

Styx noted, for they were heading away from it. He mopped his brow fretfully. It would be him who got the blame if anything went wrong . . .

The next moment, he noted something else; a tumbling of rocks; a wailing and screeching. Dark shapes were emerging from the depths of the canyon and slithering upwards towards the light.

The two figures must have noticed them too, for all at once, they were running. What was more, they had changed course. Abandoning their attempt to scale the side of the canyon, they were heading straight for the entrance to the tunnel.

'Excellent,' Orbix Xaxis purred, and Styx thought he could detect a smile behind the High Guardian's muzzle and dark-glasses. 'Run, run, as fast as you can,' he whispered.

'Hail, the Great Storm!' Orbix Xaxis cried out as, at the very same moment Xanth and Magda disappeared into the tunnel, a distant flash of lightning lit up the sky beyond the Edge. 'Hail, Demons of the Deep. Rid the Sky of its polluters, one and all!'

At that moment, the first of the dark shapes reached the shadowy hole. It paused, and sniffed round suspiciously. Others arrived behind it; a dozen, twenty, fifty . . .

Styx looked down to see the rock demons pouring into the tunnel. Their screeching had taken on a high-pitched intensity which, for all the torrid heat of the night, made the gnokgoblin's spine tingle icy-cold. Despite himself, he couldn't help hoping that the young couple might escape. Librarian or no, nobody deserved such a terrible fate.

He felt a hand on his shoulder. It was the High Guardian of Night himself, Orbix Xaxis. 'Well done, Styx,' he purred from behind the metal muzzle. 'With your skilful cage-craft, you have sealed the librarians' fate.'

·CHAPTER SIXTEEN·

THE STONE HEAD

Rook gripped his seat in anticipation. His old professor, Alquix Venvax, should have been sitting next to him, but his place was empty. Rook hadn't seen him since just before embarkation.

The barge gave a lurch to the right, then to the left. They were almost out of the sewers. Ahead, the other four barges of the Great Library fleet had already emerged from the sewer pipe into the strong current of the Edgewater River. Rook could just make out their crews rowing frantically against the current, bobbing and weaving in their desperate attempt to get up-river.

Although he had seen what had happened to the others, nothing could have prepared Rook for the sudden jolt as the choppy water struck the port side of the boat. It lurched violently, sending the cargo sliding to one side, the barge creaking and groaning in protest. Rook was soaked with water.

'Cut the buoyant-lectern net!' the barge-master cried out.

Several librarians jumped forwards, knives drawn. The net was cut and the lecterns were set bobbing about in the air above them. The vessel righted itself. Then, back in their positions, the librarians picked up their oars and brought the boat slowly round in the water until it was pointing upstream – all to the accompaniment of the barge-master's bellowed commands.

'Pull! Pull! Pull!' he shouted. 'Ten degrees to port . . . And pull! *Pull!*'

Slowly but surely, the barge began to make progress up the Edgewater River, following the rest of the fleet. It was hard work, though – for it wasn't only the currents the librarians had to contend with as they battled upstream, but also the strong headwind which tugged at the bobbing lecterns and threatened to drag the heavy barge back towards the endless falls at the Edge itself.

'Pull! Pull! Pull!' the barge-master commanded.

Rook breathed in deeply and looked around. The lights from the opposite bank glinted back at him. The fleet was keeping to the centre of the river where

the water was deepest. No-one wanted to run aground. Far, far ahead, the lofty towers of the Mire Gates were just visible. Rook felt a hand on his shoulder and looked up to see the Most High Academe looming above him.

'I see you have a spare seat,' he said. 'Do you mind if I sit?'

Rook shrugged. 'It was Alquix's place,' he said, 'but I lost sight of him as we boarded.

Cowlquape shook his head sadly. 'I feared as much, Rook, my lad,' he said, sitting down beside him.

'What?' Rook asked.

'He couldn't bring himself to leave his beloved library,' said Cowlquape simply.

'You mean he stayed behind, even though . . .' Rook felt tears sting his eyes as he thought of his kindly old professor.

'Yes, even though the eleventh hour approaches,' said Cowlquape. 'The goblins will already be entering the sewers. And the shrykes won't be far behind. Just thank Sky that *we* managed to get out in time.'

Rook nodded glumly and the pair of them stared up into the threatening sky. The dark clouds were writhing and squirming in the broken moonlight. 'We will make it, won't we?' he asked, turning to the Most High Academe.

Around them, the librarians groaned as they pulled on their oars to the barks of the barge-master.

Cowlquape continued gazing up at the sky. It was growing darker. 'According to Vox's calculations – he showed them to me himself – the dark maelstrom will strike at the eleventh hour precisely.'

Rook felt his stomach lurch uneasily, but it wasn't the motion of the barge that was unsettling him. There was something else nagging at the back of his brain. Something important that he couldn't quite put his finger on.

'Finest cloudwatcher the College of Cloud ever produced,' Cowlquape was saying. 'Vox had it all. That's why I made him my deputy all those years ago. If Vox says the eleventh hour, then the eleventh hour it will be.'

'PULL! PULL! PULL!' The barge-master's cries grew ever more insistent.

'The Tower of Night, the Mire Road, the Sanctaphrax

Forest,' Cowlquape's hand gestured across the Undertown skyline. 'Say what you like about the fat wretch, but he's certainly left his mark.' The old professor looked down at his seal of office and fiddled with it distractedly. His eyes clouded over. 'Unlike some I could mention.'

Now it was Rook's turn to place a hand on the Most High Academe's shoulder. 'Don't do yourself down,' he said. '*He* left his mark on Undertown; *you* left your mark on people's hearts. I know which is more important.'

'Sky bless you, lad,' said Cowlquape, looking up with a smile. 'There were times in the dungeons of the Tower of Night when I doubted that.'

Rook shook his fist. 'Tower of Night, *pah!* Mire Road, *pah!*' He laughed, and Cowlquape joined in as Rook continued, 'Sanctaphrax Forest, *pah!* Vox's baby – *pah!*'

Cowlquape stopped laughing. 'Vox's baby?'

'Yes,' laughed Rook. 'His latest project – a great big sphere full of bloodoak acorns and phraxdust.'

'Phraxdust,' Cowlquape gasped, the colour draining from his face.

'It's horrible stuff,' Rook went on. 'I had a bit of an accident with it down in Hestera Spikesap's kitchen. A couple of specks of dust, a drop of water and *BANG!!* The explosion was colossal.'

'And he's packed a whole sphere full of the stuff,' said Cowlquape weakly. 'Sky above, suddenly it all makes sense. The fireballs, Rook! It must have been one of those that knocked you out of the sky. Vox has clearly been experimenting for quite some time.' His voice dropped. 'But I didn't think that even Vox Verlix was capable of such a thing. He's mad! Quite mad!'

'I . . . I don't understand,' said Rook unhappily as a wave of guilt washed over him. He'd had his own part to play in the feeding of the baby. But what exactly had he done?

'Don't you see, Rook?' said Cowlquape. 'If this "baby" of Vox's, packed full of phraxdust and bloodoak acorns, is as explosive as you say . . .'

Rook nodded.

'Then setting it off,' Cowlquape continued, 'could well trigger . . .'

'The dark maelstrom,' whispered Rook.

The lightning crackled as the clouds advanced. Far above in the sky, a white raven wheeled round and round.

'So *that's* how he could predict when it would strike,' Cowlquape murmured. 'Because he himself always intended to set it off. I've been such a fool, Rook, blinded by sky-charts and calculations . . .'

'It's not your fault,' said Rook. 'It's mine for not recognizing how dangerous Vox's baby actually was, and warning you all.'

'No, Rook,' said Cowlquape, rising from his seat. 'You couldn't be expected to know that. Few of us have ever been able to read Vox's dark mind, and those of us who have tried have failed miserably.'

Cowlquape collapsed, head in his hands, moaning softly. Rook leaped to his feet.

'What is it, Most High Academe?' he asked urgently. 'What is it?'

Cowlquape looked up, his face as pale and haggard as Rook had ever seen it. 'Vox insisted that the banderbears carried him to the Mire Gates by ten hours,' he said, 'even though the maelstrom he predicted was due to strike at the eleventh. I thought nothing of it when I looked at those accursed charts and calculations, but now . . .'

'Now we know that he has the power to *cause* the dark maelstrom himself, and that we – the librarians – have arranged for him to be carried to safety!' Rook gasped.

'Yes,' said Cowlquape, gazing at the dark sky and fast flowing Edgewater. 'There's nothing to stop him launching his baby, creating the dark maelstrom, and destroying us all right now!'

'Oh, but there is,' said Rook grimly. There was steel in his voice. 'I'll stop it being launched – or die in the attempt.'

He jumped up from his seat and hurried to the side of the barge. He raised his arms.

'I'll meet you at the Mire Gates!' he called back. 'Earth and Sky willing!'

'No, Rook!' cried Cowlquape. 'I can't ask you to do this.'

'I must!' Rook cried, and he dived into the swirling Edgewater River.

Far above his head, the white raven let out a raucous shriek, turned in the air and soared off across Undertown.

'Good luck, lad!'

Cowlquape's quavering voice floated across the choppy surface of the river as the library fleet continued battling up-river towards the safety of the Mire Gates. Rook gritted his teeth. He'd need all the luck he could get.

He struck out for the far shore, praying that he might avoid the treacherous oozefish this time. After a few minutes his boots sank into the slimy bottom of the riverbed. Steadying himself and leaning into the current, Rook waded towards the bank. He emerged, quivering with exhaustion – yet there was no time to rest.

With a last glance back at the distant fleet, he dragged himself to his feet and up the muddy slope. In the distance, he could see the jagged outline of the Palace of Statues.

The shoreside buildings came closer, their lamplit windows showing him the way as the sky darkened. Rook darted down one of the narrow alleys. The palace, he calculated, must be some way to his right. He took a sharp turning, then another, and raced across a deserted square. At the far corner, he went through a narrow arch onto a broad, stately thoroughfare – and cried out with joy.

'Thank Sky!'

Looming up before him, the Palace of Statues was bathed in shadows and light. Pools of golden lampglow poured from every window, casting the statues on the balconies and the plinths on the walls outside in sharp relief. And from the top of the building a vast, circular beam shone up through the glass dome of the Leagues' Chamber, like a great chimney of light against the swirling clouds above.

'Just a little further . . .' Rook panted. 'Just a little bit more . . .'

At the palace at last, Rook dashed up the marble steps and hammered at the heavy oakwood doors with his fists. The thudding echoed loudly through the building inside, then faded away. There was no answer.

Rook groaned. Of course there was no answer, he realized. That was Speegspeel's job and, even as he stood there, locked outside, he knew that Speegspeel was high above in the Leagues' Chamber, preparing to launch the baby.

Darting back down the steps, Rook scurried round the building, checking the palace walls with every step he took. It was only when he reached the back of the building, that he saw what he was looking for.

One of the statues at ground level had toppled to one side and was leaning against the sheer, windowless reaches of the lower wall. So long as it didn't slip, he should be able to climb up it and onto the balcony above its weathered head. From there, he judged, looking up, it shouldn't be too difficult to find a route right to the very top.

The statue jolted as Rook climbed onto it. It was slippery and unstable. Up over the statue's huge stone knees he went, across to its waist and, using a fold in the leaguesman's carved robes as a foothold, pulled himself up onto the shoulders. From there he reached up again, grabbed the bars of the balcony balustrade above his head and hoiked himself up.

Below him, there was a loud *crash* as the massive statue keeled over and smashed on the paving beneath.

Rook wiped his brow and looked up. Through the thickening mist, he saw the statues. Hundreds of them. In alcoves, on ledges, lining jutting buttresses and clinging to the sides of the wall . . .

He jumped across to the statue to his right, climbed up over the stone body and onto a narrow ledge above it.

So far, so good.

He climbed up two more statues, arriving hot and sticky on a narrow flying buttress where he paused for breath. The mist had grown thicker still and swirled round in the rising wind, which whistled through the limbs of the statues and plucked at Rook's fingers as he continued to climb.

Up, up, he went. There were still four storeys to go till he reached the Leagues' Chamber at the top of the palace. *Simenon Xintax. Farquhar Armwright. Ellerex Earthclay.* The plaques at their feet gave names to the statues he was climbing up: leaguesmen, all of them.

The stone knife and chisel clutched in his hands made Leandus Leadbelly – a former master of the Gutters and Gougers – particularly easy to climb. And yet, as Rook stood on top of his angular hat of high office, he was overwhelmed by a sense of sudden unease. The next moment, something happened.

The head moved.

Rook cried out, jumped up, and just managed to grab hold of the jutting leg of a pale yellow statue above his head. He heaved himself up onto the narrow ledge it was mounted upon, and looked back down, his heart hammering in his chest, as the leaguesman's head fell.

From behind, he felt something shoving him in the back. Something cold. Something hard . . . It was the pale yellow statue! What else could it be? And it was trying to push him off the ledge!

Arms flailing wildly in the air, Rook scrambled to one side and seized the arm of the neighbouring statue. Behind him, the pale yellow statue toppled forward and hurtled to the ground. At the same moment, there was a sharp *crack!* and the arm Rook was clutching came away in his hands, pitching him off-balance again.

With a cry of horror, he twisted round. He let go of the broken arm and, pinning himself back against the wall, peered down at the falling piece of carved stone as it

turned over and over in the thick air. There was a splintering crash as it landed and, as the mist cleared for a second, Rook saw the shattered arm lying amongst the broken pieces of the other statues he'd dislodged.

He breathed deeply and steadied himself, then looked up at the stretch still to go – and the statues he needed to climb to get there.

'They're not dead leaguesmen, they're statues,' he told himself, continuing the climb. 'That's all. Just lumps of stone.'

The mist swirled round his head, a noxious sulphurous brew that made his eyes water and his throat sting. At last, he reached a statue so near to the top that, once he had scaled it, he was able to climb across to the roof itself. Pulling himself up over the carved balustrade, he landed on the safety of the vast flat roof of the Leagues' Chamber itself.

He peered down through the windows of the glass dome. He saw the wooden scaffolding; he saw the circular platform with the spherical baby resting in the narrow cradle. But where was Speegspeel?

He hurried round the dome to where the panes of glass had been smashed. Looking down into the chamber, he saw a shattered circular table with a great stone head at its centre. His blood ran cold as the dead stone eyes met his. He was looking into the carved stone face of Vox Verlix himself.

Just then he heard the butler's rasping voice ring out. 'Time for baby to fly the nest. Old Speegspeel knows. He won't let the master down, oh no. Now's the time. The tenth hour . . .'

Rook peered down to see the butler approach the cradle and insert a funnel into the spherical case. The goblin reached for the water-bottle at his side, unplugged it and prepared to pour its contents into the funnel . . .

Rook bit his lip. One drop of water, that was all it would take – and baby would be launched into the sky.

'NO!' Rook bellowed, and jumped through the glass roof's jagged opening. He fell down through the air, legs pedalling wildly, and landed heavily on the shattered table.

Speegspeel swung round with a snarl, water-bottle in one hand, a knife in the other. 'What's old Speegspeel got to deal with now?' he growled. 'The kitchen slave, isn't it?' His red eyes narrowed.

Rook crouched and grasped the stone head at his feet. 'Drop the water-bottle, Speegspeel,' he commanded.

Speegspeel hesitated, then moved towards the funnel. Rook swung his arm in an arc and let go, grunting with effort. Vox's stone head flew through the air and smashed into the hapless goblin with a sickening crunch. Speegspeel crumpled to the floor with a whimper, the contents of the water-bottle emptying by his side.

'The statues got old Speegspeel,' he rasped. 'They got old Speegspeel in the end.'

His eyes fixed on those of the stone head for a moment, then glazed over to return their lifeless stare. Rook picked himself up and stumbled over to the cradle. He laid a hand on the smooth metal side of Vox's baby and looked down at the funnel jutting out from the casing. The hot, humid air was stifling. A drop of sweat fell from the tip of his nose and pattered on the inside of the funnel.

Rook stumbled back. 'What have I done?' he gasped.

As he spoke, there came an ominous rumble and a series of urgent clicks and creaks as the whole scaffolding seemed to shift about. Rook looked up anxiously. The next moment, there was a loud *crack*, and the horizontal beams which had kept the spring-mechanism closed, shot upwards with incredible force – and the baby was hurled from its cradle into the air, through the glass dome in a shower of falling glass, and on up into the night sky above.

For a moment, the air quivered with intense silence. Then . . .

A flash of blinding light and . . .

BANG!!!

The shock waves that followed the light struck with a battering rush of roaring wind. Roofs were torn away, buildings fell, statues plunged – and Rook was picked up and tossed back across the chamber . . .

As the dust finally settled, Rook scrambled to his feet. Dazed and frightened, he looked back at the sky through the hole in the glass dome. The light in the sky had shrunk in size, yet curiously seemed to be sucking everything inside itself as it grew smaller and more intense. Finally – as bright and tiny as a dazzling star – it disappeared completely, to be replaced with a spot of blackness as intense as the light it had followed.

Like a blot of ink, the dark spot grew and grew, spreading out across the sky. It turned the clouds black and cast the land below into absolute darkness. Huge fat raindrops began to fall. They landed heavily – all over Undertown, in the courtyard of the Palace of Statues,

through the broken panes of glass in the dome . . .

The next moment it was as though the sky had turned to a mighty river. The rain became torrential, cascading from above. It was, Rook thought as he scurried for cover, like being beneath a great waterfall.

Down below him, he saw that the courtyard was already awash with water, like a great lake lapping at the fallen statues. And if it was this bad here, what must it be like for the library fleet on the Edgewater? Would any of them make it to the safety of the Mire Road?

'Earth and Sky protect you,' he murmured softly. He turned towards the door and waded across the flooded chamber. 'Earth and Sky protect us all!'

·CHAPTER SEVENTEEN·

BLOODBATH ON THE BLACKWOOD BRIDGE

The High Guardian gripped the balustrade of the upper gantry and craned his bony neck upwards. From inside his metal muzzle came the sound of sniffing.

'It is time,' he murmured. 'It is time.'

Even now, as he stood surveying the boiling cauldron of the sky, the rock demons would be infesting the sewer-tunnels in search of librarian flesh. The sewers would be cleansed, and the Great Storm would come to heal the sacred rock.

'It is time.' Every muscle in Orbix's body tensed.

Below, the jutting gantries were crowded with silent Guardians gazing up at the heaving sky. Above them, the great swirling cloud banks that had circled Undertown for months had merged into one monstrous formation like a vast and mighty anvil. The air was so thick and heavy that even breathing had become difficult.

Suddenly a low moan rippled through the crowded gantries. Orbix looked down. A great fireball was slicing through the thick air, arcing up over Undertown and heading for the centre of the mighty anvil.

From inside the metal muzzle, there came a gasp. 'Sky be praised,' he breathed.

The fireball disappeared into the midst of the swirling cloud and, for a moment, there was an unearthly silence. The air burnt the High Guardian's lungs as he took a rasping breath.

Suddenly, from the very heart of the anvil, a cataclysmic explosion ripped across the sky – first dazzling white, then black as pitch. Deafened by the tumultuous percussion of the mighty thunderclap, Orbix raised his arms up high.

'Hail, the Great Storm!' he screeched.

'Hail, the Great Storm! Hail, the Great Storm!' The chorus of voices echoed round the Tower of Night. 'Hail, the Great Storm!'

All round, the black cloud fizzed and crackled with tendrils of lightning which zig-zagged off in all directions, a network of fiery veins, dazzling and jagged. As each individual lightning-bolt faded, so the deafening thunder rumbled across the sky, like a mighty hammelhorn stampede.

'Midnight's Spike!' Orbix Xaxis bellowed above the barrage of noise. He looked up from the upper lookout-platform at the figure of Mollus Leddix, poised on the spike-ledge, waiting for the command. 'Raise the spike!'

Leddix raised his hand in assent, and crouched down next to the winch-mechanism. Observing him from below, Orbix was struck in the face by a huge raindrop. As he wiped it away with his sleeve, another clanged against his muzzle – followed by another, and another.

Within moments, the rain had become torrential and the anvil had flattened out into a huge swirling disc above the Tower of Night, like the wheel of some huge wagon. Tendrils of lightning flickered and crackled round its rim.

'Hail, the Great Storm!' shouted the Guardians excitedly. 'Hail, the Great Storm!'

There was no time to lose. The healing power of the lightning had to be harnessed. Orbix brought a fist down heavily on the balustrade.

'Faster, Leddix!' he bellowed. 'Faster!'

Leddix cursed beneath his breath as he worked the winch-mechanism. This should have been that pasty-faced whelp Xanth's job, not his! The spike rose slowly from its oiled sheath and up into the boiling air.

Leddix fought to catch his breath.

'Nearly there,' he gasped. 'Nearly . . .'

Clang!

The spike was fully extended, the winch-mechanism straining beneath his hands. Leddix reached out for the deadbolt, hanging from a hook beside him. His hand grasped at thin air.

'What's this?' he yelped, straining to keep the winch handle from spinning back with his other hand while he felt around beneath the hook. 'It can't be . . .'

The deadbolt – long, pointed at one end and decorated with the gleaming head of a gloamglozer at the other – was gone. Leddix threw his head back, the rain splashing against his snarling face.

'Sky curse you, Xanth Filatine!' he roared.

Unable to hold the heavy mechanism for more than a moment without the deadbolt, Leddix's arms gave out. The winch-handle slipped from his sweating hands and rattled noisily back. Above him, the spike slid slowly down into the sheath.

Clang!

The sky crackled and flashed. The muzzled figure of the High Guardian appeared on the spike-ledge, his arms flailing in a demonic fury.

'I said, raise the spike! Leddix!' he screamed above the deafening thunderclaps. He grasped the cowering cage-master with claw-like hands and thrust his muzzle into his white face.

'C . . . c . . . can't,' Leddix whimpered. 'The . . . the . . . deadbolt . . . G . . . g . . . gone!'

'Then so are you!' the High Guardian's voice rasped through his muzzle. The claw-like hands tightened their grip as the High Guardian raised the struggling Leddix high above his head, and threw him from the Spike-Ledge. The cage-master's scream was drowned out by another huge clap of thunder.

'Hail, the Great Storm! Hail, the Great Storm!' Below, the Guardians' cries were reaching fever-pitch.

Above the great tower, the clouds were swirling like a vast cauldron of inky stew stirred by a great ladle. The lightning bolts converged, twisting together into a knot of fizzing light.

'Hail, the Great Storm . . .'

There was no time to winch the spike up from its sheath, Orbix realized, but he could not let the storm simply pass by. With a howl of rage and desperation, he leaped onto the top of the winching-mechanism and stood up, arms outstretched.

At that moment, the storm exploded with a sudden blinding flash. A single lightning-bolt – coiled and charged – hurtled down from the raging maelstrom above. It sliced through the black air like a mighty spear.

'Hail, the Great Storm!' Orbix cried out. 'Hail . . .'

The lightning struck – and with such violence that the Tower of Night shook from top to bottom, sending walls crashing and gantries falling. Guardians toppled, screaming, from their perches through the blue, flashing air. And as the mighty power of the lightning held everything momentarily in its deadly embrace, the wooden tower smouldered, the diseased rock it stood upon crackled and oozed – and from high above, Orbix Xaxis, High Guardian of the Tower of Night, let out a terrible unearthly scream . . .

*

'Do you think we've lost them?' Magda whispered.

Xanth knelt beside her in the small sewer pipe above the Southern Transverse. 'I'm not sure,' he said. 'I . . .' He hesitated. 'I think so.'

He was drenched in sweat. There had been times, with the rock demons scuttling after them, when he'd thought they wouldn't make it. But Magda, Sky bless her, had been as diligent about her sewer studies as everything else. She'd sought refuge in the narrowest, most awkward pipes in the system whilst their bigger pursuers had shrieked their frustration in the larger pipes behind. And now they'd emerged, just as Magda had promised they would, above the Southern Transverse, just in sight of the Central Tunnel and the entrance to the Great Library itself.

'What's that?' whispered Xanth.

Magda frowned. She'd noticed it too. From up ahead, there came a low, regular, pounding noise, overlaid with a strange jangling, like the clatter of metal. They both listened. Xanth turned to Magda, his face ashen grey.

'What *is* it?' he whispered.

Magda shook her head nervously. They couldn't go back – not with the rock demons behind them. She seized Xanth's hand and together the pair of them advanced towards the end of the transverse tunnel. Water trickled past beneath their feet.

At the junction with the Central Tunnel, they stopped again and peered out. Pouring from the mouth of a steeply sloping pipe ahead, into the Central Tunnel itself, were goblins – flatheads, tufteds, longhairs and, massing at the east doors of the Great Storm Chamber Library itself, the metal-clad ranks of the hammerhead guard.

'A goblin army?' Magda gasped, her hand shooting up to her mouth in horror. 'At the door to the Great Library?'

'Goblins to the front, rock demons behind,' Xanth whispered. 'We're trapped!'

Magda crumpled to her knees, her head in her hands. Silent sobs convulsed her body. 'It's over, Xanth.' Magda's voice was thick with tears. 'I can't go on.'

'But you must,' came a frail voice behind them. Xanth spun round, his fist raised – but Magda grasped his arm as an elderly librarian stepped out of the shadows.

'Alquix? Is that you?' Magda rushed to the professor and embraced him, her sobs returning.

'There, there,' said Alquix kindly, stroking her head. 'I feared we had lost you, just like Rook, but now I find you have returned – just as he did.'

Magda's sobs ceased, and she drew back. 'You mean Rook is alive?'

'Yes, my dear young librarian,' said Alquix. 'And not only is he alive, but thanks to him, our Great Library has been saved from these barbaric hordes.'

'I . . . I don't understand,' Magda began, but Alquix silenced her with a raised finger.

'There'll be time enough for explanations when you join the librarians at the Mire Gates,' he told her. 'But you must hurry. Already the sewers are beginning to flood.'

Xanth looked down at his feet. It was true. In just the short time they'd been standing in the narrow tunnel,

the trickle of water at their feet had turned to a steady stream. Alquix stepped up to the pipe's entrance and peered out.

'You there, lad,' he said, addressing Xanth directly for the first time. 'Do you think you and Magda here can make it across the Central Tunnel to that small culvert over there? It will take you to a little sewer grate up in East Undertown.'

Xanth looked. 'But the goblins!' he said. 'We'll be in plain view of the library entrance . . .'

'You leave the goblins to me, lad,' Alquix told him. 'Just make sure you both make it to the Mire Gates. The library has need of brave young librarians if it is to make it to the Free Glades.'

'Alquix, no!' Magda embraced the old professor again. 'We can't leave you here.'

Alquix pushed her gently away. 'I am old,' he said, smiling sadly. 'I've spent the best part of my life there in the Storm Chamber Library. Why, I helped build the Blackwood Bridge with my own hands before you were born. I cannot leave it, even now.' Tears were streaming down the librarian's face. 'Now, go!'

With that, he pushed past them and strode down the Central Tunnel towards the library entrance, raising his staff as he did so and bringing it clanging down against the walls.

'Long live the Great Storm Chamber Library!' he roared at the massed ranks of goblins before him.

Behind him, unnoticed, two figures – one hunched and supported by the other – slipped across the Central Tunnel and into a small culvert on the other side.

'Seize him!' General Tytugg's command rang out from the doors to the Great Library, which were being pounded by a huge battering-ram.

A phalanx of tufted goblins surrounded the old librarian, their razor-sharp spears at his throat. A thick-set hammerhead guard barged his way through the crowds still pouring into the Central Tunnel and seized Alquix, lifting him bodily above his head and carrying him back towards the library doors. Tytugg smiled as Alquix was dumped roughly at his feet.

'Our first librarian,' he sneered, turning to the ranks of sweating hammerheads, the huge battering ram poised to strike the library doors raised high above their heads.

'The rest of his kind are cowering behind these puny doors. We shall reunite him with them! He shall be our battle banner!'

He clicked his fingers and two flathead standard-bearers leaped forwards and grabbed Alquix roughly, strapping the frail figure to a long carved pole with a hover worm crest.

'Attack!' roared the general as the old librarian was hoisted high above the seething mass of goblins.

The hammerheads surged forwards, swinging the battering ram with incredible force against the library doors, which splintered like matchwood.

'Victory to the goblins!' Tytugg roared.

'Victory to the goblins!' the great army roared back as it poured into the Storm Chamber Library. 'Victory to the goblins!'

In front, the hammerhead guard marched forward, their shields interlocking in a solid wall, Alquix held high on the hover worm standard in their midst. They thundered across the Blackwood Bridge as, above and below them, the tufteds and longhairs swarmed onto the gantries and over the Lufwood Bridge, their ranks bristling with spears and crossbows.

Tytugg and his captains stepped through the shattered gates and surveyed the scene.

'I don't understand it,' the general muttered. He looked up at Alquix. 'Where are the librarians?'

A thousand goblin eyes turned to the old librarian. For a moment there was utter silence. Then Alquix's thin, reedy laugh rang out.

'They are safe!' he cackled. 'The library has been saved! Long live the Great Library . . .'

Just then, there was a blur of movement from one of the jutting gantries overhead and a flash of yellow and blue whistled down through the air. Then another. And two arrows buried themselves in the old librarian's heart.

Dumbstruck, the goblins stared at their standard in disbelief as Alquix's head slumped and blood poured down his chest.

'Shryke arrows,' the standard-bearer roared, brandishing a fist at the upper gantry opposite. 'And they came from up th . . .'

Before he could finish his words, a brightly tufted arrow embedded itself in his neck. He fell to his knees, blood gurgling from the gaping wound . . .

'What treachery is this?' General Tytugg's voice echoed round the great chamber. 'Take out the shryke scum on the gantries!'

As if responding to the general's commands themselves, shrykes suddenly appeared on every upper gantry, helmets and breastplates gleaming. They screeched loudly, raised their bows and the air hissed with the sound of flying arrows. At the far end of the

Blackwood Bridge, Slad the hammerhead fell to his knees and pulled the cross-bow round from his back.

'Cover me,' he hissed to his comrade.

Dunkrigg raised his shield.

Slad primed the cross-bow and looked through the sight. The plump gaudy chest of a brightly-coloured shryke appeared behind the cross of the viewfinder. Slad smiled and squeezed the trigger.

The bolt found its mark. The shryke's chest exploded in a flurry of feathers and blood. The bird-creature toppled off the gantry, hurtled down through the air and landed with a sickening *crunch* on the Blackwood Bridge.

'First blood!' Slad cried. He raised his crossbow a second time, taking care to remain behind Dunkrigg's shield as a volley of shryke-arrows flew in from all sides.

He ratcheted the bow-string back. He took aim. He pressed his finger gently against the trigger, and . . .

All at once, the great doors at the west end of the bridge flew open. Slad gasped. In front of the phalanx of hammerheads, pouring in through the west doors, were shrykes. Hundreds of them. Each one armed to the teeth and massing into flailing, screeching battle-flock formations.

From behind the shield wall, Slad braced himself and drew his sword; a magnificent two-handed hookblade.

'By Sky, old Cleave-in-Twain, you shall drink shryke blood tonight!' he said.

Around him, the other hammerheads in the phalanx drew their serrated blades and muttered battle oaths of their own. In front, the battle-flocks surged forwards like a cresting wave about to break on the solid bank of shields. The shrykes were armed with bows and arrows, pikes, whips and flails – but Slad knew it was their glinting beaks and gleaming talons he had most to fear from.

The shryke wave hit the shield wall and recoiled with a deafening howl, splatters of vivid shryke blood showering the front ranks. Here and there, ahead of Slad, hammerheads sank to their knees with low groans and the same look of shock and slow astonishment as they discovered that the blood pouring down over their breastplates was their own; their necks talon-slashed.

'Come, Dunkrigg,' growled Slad, advancing to plug the gap. 'Here they come again!'

Another battle-flock broke against the hammerhead phalanx – and tore it apart.

Slad found himself staring into a pair of yellow eyes as, either side of him, his comrades' severed heads shot high up into their air and their bodies crumpled to the floor, staining the Blackwood boards red. Dunkrigg lunged forwards, his shield deflecting the razor-sharp talon that was inches from Slad's throat.

With a roar of rage, Slad swung Cleave-in-Twain at the huge shryke battle-sister looming over him. The brightly plumed shryke swerved left and Cleave-in-Twain beheaded her flail-swinging companion behind.

From over his shoulder, Slad heard Dunkrigg groan and he turned to see his comrade's breastplate punctured and spurting blood. The shryke battle-sister's beak dripped with his blood as she rounded on Slad.

'NO!' he howled, blind with fury. He swung Cleave-in-Twain so hard and so fast that he sliced the bird-creature in two before her deadly beak could strike again.

He glanced down at Dunkrigg, his friend. He was already dead. Now Slad wanted revenge.

'*WHOOOAAAAA!!!*' he roared, striding forward.

With a piercing shriek, Sister Slashtalon leaped up and lashed out with her heel-talons. An expression of utter bewilderment spread across her flathead opponent's lumpen features as he looked down to see his breastplate sliced in two, blood pouring from it. Sister Slashtalon stepped forwards and savagely shoved him with her pike. The goblin keeled over the balustrade of the Blackwood Bridge and into the rapidly rising water.

'More! More!' she growled, a loop of drool hanging from the edge of her beak. The hunger was coming upon her.

Out of the corner of her eye, she saw a flash of steel as a long-haired goblin swung a great ball-and-chain at her head. Sister Slashtalon drew back and spat, venomously.

The green bile splattered into the long-haired goblin's face with a soft hiss. 'My eyes!' he screamed. 'My eyes!'

Slashtalon brought her beak sharply down, splitting the goblin open from sternum to stomach. With a jerk of her head, she plucked out the still-beating heart and swallowed it whole. Yes! Sister Slashtalon shuddered, her feathers standing on end; the hunger *was* upon her!

A huge hulk of a hammerhead goblin stormed towards her. His entire body was covered in blood; the blood of others. Sister Slashtalon reared up, talons bared, and stood her ground.

Slad's eyes were rolling; froth bubbled at the corners of his mouth. He stared at the vicious, blood-spattered bird-creature through a raging haze of crimson.

'WHOOOAAAAA!' he roared, hurling himself at the shryke, Cleave-in-Twain clasped in his bloodied hand.

Slashtalon leaped forwards, all four sets of talo slashing at once.

They met in mid-air at the very centre of the Blackwood Bridge with a horrifying *crash*.

At the east doors, the remnants of the hammerhead guard had clustered round Tytugg. At the west doors, the ragged remains of the battle-flocks squawked and flapped around Muleclaw's banner. On the bridge itself, the mounds of dead covered the boards and, in places, rose above the balustrades. Below, the central sewer was fast flooding; the Lufwood Bridge was already submerged and goblins and shrykes alike clung to the lower gantries as the waters rose.

Slad's roar and Slashtalon's shriek intermingled as, for a moment, they stared into each other's eyes. Cleave-in-Twain was embedded in Slashtalon's gizzard as deeply as her talons had sliced into Slad's throat. Slowly, gently, the hammerhead and the shryke-sister sank to their knees where they remained, motionless, in their deadly embrace.

An eerie silence fell across the Blackwood Bridge.

High above the bloodbath, dark creatures appeared at the cracks in the vaulted roof and crawled through into the chamber. There, black against the white stone, they clung on upside down and sniffed the rich air, their eyes glowing. Calling to one another, they were joined by more, and more; pouring in through every crack and spreading out across the ceiling.

Suddenly, as if to some unheard command, the entire flock of rock demons launched itself from the ceiling as one and spiralled down through the air on leathery wings.

Across the bridge, goblin stared at shryke, and shryke at goblin. They all looked up as, like a black curtain falling on a red stage, the rock demons landed.

·CHAPTER EIGHTEEN·

The Ghosts of Screetown

Past rows of statues Rook ran, hurtling down the palace stairs two at a time. From outside came the distant crash of stone against stone as the deluge stripped the outer walls of their statues. He thudded down onto the final landing, skidded round – and stopped dead in his tracks. Hestera Spikesap was hurrying across the marble hallway below, heading for the staircase.

Rook took a step back and knocked into a statue which rocked on its base, then toppled forward, taking three of its companions with it.

'Hestera! Look out!' he shouted as the statues hurtled down towards the marble floor.

The old goblin didn't look up. Nor, as the statues shattered on the floor in front of her, did she miss her stride. She reached the stairs and began climbing. Rook noticed that she'd lost her bonnet. Her balding, scabby scalp glistened and her clothes were wet.

'I'm coming,' she crooned, as if soothing an infant. 'I'm coming, my sweetness . . .'

She brushed past Rook, her small red eyes looking right through him, and continued up the staircase. In her arms, she cradled a large red bottle, with a label marked *Oblivion: Special Vintage*.

Without looking back, Rook raced down the last flight of stairs to the marble hallway, almost losing his footing on the wet, slippery floor. Water was bubbling up from the kitchen door and spreading across the hall. Sodden recipes, pots, pans and potion bottles bobbed on its surface. Rook looked down as a green bottle marked *Retching Cordial* floated past.

He splashed across to the great woodoak door and seized its handle. From behind it came the sound of hissing which, as he pulled, grew to a mighty rushing roar.

A torrent of water rushed into the hallway from the street outside, knocking Rook back across the floor and drenching him to the skin. Above him, the statues on the staircase were toppling in twos and threes, splashing into the swirling water. Rook staggered to his feet and fought his way back to the door and out into the street.

The rain was like nothing he had ever seen before. It was torrential, a deluge; falling so hard and so fast that it resembled myriad silver wires, strung out taut between the ground and the boiling clouds overhead. And, as the tempestuous wind thrashed and spun, so the raindrops merged to form rippling, shifting sheets of water which slapped at the sides of the buildings and slammed down into the rising floodwater below.

'Sky guide and watch over me,' Rook muttered grimly as he waded through the ankle-deep water.

The rain forced him to lower his head protectively as it hammered down on his skull and shoulders, and ran down the back of his neck. Raising an arm against the battering downpour, he tried to take his bearings. Undertown had been transformed, its streets and alleys now deep canals of swirling, muddy water. In the distance he could just make out the towers of the Mire Gates peeking up above the muted skyline.

Had the library fleet made it? he wondered.

As he battled through the flooded streets, he became aware of other shapes, blurred and indistinct through the shimmering curtain of rain. They were ahead and behind him, in the alleys and lanes on either side; all moving along in a growing procession in the same direction as himself.

'Undertowners,' Rook murmured.

Just above his head, a whirring noise made him look up. A white shape, a blur of movement, shot from one

sloping roof to another on the other side of the street. A piercing whistle cut through the roar of the rain and was answered by three more from further up the street.

Rook waded on, finding a brief respite from the lashing rain behind the massive forms of a party of cloddertrogs.

'The Mire Gates – we'll be safe there, Duldug,' one called to his neighbour. 'The Ghosts of Screetown'll guide us, don't you worry.'

'What did you say?' Rook cried out, unable to conceal his excitement.

The cloddertrogs ignored him, pressing on through the downpour, and Rook was jostled from behind as other Undertowners brushed past him impatiently. He was in the middle of a vast crowd now and had to struggle to stay on his feet as it surged forwards. Just to one side of him, a gnokgoblin, a young'un in her arms, stumbled and let out a cry as she lost her balance.

Before Rook could do anything, a white figure swept down from a rooftop opposite. It landed with a splash, and grabbed mother and child. Rook could make out a bleached muglump-leather jacket, patched and mended, a white ratskin hat and a grappling-hook clutched in a white, bony hand.

'Run along now and take care,' the figure said, setting the gnokgoblin safely down.

'Bless you, sir,' murmured the gnokgoblin. 'Bless you.'

Rook stared open-mouthed at the figure before him. 'You're . . . you're one of them . . .' he spluttered, fighting against the force of the crowd. 'A ghost of Undertown.'

For an instant, the figure turned towards him and Rook saw the weather-beaten face of a mobgnome with piercing blue eyes looking into his own.

'Just keep moving, lad,' the mobgnome smiled, sending the grappling-hook arcing through the air with one graceful sweep of his arm. As the hook clanged onto a rooftop, the ghost pulled the rope taut and swung up through the air as if fired from a catapult, riding its springing recoil.

'Wait!' Rook called. 'I have a friend, Felix. Perhaps you . . .'

The ghost disappeared over the rooftops.

'. . . know him.'

Ahead, the street opened up into a square and, through the flapping sheets of torrential rain, Rook could see the Mire Gates looming up before him. The huge crowd was streaming into the square from all corners of Undertown. Groups of cloddertrogs, families of gnokgoblins, artisans and merchants; former slaves – all guided by the whistles of the ghostly white figures who

stood out against the black silhouettes of the rooftops all around.

A cloddertrog matron, swathed in a black raincloak, paused for a moment to check that her brood of young'uns was keeping up. A fearful-looking lugtroll – a gash down one cheek and nursing a swollen arm – hurried past her, muttering under his breath, 'Curse you, Tytugg. Curse all hammerheads!' Behind him came a stooped rheumy-eyed gnokgoblin who was being guided by her granddaughter, a youngster with stubby waxen plaits, a broad nose, and clutching a wrapped sword to her chest.

At the square, the Undertowners jostled against the Mire Gates, causing them to sway back and forth – and from behind them came the trilling and squawking of shryke-mates and fledglings.

As Rook eased himself through the seething crowds, he craned his neck to get a better view. He had to get to the jetty that lay just on the other side of the Mire Gates – for there, where the Edgewater River met the mudflats of the Mire, he hoped against hope that he would find the library fleet, safe and waiting for him.

From overhead came whirring sounds followed by sharp thuds as grappling-hooks struck the wood of the Mire Gates. In an instant, high up at the top of the gates, the white Ghosts of Screetown appeared. They stood there for a moment, swaying slightly before dropping down, as one, on the other side.

For a moment, the cheers of the Undertowners mingled with the piercing shrieks and cries of shryke-mates and fledglings. Then the huge gates slowly swung back.

Rook was carried forward as the crowd burst through the gates and spread out across the vast wooden platform beyond. He looked up and gasped at the sight of the Mire Road snaking out into the endless white mudflats before him.

Here on the other side of the gates, the rain was merely a light drizzle and the Undertowners broke up into excited groups; some dancing little jigs of celebration, some hugging each other, while others simply slumped to their knees and gave thanks. To his right, Rook could see a walkway winding down from the platform to the Edgewater Jetty.

He glanced back, and his heart lurched in his chest as he saw the Undertown skyline crumbling beneath the swirling black cloud of the dark maelstrom and its impenetrable sheet of rain. In the far distance, despite the deluge, the Tower of Night blazed like a mighty torch, the flames fed by great forks of lightning which crackled about it. It was a scene out of a nightmare; a nightmare that he, Rook, had unwittingly brought about.

For a moment, he forgot about the library fleet and sank to his knees. He had fed Vox's baby, the terrible fireball, with his own hands. Worse than that; it was he – *he*, Rook Barkwater, who had done everything to prevent it – who had triggered the dark maelstrom. His fists pounded the boards of the Mire Road with a mixture of fury, misery and despair. Above him, a white raven swooped low and hovered, letting out a raucous cry.

'Waaaark!' it screeched. 'Rook. Greetings!'

Rook looked up as the white raven landed beside him.

'Gaarn,' he said, managing a weak smile. He wiped his eyes. 'Is Felix with you?'

'Never far behind!' came a familiar voice and Felix – tall, powerful, clad in white muglump leather – strode across the platform, flanked on either side by Ghosts of Screetown.

'Oh, Felix!' Rook cried, and leaped to his feet. 'So much has happened since we last met!'

'So it has, Rook, my friend,' laughed Felix, clamping an arm round Rook's shoulder. 'Undertown is finished. Our future – yours and mine, and all these brave souls' – lies out there.' He gestured with a sweep of his arm. 'In the Free Glades!'

A cheer went round the crowd that had gathered about them.

'But you don't understand,' Rook said miserably. 'This is all my fault. I could have prevented this terrible storm, but I failed. Not only that, but . . .' He bit his lip as tears welled up again.

Felix patted Rook's shoulder, a look of concern clouding his features. 'I can't pretend I understand you, Rook, but I can see this has hit you hard. It can't have been easy down there in the sewers when this storm struck. Did any other librarians make it out alive?'

Rook started back. The librarians! He spun round and started running towards the walkway that led to the Edgewater Jetty. 'They made it out of the sewers in a fleet of library barges, and onto the Edgewater,' he called back over his shoulder. 'I said I'd meet them here at the Mire Gates, if . . .' – he stopped and slowly turned round – '. . . we survived.'

Felix turned to the white raven which now nestled in its familiar position on his shoulder. 'Gaarn,' he said. 'Go, seek and return!'

With a cry, the white raven launched itself into the air and wheeled round, heading off towards the dark skies over the Edgewater.

'Come, Rook,' said Felix, pointing towards the walkway, his voice choked. 'You have an appointment to keep.'

Rook looked down from the balustrade and shuddered. On his sky-patrols, he was used to seeing the sluggish Edgewater snaking its way through the channels of mud. Tonight, however, it had grown so broad and so deep that it raged and frothed below him, threatening at any moment to pluck the support-beams away and hurl the whole jetty into the perilous waters.

Sick with worry, Rook scanned the river, the bank, the raised walkways – *everywhere*; desperate for some sign of the missing library fleet. Surely they should have made it by now! Gripping tightly hold of the balustrade, he leaned out, neck craned, scanning the curve of the river . . .

'And they're all out there?' asked Felix, the choking sound still in his voice. 'The whole council? Varis . . ? And my father?'

'Yes,' said Rook. 'The two of them were both in the fourth barge.'

They looked out at the furious waters in silence. Above them, on the Mire Gates platform, the ghosts were organizing the Undertowners for the great exodus down the Mire Road. Felix looked over his shoulder, then back at the Edgewater. Beneath their feet, the jetty shuddered.

'You know,' he said, slowly. 'We haven't got long, Rook. This jetty's giving way and the Mire Gates will follow. If we don't set off soon, we'll all be lost . . .'

'Just a little longer,' Rook pleaded. 'After all, it's your sister and father out there, Felix. You're acting as if you don't care!'

Felix looked down at his feet, the muscles in his jaw flexed and unflexed. 'All I've ever wanted,' he said quietly, 'is for my father to be proud of me, Rook. And now, just when I might have proved myself to him at last, he is lost out there. Don't you think *I* want to wait longer?' His fist slammed against the balustrade.

'I'm sorry,' said Rook. 'It's just . . .'

'I know, I know,' said Felix, clearing his throat. The jetty lurched again. Above them, shouts rang out and a group of ghosts marched down the walkway, escorting two struggling black-robed Guardians.

'We found these two by the Mire Gates, Felix,' the mobgnome ghost reported. 'Shall we slit their throats and dump them in the Edgewater? It'd be kinder than letting the Undertowners loose on them.'

The Guardians stopped struggling as Felix stepped forward and pulled down their hoods.

Rook gasped. 'Magda! And . . . Xanth!'

'Release them, Lemlop,' said Felix. 'This one's got a flight-suit on beneath her robes – she's a librarian, you fool! And this one . . .'

'I can vouch for him,' Magda said boldly, her eyes flashing.

'You can?' said Rook.

'He saved my life, Rook.'

'Felix,' said the mobgnome ghost urgently. 'We've got to get out of here . . .'

'I know, Lemlop,' said Felix, turning to go.

Reluctantly, Rook turned away from the balustrade, his head hanging. Magda fell into step beside him as they mounted the walkway to make their way back to the Mire Gates platform.

'Rook, what's happened? Where is everybody?' she said. 'There are rock demons loose in the sewers and a goblin army in the Great Library. We were expecting to meet the library fleet here . . .'

'I was, too,' said Rook. 'Oh, Magda . . . The librarians . . .'

'Librarians! Librarians!' A cry went up. Above them, the crowd of Undertowners thronged the Mire Gates platform, shouting and pointing excitedly.

Rook turned to follow their gaze. 'It's them!' he exclaimed. 'It's the Great Library Fleet! They've made it!'

The first great barge rounded the bend in a flash of oars, a clatter of bobbing buoyant lecterns and the regular cries of the barge-master urging the librarians on. A white raven flapped above it, cawing loudly. The second barge came into view, followed by the third, the fourth, the fifth – and Rook saw that they had all been lashed together with long ropes.

So typical of the librarians, he thought. All of them had to make it to safety – or none.

Hurrying back down the rickety steps of the walkway, Rook raised his cupped hands to his mouth and bellowed across to the approaching barge. 'Throw me your tolley-rope!' he shouted. 'Quickly, there isn't much time!'

No reply came, but the barge shifted direction. It was heading straight for the jetty.

'Stroke! Stroke! Stroke!' The gruff cry of the barge-master echoed over the roaring of the water.

The Ghosts of Screetown hurried down the steps onto the jetty and, as the fleet came alongside, they grabbed the coils of tolley-rope tossed to them and tied them securely to the mooring rings which lined the sides.

One by one, the librarians disembarked. They looked utterly exhausted. Silent and dazed, their muscles throbbing with pain, they staggered onto the jetty, which threatened to collapse at any moment. As Fenbrus Lodd stepped out of the fifth barge, the wooden pillars set into the mudflats below creaked loudly and the landing-platform trembled.

'Unload the barges!' he roared, above the weary chorus of moans and groans. 'As quickly as you can!'

The librarians set to it, helped by the ghosts and a contingent of large cloddertrogs who, with their powerful bulk, made short work of the task. Rook, together with Magda and Xanth, who had discarded their black robes, tossing them contemptuously into the swirling waters of the Edgewater, all pitched in. As the final sky-craft and buoyant lecterns were being carried on to the Mire Gates platform, the jetty collapsed and disappeared, along with the empty barges, back into the inky blackness of Undertown.

The whole council, flanked by Felix's ghosts holding burning torches, was now gathered in the centre of the platform. Tallus Penitax, the Professor of Darkness, stood beside Ulbus Vespius, the Professor of Light, and beside them, Varis Lodd. Cowlquape – looking older and more haggard than ever – sat in the centre, on an ornately carved trunk. Next to him stood the High Librarian, Fenbrus, his arm raised for silence.

'My dear librarians!' His voice had lost none of its power or authority. 'Earth and Sky be praised we have made it this far. A long journey still lies ahead of us, but we are indeed blessed to be able to share its dangers with the good people of Undertown. And for this, we, and they, have to thank, the ... *errm* ... I believe they're known as ... the Ghosts of Screetown! And their leader ...'

A huge cheer went up from the Undertowners as Felix stepped into the torchlight.

'Ah, yes,' said Fenbrus, 'their leader, who is . . . What is your name, my brave young fellow?'

Felix's eyes met his father's.

Fenbrus blinked. His mouth fell open . . . 'Felix? . . .' the High Librarian spluttered.

Felix smiled, a look of eager anticipation on his face. He held out his arms to embrace his father.

A tear trickled down the High Librarian's cheek. 'I . . . I . . . I don't know what to say . . .' His face coloured with embarrassment. He cleared his throat noisily and patted Felix stiffly on the shoulder.

There was an awkward silence. Felix's face fell.

Was that it? he wondered. The reunion he had, for so many years, both dreaded and longed for . . . A pat on the shoulder!

Varis rushed forwards and embraced her brother, but he didn't seem to notice, his eyes still fixed on his father's face – and a look of hurt and disappointment on his own.

'My dear librarians, Undertowners and ghosts,' Fenbrus's voice rang out, strong and clear, once more. 'Our journey shall be long and difficult but, if we all work together and look out for one another, at its end we shall have earned the right to a fresh start, not as librarians, or Undertowners, or ghosts – but as Freegladers, one and all!'

Rook joined in the chorus as, all around, Undertowners picked up their belongings, librarians shouldered backpacks and commandeered shryke wagons, and ghosts with flaming torches prepared for the long march down the Great Mire Road.

Rook, Magda and Xanth fell in behind Felix. His dark expression suggested he didn't want to talk. They made their way silently towards the front of the mighty procession. As they pushed through the empty shryke tally-hut and out onto the Mire Road itself, Rook breathed in sharply with astonishment, then let out a cry of joy.

Ahead of them, a short distance away, was Vox's bower, carried by his banderbear friends.

'Weeg! Wuralo!' Rook called. 'Wumeru! Molleen! Weera-lowa. Wuh-wuh weega!' *Your burden is great. Let others take it now!*

But something was wrong. The banderbears didn't respond to his yodelled greeting, but instead continued their slow, shambling march up the Mire Road.

The curtains of the bower twitched. *All's well, my friends,* an icy voice sounded in Rook's head. *Let us go on our way . . .*

Rook turned to Felix and grabbed him. There was a

glassy look in his friend's eyes. 'All's well,' he was mumbling. '. . . Go on their way . . .'

'NO!' shouted Rook. He grabbed Felix's grappling-hook and threw it at the bower. It snagged on a wooden upright and Rook felt the rope pull taut as he lashed the other end to a Mire Road balustrade.

The banderbears continued carrying the bower, straining against the rope until – with the sound of splintering wood – the upright came away. The banderbears collapsed onto the wreckage of the bower, crushing the frame and snapping the carrying-poles in two. Rook came running up, followed by Magda, Xanth and Felix.

'I don't know what came over me,' Felix said, shaking his head.

'I think I do,' said Rook, 'but I'm not sure I understand it. You see, this is the bower Cowlquape sent to carry Vox to safety . . .'

The banderbears were clambering to their feet, shaking their heads in turn and yodelling softly.

'Weega-wurra-loora,' murmured Wumeru, her fingers fluttering. *A dark forest dream has lifted like a mist.*

'Wuh-wuh, wugeera. Luh-weeg,' added Molleen, with a shudder. *My mind now comes back to me. Before are only windswept echoes.*

Rook patted the backs of the banderbears reassuringly. 'Weg-weeg. Weegera, weera, wuh-wuh,' he yodelled, and touched the tips of his fingers to his chest. *Do not fear. No harm has come of your sleepwalking, friends of my heart.*

'Vox?' came a querulous voice behind them. 'Is that you, Vox? We kept our side of the bargain, yet *still* you planned to destroy us! Shame on you!'

The frail figure of Cowlquape, followed by the High Council, marched forward to join them round the wreckage. Cowlquape stopped and looked from the banderbears to the bower and back again.

'Oh, dear,' he said, a smile coming to his lips. 'There seems to have been an accident. Is anyone hurt? No? How about you, Vox?'

Cowlquape pulled aside the length of heavy curtain that was covering a great quivering bulge. There, sitting cradling a dazed-looking ghostwaif in her massive fleshy arms, was the figure of Flambusia Flodfox.

'Speak to me, Ambey, dear,' she clucked. 'Speak to me!'

Rook walked over to the Mire Road balustrade and untied the rope. He looked back at Undertown, almost totally obscured by the terrible dark maelstrom. It was all over, he thought, but the heavy weight that had been pressing down on his chest for days seemed to have lifted.

He was with his dearest friends again; Felix, Magda, the banderbears, even Xanth – and ahead lay the greatest adventure of his life.

He gripped the balustrade tightly for a moment, his knuckles white. Was that the Palace of Statues crumbling in the distance?

Relaxing his grip, he turned back to the others, a smile on his face. Undertowners, librarians and the Ghosts of Screetown filed past in an endless procession down the Mire Road. Rook's gaze followed them.

'Freegladers,' he murmured.

*

'Amberfuce,' said Vox, his voice barely more than a whisper as the awful truth dawned.

'I gave him some of my special medicine, and he got Speegspeel to slip it in your oblivion, dearie.' Hestera smiled. 'Then he took your bower. Flambusia begged me to go with them,' she said, 'but I told them I'd rather stay.' She smiled again, her face creasing up into unfamiliar folds. 'I wouldn't leave you, my sweetness. Not ever.'

The palace shuddered as yet another buttress crumbled into the surging torrent below. The whole west side of the building was now gone, and the wind and rain howled through the massive cracks opening up in the walls.

'Betrayed,' Vox murmured. He slumped to the floor and held his head in his hands. 'Betrayed!' A huge sob wracked his bloated body.

Hestera crouched down beside him, and rested a hand tentatively on his arm. Above them, the ceiling cracked, and the dripping water turned to a steady stream. Vox's sobbing suddenly stopped. He looked up, his small eyes narrowed to mean, murderous slits.

'*You*,' he muttered. '*You* gave Amberfuce some of *your* special medicine . . .'

'That's right, my sweetness,' said Hestera, uncorking the bottle marked *Oblivion: Special Vintage*.

'You mean,' spluttered Vox, 'you *knew* of his plans – and you didn't tell me!'

Hestera grabbed Vox by one wobbling, fleshy jowl and squeezed with an iron grip.

'Ooowww!' Vox screamed, his fat hands attempting to slap the goblin away.

'Of course I didn't tell you, my sweetness,' Hestera crooned, jamming the bottle into Vox's gaping mouth.

Vox's hands stopped flapping as Hestera held the glugging bottle firmly in place. His eyes dulled and closed; his head lolled to one side. The crack travelled from the ceiling, down the wall and snaked across the floor. The great chamber shuddered.

'It's what I've always wanted. A dream come true, Vox, my loverly,' said Hestera, cradling his massive head in her apron and rocking gently from side to side. 'You, my sweetness, all to myself.'